AGES OF
AENYA

Nick Alimonos

ISBN: 0692957006
ISBN 13: 9780692957004
Library of Congress Control Number: 2017914920
Ages of Aenya, Tarpon Springs, FL

ACKNOWLEDGMENTS

This is for my wife, Hynde, who never lost faith in this project, who put up with me during the ups and downs of the long creative process. I would also like to thank my friends and fans, my tireless beta-reader, David Pasco, whose enthusiasm for Aenya often rivals my own, and Heather Zanitsch, whose literary knowledge keeps my mind from dulling. And to everyone who's ever given me a word of encouragement, I give my regards, from Dean Ristich, who taught me to see the magic in the world, to my third-grade Creative Writing teacher, who inspired me to pursue my dream. Of course, I can't forget my partner in crime, my editor, Ava Justine Coibion, whose insights have helped make Ages of Aenya the best it could be.

There is a land called Ilmarinen, between
the Light and the Dark Hemispheres, named
after the flower of orange and violet. In
Ilmarinen, it is said, there is no poverty or
war. Grasses brush softly so that children
might chase through fields unblemished
and aeons-weathered boulders make beds for
lovers and poets and stargazers. There the
Monastery of Alashiya stands, ancient beyond
memory, repository of forbidden knowledge.
Of all Aenya's peoples, only the Ilmar
remember the age before the Greater
Moon, when we failed to save the world
from Cataclysm. In memory of song, they
remember us, our hubris and our wisdom.

—From the *Ages of Aenya, Volume II,*
as recorded by Eldin

T he blood rushing to her head made her skull
ache. She could feel the throb of her heart, flowing through her limbs, bringing spasms of pain to
her ribcage. Dizzy with dread, she glanced back and saw
it—not far now—a blur of crimson. The halfman was still
following.

Dapples of sunlight percolated from the treetops. The
leaves were wet and slick with dew and stuck to her soles.
Soft dirt came up between her toes, slowing, weakening
her grip on the earth. Arrows jostled in her quiver, eager to
fly in every direction. A bow of twine and oak smacked her
backside at every rock and ravine impeding her passage.

Without slowing pace, she fumbled at the harness between her breasts, discarding the bundle of arrows, and the bow, which followed in the dirt. She kept on, free of everything but muscle and skin—a true Ilmarin born of Nature—her auburn braid swaying like a banner caught in a storm.

She could hear the arrows snapping like twigs with heavy, inhuman footfalls, and knew the halfman was close behind. Strengthened by fear, she kept momentum as brambles reached for her ankles and river rocks cut into her soles. She would never tire, or waver. After all, she was not like other humans. Her sense of touch was as keen as her vision. She could feel the Goddess everywhere, in the rain, in the wind, as part of the wood and part of her.

But she was far from the wood she knew.

An immense camphor tree stood in a depression of leaves like a parent over the forest. Her fingers and toes were still covered in sap from sleeping in the branches. The stickiness helped her dig into the brittle bark, scurry up the sheer trunk with little effort. She came up through the foliage into the open sky where she squatted along a bed of swaying twigs.

Certain the halfman could not follow, she placed a hand to her breast, feeling her heart grow calm, her breathing settle into rhythm. No more running. She had lost him in the high places like so many other predators that had stalked her in the past.

Shades of green stretched below, split by a deep, waterfall-studded gorge, which fed into the azure ribbon that was the Potamis River. The river spilled into the turquoise moon that filled the horizon. The smaller moon swam like a purple fish across the face of the greater, marking the passings till nightfall.

In quiet moments when she was in hiding, she doted on the ilm her father had given her, now lost in the quiver with her arrows. The scent of the flower conjured memories of home, and she would never think to eat it or make it into a tea, unless gravely injured. Jagged rocks punished her soles often, when she neglected to watch where she was running, and the branches of some trees left scrape marks across her shoulders and forearms and sometimes her cheeks, but these were mild discomforts she learned to ignore and did not warrant use of the ilm's healing properties. When she was confident that the halfman was gone, she would go down and look for the flower, and when she had it in her palm again she would try and recall the orange and purple that colored the hills of her homeland.

How many eclipses had come and gone since leaving home? For cycles, she followed the Potamis, maintaining a southerly course, keeping the greater moon to her left. The river served as a guide on her journey, but also a source for drink and bathing. When the waterway dipped through barren valleys, her sustenance consisted of grubs and beetles, but in the wood she drank dew from leaves and relied on her marksmanship to sate her hunger. Despite their efforts, her parents could not have prepared her for the vast, nameless stretches of Aenya. They could not have known of the unfamiliar and ever-changing flora, of the fruits their daughter could only guess the relative safety of, fruit which could either soothe the hollowness in her belly or leave her aching and vomiting. The farther from home, the harsher the touch of the world. Days were scorching and nights made her shudder. Dragon-mosquitoes found her blood sweet as she slept in the trees, and even the flowers had thorns. But she refused to mask her body in the protective covering her mother had given her. Even the occasional thorn was preferable to the constant grating, the heaviness and sultriness and numbness, brought on by clothing. The outside world was unlike Ilmarinen, but every new sensation—even the painful ones—heightened her awareness of life, of the Goddess that resided in all things.

The darkness that came with the fully eclipsed sun, the depth of night, seemed to belong to other gods. In Ilmarinen, she had lain down on the roof of her father's house under a universe of twinkling fires, her eleven siblings slumbering below before a warm hearth. But here, lonesome but for the surrounding trees, she shut her eyes and willed sleep to come, fitfully separating the harmless noises from invisible things that hunted in the dark.

Leaves whispered and branches crackled, rousing her from her thoughts. Her foundation began to sway violently, threatening to fling her hundreds of feet to the ground. Something was making its way up towards her. As it burst through the foliage, she caught a glimpse of howling teeth and fur like the color of blood.

She scurried away like a four-legged animal. Without realizing it, she was in the adjoining tree. He was in the other, growling in his guttural language, shaking the bone talisman in his fist. Careful to watch his footing, he moved uneasily across the makeshift bridge of touching branches. She reached for her bow only to realize she'd thrown it away. The limbs of the trees groaned in protest as she pulled herself to the twig-like fringes of the camphor's height. The wind gushed fiercely about her, testing her balance. Being twice her size, she was certain that the halfman could not follow, that the branches would snap under his weight. But he could still reach—she could feel him, clawing her heels, drawing blood with his nails. She navigated through the maze of branches, finally evading him and locating a way in which she could move down and backwards, blindly reaching for anything to hold onto, clutching at twigs no thicker than her fingers. When she could no longer see his red hide, she allowed herself a moment to breathe, and then the halfman dropped from above. She slinked away again, her feet kicking empty air, and suddenly her stomach lurched into her ribcage as the sound of splintering timber rounded in her ears.

She broke through the branches as she fell. The ground was strewn with leaves, but hit harder than dirt. Lifting herself carefully, she tested her body for pain, for broken bones—and was off again, her feet slapping against a flat unyielding surface. In a blur of stone and iron, she could feel the strangeness of her surroundings, the runes etched into the floor, the obelisks and massive rings, tall as trees, teasing her curiosity as she gasped for air. Vague human shapes towered over her, faceless giants lining the path. *Golems*, her people called the statues—they were everywhere, even in Ilmarinen, masquerading as boulders. But she'd never seen so many, standing upright like sentinels. The place was old beyond memory—a great city from aeons ago, from before the greater moon. Every stone in every courtyard echoed with the memories of the dead. But the forest was reclaiming it. Grasses sprouted between tiles. Roots cut through walls without doors or rooftops. Yet, she had no time to wonder at it all—she could not hope to lose the halfman here, in the open.

Turning toward a broken archway, beyond the watchful faces of stone, she flew deep into the thick of the wood, hoping to be concealed by the fan-shaped leaves. She moved with the grace of a hunted treer, navigating streams and slopes and thickets as though she had run through them a hundred times before. But the halfman was not giving up the chase. Any moment, her legs would give out, and he would be on top of her. Hiding had failed her and running no longer seemed the wisest course. If there was any chance to fight, it could not happen with her back to it. But there was no hope of turning. Even now, its monstrous breathing was raising the hairs of her neck. The shock of its raking claws threw her off balance and she collapsed hard, repeatedly punished as she rolled across the uneven, volcanic terrain.

She could feel the heat of his growl, smell the undigested meat between his oversized molars. The halfman overshadowed her, beating his muscled breast with arms thicker than her waist. But she did not show fear. With equal ferocity she returned his glare, with eyes of green fire, giving the monster pause. But her fists would not be enough. She frantically searched her surroundings, looking for anything she could use to do harm—a rock, a branch, anything at all. She was touching it before her eyes could follow. Spreading beneath her feet were hundreds of volcanic shards. Never having worn shoes, her soles were tough as aurochs' leather, but she could still feel the jagged pieces prickling her instep. She groped for the largest fragment. The obsidian edge cut into her palm as she lifted her arm to the moon and down again, the shimmering blade plunging between the halfman's eye and nostril. His howl stung her ears, and she stumbled away, mesmerized by the horror of it, by the black glass jutting from the mutilated face.

You should be running.

Before she could see it happen, his meaty fingers closed about her wrist and yanked hard, snapping her body like a doll. Tendrils of pain shot through her shoulder. She could not hope to wrestle free, even with two good arms. The halfman roared, pounding his chest again. She winced as it flexed for the killing blow. Her final thoughts were of home, of the brothers and sisters she would never see again. But the blow never came.

The halfman's grip died away, and her arm flopped lifelessly. His ape face, she could now see, was contorted in a mix of rage and confusion. An arrowhead jutted from its throat.

She blinked through the pain at the shapes emerging from the haze, hardly recognizing them for what they were. Human bodies were supple and hairy and did not gleam in the sunlight—at least not the kind of human bodies she was familiar with.

"The rumors appear to be true, Captain Dantes," one of the men said to the other. "Halfmen," he added, nudging the lifeless mass of fur with his boot, "and so close to camp."

"Aye," said the man on the right, tilting his faceplate open, "but what of *this* one?" He fixed his shaggy brows on her, astonishment showing through his age-sunken eyes.

She felt suddenly very young, lost and vulnerable, her gaze wandering with intense curiosity over the leather and bronze of their armor, over their belts and boots and gloves, as if never having seen clothing before. But outsiders were not entirely unknown to her people. It was what had brought her so far from home.

"Why, she's bare as a newborn!" the older man exclaimed. "It's a wood nymph if ever I saw one!"

"Her grace kindles the heart, indeed, Torgin," the Captain replied, "but she's just a girl, a feral child, perhaps, lost to the wood when the bogrens came to her village. And she's hurt."

She felt their stares, and though she could see they were branding her every curve to memory, she did not know to feel shame any more than a fish can know what it means to be wet. She simply stood, awaiting her next move, focused on holding herself still as a morning dewdrop, her right arm limp against her side.

The man called Captain pulled off his helmet. He had dark eyes and an ebony beard and was pleasing to look at, and did not seem capable of hating her, despite her parents' warning. Her instinct was to dash into the wood, but she did not flinch as he unhinged his cloak and stepped closer, wrapping her in it. She tugged at the hem, finding the fabric richer and more finely worked than her mother's tunic. He pulled a jeweled dagger from his belt, the finest blade she had ever seen, and with a single stroke cut a long strip from the edge of his cloak to fasten about her palm, staunching the flow of blood.

"Do you have a name?"

My name is Thelana.

"Can you speak?"

Yes.

Words did not leave her mouth and she did not know why. She understood most of what was spoken to her. It was a dialect similar to the one used by Aola, the outsider who taught her the way of the bow. But it'd been so long since speaking with anyone. Perhaps she'd forgotten how.

THE FIRST OMEN

OMEN

City by the Sea

1

A COMPASS FOR MISERIES

*If the body is offensive, then it
is offensive to be human.*

—Kjus

Again he planted his battle ax into the gelatinous head, squeezing slime from an antenna as he wrestled to stay seated aloft the snail's olive-green shell. With that final stroke, the cloven head submerged without a squeal and the warrior slid from its neck to the rim of the marsh. Under the turquoise moon, he gazed over his kill—at the monster that had fed on so many passersby—and spat.

Emmaxis reached over his shoulder, the skull-face trapped in the steel quivering with lust. He could feel the sword's eagerness like a flame coursing through him to his ankles. But it would not taste blood today. The attack had come from beneath the murky waters, offering little time to unsheathe the great sword.

Aside from the baldric he wore to carry his weapons, his clothing was the mud caking the muscled clefts of his torso, the leeches clinging to days' old blood, the dirt and twigs crowning the long blond tangles of his hair and beard. Standing in the midst of the swamp, he was like a statue worn by the ages, where the granite is chipped and made coarse. He gazed down at the reflection forming on the now still water. Only his eyes were soft, untarnished, seeming to belong to a different man.

A maple leaf, curled and brittle, was sticking to his shoulder. The tree that had dropped it did not belong to the swamp.

What winds brought this to me? From how far have you traveled? The gale carried the leaf from his fingertips, over and beyond the brambles of the marsh. Another shape was soaring in the crimson sky, a wing taking form as it approached. He shielded his brow from the eclipsing sun and there was now a creature where the shape had been, a man feathered from crested scalp to winged heel.

Familiarity loosened the grip he had on his ax. "Ouranos!" he called through gold tangles of beard, his voice hoarse, thirsting.

The avian shifted into a glide, taloned feet pointed earthward, the feathery membranes between his hips and wrists waxing to fullness. Ouranos shimmered, flexing his wing beyond his fingertips, changing hues like a peacock from silver gray to shades of blue.

"What brings you from Nimbos, Ouranos?"

The avian studied him, disappointment stretched across his angular face. "Always to the point with you, eh,

Xandr? No time wasted on mere formalities? No polite chatter regarding myself or the nest mate?"

Xandr betrayed nothing as he scraped the muck from his chest to reveal the long, winding scar that defined him. He had many similar scars, like pink script, tales of battle written across his body.

"I should have known to find you in such a place," Ouranos continued. "Drowning your miseries in misery."

Xandr knew the bird man hated the swamp. Growth choked the air with muddied greens and browns—moss-coated willows weeping like maids in mourning and boughs that twisted at odd angles to meet the sky. Only the smaller violet moon hemming the tree-line beckoned with a promise of hospitable lands beyond.

"This is no home for a human," the bird man admonished. "When will you return to the family of men?"

"Men are cruel and stupid things and no longer interest me," Xandr replied, amid the ear-pinching whine of a fist-sized dragon mosquito—a poisonous shade of green with wiry tendrils—which floated up from the moon to drink from the snail's corpse.

"So you are satisfied here, in this *Marsh of Melancholy?* You would be king among the . . . the mosquitoes?"

The avian could see that Xandr was unmoved, so he tried again, twittering in a gentler tone. "How have your wounds healed since last we parted?"

"I still have scars to remember you by," said Xandr, taking an overgrown root for a seat.

The avian made a noise strange to the Ilmarin's ear, an amalgam of human laughter and a parrot's squawking.

"How does the world look from above?" Xandr asked, letting his wet braid fall against his collarbone.

"All the lands are in disarray," Ouranos replied. "Everywhere I look . . . there is suffering."

"Yes, that much I am able to assume. But what is it to me? That is the way of things." Pulling the sword from his shoulder, Xandr impaled the ground between them. Xandr watched Ouranos eyeing his own reflection in the sword, and could sense that the avian hated the way the folds of the metallic skull face twisted the image of his face. The blade was a mirror surface, free of nicks or smudges, as if it were just born from a blacksmith's molten fire. Xandr cleared his throat. "The people can keep their miseries. I am done with them."

"Are your senses still attuned to the elements? Feel about you," the avian implored. "There is great change in the air. The middle lands grow colder . . . Omens of change abound."

Xandr's braid whipped about as he turned away. "Leave me alone." Somewhere in the heart of the marsh, a beast brayed with agony as something massive snarled and stomped. Numerous other creatures raised their voices in a fearful clamor, but Xandr paid them no heed. Only Ouranos' milky white-on-white pupils darted with apprehension—his bones were hollow and many an animal considered him prey.

"When will you stop wandering?" Ouranos persisted, reaching out to him with his feathered palm. "You cannot hope to outrun the gods, nor unfasten the strings of Fate."

"What do you know of human gods? Or of my fate?"

"I am your only friend. Who but I would know? It is ignoble to hold to the memory of the dead."

Xandr stared off into the distance, to a place he knew Ouranos could not see. "The dead are all I have."

"No!" Ouranos objected. "There are others like you. I have seen them, I—"

"Have you come here to torment me?" Xandr cried, the blue of his eyes receding under an angry brow.

"No, I've come to deliver a message."

"A message?" Xandr could not imagine who would do this. For nearly ten years he'd lived as a recluse, avoiding civilization, scavenging for food, sleeping—whenever fortunate—under shade of the wood.

"Two cycles past, a human came to the Tower of Heaven. He scaled Mount Spire to address our council, a feat we believed impossible. He hailed from the city by the Sea, from the capitol of the Hedonian Empire. They were at war, he told us, with the waterlings, with those they call *merquid*. It is strange that this should happen now, that waterlings should rise against groundlings when the two have coexisted for untold millennia. I fear it is a sign of the darkening times. The Hedonian spoke of a *Batal of Legend*. He offered a talent of gold so that we might seek him out, and so I knew I had to find you, as you are the only one who has spoken this name to me."

The name floated between them, no less poisonous than the dragon mosquitoes gathering at the corpse of the sinking snail.

"The bones of Batals have long become dust," Xandr replied. "For all anyone knows, they may never have existed at all."

"I was sent to find this Batal," Ouranos screeched, "to deliver the plea of Urukjinn! And since I believe you are this person, to your ears shall this plea fall!"

"Urukjinn? Should I know him?"

"He is the High Priest of the Sargonus Temple. Lead a contingent of hoplites against the merquid and he promises his virgin daughter to you, with such a dowry as to make a man king."

"Dowries and spoon fed princesses do not entice me. What of Nimbos? Is the Ascendency too cowardly to lend arms?"

"Since the Age of the Septhera we've kept to the mountains, and as a result we have never seen the face of war. You know this, Xandr. No groundling or waterling has ever posed a threat to us. If we were besieged, perhaps . . ."

"Avian cowards!" Xandr spat. "Your tongues should be cut off to speak of heroism! Even so, there's no Batal—it is a fiction born of hope, by desperate men." He tugged his sword southward, but the blade remained fixed in the damp soil. "I shall go my own way!" he barked, half-speaking to the weapon. With that, Emmaxis surrendered into a wild arc, nearly kissing Ouranos' lip. Still gripping the hilt, Xandr turned on his heel like a weathervane against a changing wind, the sword parallel to the horizon. A shaft of sun ran platinum white along its side, its tip shining like a jewel. He could feel Ouranos' eyes, amused and righteous, on his back.

"The sword directs you south, to Hedonia."

The Batal cursed and spat as he wrestled with the weapon.

"It is your destined path."

"No, Emmaxis follows blood. It is," he added tiredly, "a compass for miseries. Remember that its name means *blood spiller* in the Ilmarin tongue. It senses war, an opportunity for slaughter."

"In that case, that sword is a wicked thing. Why not toss it in the swamp and have done with it? It is unbecoming for one of your race."

Xandr's eyes fixed on the devilish intricacies of the skull face as though looking upon a long-departed friend. "If I do not carry it, who will? It is my *purpose*."

"You do not know that for certain, Batal," Ouranos said, "but if that is so, I suggest you do as it wills."

"Should I have done so," Xandr replied, "you would already be dead." But Xandr could not deny the bird man's reasoning. If the sword was his purpose, he would have to follow it.

"Hedonia is the greatest of all cities," Ouranos chirped softly. "If you go there, you may even find . . . whatever you seek."

Xandr maintained his gaze, a painter before an empty canvas, saying, with finality, "Yes. Perhaps there is something there for me in Hedonia."

"I am uplifted by your change of heart and shall tarry no longer," Ouranos replied. "Farewell, my friend, and good journey." The avian caught the gale, his feathers bristling and billowing with fullness, and with a sweep of his arms he was distant again.

The village was like any other. Irrigation channels radiated like the spokes of a wheel, splitting the fields, but the channels ran shallow or dusty. The huts that followed the riverbed were of thatched straw and stacked dung, with spaces left open for windows. Lone doors hung open, captive to the irregular whims of the wind, and age-old chips of paint hinted at better days. A three-legged beet dog looped in circles about the village square, losing a race to a lanky rooster.

The children were curious to approach him. Their ragged tunics were colored by age and human excess. Too poor for shoes, they pocked the hard dry earth with bare feet as they gathered, staring aghast at the man who wore no clothes but a baldric for his sword and ax, his weapons chiming with each step. Mothers and women of marrying age moved about hastily, their wicker baskets teetering overhead, embarrassed stares hidden under their shawls, as fathers and sons labored in the field, hacking at lifeless clay, dredging up water from wherever it could be found. After a short while, the children with older relatives were pulled away from the gathering, led back to the safety of their adobe domiciles with frightful whispering and hushes. No one else greeted him.

From the time he stumbled out of Ilmarinen as a boy, his nakedness was met with averted eyes, shouted insults, sometimes stones. They called him savage, and spoke of primitive people, like the Ilmar, as if less than human, so that in time he learned that the outside world despised him and his ilk. *Mankind should share no affinity to animals or the lesser species.* Civilized gods taught that humans reigned above other life forms, fashioned by the divine from a different substance. But his gods were not theirs. In cities, they worshiped before altars of stone, venerating symbols, idols of gold and silver and all that was rare beneath the earth. To the Ilmar, only things that grew were precious—*life*—and so Xandr rejected the local taboos, choosing seclusion over conformity, living far from the places where populations amassed. He was a man without home, without country, without kin. Having nothing, he feared nothing. Fearlessness served him in the untamed lands, in the dark, wild, lost places of Aenya, where the city-born went to die. But if he were to enter into Hedonia, the very heart of the civilized world, he knew he could not go as himself. Xandr would need to hide behind custom, become familiar again with the trappings of men. Learning to wear clothing would not be enough. Having survived, until now, by hunting and gathering, he had no currency and nothing with which to barter. His only possessions were his body and his weapons.

Finding no inn or tavern, he accosted a man hacking at rows of dirt with a rust-flaked hoe. Beside him, a hump-backed aurochs shackled to a plough hoofed at the clay, its frilled horns crisscrossing above the two men. "Blasted scrabs," Xandr heard him grumble. "They're more each year!"

"What place is this?" Xandr asked the farmer.

The man nudged the brim of his hat to better look at the stranger. "No place you'd want to be, I can assure you," he said, his nose dipping under his lip. "Most folk that pass through here don't know they did. But should anyone ask, this here's Akkad."

"You are different from the others in your village."

"And how's that?"

"You do not fear me."

"Should I?" A chuckle caught in his throat. "Fools just haven't been around as long as me. On the planet, that is. It's all in the eyes. Only Ilmarin-folk have eyes so fair."

Xandr smiled. "You have a gift."

"And you're a well-built fellow, even for a wild man," he replied, straining under a crooked spine. "You might not be some kind of god now, are you?"

"I confess I am not."

"Always good to be kind to strangers, see—never know when they might be a god."

"You have nothing to fear from me. Your kindness is your own." Even as he said this, Xandr could sense the man's growing unease. It was not an uncommon reaction. But the farmer was more intrepid than most, and Xandr did not have to guess the reason. Loss was camouflaged beneath the old man's unassuming demeanor—a plague or a raid had likely stolen his wife and children, and such men feared neither the loom of Fate nor the scythe of the Taker.

"How grow the crops this season?"

"Scrabs," he replied. "I'll be damned if you don't need a pickax to crack those buggers. They chew up my roots, but you can turn 'em into a nice soup and bowl. I only just got planting—ollyps, blums, watermelon grapes, napshins, hockenberries, tomatoes, the usual sort of thing—but harvest is smaller each year. I say—we're headed for famine again."

"Perhaps the Goddess shall favor you."

"Well, sure's hot today," he answered, with a wipe of his brow, most likely unsure of which goddess was meant. "I'd be grateful just for a cool breeze."

"Can you show me the way to Hedonia?"

"You mean you don't know? All roads lead to the city, or so they say. Don't you see it?" Silhouettes stretched across the turquoise moon, no bigger than the hairs on his arm. The shapes were unnatural, angular, like a ghostly fleet drifting in the ether. "You only have to follow the Phayus to the Sea."

"I am glad it's so near. I expected another cycle of walking."

"Three, I'd wager, if you got strong legs and keep a good pace," he said. "Or you could go by boat, if you had the coin for the ferryman. On a clear day like this, those monuments rise like mountains."

"I see."

"Tell me, son, why go to Hedonia?" His bitterness was evident, and even his aurochs seemed to agree, rattling in its harness and braying with distaste.

"I am summoned there."

"Well, you can't go as you are!" He attempted a laugh, but his mouth was too full of dust. "You'll be turned away at the gate! I was, once, when my wife was ill. Dressed too much like a beggar, they told me. Haven't you anything at all to wear?"

"I am Ilmar—we do not need *clothing*," he replied sharply, defensively, and immediately felt the fool, knowing he could not go without. Apologetically, he added, "I have long to join the company of men."

"Don't trouble yourself. I've got sandals to spare, made from my own hide. Well, not *my own* hide, but you figure my meaning. On lunar days I work as a tanner, when so many shoe worn travelers pass through here seeking the city."

Xandr could not tell whether the offer was purely out of kindness, a plea for self-preservation, or some measure of both. "I am grateful, but have no coin for it."

"Alas," he said with pity, "there are no poorer folk than Ilmarin-folk."

"I am not—we are not poor! No man is poor who wants for nothing. But I will return the favor, somehow."

"Pff!" He gestured him away. "*Blessed by Sargonus are those who show kindness to strangers.* But be forewarned—should you find yourself caught in the wheels of civilization, sooner than you realize you'll be laboring like my beast to repay some debt. It is a land of riches, to be sure, but those who go there hunger for want of the soul, living to forever quench their greed, their appetite for wine and meat, their lust. See what the name itself has come to mean—*hedonist.*"

"Do not preach to me," Xandr said. "When my people made their exodus from their lands, the men were made beggars and the women forced into bondage. I know of what it means to be civilized."

"Now I meant no offense, and you have my apologies. But my offer still stands. Come daybreak, I can provide you with footwear and something to gird your loins. Until then, may Sargonus watch over you."

With the farmer's words fresh in his ears, Xandr took shelter under a eucalyptus tree, which sprang from the riverbank. Bathing in the Potamis—what was here called the Phayus—could wait until sunrise.

Solos melted like the yoke of an egg into the surface of the greater moon in the celestial ritual that turned day to night, and slowly he drew forth Emmaxis, gazing at his distorted reflection. He had days to succumb to the lure of sleep. Gold and turquoise and violet streaked the dying sky and in shifting clouds he sought familiar faces. And one by one, the stars emerged, glinting like tips of daggers.

Watch the sky.

Those had been the last words of his mentor.

2

DREAMS OF ILMARINEN

Let me run the hills of Ilmarinen
With soles in soil and grass
Where braids play the gale
And sun splashes sharp shoulders.
I wrap the sky around me
And birth myself to freedom.
Let the universe swell my lungs
And stars scorch my heart.
My feet pound the river rock
as I run the hills of Ilmarinen.

—A song of the Solstice Night

Hand over foot, the young boy managed his way to the top of the plateau. The air was crisp about his pores and the green scent of the Goddess filled his lungs. His arms spread across the horizon, across the turquoise crescent that was Infinity, the greater moon. The other moon, Eon, glittered like an amethyst in the morning sky. Melting snow cascaded beneath his battered soles, vanishing into mists below. All around him, water could be seen pooling over sheets of rock, feeding into the sun gilded Potamis River. A thousand shades met his eyes, from the jade of the leaves to the amber of the oaks to the purple of the ilms. To the north, the Mountains of Ukko met the heavens like strokes of gray-white chalk.

Apart from his wooden sword's baldric and the lapis lazuli in his braid, the young monk was clad in nothing but sky, with all the ground his shoes and the sun his coat. The sparring weapon and the blue mineral were his only accouterments, but in this moment, he was more interested in the stone, remembering the River Girl who had given it to him—she had a pleasing face and an easy gait and he had admired the skill with which her henna was applied, the pattern running up her thigh to form an arrow between her breasts.

Effortlessly, his hands and feet met the nooks in the olive tree's roots. Descending the hill, he spotted his mentor rounding the path.

"Queffi!" the boy called. "I am here!"

Xandr was well aware that Quasil did not appreciate his sudden disappearances, yet his mentor never punished his boyish eagerness to explore. Blinded by the sunbeam reflecting off the old man's scalp, the boy suppressed the urge to laugh. It was not that his mentor lacked for hair— his ash white locks reached to the middle of his back and his silver streaked beard concealed the whole of his collarbone. But the top of his head was as barren as the western hemisphere.

"Recite the names again," his mentor droned, steadying himself on his quarterstaff.

What enthusiasm Xandr had shown earlier that morning drained from his voice. Not ecology. Again. Why couldn't they learn more about saurians or mammoths or horgs? He doubted he would ever face mortal danger from an elm.

"High in the canopy there, I see a camphor tree, with elms all about it."

"Good."

But these trees were easy to name. Oak and camphor were made into homes, the walls of each room integrated with the living whole, a good example, Quasil loved to remind him, of how every life is connected to another. Lesser known flora, like the dead looking baobab tree, Xandr mistook for a fledgling oak, for which his mentor had rapped him on the head.

They continued on, the boy directing his mentor to things he was certain to recognize, through a grove of twisting bark with dull green leaves. ". . . and these here, of course, are olive trees . . ." The fruits were small and flat, not yet ripe for the beating. It's odd, he mused, how the younger limbs are smooth but the trunk and the older branches are rough and gnarled . . .

"Xandr!" a voice rumbled. "Focus! What of these flowers here?"

The boy suppressed a groan. "Um . . . blue orchids?"

"They are blue, indeed, but are only similar to orchids in their appearance. Did you forget?" Disappointment gnarled his mentor's face, making him look more like an olive tree. "You must not forget the names of the Goddess, or she will forget you."

"Yes Queffi, that *is* true, but—"

QuasiI bent to examine a sapling, pressing the tiny leaves between thumb and forefinger. He was not so different from his pupil, often distracted, aloof, but Xandr's respect for him never lessened. Despite his great age, his mentor's hands looked strong enough to squeeze water from a rock. And QuasiI knew things no one else did. He could tell when rain was to fall days in advance, knew the age of any plant by touch alone, and he referred to each animal as part of a great family, explaining how the rabbit was cousin to the deer and the deer to the ornith.

Every year on the morning of the Solstice, the keepers would descend to the village to select among the wisest of the youth a protégé to be raised in the monastery. A boy or girl showing an aptitude for metallurgy was taught the secrets of metals, and after a lifetime of study was expected to replace their mentor as Keeper of Metallurgy. So it went with all the secrets of the universe. But Xandr was unlike the others. For as long as he could remember, he lived with the keepers, and though he cared little for plants, he was expected to know everything about them. As QuasiI often reminded him, the discipline of ecology was the greatest of all the sciences, but Xandr could not bring himself to agree. He much preferred tales of the Zo, with their planet-spanning cities and fantastic machines and weapons. The boy could not understand why the Ilmar, despite seemingly limitless knowledge, had no such things as the Zo—why the Ilmar were, in fact, forbidden possessions of any kind. Whenever he asked the keepers about it, he was simply told, "You are the Batal," and nothing more.

"Shall we go over flowers, then?" QuasiI suggested.

Leaves crackled and seeds popped underfoot as the boy circled. Xandr was a jumble of energy, nimbly ducking branches and hopping roots. "Queffi . . . there are things I wish you to teach me that you never have."

"Such as?" He arched a bushy eyebrow, and the boy understood that his mentor knew what weighed upon his heart, and was testing him.

Xandr settled on a simple question, in order to loosen his mentor's tongue. "I want to know of the things beyond Ilmarinen. Is it true that people south of the river must hide their bodies?"

"It is true," he replied matter-of-factly. "Clothing, or fabric, is woven from many different plants, animal skins as well. The most common method is the loom, by which—"

"Queffi!" the boy interrupted. "That is not what I wanted to know."

QuasiI feigned confusion, but the boy remained adamant, rooted to a mossy boulder. "With whom have you been speaking?"

"Brother Zoab," the boy admitted.

"I should have known." He cleared his throat, as though he were about to recite from the philosophers. "We are as diverse as the flowers, Xandr. Just as the soft soil suits the ilm so that it may flourish, so do human customs vary. Ice does not fall here as in the Dark Hemisphere, nor does the sun scorch the flesh as in the West. Here in the *Womb of Alashiya*, we live as simply as we are born, as Kjus teaches."

"But Queffi," the boy went on, hopping from his perch, "Brother Zoab told me that the Ilmar cannot venture beyond our borders without clothing, that we are hated otherwise, that the women in some cultures may even be killed—with stones—should their bodies be seen. I do not understand these things, Queffi. I asked Brother Zoab about it, but he gave no answer." The boy stood in silence, staring into his own palm, wondering at its complexity, at the faint blue lines beneath the skin. "Are we not to roam freely about the world? Or is there some flaw in the people of the outer world?"

"No," Quasil asserted. "The body is an absolute good. Mankind is born of the Mother Goddess, just as our cousins, the merquid and the avian. We are lovingly and minutely refined over the aeons. The flaw is not in us—I fear—but in the stars. Since time immemorial, before the greater moon loomed in the heavens, we were all Ilmar. For hundreds of millennia, humanity knew nothing of want or possessions."

"What happened?" Xandr asked a little too loudly. "Was it the *Cataclysm*?"

"No." he paused, addressing Xandr with uncertainty, with half-truths. "It was not the external world that changed us. It came from within. The Zo ate of the fruit of knowledge, but did not drink from the well of wisdom. They looked upon themselves and saw that they were fauna, and became ashamed, and in their hubris longed to separate from the Mother Goddess, to become gods themselves. Of all the species of this world, only humans reject what they are. This shame is a perversion. If one does not see the Goddess within himself, he will not see it in others.

If man can hate himself, he will hate others of his kind ... and even those not of his kind. "

The boy rocked uneasily, disappointed. He never cared for abstractions, for ideologies that forced him to ponder until his head hurt. For once, he wished for concrete truths. The history of Aenya was a puzzle, one in which many of the pieces were missing.

"But Queffi," he began, squaring his shoulders and choosing his words carefully, "when the greater moon came into being after the Cataclysm, something changed. Man changed. How? Did it have something to do with what Brother Zoab told me, about the star called *The Wandering God?*"

QuasiI paused to glare at him, then hurried off, his staff clacking against the stones. "I am not so certain Zoab should speak to you of such things. You are not yet a man."

Xandr held his anger in his fists so that it not show on his face. He was no longer a child. When a boy or girl began to show hair about the loins, they would partake in the rituals of the Solstice Night. Though Xandr had yet to jump the sacred bonfire hand-in-hand with a girl that was to be joined to him, the time was upon him, as evidenced by his maturing body. "No," he protested, "my hair has grown and my chin is coarse. Soon I'll be bearded, and a man!" Xandr had never challenged his mentor so openly before, but he still lacked the courage to meet the deep well of wisdom that were his mentor's eyes.

"Have you been practicing the technique we went over?"

Devoid of thought, a hand flied to the pommel at his hip. "The *delayed counter*?" Yes, I have. Every day and night!"

"Show me."

"Wait! You always trick me into forgetting my questions this way. But not this time." And he folded his arms defiantly.

"So the Batal has come of age, eh?" It was more a question than a statement. "Come." Without a further word, they followed a path clear of vegetation, formed by years of treading feet.

Layers of limestone rose above the tree line. An immense white willow grew at its peak. Its trunk always made Xandr think of a bent woman with a cane. It was a place for bloodless battles, long discourses on philosophy, and an observatory for the Zo, Alashiya, and Skullgrin constellations. As was their custom, QuasiI let his staff against the mossy stone and was seated. Xandr folded his legs atop the boulder below, tucking his manhood between his thighs, a thing which had become a bother lately, especially when the young girls bathing in the waterfalls in the valley below crept into his mind's eye. He assumed it was a part of his growing to maturity, but he was destined to be the Batal, which made him wonder whether he would ever join in the festivities of the Solstice Night.

"The sapling," QuasiI began, "too feeble for the outer world, remains safe within its seed. There it waits till ready, till strong enough to break its shell and lay roots in the earth."

More metaphors! If there was one thing Xandr disliked more than abstract answers, it was metaphors. "But teacher," Xandr objected, "I've already bested you with my sword!"

The old monk waved a dismissive hand. "That is not what matters. Do not forget the sayings of Kjus— 'knowledge not tempered by wisdom sows destruction'. I may know to destroy this jasmine," he added, caressing the violet bulbs of a flower sprouting from between the crevices in the rock, "yet I may not have the wisdom to hear it speak to me."

Xandr threw his shoulders back, the sunlight turning his hair to gold. "But I am ready, Queffi. Ready to leave Ilmarinen, to become the Batal."

"And how can you be so certain, my son, when you do not know what lies beyond the Potamis? Look there." Quasil pointed to a tree as tall as the sky, with branches thick enough to walk upon. "The Batal is like the mighty camphor. It begins as a berry no bigger than your thumb, but then it grows, becoming a home to many species . . ."

Having heard the lecture countless times, Xandr's mind drifted. Quasil was either stubbornly repeating himself or becoming forgetful. The boy longed for Brother Zoab's tales of magic and monsters and heroism.

Shifting in his limestone seat, he pulled at his ankle to study his sole. The underside of his foot was black as tar and rough as bark, the cracks in it like some form of lettering. In his fourteen years of pounding up the jagged slopes to his monastery home, of navigating the river rocks lining Ilmarinen's southern border, of stomping through raw earth and twigs, his feet could have borne him across half the planet. But today—he could not remember from when or where—a sharp sensation followed his steps. Being Ilmarin, it had to have been a long splinter for him to notice. Running a thumbnail to his heel, he discovered what he'd taken for a splinter was in fact a knife-edged seedling. His fingernails drew blood as he worked to remove it.

After his mentor was finished speaking, he looked up from his sole, saying, "But am I not already the Batal?"

QuasiI rubbed his skull, forming new folds of flesh. "No. Not yet." He gazed into the sunrise, drawing images with his hands. "Only by relinquishing pride, by surrendering possessions, can one hope to escape the mistakes of the past. It is why the Goddess chose *us*, for of all the world's peoples, only the Ilmar desire nothing."

"But will you not tell me, plainly, what I am meant to do?"

The wizened monk drew a long, tired breath. "You will know when you learn to listen to the trees, to hear the voices of Alashiya."

As if remembering something urgent, the old monk's attention came away and they became aware of it—between the turquoise moon and the violet glow of the smaller—a gray ribbon of smoke was diffusing over the orange sky.

Xandr could see the turmoil in his mentor's eyes, but his own imagination did not lend itself easily to horror. "What could it mean?"

"No. Not this," he murmured, never straying from the ribbon of smoke. Instantly, the staff was in his hand, no longer a stick for walking but a weapon, as QuasiI transformed into a warrior of commanding presence. "We've been found! Hurry, Xandr! Today you prove yourself!"

And for the first time the boy sensed real fear in his teacher's voice.

3

JEWEL OF THE SEA

*Cities rise and fall with the tide. Gods of
stone and symbol vanish in the winds of ages.
But the children of Alashiya are eternal.*

—Kjus

Banners rippled in the air, blue and tapered and hemmed with tassels, each with a truncated trident emblazoned in gold. Bridging each tower, battlements rose and fell with the slope of the land, atop which hippocampus-driven chariots patrolled two-by-two.

In a canvas of disparate humanity, a multitude of peoples crashed like waves against the city's arches—moneylenders from Thetis, fish mongers from Thalassar, craftsmen from Northendell, and traders from the far eastern provinces of Shemselinihar. Lizard jerkins mingled with distantly embroidered muslin tunics, while pleated kilts married striped djellabas and clanking chain mail challenged revealing chitons. Many were of a displaced people,

Xandr knew, populations which, due to invasion or famine, no longer possessed lands to call their own. Whether any were of his race, there was little way of knowing. Despite the plethora of customs on display, only Ilmarin fashion— or rather the complete absence of it—was shunned here. Individuals attired in clothing from a hundred different cultures coexisted in a semblance of harmony, but the sight of a human body was to be abhorred or pitied, as one would an animal, a beggar or a slave.

He tugged at his kilt, the one the farmer in Akkad had been kind enough to give, keenly aware of each and every loose stitch—it grated his skin and was damp with his sweat, and the seams pulled in opposition with his movement, the constant sensation almost unbearable. But the girdle about his waist was a far greater discomfort, roping him like a man on the gallows, stemming the tide of blood to his loins. He supposed that he would learn to adapt, as he had learned to ignore his baldric and the weight of his weapons. Splashes of morning sun warmed his bare shoulders, and a cool mist from the Sea rolled over and around his upper body, but the lower half of him was numb to the touch of the world. Bound in sandals, he could not feel the hill beneath him, the soft shifting sands, the sunbaked limestone, the dew from the tall coastal grasses that grew between the rocks. There was only the dull leather sole, step after step.

Continuing down to the coastline, a multitude of tongues jarred his eardrums, as few could be counted to converse in the same dialect. Hedonian speech, which to the Ilmarin sounded overly syllabic and flowery, was omnipresent, contorted to suit the enunciations of conquered languages. Adding to the noise was the twang of the sitar player's F-string, the trombone-like bray of a saurian as it tugged at the chains tethered to its three gilded horns, the purr of the green-striped saber tooth pacing in its cart, and the sympathetic applause for a strongman swinging his daughter from the rope in his teeth. The chiming of the merchant nomads' wares—from ivory prayer beads to wards of eyeball-and-hand—added to the cacophony.

Under the dizzying height of the central gate's topstone, centurions directed the traffic of emigrants, gleaming like bronze golems, abstracts of tridents emblazoned along their convex arms. It was not long before Xandr's weapons drew attention. Two men accosted him. Their horsehair crested helmets, too hot for peacetime, were tilted away from their faces. One was newly ripened to manhood, and though weighted and stewing in his bronze, hopped from sandal to sandal with naïve exuberance. The other was in his middle years, idling against the lip of his hoplon. He had a wary look about him and his breastplate with its dull polish and clawed grooves gave evidence of battle.

"From what land do you hail?" he asked, swatting at mammoth-flies with his miniature cat-o'-nine-tails.

"I am from a far off land," Xandr replied.

"And what business do you have in the capital?" he droned, grown bored with the words.

"I was summoned by your priest."

"There are some three hundred clerics here. You will have to give me a name, or—"

"Urukjinn," Xandr intoned, hiding, as best as he could manage, his newfound longing to tear the soldier's head from the collarbone.

"What?" the fresh-faced soldier interrupted, "Do you mean to say the High Priest of the Sargonus Temple summoned you?" Incredulously, he glanced toward his companion.

Ignoring the youth's presence entirely, the hoplite studied Xandr with a mix of contempt and revulsion. "The priest does not summon . . ." he began, but Xandr could see him taking in the kilt and sandals, the immense sword mirroring his face, clearly unable to decide whether to call him beggar or barbarian.

"I am . . . *the Batal*," he admitted through clenched teeth. "Now let me through."

"You!" the younger man exclaimed. "*You* are the Batal? I'd heard you were eleven feet tall."

"Please, Finias, no one asked what you've heard, nor does anyone care."

A man at the dusk of boyhood, Xandr eyed him. Brother Zoab taught how worlds existed with only one moon or none at all. On Aenya, the greater and smaller moon affected every aspect of culture and language. Infinity was synonymous with the positive, greater attributes, whereas the small moon served as a metaphor for the lesser. A child of ill-health was born under Eon. A man of sizeable stature was named after Infinity. But this *Finias* displayed no characteristic one could call greater. His greaves, breastplate and helm boasted more intricate etching than those of his comrade, but they fit him loosely. No doubt he was of an aristocratic house, his armor a family heirloom.

"Well, what do you think?" Finias asked sheepishly. "Should we let him through? Could he be the Batal of Legend?"

"Oh, I'm certain of it!" the other man answered, swinging and missing the mammoth fly buzzing at his ear. "As are the other dozen Batals raving in our streets! You've been filling your head with too much bard shit, kid. But as I'm in no mood to scuffle with muscled lunatics, there's no sense turning him away. Escort him to First Commander. He'll have fun with him." Eyeballing Xandr, he added, "I warn you, vagrants coming here making brouhaha end up dead, or worse, in the dungeons."

Sunbaked roof tiles and fluted marble sprawled across their plane of view as Xandr and Finias passed under the arch and into the city. Xandr allowed his senses to drown in the exotic. Carpets of obscene complexity lay draped in loose piles, and children perched in niches high above the streets, tapping bronze into plate-ware. Housewives sat on carved benches, fingering spinning mud into pottery. Aromas from a thousand different nations confounded his nostrils, from mounds of powdered saffron to barrels of almonds.

"This is the market district," Finias remarked. "Long ago it was a temple complex, I think, but it's turned to ruin.

"Um, there are many things to do here," he went on, stealing nervous glances at Xandr, who towered by his side. "From the looks of you, you've never seen a city."

"I have," Xandr replied.

"Ah, but no city like Hedonia, I'd wager. All the delights of the world can be found here. That's why Hedonia's called the *Jewel of the Sea*! If you like, we can go to the stadium to see the chariots, or perhaps the gladiators would better suit someone of your . . . er, profession. Father took me to the fights when I was little, said it would make me a man, but I was sickened by the blood. He also took me to the races. I liked it better."

"I have no interest in any of that," said Xandr. "Just show me to the priest."

"Yes, sir." Finias shifted uncomfortably under his shoulder plates. "I don't suppose you'd care for the theater? There are several performances showing right now by some of our finest dramatists. One of them, I believe, is about you."

Xandr paused in mid-stride, noticing the second wall curtaining the horizon. "About me?"

"Truly!" he said, beaming with enthusiasm. "It's called, *Batal and the Floating City of Abu-Zabu.* I mean, the actor doesn't share your build, of course, but actors are meant for acting, not brawling. He does have a booming voice though . . . you can hear him all the way in the two-mite seats, which is good because I can scarcely afford better. But it's quite a riot—I've watched it seven times already. It's about your adventures. About how you slew the two-headed giant of Abu-Zabu."

"Did I now?" Xandr's lips eased into a smile. "I was not aware of that."

Courage crept into Finias' voice, though he still failed to make eye contact. "So, did you really slay the two-headed giant of Abu-Zabu?"

"No. I've never seen a two-headed giant, nor heard of a place called Abu-Zabu."

"Oh." Drained of his eagerness, the boy engrossed himself in the pavers on the street, counting the ones that were missing. "But if you didn't slay the giant," he went on, tapping a pebble from his sandal, "you must not be the one we hoped for, the Batal of Legend, I mean."

"You are fond of speech," Xandr admitted.

"Oh, that's true, sir."

When they arrived before the shadow of the second gate, Xandr peered down the alleyway framed by the face of an old library and the inner city wall. Under dimly glowing lanterns, he could make out the tents that served as homes and the peasants in their soiled and tattered clothing.

"Do not go that way!" Finias called out. "It is a wretched place . . ."

An aged man sat amid his possessions, rattling a pair of obol in his tin. With a shift of his head, the man recited, "Good sirs, sit a spell and be moved, if you will. I am no mere beggar, but a proud legionnaire of the Stygian campaign, who lost his sight to heathen hands. Alas, I cannot longer work, and only ask a pittance for a respectable burial."

Finias lurched suddenly, kicking the man with his greave. "Get moving, worm! And take your rubbish with you. You know you can't make your homes here."

"Let him be!" Xandr cried, surprised by the youth's sudden assertiveness. But already the old man was fleeing, making a trail of his belongings.

"But . . ." Finias muttered, "they're the basest class! They sleep in their own piss!"

"He said he was a legionnaire."

"Oh, they all say that. And they don't belong here along the tower wall, Demacharon said so. Muck up the whole place with their filth. Besides, he could have robbed you."

"If I am here to face merquid, feeble paupers should hardly pose a threat to me. Do that again and you shall know my might, firsthand."

The Hedonian shrank away. "Forgive me."

Xandr scowled. Could someone of Ilmarin birth have been treated here with such cruelty? "I thought such men were turned away at the gates."

"That's the whole point, isn't it? Hedonia's bursting with such riffraff. Can't keep them all out, you know. It's a big city, and now we have gill knocking on our gates from the other side."

"Have you seen them?"

"Who? The gill?" he said. "No, not yet, but from what I've heard, well . . . they do give me the creeps."

Despite Finias' protests, Xandr ventured deeper into the shadows, where the glow of sun and moons was absent. His guide kept close behind as disturbing revelations set upon his innocent eyes.

"I've never been this far in," Finias admitted. "I'm no longer a guide here."

The Ilmarin paid him no heed. "So . . . this is where Hedonia hides its poor and downtrodden," he said quietly. "Did your father never show you this?"

"No, sir. He died a long time ago, on a campaign to liberate the barbarians."

Children huddled near a flame to roast pigeons and rodents. Peasants mottled with boils shuddered with fever. A few bodies lay wedged between stone embankments as feasts for mammoth flies. A newborn wailed like a distant squawking bird, its pleas going unanswered.

Someone called to them from below in a voice so strained from lack of use it could hardly be recognized as a woman's. She had not reached the third season of her life, yet her face was split from years of worry, where soot had set too deeply to be washed away. Dark strands, never knowing the touch of a blade, reached long across her face, and many spindly legs skittered freely between each hair. Finias stepped away, shielding his nostrils with a raised forearm, but Xandr knelt beside the woman, gazing honestly upon her. Her eyes were clear, he could see, as they were so often washed by tears.

"What do you want?" he asked her.

She straightened, letting the ox hide slip from her knee to reveal a thigh. "One copper drachma," she answered, pointing to the upturned helmet in her lap, "for half a passing." She worked up a smile but it was hardly sincere.

Xandr turned to his companion. "Give her what money you have."

"B-But, sir!" he stammered. "If this is what you crave, I assure you, there are better women to be had in Hedonia! This is not the place for us! Come away with me to the Temple of Irene, choose from the youngest stock, from the most lovely females the Empire has to offer, any shape you fancy . . ." but seeing how the barbarian remained unmoved, the Hedonian added, "For the right price, there are the sacred virgins, trained in the arts of love without ever knowing a man's touch."

"I care not for whores!" Xandr cried. "Give her what money you have and I will repay you in blood on the battlefield."

The soldier emptied his purse into the woman's lap. Falling on her hands and knees, she poured the contents onto the cobblestone, counting four gold drachmae and two copper. Fearing she might be deceived, she hurried the gold into her mouth, bent the soft metal between her molars. With that, she lifted her eyes to Xandr, awestruck.

As he motioned to leave, she loosened her tunic, and they could see her pale flesh stretching tightly over her ribs.

"No," he said, turning again.

"Please, kind sir," she murmured, "do not shame me. Of all the times I've lent this body for copper, let it now be for gold."

He snatched up the garment, thrusting it violently into her arms.

"Mercy." Casting her face in shame and shadow, she motioned to a bundle against the crumbling wall. "Would you like . . . my daughter instead? S-She's older than she looks, and she has experience . . ."

With that, Xandr felt his face grow hot, and his fists clench, so that even Finias was made to tremble. "Away from me, whore! And with this," he added, indicating the coins in her hand, "buy back, if you can, her innocence."

As the two strangers retreated to the façade that was Hedonia, a pair of eyes followed, shining like emeralds amid the squalor and the shadows, hidden in that den of man's waste and the waste that had been made of men.

Throughout the city, in bronze relief across doorways and on marble pedestals, in armor donned by stone goddesses and flesh and blood soldiers, almost everywhere a traveler could look, Xandr noticed the varied forms of the trident.

In some instances, the standard of Hedonia was garlanded by laurel leaves. Elsewhere, the trident included flanking hippocampi. But as they neared the Coast of Sarnath, it was more often a rising sail from the mast of a trireme. The *naval trident,* as Finias called it, greeted them at the door of the First Commander.

Demacharon was a broken man. It was clear to see upon meeting him, though Xandr could not tell what had broken him. Weaving across his handsome face, a violet discoloration divided his cheek and chin—a scar that had not healed properly. But it was little clue to his brokenness, as Demacharon wore the deformity like a medal of honor.

"What have you brought me now, Finias?" he asked without ceremony. "Another cliché?" A map spread across the granite slab between them and Xandr noticed the Empire's chalk outline, which the neighboring kingdoms could never have agreed to. Hedonia encompassed all the lands from the Dead Zones in the West to the Dark Hemisphere in the East.

"This is Xander," Finias stammered. "He claims to be the *Batal of Legend.*"

"Excellent," the commander replied. "In that case, we are saved."

"Yes, um, and he seeks audience with the High Priest."

"Oh?" He sighed with distaste, lifting his eyes to study the newcomer. "Few men look upon the High Priest. What makes you believe you're worthy of the honor?"

"It is no honor for me," said Xandr. "I merely answered a summons."

"A summons?" he replied, and as if there was no reasonable way to reply, he turned to the young escort. "Finias, go do something useful, will you? Go groom my steed."

"Yes, sir!" he exclaimed, slamming a fist against his breastplate. "*Strength and Honor*, sir!" he cried, making an overly dramatic about-face before marching out of the room.

"Yes, yes, strength and honor," Demacharon said warily, waving him off.

As the sound of Finias' clanking bronze softened, Demacharon leaned across the empire. "You're a long way from home. Yes, I know what you are—the refugees we've taken in over the years have difficulty adjusting to . . . *modesty*."

"To modesty or shame?" The thought of other Ilmar passing through the city made his heart thrum, but Xandr's hardened face betrayed no emotion.

"And what would you know of shame? Or anything pertaining to civilized matters?" Demacharon demanded. "Your kind prefer living where deserters go in exile." He stood, revealing the naval emblem of trident and trireme across a bronze breast, his wine dark cape swaying from his shoulders. "But you can fornicate with swine for all anyone cares. Leave the moralizing to the moralists, I say. My citizens and I fear only one thing, and we have it in great supply: xenophobia—a distrust of strangers, especially those with points of view."

Despite the commander's harsh words, Demacharon did not elicit the same reaction as the guard at the wall. There was sincerity in his convictions that made it difficult for Xandr to hate the man. "So what's your story?" he went on. "Witness many awful things in the untamed lands?"

"No worse than on your campaigns," Xandr replied. "Though my hands are clean of innocent blood."

The commander grinned appreciatively. "We've beaten back the wild so that men might live free of terror. The lives of a few short-sighted dissenters are a small price to pay. Besides, our hands rinse clean in the holy waters of the Sargonus Temple."

"Do they?"

Demacharon stood by the tower window. A glorious vista spread before him, the center of the city, and beyond it, the surrounding cityscape with its gleaming marble colonnades, magnificent rotundas, and pediments lined with gods. At its extremity, the land sloped to the opposing city wall, where blue and white roared and rocked against silhouettes of long narrow hulls and masts as numerous as shafts of wheat in a field. Xandr was no stranger to the Sea, yet so much water never failed to impress him. Even at such distance, the salty air was intoxicating.

"My father was a legionnaire," he said slowly, "as his father before him. The cause has been in my family for generations, and you think to barge into my chambers, lob a few pointed words at me and alter my loyalties?"

Xandr was tempted to argue but chose the course of discretion.

Now he could see, through the opening in the wall, the monument complex casting its shadow over the city. In a perfect rectangle of green, the Temple of Sargonus stood in gleaming white and gold, mirrored in a pool of equal dimension, flanked by six obelisks that stabbed at the turquoise moon. It was a three-sided pyramid flat at the apex, with a ramp of steps ascending from its base to the arched recess at its center.

The Ilmarin was dumbfounded, speaking only as words came to mind. "What giants could have built such a thing?"

"None," Demacharon replied. "Unless men can be called giants. Slaves and freemasons, tens of thousands, laboring for decades before the time of the High Priest Callusa. Impressive, isn't it? I've dragged holy men prepared to meet the Taker before the Temple and watched them renounce their gods, watched them grovel in humility." After a pause, he added, "I don't know what his Eminence thinks you can achieve—even if you *were* sent from Nimbos. I never would have thought it possible, the Batal an Ilmar, a small degree above animal. Yet if his Eminence believes, I must also. But mind your tongue before him. Nature worship is a heresy in Hedonia, and heresy is punished by death."

4

THE SECRET

Knowledge is mastery.

—Kjus

Hundreds of feet below her, night fires spread like constellations. Street lamps gave shape to roads. Torches revealed angled temples, domes of courthouses and the elliptical walls of amphitheaters. Mirroring the cityscape, the velvet sky welcomed her with its familiarity, made her dream of nights sleeping on rooftops. But if not for the moon painting her skin green with its glow, she doubted she would see the rope running down the slope to her waist. It was a perfect night for a crime against god.

Climbing the pyramidal structure of the Sargonus Temple would be considered suicide by most. Dantes would have surely dissuaded her, she was certain, but his body was lying on a battlefield in the Plains of Narth, and so there was no longer anyone to keep her recklessness in check.

All was silent but for the hush of distant waves. An icy wind came before it, like lightning before thunder, and she clutched her jade cloak more tightly to keep from shuddering. She had never seen the Sea like this, and even now her mind reeled at the vast stretch of water reaching for the horizon.

What am I doing here?

It was a question she kept asking herself, even though she knew the answer. Other thieves might rob from the market district, but Thelana was not them. She knew the fruit vendor's newborn daughter by name, and that the carpet weaver's son was gathering coin for his wedding feast. The merchants' coffers were only a little heavier than hers and they were not without hungry mouths. In her eyes, Hedonia's villains were the tax collectors, robbing the crop of the peoples' labor to lavish upon the temple. But taking even a mite from the priesthood was a thing unheard of and, as for stealing from the idol itself, that was lunacy. The city god, however, was not hers to fear. If she were to steal from him his pearl eyes, how could it matter? Sargonus was a blind god, never seeing the suffering of the downtrodden in the alleyways

Perhaps it wasn't so much the treasure, but the climb that seduced her, with its slick incline and pinnacle as high as a mountaintop. How often had she taken up similarly unreasonable challenges, finding herself sitting in places her siblings considered beyond reach? How often had she underestimated the strength of a branch only to be punished with a broken arm and no dinner? Was she, as Dantes was so fond of espousing, as stubborn as an aurochs? *I can climb that*, she heard herself saying, under the shadow of that beautiful bough in her memory, to goading brothers who never seemed to care one whit whether she plummeted to a broken neck. *I can climb anything.*

Where others had slid—rather than fallen—to their deaths, or had been shot down at the onset, Thelana had succeeded, scaling the pyramid under the cover of night with only a knotted rope and her bare feet. Now, more threatening than the known, was the unknown, what only the most exalted of the priesthood ever laid eyes upon: the defenses of the temple's inner sanctum. Surely, there would be guards, unless the priesthood never bothered to prepare for such sacrilege, which, from what she understood of Hedonians, was possible. No danger could dissuade her, however, for surviving improbable odds proved a better bet than the certainty of shame and impoverishment should she fail.

She reached between her slender shoulders, feeling the smooth treasure that once belonged to Kinj Sonoma, the master thief and metal smith. The gold in her hands glittered in the dim city lights and with the click of a jade-tipped button, its two halves split apart, revealing a system of tightly-wound spools and pulleys. Like a bat unfolding its wings, her sword spread into a bow.

Digging her toes between the stones, chipping at surfaces untouched for millennia, she drew herself over the lip and into shadow. There she would bide her time until both eclipses were past, until sun and moon wheeled behind the turquoise giant, thus turning the world black. Drawing into a bundle of jade, she fended off the cold sea air, and picked at the string of her bow like a lutenist as her mind meandered paths of days long gone.

"Thelana, are you listening?"

The little girl turned, her chestnut braid swaying, the wooden bow slack against her thighs. "I *am* trying," she said to the Nibian woman, "but I'm just no good!"

In the distance, Thelana could feel the man's eyes riding the curves of her backside. *Why does he look at me so? Is there something wrong with me?*

"Let her be, Aola. She's just a little scamp." His tone was made more degrading by the chewing noises escaping his lips.

From the time of the outsiders' arrival, Brutus treated her family like creatures who had crawled out from under some rock. But they were just as strange to her as she was to them. For Thelana, they were little more than faces and arms. Sometimes she wondered whether they possessed bodies at all. Like turtles, they were never without their shells, and she could not imagine what they could be hiding. The outsiders called her Ilmar—*human*—which made her wonder what part of nature they belonged to. Brutus was the least humanlike of all. She'd never seen such a round belly on a person or such meaty jowls, which jiggled when he chewed his food, which he did continuously, like a creature that did not know when it was full, and he could sit and sit for passings, croaking insults. She called him the toad.

Captain Aola was altogether different and fast became her friend. Often, Thelana caught herself marveling at the woman's beauty, at the complex array of tight fitting leathers, at the glittering ring mail, at the silky blood-red cape that fell from shoulder plate to heel. Against Baba's will, the young Ilmarin asked the strangers about the tools they brought, about the sword and the bow. She even managed to learn, with a speed that astonished family and foreigner alike, the Kratan language. "Retrieve your arrows, Thelana, and let's give it another shot."

Thelana searched among the reeds, mumbling curses to the gods that there should be so much flora resembling arrow shafts growing around her home. Something red caught her eye then, like the tail of a finch, and she pinched the arrow up and went in search of the rest. The victim of her aim was a green pomegranate fit snugly between the folds of an olive tree, but only three arrows jutted from its gnarled bark. Even after ten shots, she'd failed miserably to split the fruit.

"No, Thelana," she heard Aola say. "Other side, arrow should be on the inside, single feather out."

"Looks like you have a lot of work ahead of you, Captain, if she can't even tell her right from her left!" He laughed, forgot to chew, and coughed up a sliver of apple.

Thelana tried to concentrate, to quiet her mind, but the toad's banter was incessant.

"Pay him no heed," said Aola, "he's an ass."

Thelana nodded. *Alright.* With her eyes clamped tight, she watched the events unfold in her mind: the string snapping with a faint buzz, the bronze point speeding away, the fruit bursting into a juicy mist.

"Don't look so nervous," her teacher added. "Be loose. Steady your breathing. Just remember: draw to your cheek, elbow up, and release quickly."

"What about wind and distance?" Brutus remarked.

Aola waved him off. "Doesn't matter at three paces. Now shut up."

Steady your breathing. Air funneled through her lips, swirled like a fire in her bosom, escaped back into the world.

Adjust for wind. She became acutely aware of the bowing reeds, of every hair along her body leaning eastward. She fitted the arrow along the bow, nocked the tail into the string, lifted and pulled.

"Not with your thumb!" Aola corrected. "Three fingers, Thelana."

Her elbow bent to its extremity, already sore from the day's weeding, and she held it and held it, the bow pregnant with arrow.

"Don't hesitate," said Aola. "Quick release!"

But it was too late. Thelana's arms drifted from her face, the string became too tight to keep steady, and the arrow—distanced from the bow—flipped over and around, flying between her toes into a tangle of weeds. Laughter erupted, crushing her.

Brutus' engorged cheeks flushed the color of his apple as he continued to laugh and choke. "What a scamp!" he managed, his eyes wet with tears, chin sopping with cider. "Even if you did manage to teach her the bow, where would she keep her arrows? You try to dress up these savages and they squeal like hogs!"

"Easy, Brutus," the Captain urged. "It's my composite bow, after all. The pull must be half her weight."

"You're wasting your time, Captain," he went on. "Just look at her! At least my mother had the good sense not to let her daughters go prancing like whores before all that's holy. She'd have a stiff board for their bottoms, my mother would."

"We're not in Kratos, Brutus," she said sharply. "This is their land, and so long as we are their guests, we will respect their customs, however unorthodox they may seem to you."

"Really?" he said with sarcasm, crunching into the core of his apple. "I didn't know we'd stumbled upon so great nation! A kingdom to be respected! Of proud history and lineage! Marvel at the architecture, will you . . ." he intoned, addressing the trees.

"We've lost many good men," she admitted, her icy demeanor framed by golden curls, "but I am still in command here, Brutus, and so long as that is, you will refrain from such comments."

"Point taken," he conceded. "Just don't expect her to be replacing any of my brothers, or being of any use to us, unless you plan to use her as bait."

"If the drought comes, and the Great Moon does cover this place, they'll need hunting skills to survive, and what better tool can we give them than the bow? At least this one is willing to learn. Now silence your tongue," she added, cutting him with a sharp glance, "or I'll silence it for you!"

Thelana fought to shut out their words. The arrow plopped from her bow another three times and her heart sank. *I don't want to be Ilmarin anymore. I don't want to be a scamp. I want to be a warrior. Then they'd see, then they wouldn't make jokes.*

When every arrow found purchase among the reeds, not a one making its home within the olive tree, the pomegranate began to blur in Thelana's sight, and her cheeks dampened. "I can't do it!" she cried, tossing the bow aside. "Brutus is right. I'm nothing but a worthless little scamp."

The Kratan woman bent down, and with a mail-sheathed finger she brushed away the tears. "Thelana, you don't even know what those words mean."

"Yes I do," she said. "That I'm different, me and my family. That we're not like you."

Aola connected the freckles of her cheeks, combed strands of hair away from her face. "Words don't mean anything unless they mean something to you. Being different doesn't make you any less of a person."

"Then why can't I do what you can?"

"Thelana," she answered, as tenderly as any mother, "you may not fully grasp this now, but I am going to tell you a secret which I learned only after many years of failure. People will mock you, because they fear that you might someday become better than them. No one is born to greatness. It comes from your will to succeed, your ability to ignore the jeers and wade through rivers of disappointment. It comes from the courage to be lonesome in the steadfast belief in yourself. Do you understand, Thelana?"

She forced a tiny nod. "I think so."

"Good," she said, handing the bow back to her. "Now try again."

The arrow erupted, arching over the tips of the reeds, traveling beyond time and space, coming down in the darkness across the ages. The hoplite gasped, drawing his hand—slick with blood—from his throat. His torch clacked against the parapet. Red smeared the temple wall as he reached to steady himself, failing, slumping into a heap beside the fallen flame which flickered in his eyes.

5

THE PRIEST AND THE BARBARIAN

*No fear of gods or man can stem
the evil in men's hearts.*

—Kjus

At the topmost step of the Temple, where the wind from the Sea blew freely and fiercely and the air dipped to a chill, Xandr surveyed the whole of the Hedonian sprawl. The Legion Commander stood at the triangular arms of the pyramid's gate, awaiting the procession of the courtesans who had washed, trimmed, and dressed him only moments ago. Gold glittered from their armbands and flower petals adorned their hair, and the silk from their sleeves rippled like moving water. With a half-hearted salute, Demacharon departed to his duties, leaving the courtesans to usher Xandr through the arch and into the hallway.

On each side of him, captured in high stone relief, faces twisted in agony and terror: chariots and horses, scenes of battle lost to the ages. Centaurs, dragons, and grotesque distortions of beast and man added to the cavalcade of myth and history. Before one such figure, Xandr paused gloomily. The hips and breasts suggested a woman, but the serpents that tangled and curled from the root of her scalp proved otherwise. The relief continued inward, toward an expanse of marble where, somewhere further down, faint voices could be heard.

Impressions of waves and fish spread beneath his feet in mosaics of chalcedony, beryl, sardonyx and other precious stones Xandr could not name. The echo of his sandals mixed with the sound of chanting, but the priests did nothing to acknowledge his presence as he entered the large hall. It was the strangest sight yet: a dozen men with fluttering eyelids and babbling tongues, swaying beards and red, oddly cut copes. Some lay prostrate in worship, while others danced in circles with arms outstretched as might a small child, their eyes rolled white and their lips foaming. Xandr saw objects in their hands he did not understand: rectangular frames with neat rows of beads strung along them, globes of glass marked with stars, and metallic folding shapes etched with runes. It was a mathematical, opiate-enhanced ritual. On the wall opposite them, a single sail and a double tier of oars battled wind and waves. The nautical scene was so massive, Xandr felt he could have boarded the ship of pigments.

"It is the *Aea*." The voice was deep, and calm.

Xandr turned, expecting a man of great stature. Instead, a gaunt pillar-like form blocked his view, made taller by a round, pointed miter. His vestments were of white samite interwoven with gold thread. A nose sharp as a knife formed from the creases between his knobby cheeks and an apple-shaped lump jut from his deeply pitted throat.

"It is the *Aea*," he said again, his eyes as dark and shining as a black pearl. "The ship that brought the founders of Hedonia, ages ago. Our city was once their colony."

"And what of those men there?" Xandr asked. Sages or madmen, they did not acknowledge the High Priest's entrance. "What in the gods' names are they doing?"

"Those are the *red mystics*," he replied. "They have delved into their own minds, seeking the mysteries of the universe. You need not concern yourself with them. I am the man you seek, the man who summoned you."

"Urukjinn." The name climbed the walls, vanishing softly to the ceiling. "Ruler of Hedonia?"

"Ruler?" he echoed, aghast. "Speak not such blasphemy. I am but a mouthpiece, a vessel through which Sargonus delivers his wisdom. God is, and has ever been, the Lord of Hedonia."

The Ilmarin paused, cautioning himself against making any further assumptions.

Urukjinn eyed the hilt at Xandr's shoulder. "Weapons are forbidden in the temple."

"I've relinquished my ax."

"I see," said Urukjinn. He righted his staff so that the gold trident relic at its tip rose above his miter. "Very well, then," he added with resignation, orbiting the warrior. "At least you clean up well. The kilt suits you, though I suppose a jerkin to cover that body would be asking too much of an Ilmarin, and might be a shame, also." His fingers moved like spiders across Xandr's spine. "I see you have been properly oiled and scented, befitting the temple, and the god."

Xandr recoiled with disgust. "Tell me, priest, what do you want of me? I do not care for idle chatter."

"Come. I will show you." With staff echoing amid his stride, Urukjinn led him beneath a vast archway into yet another chamber, where a lurid shaft of sunlight came down from the opening in the pyramid, crowning the marble god in a halo of gold, illuminating each muscle. He was colossal, enough to hold a man in the recess of his palm. Shadows splayed across his solemn visage as he judged those who came into his presence through eyes of pearl. The Sea was his hair, cascading and tumultuous, and clouds were his beard. In his left hand, a gilded trident directed his seashell chariot, latched by golden reins to a pair of wakefins—the kind that sank merchant galleys— as massive in stone as their living counterparts. Forming the base of the idol were the tentacles of a crimson monster half-submerged in the pool encircling the whole of the monument. Unlike the gleaming marble god, it was made of dull, time-chipped coral.

Again, the High Priest's voice boomed unexpectedly from his gaunt frame. "Behold Sargonus, Supreme God of Hedonia and the Sea."

The overall effect of the vast, octagonal chamber, with its high relief sculptures, was to induce awe. Strolling between the eight vaulted recesses and their altars, Xandr noted the various gods, some of whom he was familiar with and others whom Urukjinn was eager to illuminate upon. The four goddesses looked down upon him: Maki of War and Chastity, with sword and shield of writhing snakes, Irene of Love and Peace, with her ankle length tresses and rose petal garlands, Zoë of Wisdom and Birth, also known as the Bringer, with her quill and scroll, and Fate, the Dreaded Spinster, sitting at her loom. Then, the three male deities: Solos of the Sun, with his chariot and stallions of fire, Dak of Time and Knowledge, known also as Most Ancient and the Watcher, with his eyes of stars and altar of many candles, and Strom the Thunderer in his chariot, with his hammer and trumpet of winds. The gateway to the final church was of darkest obsidian, in which only a single candle reflected upon the black waters beneath its gold altar. Xandr recognized the idol as Skullgrin, of Death and Darkness, known also as Shimoti, and the Taker, of two sexes, whose face was split between a skull and a beautiful woman.

"Witness, *Ilmarin*, this great city, its measure, its grandeur!" Staff and voice rose up together in supplication, the idol looming within the gold loop of his trident. "Our colonies line the coast like tassels in a great tapestry, along every harbor and peninsula. Even the ancient city states of Thetis and Thalassar, which long ago ruled empires of their own, pay us tribute. With those kingdoms beyond our influence, we offer trade.

"Did you know there were once many great bodies of water, many seas? That was before the world was rearranged, when countless petty kingdoms feuded over its dominion. After the Great Cataclysm there was but One Sea, and Hedonia laid claim to it, building the greatest empire Aenya has ever known.

"But the Hedonian Empire is more than the land and its people. It is an idea! The idea of civilization! Literature, temples built to rightful gods, and laws for all that man can and cannot do. These things bring order from chaos, and with order comes the power to unite the world. Soon, civilization will spread to every continent, and the scattered remnants of barbarism will disappear."

The High Priest grew pale, drawing deep breaths as if drained by his declarations. Urukjinn could move thousands with his voice. He was a master of tone, of subtle, hypnotic persuasion. Xandr wondered how often he'd given that sermon, and to whom.

"And what if some don't wish to join your civilization?"

Urukjinn's lips twisted into a smile worse than any scowl. "We help them to see the light."

"By force?"

"That is the nature of our campaigns, to liberate humanity from depravity, through peaceful measures, or by the sword if necessary."

"If you offer them liberation, why do they resist you?"

"Inferior races do not know better. Just as your people did not know to wear clothes before leaving Ilmarinen."

The High Priest wielded words like weapons, but remembering Demacharon's warning, Xandr resisted the urge to argue. He heard himself saying only, with bitterness, "You know nothing of my people."

"I know them as they came to us, seeking refuge. They were unkempt and ill-mannered."

Now Xandr's voice pitched toward anger. He would speak his mind, blasphemy be damned. "Should I judge you by my people's customs? By my people's words?"

"Agreed, the customs of Aenya's cultures vary greatly, but your people are especially curious. You could not be faulted, of course, for knowing nothing of shame."

"Shame lies in the actions of men, rather than in their appearance." The words of his mentor shot from his lips before he could realize from whence they came. "Shouldn't your legionnaires be ashamed to tax the people they have *liberated*?"

"The tribute is a nominal fee to maintain the functions of the Empire, to build roads and ships, and temples."

He felt his face knitting into a scowl. "This temple is made of innocent blood."

Even with all his power of presence, the High Priest shrunk back. "Greatness cannot be achieved," he murmured, in half-hearted apology, "without sacrifice."

Despite his status of holiest man in the world, the High Priest was either obliviously rude or possessed by excessive vanity. "Tell me this," Xandr said. "If my people are so lacking, what do you need of me?"

"Ah!" He exhaled, relieved of the tension between them, his cheeks receding into the fleshy skull that was his face. "You, Batal of Legend, have more to do with the destiny of the Empire than you realize." His cope fluttered as he led Xandr to the foot of the idol. At such closeness, the head of Sargonus overshadowed them, and red tentacles coiled and twisted from beneath the seashell chariot as if reaching to pull Xandr under the still waters. A dais stood erected before the sacred pool, and upon it a bejeweled tome, open to an image of a nude man—mere scratches upon aged papyrus—most of the face lost to heavy strokes of chalk. The longer Xandr looked at it, the more uneasy he became. There was no mistaking the resemblance, the swaying mane, the muscular build, the two-handed sword.

"Are you versed in symbols, barbarian? Can you read?"

"No," Xandr admitted.

"They possess great power. Can change the world. For just such reason, none but the High Priest may lay eyes upon the sacred text, and he is anointed only after the death of another. So you see, I am the only man alive that has seen this. And now, you are the second."

"And you believe . . ." Xandr muttered, glancing again to the chalk on the page, ". . . *that* is me?"

"It is," Urukjinn replied. "The First Prophet Eldin, Peace Be Upon Him, foresaw your arrival thousands of years ago. It is written that the Batal of Legend would come to us as a barbarian, a man with a great sword, and— this I found most fascinating—that he would be a *naked* man. For centuries, theologians have wondered what this means. Any man, after all, can be naked given the occasion. But then I learned of the Ilmar, and I grew more in my certainty that the Prophet could have meant no other, but a man such as you."

"This is madness." But despite Xandr's distrust of the priest and of prophecies, he could not escape his yearning to know more.

"After the Great Cataclysm, the first of the Aean race arrived on our shores, bringing with them the *Ages of Aenya*, which we have kept sacred. Alas, only the scriptures between IV and VII remain. The other volumes were lost in a blaze three thousand years ago, when barbarians ransacked the city. But it is no matter. Through his writings, Eldin taught us of the gods, of Sargonus, and of the Ages of Aenya.

"It is said that in the time of the Ancients, man was immortal and all-knowing. But this resulted in vanity and hubris. The gods became angered—some even dare to say, envious. And so, from deep within the heart of the world, the gods released the elder giants: Magmus and Chaos, Havok, Tsunamis and Infinitia. Thus begat the Great Cataclysm, and the Dark Age of Aenya, and we have suffered ever since. So we have struggled throughout history, in our campaigns, through our military might, to bring about the dawn of a new age, as promised by Eldin.

"That time is upon us now. The coming of the Batal is the first omen—and so we welcome you. The other omen, however, has caused controversy for millennia. It speaks of the destruction of a great city by the sea, and the fall of an empire, but the writing is archaic, difficult to interpret. I believe the two omens are intertwined—I believe a new age will come to pass only when the Batal of Legend saves the city, for without Hedonia there can be no prosperity. And so you were summoned, to oppose that which threatens our very existence."

Xandr sighed. The High Priest had spoken too many words, avowed too much. The Ilmarin rubbed his beard, surprised by its neatness and short length, remembering with fondness the courtesans with their nimble fingers and simple smiles. "What could threaten such a city," he said at last, "with such high fortifications, with such massive armies?"

"The soldiers call them gill, but they have been known to us for millennia as *merquid*. Our libraries teem with documents concerning them—sailors turned bards have made songs of their encounters with them. But merquid have always been reclusive, making their homes in the depths of the waters. When the air is wet and heavy and the moonlight wanes, when we cannot see them, they lurch toward our walls. Our civilians were the first victims, women . . . and children, before we knew the danger, when the harbor was deemed safe.

"We've campaigned throughout the world, bringing Eldin to the people, but these briny fiends lay siege to the heart of the Empire. We slaughter them and they come again in greater number. Never did I imagine living to see it, the enemy at our infant's cradle! Should they reach beyond our fortifications, all will be lost, our fair city, civilization itself!"

"Why would creatures that live under the water attack you, and with such undying determination?" But Xandr knew there were horrors of uncompromising evil, and creatures without remorse or compassion. He could see the fields of bodies—monks from the temple—naked and deformed in tributaries of blood. And the face of the High Priest turned pale and broken, into the dying face of his mentor.

"They are evil!" the priest cried. "Must there be another reason? I have seen them, grotesque beyond imagination, reeking of brine, gibbering unintelligibly, mindless to their own destruction! For this they must be wiped out, all those spawned of Gulgola.

"This attack is but an omen, a sign of the changing of ages. As Eldin writes:

> In the beginning, there was only the cold and the darkness and it was called Chaos. And the world was covered in water, and all living things swam in it, and thus ruled

Gulgola, who is named Tentacled-One, who is named Devourer, who is named Tsunamis. And Gulgola ruled over this world that was Chaos, and over all that dwelt therein. Hither came Sargonus, strongest of gods, down from the Starry Heavens in his chariot of fire and lightning. And gazed he upon all that was, which was Chaos, and saw that it was not good. And so Sargonus smote at Gulgola with his trident of gold, imprisoning the monster in the Abyss of the Sea, and from the Chaos brought he Order, and from Order came dry land, and Solos, god of the sun, gave men warmth, so that men might thrive."

Xandr eyed the horrid mass of tentacles reflected in the pool and the god towering over it. The idol was a representation, telling a story. "That is Gulgola."

"Now your eyes have opened," the priest answered. "Sargonus released Gulgola once before, to destroy man in his hubris, and now the elder one has been released again. Why else have his minions come up from the depths to destroy us? Gulgola has risen from the Abyss!"

The Batal scratched under his chin. It was a peculiar sensation—this cutting and trimming of hair—an alien thing. Either the shave was irritating him, or talk of gods and monsters made his skin itch.

"And I am the only one that can stop this? You have armies of tens of thousands."

"It is the myth that matters, the idea of you. As it is the idea of Hedonia that makes us powerful, so does the idea of the Batal make you what you are. The tales of your exploits inspires men to courage. The enemy they face is strange and terrible. Fear is the merquid's greatest weapon. You will counter this."

"What if you're wrong, priest? What if Eldin was a madman, and I, no more than a lowly barbarian?"

"Have you no faith?" Urukjinn asked him. "No heathen gods to which you pay devotion?"

Xandr thought long and hard, the High Priest eyeing him with impatience. He chose his words carefully, before letting them ring out in the cavernous space. "My goddess is the voice in the babbling brook, the touch of the morning sun, the breath in the wind. The sky is her temple," he added, lifting Emmaxis into the light where it shone like a mirror, "and this is the Long Tooth that smites her enemies."

"A god of savages near to extinction," Urukjinn snorted. "No doubt she is equal to a god belonging to millions!" And he lifted his arms triumphantly—his trident glittering—as if raising the colossal idol of Sargonus. The presentation was more convincing than any argument he could have made. The words of QuasiI came again to his defense: *confound the senses and reason is sure to follow.* The High Priest was no more than a venomous creature, a swamp snail lurking after weak-willed prey. Regardless, something of the Hedonian myth spoke truthfully to him. And the ancient tome—with its uncanny depiction of him—could not be ignored.

After some silence, Emmaxis rang against the mosaic at Xandr's feet, resonating from wall to angled wall. If any blasphemy was to be spoken, the gods would be sure to hear it. "I will defend this city. But not for you or your gods, Sargonus be damned."

Xandr watched Urukjinn's corneas constrict with displeasure, making the priest's face all the more skeletal. "Hush!" he hissed. "Do not blaspheme Him in his own Temple!"

Six feet of steel jumped between the two of them, and now Xandr could see, reflected in the sword, real fear in the priest's eyes. He could no longer resist. "I have witnessed idols just as great as yours fall to plunderers, with no god manifesting to take vengeance. Things made of stone fracture. Even the mountain from which your city was quarried grows rounder with time, and after many eons will be ground to dust and washed away to the Sea."

Urukjinn took a step backward, his slipper catching on his cope. "I see you are a barbarian in the truest sense. Indeed, Sargonus works in mysterious ways. Nevertheless, my offer of dowry stands. You will have my daughter, Merneptes, and with her, a hundred talents of gold."

From the other side of the idol there came a sobbing, as though the god wept in a small, feminine voice. Someone had been listening.

The blue eyes of a young girl reflected in the ripples of the pool. Tears clung to her chin like morning dew, and losing their hold, formed expanding circles in the sacred waters. Startled before the High Priest, she revealed herself as she stood, the gold leaves of her chandelier-headdress chiming, her white and gold-trimmed muslin tunic clinging to her body, a seashell cupping her womanhood. Towering over her stood a monster. Its camel-like snout hung in leathery folds, and its teeth jutted like river stones from its jowls. Its eyes were black as olives. The gold boots and burgundy cape of velvet traditionally worn by the legionnaire did little to mask its hideousness. Looped in its four-fingered palm, tall as a man, was a golden hammer shaped like a bell.

The disparity between girl and monster, between daintiness and hulking brute, touched upon the extremities of description.

"Xandr of Ilmarinen," the High Priest addressed, apologetically, "permit me to introduce you to Grimosse, guardian golem. He takes care of me and my daughter."

"So this must be Merneptes," said Xandr. It occurred to him that she was more arousing in her flimsy attire, than a girl entirely stripped of clothing.

Urukjinn snatched her up by the wrist, rattled her like a marionette just as she brushed at a tear. "Merneptes, I told you this place is forbidden to women! Do you not know the punishment for sacrilege?"

"Father!" she wailed, wilting in his clutches. "Let them kill me! I care not! You can't make me join to a brute! What a disgrace is that?"

"Silence!" he roared, leaving the mark of his ring on her cheek. "How dare you speak like this in the presence of men? I am your father and master. I will judge what is best. Grimosse, off to the bower with her."

But there was no need. She fled before the monster could obey.

6

A THIEF IN THE NIGHT

It is, indeed, a great evil that men should pervert
the human form to elicit our basest instincts.

—Kjus

The young boy raced ahead of his master, leaping over bustling creeks, never minding the thorny seedling that dug deeper into his sole. Twisting boughs obscured his sight, roots impeded his passage at every turn, yet he maneuvered around them without conscious thought, letting the pull of a slope take him when it would. With each step, the smell of burning intensified, quickening the drumbeat under his chest. Whether Quasil had followed he could not tell, nor could he hear the rustle of the branches or the ballad of the sparrows. All that mattered were the notches and the footholds he knew too well, blindly meeting feet and fingertips at will.

The cylindrical monastery crowned the peak, rising from the rock like a phoenix with folded wings in a quartet of buttresses. It was the only familiar sight. Flames spread along wooden frames as blackness billowed overhead and a mob of hideous gray creatures scampered every which way, their pumpkin-sized heads bobbing urgently. Faces Xandr knew became distorted through dust and sweat. His friends were holding the field, but there were too few short swords and quarterstaffs and desperate fists to stem the tempest of blades. A whining sound pervaded his ears, like laughter, mocking the shrieks of the wounded and dying. Flames swirled about torches clutched in clawed fingers. Stones launched through mosaic windows, instantly shattering centuries of splendor. And somehow the gray, emaciated bodies found the strength to drag the fallen to a gathering, where others with daggers joined in the stabbing, raining blood over sacred earth and walls.

Bogrens.

He knew them from the lessons on species related to human. Those lessons now seemed remote, for knowing their names made them no less terrifying. But there was no time to waste. His empty sword belt struck the ground as horror gave way to rage. Instinct commanded the legs that carried him, the arm that thrust his blade between a bogren's shoulders. The squeal pained his ears and the creature slumped forward, its limbs bent at awkward angle. Streaks of black painted the silver of his sword, dripping from the tip as from an ink-dipped quill. The hilt quaked in his palm—it'd never drawn blood. But despite the bogren's hideousness and the awfulness of its deeds,

its death brought the boy little satisfaction. The slain bogren had taken something from him, a peace he would
never know again. But in the madness of battle, loss gave
way to the euphoria pulsing through his veins.

A host of Gray Ones turned from their most recent victim, shaking their blades clean of entrails, measuring the
boy through folded pupils. Paying their fallen comrade
no mind, they advanced with daggers hooked like talons,
speaking in tortured syllables. Xandr moved his blade between himself and the points directed at his underbelly.
Chrome flashed, arched in semi-circles and twisted back
in figure S's, dancing to the ring of metal. The bogrens
were swift but he was a blur of naked flesh. Mired in gore,
he fought with a ferocity and desperation never observed
in him by his fellow monks. For never, in all his years of
sparring, had he known the company of the Taker. Now
the God of Death became his shadow, patient as a vulture
as one bogren after another crumpled at the boy's feet.
And always were the lessons guiding his hands: *you must
be everywhere and nowhere, faster than thought, than perception
permits.*

Two fell under him in a single stroke, one scalped from
the horns, the other gutted through the ribcage, its plum-
sized heart split across the middle. At the sight of this, the
remaining two wailed and scampered off on all fours.

But Xandr soon learned that they were not retreating,
but regrouping. Every evil eye fell upon him. Like locusts
they swarmed him, grinding shoulder-bones as they joined
together, every pointed dagger a gesture how a man might
be butchered.

CRACK!

64

Wood split in his ears and Xandr knew he was not alone. Tendons became unfastened and vertebrae snapped and grew limp. Eyeballs smashed into brains. The old man fought through the horde with total economy of movement, not a blow wasted, not an incoming blade left to chance. He turned their attacks as easily as a parent swatting an infant's hand. The staff was everywhere and nowhere simultaneously, at once vertical and immobile as a cedar, at once horizontal and devastating as a tidal wave. Out of decades' training and centuries' tradition, the staff painted Ancient symbols of power in the old man's nimble hands. QuasiI was *Keeper of Flowers*, the greatest of the warrior monks, and the bogrens must have sensed it from the moment he appeared.

Side-by-side with his teacher, Xandr believed himself indomitable. Together they would drive back the attackers, send them cowering from whence they came. But his thoughts strayed to his friends. Who among them was gasping through punctured lungs or spilling their last into the dirt? Which of his mentors somewhere called his name? And there was the ultimate question of why, reverberating in his skull, tearing at the tissue of his reasoning. *Why is this happening.*

With staff and sword they fended the onslaught, but as bodies piled at their heels, more bogrens came as if from nowhere, clawing with abandon over the dead and injured, redrawing the circle of battle to narrower confines.

"Xandr, the sword!"

It was QuasiI, his voice muffled by dying squeals and the crack of wood and the indistinctive din of battle, but his meaning rang clear. He could have meant only one.

The sword.

His bed sheet was damp with sweat. Casting the sheet into a bundle at the foot of his bed, the cool night air rushed across his body from a lone window. Memories pelted him like sling stones. The knowledge of where he was, and how he came to be there, came piece by piece into his mind. He remembered mulling over the High Priest's words and pacing through his bedchambers in the nightly ritual of purging his mind of the dead and dying. Sometimes his dreams were more vivid than the waking world, despite the fact that what haunted him in the night were things long absent.

He turned to his own face, disheveled despite the courtesans' efforts. They could do nothing to erase years of restless sleep and wandering. Emmaxis was smooth as milk and shone like polished silver, but it never showed a face he wished to see, only strange distortions.

"Xandr!"

The shout came from the hall beyond. Realizing that he could not leave his chambers as he slept, he quickly laced up his sandals and put on his kilt, before sliding the bolt from his door. Finias stood trembling in the hallway.

"Xandr!" he cried. "Murder most foul! In our very temple! Come quick! The High Priest summons you." At least those were the words Xandr thought he heard, as images of monks and bogrens still swam in his head.

"What is it now?"

"A terrible omen!" Finias exclaimed. "Terrible! Follow me post-haste!"

Zaboa had been his name. What remained of him lay in a crumpled heap of cloth, the red of his cope bleeding onto the floor, the tail end of an arrow between his rigid fingers. A host stood assembled around his corpse, a sleepy High Priest and a contingent of soldiers. Such was the scene as Xandr and Finias arrived. They had come in through the underground tunnel from the palatial complex, which consisted of the cloister and the barracks. Nobody remained overnight in the Temple but the guards, and the red mystics, who were said to never sleep.

But it was not the dead mystic that drew the attention of the gathering, but the wall against which he had fallen, where the singular word *doom* was written in blood.

"What is the meaning of this?" Urukjinn cried, upset by the intrusion of his sleep.

A soldier in full regalia stood near the body. His armor was ornate, as polished as Demacharon's. He resembled a bear, with arms, face, and neck black with hair. "Nothing superstitious here, your Holiness," he said. "We have an intruder."

"An intruder?" he echoed, stepping carefully over the growing pool of blood. "Here? That is not possible."

"The evidence would suggest it, your Holiness," the soldier replied. "This mystic was shot. No doubt of it."

Murmuring ensued. Some questioned whether it was an act of merquid terrorism and others, in hushed voices, spoke of the prophecy of destruction. The High Priest was visibly annoyed. "Captain Sarpedon," he barked, "split your men up. Find this intruder. He must pay for this blasphemy. And find someone to clean this mess. Blood may not be shed in the temple."

As the host grew thin, Xandr knelt beside the corpse. The mystic was tattooed in runes from forehead to chin, and his beard was nearer to white than gray. "What was this man doing before he died?"

Urukjinn loomed over him. "What does that matter? He's dead. Committing blasphemy with his blood."

Xandr fingered his chin, as though answers could be found in his beard. He then ran a hand under the ribbon of the dead man's garb. "This is not his blood."

"What?" The mouthpiece of Sargonus was empty of divine insight.

"What ritual was the mystic enacting?"

"Zaboa was our oldest and most venerable." Urukjinn hesitated. "He was greatly concerned with prophecy. With divining the future." His tone grew darker with each syllable, as if contemplating for the first time the message scrawled in blood.

But it was the boy, Finias, who spoke. "It says *doom! Doom!* The prophecy is coming to pass!"

"Silence!" Urukjinn commanded. "You must not speak of that which you know nothing."

Prying loose the bloody arrow, Xandr noted its simple design, the twine with which the feathers were fastened to the shaft. "This is birch," he said. "It doesn't grow around here." But a common sight in Ilmarinen. "And these feathers, where would merquid get bird feathers?"

"We must not question these things," Urukjinn replied, "but accept them as the will of the gods, as a test of faith, and act accordingly. Zaboa did not question this. He died knowingly."

Shouts rang out, echoing from the shrine, cutting the discussion short. Those gathered about the body were quick off their heels, Xandr leading them away.

The din was like that of battle, of men in a confused, desperate uproar. Except no commands were being issued, nor was there the familiar scream, unmistakable to those who have heard it, of a man when the Taker comes to him unexpectedly.

Carried by the shouts through the arch at the pyramid's center, Emmaxis quivered with lust, but Xandr found only two men—hoplites by the look of their spears and shields— their necks craned beneath the shadow of the stone god.

"A demon!" one of them cried, with spear at the ready, "A demon in our very midst, in this holiest of places!"

"Sacrilege!" the priest spat. "Get her down at once!"

"But how?" said the soldier. "We dare not hit the idol!"

". . . and be damned for all eternity!" the other man added.

It was, Xandr realized, a moral dilemma. The humor of the situation did not escape him.

"Either way, my children," Urukjinn mused, "we're all damned."

Twirling from head to heel from the angled ceiling, she revealed herself, a flash of bronze flesh, with hair of chestnut, like leaves after long eclipses, pleated into a single swaying braid. She wore only a scabbard, and a rope. Unfastening the knot at her waist, she dove headfirst onto the idol, perching with cat-like grace atop its nose. Fortunately, Sargonus possessed a broad, straight proboscis, befitting his godhood.

Xandr's heart hammered with curiosity, to know who she was, and with dread also, at what Urukjinn might do to her. By the tone of her skin, and the ease with which she moved in her unclad body, he knew at once she was Ilmarin, if unlike any he could have dreamt of. Stealing from the Temple was beyond audacious, and the Ilmar were never known to become thieves, or to murder.

"It's no demon," he remarked.

"A woman!" Urukjinn cried, as if a demon was preferable, as if the very word offended him. "No! Impossible! What can a woman do? It has taken a woman's guise, to beguile us, to tempt us with wicked thoughts."

"You don't know *our* women," said Xandr, biting his tongue as the words escaped it, for there was no doubt the intruder was Ilmarin, a fact he wished not to implicate him. What she was doing, he could scarcely imagine. But the High Priest either did not hear him over his own sermon, or did not catch his meaning.

Her sacrilege did not stop at mere intrusion, however, as from her shoulders she slipped a jade and gold sword, wedging the blade into the tear duct, at the pearl orb of Sargonus' eye.

"What would be the greater evil," Xandr said to Urukjinn, "having her remove the eye, or pitting the idol with spear points?"

"It is said that when Sargonus no longer looks out to protect the city, and that all is doomed. Men, as I am the mouthpiece of God, fear not. Hurl your spears, but damage His image at the risk of your own souls."

Their spears climbed sluggishly, as the men were ill-trained to strike at something so directly above them, or lacked the will to damage their deity. The first spear passed the god's cheek, clacking on the opposite side. Twirling on the balls of her heels, her sword opened like a butterfly and a chord stretched tightly between the tips of its wings, and then a short arrow slid at the ready from its confines. As a second spear wobbled up into the air, she snatched and tossed it aside.

In speaking with Demacharon, Xandr had learned that the pious gathered upon this very spot from all corners of the Empire, many after year-long pilgrimages, to venerate the god. They prayed for the souls of the recently departed, and for the sick, and for the wounded. Rumors spread throughout the colonies and lands beyond of miracles, of men and women who laid eyes upon the idol and were healed, or drank of its holy waters and became free of afflictions. Vials of its waters were sold in every bazaar, whether authentic or counterfeit. And now this girl traversed the idol with her bare feet, nimbly navigating the threads of muscle along the god's outstretched arm, leaping onto Sargonus' shoulder. He could understand the level of blasphemy, could fathom the Hedonians' outrage, but could not help the laughter that stifled in his throat.

"Finias!" the priest bellowed. "Your spear!"

In a single motion, she crouched into an archer's stance and loosed her arrow. The bow twanged like a lute out of tune. The bronze point punched through the wooden periphery of the Hedonian's shield, a thumb's length from his eye.

"She's using some kind of cursed bow!" said the hoplite, wheeling his shield around.

A second arrow came whistling down, trailing the first. Hurling himself before the High Priest, the second hoplite crumpled with a howl, his metal ringing against the marble. Feathers from a red tailed finch protruded from his breastplate, and he pawed at it clumsily, gasping for air that did not come without agony.

Astonishment marred Urukjinn's skeletal face, as he stepped away from the body. "Blood," he murmured. "There must be no bloodshed in the temple! Finias, take the fallen into the street."

"But your Holiness," he stammered, "we . . . should we not first help him?"

"I did not miss." The unique architecture of angled walls and vaulted ceiling carried her voice, as though from the idol itself. With her every action, the strange girl was inventing new blasphemies. "My arrow is three fingers from his heart. Consider it mercy."

She was using their fear against them. Nobody was that good.

"It's no use!" Urukjinn cried, distancing himself from her bow, to what he believed a safe distance. "Finias, make haste! Call the archers!"

He could see that she had no way of escaping and, despite her thieving and murdering, Xandr was certain of one thing: he would not allow her to die. But how to save her from a city of enemies? Without revealing himself an ally? Should she manage to escape beyond the Temple, she would be hunted and caught. The Hedonians, being a people of pomp and legality, would make a spectacle of her torture and execution.

"Urukjinn," he said, "allow me." Even now, the High Priest winced at the blatant use of his name, yet he did not interrupt. Xandr slipped the helmet from the dying man and approached the lip of the sacred pool.

The bow went slack against her thighs, and her toes crept closer to the edge of the stone arm, to better look upon him. He became acutely aware of his bare breast, of the fact that he was armed only with a helmet. "Come now, you jest," she said.

"Even if you could reach the pearls," he called, using words the others could not understand, "you have nowhere to go. Play along, or you die."

Her eyes sparked with recognition. The helmet spun from his fingertips like a discus, whirling crest over cheek-guard. Whether stunned by his revelation, or due to her willingness to trust him, the plumed hollow collided with her shin and knocked her from her perch. She plummeted into the sacred pool, soiling its sacred waters with heathen sweat. Her bow, all the while, glanced off the idol's knee with a clamor, resting in the shape of a sword in the arms of the Tentacled One.

"Excellent," Urukjinn told Xandr. "The scriptures speak truly of you."

As quickly as she had fallen, she arose, her braid damp and heavy across her slender form. Her body told her story, scars that spoke of battle, underdeveloped breasts suggesting a childhood of malnourishment, yet her well-defined thighs and calf muscles revealed strength—a life spent in pursuit of prey, or in flight from enemies. But it was her eyes that captured his, moving him unwittingly closer. Only the eyes of his people could be so clear, so green, like rainwater beads on a leaf of clover. The two stood a breath's length from each other, the world becoming mute, no one existing but she—he could smell her fear, feel the power of her heart beneath her slim, throbbing ribcage. She was so close, and so distant. Her face filled him, lips cracked from thirst of yesterdays, nose like a thimble, sunspots adorning her cheeks. She was like the ilm that grows among weeds. He reached for an arm, to feel her flesh against his—to seize the intruder—but she wriggled past, making for an unguarded passage, gliding across the marble as if it were a sheet of ice.

"Don't let her get away!" the priest roared.

What was she doing? Did she not understand? Xandr gave chase, but his plodding boots were hopelessly outmatched by her slick, bare feet.

She tugged at the fish-shaped handles of a door, leaned with all her weight, when she was suddenly and violently thrown back. Sarpedon burst through the opening, flanked by archers. She flailed in his arms, as though caught in a fisherman's net, a litany of obscenities spewing from her mouth.

"Look what we have here . . . a barbarian whore!" he exclaimed, a grin on his bush of a face. "My favorite kind."

She answered him with her forehead. It collided with the bridge of his nose, and he was stunned, blood reddening the black coils of his beard.

"I am no whore!" she wailed, her voice returning from the angled walls tenfold.

In his burly arms, she was a flurry of elbows and knees, teeth and fingernails. But he was unyielding. No ordinary man could subdue her, but Sarpedon was born to immense strength—a giant of a man—a man who could wrestle a wolf.

Accepting her powerlessness, she turned at last to Xandr, imploring him in their language, in words meant only for his ears. "You are like me, are you not?"

"Take her away!" Urukjinn scoffed. "And cover her loins lest she tempt the guards with her decadent wiles!"

Xandr looked on, tormented with an urge to rush forward, but said nothing. Any chance to save her would depend on secrecy, on silence. *I will come for you. I swear it.*

"What did she say to you?" said Urukjinn, staffing towards him.

"I do not know, your Eminence," Xandr replied. "She is not . . . my kind."

"I thought I heard you speaking to her."

"No," Xandr answered, staring back at the pool, at the squid-like god. "I merely thought . . . she might understand me."

"But she is naked, and looks . . . freely so."

"She is a barbarian," Xandr continued, "but not Ilmarin." Every lie pressed him. Deception was a poison, a learned evil. Hiding truth was an anathema to the Ilmarin way of life.

The High Priest sighed with resignation. "There are so many thousands of these tribes, each with their own dialect. Such a mess to sort through, so difficult to unite."

"What will happen to her?" he asked, as Sarpedon and his men wrestled her into the shadows, leaving only screams to echo.

"She will die, of course. She was destined for the Taker the moment she looked upon this shrine. No heathen eyes may behold Sargonus and live."

His mind teemed with nooses and stumps, with crucifixes and ropes for drawing and quartering, things Xandr had witnessed men endure and believed his heart was hardened to. Imagining her in such devices made his stomach sick, and he knew he had to find her—this last Ilmarin woman—if not to save their people, at least to learn her name, her story.

"Does that . . . *concern you?*" said the High Priest. His voice was high and calculating, dipped in venom.

Footsteps echoed anew in the idol chamber before Xandr could betray his heart again. It was Finias. There was a different kind of dread in his eyes, with a greater urgency than before. Demacharon stood beside him, the red of his horsehair crest bristling like flame from the wakefin leaping his helmet, the tigers of his armor growling in the torchlight, the scar coursing through his eye deepening in the dimness.

"Xandr," said Finias, "I thank the gods that the demonness caused you no harm. I feared Gulgola had sent her to kill you."

Grim determination defined the commander's face. It was unmistakable to the Ilmarin, the look bourn by men of battle. "Batal or not, we could use every good fighter in the city."

Unwillingly, Xandr tore his mind from the captive girl. "Speak!"

"Take up your arms," Demacharon said. "The night is black and merquid stalk the shores of Sarnath."

7

OF MEN AND MERQUID

The Gulf of Sarnath opened southward to the Sea, its coastal arms stretching half a day's ride. On the northeastern tip of the harbor, the city of Hedonia sat like a jewel.

The procession that moved through the streets was like fireflies in the night. With a kiss and a torch, they bid weeping wives and sleeping children farewell. They gathered bronze as they went, forming lines behind their commanders. From the parapets, teams of archers turned the sky ablaze, volleys of flame-tipped arrows falling and smothering to wisps of smoke against the silver sand.

Trikes lumbered atop the wall, turning spools of chain to raise the latticed portcullis of the southern gate. As it lifted, throngs of thousands poured with remarkable economy into squares, bronze tips staked upright, hoplon shields hanging from mailed knee to sandaled foot. It was a phalanx of pikemen, with their eight foot pikes, and hoplites, who, with shield and spear, fought at the front and sidelines.

Emmaxis quivered at the preparations for war. Xandr could feel it along his spine, and knew that soon the Taker would come to have his fill. But he was a warrior with no love for war. Violence was anathema to his people, an unknown evil before the coming of the bogren. But as unaccustomed as his people were to slaughter, so the more embittered and hardened did they become by it. Bards sang of Ilmarin nomads, conscripted into foreign armies, proving ferocious beyond equal.

The greater the blight, the greater the reprisal.

Hooves clomped through wet sand, rousing Xandr from his musings. A hippocampus stopped directly before him and snorted, flaring its equine nostrils. The beast was ice blue and smooth as a dolphin, crowned by a single dorsal fin from head to neck. Demacharon was saddled upon it, tugging at the reins, maneuvering the beast into position.

"Xandr, I've been told you fought in the Kratos campaigns."

"You heard true."

"Krats fight like women," he replied. "We are masters of war. Do you see these soldiers, how they are arranged? Hoplites carry short spears to shield the pikemen. Each man protects the other beside him. If you cannot join our ranks in formation, you must fight as a straggler, with the peasant militia, with the other barbarians."

Before the Ilmarin could respond, a second hippocampus came into view. The young rider wore no helmet, his hair cascading in thick, sun-gold curls. He rode across the lines of men waving his spear, and hurrahs rolled along the beach like thunder. Even at a distance, Xandr could see how he was admired for the perfect symmetry of his face and his princely smile, but Demacharon eyed him with something like suspicion.

"Aeonus," the First Commander addressed him as their two beasts met, "what do you have to report? I pray this is not another false sighting. The men grow weary of it and lose heart."

"No, commander—we are quite certain this time. The lighthouse sent us the signal, and we found webbed prints in the sand. Attack is imminent."

Now Sarpedon rode up to join the other two. His mount was appropriately massive to suit his bulk, bucking and snorting as though cruelly driven. "Oh, they'll come," Sarpedon spat. "This is the time, when the moons hide and the darkness grows deep, and the air is wet and heavy."

A fourth commander was soon among them, revealing a half-ring of teeth marks along his thigh, a bite from a creature Xandr did not recognize. Demacharon saluted him, asking, "How many are we, Polydorus?"

"All accounted for, First Commander. Forty-thousand on the beach, four legions. That does not include sentries, archers, or stragglers."

Sarpedon tugged at the reins to steady his hippocampus, for the beast was strong-willed and rebellious. It reminded Xandr of the Ilmarin girl and the way she struggled in his grasp. "Morale is low," he said. "The men are drained of sleep, spooked by the dark, and many replacements are new to battle—never shed blood or saw gill but on temple walls."

"Truly," Demacharon replied, partly to himself, "the merquid haunt all of our dreams."

"The men are as ready as they'll ever be," Polydorus asserted, "but what of this prophecy the High Priest speaks of?"

Demacharon scowled, his disfiguring scar making him all the more unpleasant to look upon. With a shrug of the shoulders, he gestured toward the barbarian, who had till now remained invisible. "Here: the *Batal of Legend*. The hero that has come to save us."

"Him!" Spittle clung to Sarpedon's beard, dripped in globs from his cheek guard. "One barbarian? I've killed men like him by the score."

Polydorus maneuvered his steed in a circle about the Ilmarin. "Tell me, *Batal of Legend*, are you bringing that oar into battle?"

As all but Demacharon laughed, Xandr slid the shaft of steel from the baldric at his shoulder and staked it into the ground. The skull face gleamed menacingly, nodes of chrome and pits of shadow swimming in the dim light of the moons. "We have big monsters in the North," he answered. "We need big swords."

"No man can use that properly," answered Demacharon. "Barbarian swords wound, but a short blade—a Hedonian gladius—kills."

"Or when fighting fish folk," Sarpedon added, brandishing his three-pronged spear, "a trident will do nicely."

Aeonus' teeth flashed white and Xandr imagined maids across the Empire swooning into his bed. His armor was no less splendid, with histories of battles etched in gold across the breastplate. "Let him prove his worth," he said. "Let him fight in front, lead our ranks. If he is

Batal, he will inspire us with his cunning, and if he falls, we will be rid of an imposter."

"Yes," Polydorus agreed with a wicked grin, "and let him give a speech to rouse the men. Surely they have seen the plays and know Batal speaks with the tongue of a god."

Demacharon nodded stoically. "Go then, *Batal*, give us a speech." And then, without a hint of mockery, he added, "Strength and Honor."

Xandr's veins were simmering. He was no fool and knew when he was being ridiculed. He wished to abandon them to their doom, loose Emmaxis upon their smug faces to satisfy the sword's appetite. Instead, he consumed his pride, stilling the rage coursing through his heart. With a silent prayer, he searched the black of the sky for answers.

Fluttering down from that bleak heaven was the vivid blue, orange and white of the phoenix. It was a sacred bird in Ilmarinen, an avatar of the Goddess. Sailing among the legions for all to witness, even those who did not know it believed it was a good omen. Xandr closed his eyes and reached out for her, sensing his connection to her and to the air around her, to the sand at his heels, to the rhythm of the tide. He could feel the water as it stroked the beach, feel the strength of the phoenix' heart as she beat her colorful wings. When Xandr looked again, he did not see Hedonians, did not see the bronze hoplons or the horsehair crests or the breastplates—there were only faces now, of men, and boys.

Finias, a hoplite, stood at the forefront of the assembly. He could not break formation, so he wet himself where he stood, urine dripping from his kilt to his sandals. He was one among many thousands, quaking in his armor, unseasoned for the coming bloodshed.

"I have heard you," Xandr called out, walking along the line of faces, "whispering amongst yourselves. Let me shed light on your rumors. It is just as your legends have foretold. I am the Batal of Legend."

He waited for his voice to carry across the beach, waited as a collective murmur rolled like a wave through the ranks of men.

"I have journeyed from the Dark Hemisphere to the sun-scorched Dead Zones. I have battled bogrens and horgs, have slain dragons and the giant of Abu-Zabu. Now I have come to you, in this city by the Sea, hearing of the strange and terrible enemy you face. But what is it you fear, that you do not face each day? Is there any man, woman or child that may escape the Taker?

"With each passing of the moon, with every breath for life, we die. We cling to existence as it slips away, are never younger than we were. We are perpetually a stranger to ourselves as we age, as we become infirm and wretched. Bones and dust is the fate of us all. And if *that* is what you fear, I say, let it come! Heroes do not fear the Taker! For heroes know what matters is that you are remembered well, by the friends that keep you in their hearts, by the children that possess your faces. But if you must, fear for what you leave in this world. If you have mothers and fathers, wives or children, fear for them. If you should be struck down today, how better to be remembered than in the defense of your home? Is there no greater honor? Would any among you leave your post to live in shame? To grow feeble and foolish with each passing day, forever having men call you craven, saying that you surrendered Hedonia, your mother city? Fight, for your mothers and wives and children, fight for your own name, that it may become immortal in the *Song of Batal*. This day, let us make war together, and let gill suffer our steel!"

Xandr did not know from where his words had come, or whether they belonged to him. But in saying them, he could not help but recall the wisdom of QuasiI, the tales of Zoab, or his own bloody encounter with bogrens. His memories were like kindling in his heart, his words like a fire, erupting from his lips and spreading across the minds of the masses. The roar of forty-thousand men sounded like thunder. Dread and hope gave way to lust for battle.

"I will kill me a hundred gill!" Finias exclaimed, drumming his spear and shield together.

"You'll be watching my backside as I rush to the slaughter!" the man beside him boasted. There were many hurrahs and much slapping of shoulders and banging of shields, and everyone's spirits were lifted. But it would not remain. Each voice was hushed, like a changing wind, and there was silence.

A white specter came into their midst, a shroud drifting ghost-like toward the circle of commanders. She reached for Demacharon, trembling like a hag, her wrist as pale and slender as bleached bone. And then her shawl slipped to her shoulder, revealing a young woman. Standing under him, she became as still as the many statues adorning the city, clutching the bridle of his hippocampus as if a gust from the Sea might carry her to oblivion.

Demacharon held her gaze, the scar splitting his face dipping into wells of shadow. "You should not be here."

"Remember what they did," she said to him. Her voice was drained of life, barely possessing substance.

"How can I forget, madam? It is my being. My purpose."

"Kill them all," she murmured. "Kill them for me."

The hard edges of his face softened, became less stoic, and Xandr was taken aback by his sudden tenderness. "I shall not fail you, madam."

A long, low bray of horns sounded from the walls. The woman faded like the white in a crashing wave as he steered his mount toward the Sea. "Xandr, whatever you see out there, do not hesitate. Understood?"

Words were unnecessary. Xandr released Emmaxis, as Sarpedon, Aeonus, and Polydorus followed Demacharon, kicking their mounts to the head of their legions. Behind him, young boys breathed music into pan flutes as others thrummed the stretched lambskin drums about their waists. Ten thousand pairs of feet stamped the sand, with pikes moving and bristling like a monstrous porcupine.

High in the moonless night, the black of the sky divided and took shape, and shapes began to fall. Men moved frantically into formation, hoisting their shields overhead as spiny spheres shattered into splinters. Those hesitant to the danger, the young and less trained, were slashed where the armor did not cover, at the forearm and ankle. The least fortunate were impaled, through multiple parts of the body, by the long spines. With no shield, Xandr could only watch as the things pelted the sand and rolled around him. *Giant urchins? It's raining giant urchins!* Screams followed, of panic and pain. Of war. The city answered with volleys of fire, as brilliant and numerous as the stars, rising from the parapets to arch over the legions, falling against the dark shapes in the Sea.

When the urchin onslaught subsided, most of the men suffered only shallow cuts and soldiered on, but a few lay crippled in the sand, and a smaller number still, having lost courage, were paralyzed.

Demacharon wrestled his mount to greater speeds, brandishing his spear and shouting. He routed his phalanx back into square formation just as it began to disperse into chaos. Those unable or unwilling to fight were trampled, their positions replaced.

Forward they marched, as if making war with the Sea, where something violet glittered on the water. Torchbearers ignited their fires, one for every ten men, and pools of darkness formed between the glow, and where the light hit the sand long shadows were born of shield and pike. Inexplicably, men began to drop by the hundreds, their enemy invisible. Mid-stride they froze, groaning and clutching at their sides, before crashing at the feet of their companions.

"By Sargonus, we've never seen the likes of this!" Demacharon cried, riding up beside Xandr. "The urchins! Poisoned! Only a scratch and it killed them! We must get closer, under the range of their . . . whatever they are! The time is now, Batal! Spur them! Spur them to battle!"

The phalanx was invented to fight men, not merquid. Assembled in squares, the Hedonians were like schools of fish in a fisher's net. Already Demacharon was shouting for them to disband. But his voice was muffled by the waves and the winds and by the din of battle. Hysteria and confusion ruled the night. As men argued and wrestled to break free of the phalanx, others did likewise to hold the line.

Where the sand became hard-packed and wet with the tide, Xandr could see them, silhouettes of things colossal and crustacean, unthinkable living devices. Other things were out there also, shambling upright in the waxing moonlight, with bodies and limbs like men, but were not men. A putrid stench fouled the air, like the decay of a fisherman's spoils. Xandr pitched backwards, his nostrils aflame, and the world blurred. He clamped his eyelids shut as Emmaxis lashed about, pulsing with hunger. The sand shifted with alien footfalls, and when he looked again, the pale, lifeless bulbs of a merquid's eyes were upon him, the slick green-gray scales of its face glistening and wet, its mouth wide with rows behind rows of chipped teeth. Xandr recoiled from its hideousness and struck again, his steel coursing through soft membranes and cartilage. With a gurgling wail and clear blood oozing from the gaping wound in its torso, the merquid slumped in the sand and writhed, its eyes looking no more dead than when it was alive.

Where water met earth, men continued to clash with merquid. The amphibious host did not walk or run, but moved in an awkward, inhuman gait against the wall of shields, flinging gangly limbs and supple bodies onto the bristling pikes. Torchbearers knelt with bows, setting merquid ablaze with arrows and secret alchemies—burning merquid moved through crowds of friend and foe in streams of reds and oranges, their scales singed and flaking. The stench made breathing unbearable. And Xandr could see that this was not a battle among equals, but a slaughter.

Demacharon's hippocampus charged along the beach, wreathed with foam. His voice sounded like a trumpet as he launched his spear. "Drive them back! Back to the Sea from whence they came!"

As the colossal silhouettes moved, the Sea rolled into hills about their extremities, and men fighting close to the shore were tossed up in the water. Crustacean claws pinched men by the dozen, swallowing them in darkness, tearing limbs, splitting hips from torsos. Blood and human entrails rained from above. As the Hedonian forces retreated from the monstrous gathering, thousands of merquid emerged from the waves, their bulbous eyes glowering. Like the tide surging back to the land, they fell upon the humans, with webbed claws and rows of teeth and barbed stingers. Living missiles launched from unseen artillery. Gelatinous shapes dissolved armor, burned away skin and eyes, sent men gasping to the ground. Hoplites fought masses of tentacles with sword and spear, holding the enemy at bay by shield. But for every merquid felled, another three arose.

Xandr watched as men were disemboweled, as jugular veins were torn from throats in splendid showers of blood, and his heart turned from dread to rage. He rushed headlong into the amphibian host, moving Emmaxis into a low, wide arc, hewing merquid down by the score, dipping his sword through scale and fin, splitting hips from thighs and shoulders from arms, leaving briny heads to be reclaimed by the Sea. Against the crashing tide he battled, in a mist of foam and blood.

Charging across the Gulf of Sarnath, Demacharon cut his way through the bodies, his gladius slick with the ichor of merquid. "Fall back!" Xandr could hear him saying, the spear in his other hand turned toward the monstrous,

rising shapes in the Sea. "Pikemen, fall back! We're helpless against those demons!"

Ten thousand men arranged themselves into the shape
of a tortoise, each shield a part of the shell, their pikes like
the spines of an urchin, and in this form they marched
backward from the shore. Archers crept to the front, their
flaming arrows bursting against the dark shapes, revealing flashes of intricate joints and pitted shells. Pincers
swatted down in retaliation, making tombs out of armor
and scattering those fortunate enough to retreat. Rearing
about, Demacharon let go his spear. It carried the power
of his arm and his hippocampus, and where the point of it
vanished, some vital organ popped, and one of the colossal crustaceans faded into the gloom.

In immediate response, merquid swamped about the
commander, tearing ribbons of flesh from his mount with
their hooked fingers. The hippocampus bucked, whicker-
ing with agony, and Demacharon was tossed into the surf.
Distraught at the sight of their fallen commander, the legion broke position, fearing more for his life than their
own. Spears soared like flocks of birds, impaling merquid
into the sand. Finias led the wedge, thrusting into the
multitude of scales, the swords of his countrymen cutting the enemy down like weeds against the scythe. But
Demacharon was too deeply entrenched. Stealing a spear
from dead fingers, he split the ribs of his attacker, yet the
bronze tip became fixed upon the soft vertebrae. As he
wrestled to free the weapon, he reeled in pain, sinking
ankle deep into the gray slush of the shore. His helmet
appeared to absorb the brunt of the rock's impact, but
now other merquid were backing away and groping for

stones. Another blow and Demacharon was knocked on his elbows, his plume and cape muddied, the tide sloshing within his breastplate. Merquid were upon him, their webbed fingers clawing his helmet, forcing his nose and mouth into the muck. He writhed violently, and then a war cry sounded, giving the merquid pause. Sarpedon came charging, snagging innards by the prongs of his trident, the legion under his command hacking merquid in his wake. But it was Xandr, fighting from the other side, who reached the commander first.

"Demacharon," Xandr intoned, clasping his hand. "Are you all right?"

Coughing out the mud in his throat, Demacharon found his voice. "Thanks to you, my friend."

"Here," said Sarpedon, leaping to his feet. "Take my steed. You are the best of us."

"No, brave commander," answered Demacharon. "A hippocampus is as dear to a man as his wife. I cannot take her. But tell me, what do you have to report?"

"All is not well, Sir. Brave Polydorus is lost! Having spent his arrows, the gill pulled him from his mount, and though he fought bravely on foot, they stripped him of his armor and beat him with coral and gashed him with their stingers, and in the salty sea the life flowed out of him. Leaderless, his legion lost hope and were cut down, and the merquid pushed to the wall!"

"What of Aeonus and his legion?"

"I cannot say, commander."

He turned then to Xandr. "I am injured, Ilmarin, and must remain here. You must lead my legion. Go to it now, away to Hedonia!"

As the tide pulled away, red with blood, pregnant with splints and spears and bodies, waves of merquid emerged anew. Xandr retreated with Demacharon's legion in tow, far fewer in number than they had been in the pitch of night. Legs and arms were weighed with fatigue, hearts made heavy by loss. There was no place a man could look and not see the dead or mortally wounded.

By the light of the sentry fires, Xandr could see the enemy scaling the walls, slowly but steadily, without rope or ladder. Archers on the battlements impeded their passage with showers of arrows and tipping cauldrons of boiling oil, educing shrieks from gilled throats and clouds of pungent vapors.

Xandr's legion arrived at their backs, pinning the merquid between stone walls and bronze shields. The amphibious invaders fell atop pikes and were trampled, and the earth became slick with their blood. With Emmaxis in hand, its skull face delighting in death, Xandr fought and killed and no adversary could withstand him. With a fierce cry, he pursued those that fled from him, ending their lives with a downward thrust. He paused only once, when a merquid dropped prostrate to gaze upon him. A woeful glimmer could be seen in those bulbous eyes, like the hope in a man begging for mercy. But in the surrounding gore, the Ilmarin's heart was hard and unfeeling—its connection to the world, to the Mother Goddess, severed.

As the dead piled at his sandals, merquid scrambled over their own to escape him, only to be cut down. Upon a hill of enemies, Xandr raised the skull of the merquid who had sought mercy, and shouted, "Do not fear these *bogrens*, my friends—they die like worms at our feet! Fight I say!

Envy your comrades who have fallen here! Envy them that you might attain such honor!"

After a time, the moons reemerged among the heavens, and the darkness began to recede into the light, and Emmaxis grew heavy in Xandr's arms, so that he toppled atop a breast of scales, a breath's length from the flat and hideous face of his enemy. Spitting gobs of blood at him, the dying merquid gasped its final bit of life, snarling, "Damn you, human!"

Xandr staggered to his feet, shuddering with horror. *It spoke! By Alashiya, the thing spoke in a human tongue!*

As Solos took his seat atop the horizon, the first ray of sun touched upon the land, shedding light upon the bodies, inert and glittering and grotesque, one upon the other like seashells covering the beach. None lived that Xandr could see. Worn with fatigue, his blood cooled. *Why? Why would they do this? Do not things that speak also reason? Do not things that reason possess compassion? If they can speak, and think and feel like men—why throw their lives away like foam in a wave? Where is the reason, Quasil? I need your wisdom.*

Xandr gazed long at the red streaking his hands, and longed to weep, but there were no tears in his body to shed. Was he not Ilmarin? A learned monk? Yet he had fought, and killed, with all the callousness and ferocity of a Hedonian. He studied the blue and gold of his Hedonian kilt, now caked in human blood and the clear ichor of merquid, and wondered whether it would be washed clean in the pool of the Sargonus Temple.

The battle was finished. Demacharon, Sarpedon, and Aeonus returned upon their hippocampi, bearing the body of Polydorus upon a gilded bier. The Gates of

Sarnath lifted to receive him and the sentry behind the walls joined the survivors to search among the dead. It was the worst part of battle. Xandr remembered the words of his mentor then, which had once been the words of Kjus: *No warrior can seek among the dead without doubting his reasons for war.*

Xandr waded through a sea of broken bodies, through parts of men pleading for help, abandoning those beyond hope. In a mess of the boy's own remains, he found Finias.

"Batal!" the young voice called out, calm and steady. "I did not stop believing in you."

Xandr knelt before him. *By Alashiya, he's no older than when I fled from Ilmarinen.* "Do you feel any pain?"

"No," Finias admitted. "I feel nothing, but . . . I am a little cold."

"I will take you by the fire."

"No," said Finias, "I doubt that will help. I am not blind. I can see that I won't last a passing." Even now, Xandr could hear his reverence for the Batal.

"You fought bravely today," Xandr answered, sensing the wetness behind his eyes, though he would not allow it to flow. *I should have fought by him. But he is just one of so many.*

The boy tried to move, realized he could not, and set his head back against the sandbank. "Batal, would you sit a while, and tell me stories?"

"If you wish. Which tale do you want to hear?"

"Batal," he said, suddenly trembling, "I see him, the Taker! He stands before me now, just over your shoulder . . . he waits. Oh, he is skull and horns and eyes of fire and smiles horribly. He beckons me to the dark, but . . . I don't want to go. I don't want to go into the dark."

"Do not be afraid," Xandr said softly. "Sargonus welcomes you to the isle of brave warriors—to see new horizons—to return to the earth and to the womb of a new mother. Sleep, dear Finias, and forget the heaviness of the world."

But, Xandr could see, the boy could no longer hear him.

8

THE CELL

Pain, darkness and cold permeated her being, defined her reality, but for how long she lay there she did not know. Her consciousness drifted continuously from awareness to uncertainty.

Am I sleeping? Where am I? What's happened?

The questions radiated painfully from her hair to her toes—a sore, numbing feeling, but it was something on which she could focus, hold fast to.

She'd known worse pain: the swelling pustule from the bite of a dragon mosquito, the edge of a bastard sword cutting across her thigh, the blunt teeth of a rakar taking chunks of her. But pain could be dissected and analyzed, like the spools and pulleys in her bow-sword, rendering it ineffectual. The drop in temperature was another matter.

There were different kinds of cold. In a blizzard, on the peaks of Mount Ukko, the temperature stabbed at the body like icy daggers and could kill. But the cold of her cell was of another kind, a dull sensation erasing even the memory of sunshine, like all the warmth had gone out of her body, as if she were already dead. Her body felt strangely unfamiliar, as if she were touching a corpse. Her fingers brought new pain to the tender parts, to her breasts, to the ribs framing her stomach, offering some sense of self. Though her homeland did not know the long absences of sun like other lands, or the wintry eclipses which brought the snows, the cold could be endured, for Ilmar were a tough-skinned people. Curling into herself, like a newborn left to shiver on a cold stone floor, she reminded herself of that fact again and again, forcing herself to believe it. Her people persevered, and so would she.

Ilmarinen did not exist on any map or in any volume of history that she knew. No great monuments of stone had ever been erected in the valleys of Ukko, only houses of thatch and oak, gifts of nature that nature would soon reclaim. It was the people that made the land what it was. The Ilmar existed for it, keeping the name of their homeland alive on their tongues. So long as she lived, Ilmarinen would not fade into the dark recesses of prehistory. The language, the songs, the exquisite woodcraft, the dances by the bonfires of Solstice Night—she would keep these for her children to pass to theirs. If only she could survive. But to that end she was blind, for the darkness kept secret any chance of freedom.

Darkness.

It was what she could not suffer. Her people soaked up sensations like no other people, were intimately aware of Earth, Wind, Water, and Sun. But this place was cut off from the Mother Goddess entirely. Smooth worked stone met her knees and fingertips, having not known the touch of life for centuries. The air was dead, lacking the caress of running water, the kiss of sun, the smell of it nearly non-existent but for the faintest trace of dank rock. The only sound was from the subtle shift of her weight, the heart in her ribs thrumming like a distant drum, her breath, drawing air across the cracks of her lips.

She stared so long into nothing that the darkness took on a tangible quality. She could touch it. Taste it like bitter syrup.

She found comfort in memory, when remembering did not pummel her with pain. Did they beat her? Force themselves upon her? No. She would have felt the intrusion between her thighs—she had fought them off and they had thrown her in this prison of prisons to await execution and, the death of the Ilmar, unless that man in the temple truly was Ilmarin. But he couldn't be. He was allied with the Hedonians. Why? Was he a slave? Or a traitor? The recollection brought thoughts, and those thoughts punished her, made her skull throb more intensely. Still, it was her only recourse, to search her mind for answers, and in doing so, begin the monologue that after many lonely years had become a dialogue with herself.

What a predicament this is! You've never been in a mess like this, Thelana. I suppose you're to blame for it, going after such a prize . . . foolish girl! What were you thinking?

My coffers were bare of drachma. What should I have done?

But was it need or pride that drove you? You could have robbed any of the merchants in the bazaar.

No. Why take from others who also struggle? Merchants have children, after all, and the temple priests don't need all that gold hanging from their ears, those bejeweled relics and giant pearls, to flaunt and mock us who have nothing! Barbarian hands worked that stone, raised those monuments, and by common law it is ours—mine—to take! She argued herself into a rage, clenched fists against imagined hatreds, and collapsed against the cold stone arms of her cell.

Aimless as a lone feather, a thought, a word, drifted into her consciousness: *escape.* Her numbed body resisted the urge to action, her aching knees warped with her weight, but she shrugged it off, forced the blood to flow into her fingers, and groped blindly at the air. It did not take more than a step to reach the adjoining wall. It was a cube built for one, with barely enough room for two to stand abreast.

But where was the door? Her fingertips brushed the stonework, trembling, painfully aware, and found nothing but dust and gravel. The dungeon was old. Others had died here, or soon after being moved from here. The thought made her shudder. Fate could not have chosen a crueler path. To have been killed fighting, to have fallen to the temple floor to blaspheme their gods with her blood, or better still, to be buried under Old Man oak, beside her family, for her body to flower into ilms where future children might play . . . any of these would have been preferable. But this?

There must be a way out. There must be a door! She searched again, dug her fingernails between the cracks for a seam, a lever, anything.

There must be a door. There must be a door.

The words spilled from her lips in whispers, in gasps for breath. She analyzed the meaning of each word until they sounded like gibberish in her ears, like an incantation, a mantra for rescue. Realization crippled her. She'd rounded the room a dozen times already. From the cold stone floor she wept. There was no door. It did not exist, nor did a way out.

Oh Mother Goddess, how long have I been here? Days? Years? How hard did they hit me?

Her fists smacked the wall, removing centuries of dust. The thick masonry registered no sound or vibration. Frustration turned to screaming, her voice reverberating in her ears. There was only one way out, she knew—the way of desperation, the final way. She would curl back into herself like a fetus, shun the cold and darkness and pain, and find escape within her being.

Hunger. A new sensation, it triumphed over all the others now, impossible to disregard, waking her to misery. *Do they not feed prisoners? Or is it heretics they do not feed?* She floated upwards, imagining herself a will-o-wisp, and followed the hunger to an open doorway, where light and warmth awaited her.

Everyone she cared about was present around the dining table, the one that grew from the roots of Old Man Oak. Most of her sisters were prettied up in elaborate braids, in beads of rich blue lapis lazuli, in garlands of jasmine and ilm, their bodies intricately patterned from head to heel in swirls of henna. The boys, as was the tradition, wore tusks or horns.

Amina was there, the most fully developed of her sisters. Her hips and buttocks were broad, ideal for childbearing, and her breasts were like melons, which would keep her newborns alive in time of famine. Thelana would never admit her envy.

Aliaa sat beside her, her hair like ebony against her shoulder, the wood carving she'd been whittling for days in her palm. Her vision was too poor for scavenging, but she could name every flower, spice bush, and tree, could tell you what was good for eating, planting, and what was poisonous. Thelana assumed Aliaa would be chosen for keeper someday, but Mother was torn. Could she part so soon from her child? And might not Aliaa be happier as a wife and mother among other river folk? Mountain People were not simple. Their ways were strange.

Anja kept herself as far as possible from the boys, grumbling whenever she touched elbows with her boyish sisters. She never passed a reflection she did not pause to stare into. Her braids were like golden ropes swaying down to her bellybutton, and her skin was supple and fair, like an infant's. She had yet to sacrifice her blood to the river nymphs, but Thelana knew, despite the immaturity of her body, that Anja would be the first to jump the fire. No man will deny you, Father warned, which was why—and Thelana thought it peculiar—the older boys were never left alone with her. But why any girl would desire to be taken by a boy, to be given to another family, was beyond Thelana's comprehension. Next to Anja was Nicola, the last born, who was still new to the world and searching for faeries.

The sister she loved most was Britannia. She was nearly Thelana's twin, with the slender physique of a girl, but all the mannerisms of a boy. Like her brothers, Britannia shied away from henna and garlands, preferring bangles of teeth and bone. Beneath layers of mud, clay, and dirt, her skin was an indistinct tone, a patchwork of river gray and earthy blacks and white granite dust. Mother flew into a rage whenever Britannia came home after eclipse having neglected to bathe in the river, looking so savage—like the worst of the boys, sometimes worse. More often than not, Thelana was out with her, seeking discovery in the same mucky places, where—should either break a bone— no one could hope to find them. Come nightfall, they'd come running home, hand-in-hand, making footprints all over the porch, pulling twigs from each other's hair and spurs from each other's heels. Once, Britannia returned from the woods with bright green skin. "Camouflage!" she explained. Mother was not amused, dragging her by the ear to the Potamis. She was scrubbed until it hurt, until resembling a human again. Amina had been eager, as always, to help out—much to Britannia's humiliation. *No family will ever want you for their son,* Mother would cry, *if you don't wash that dirt off!* She would then point to Amina, Aliaa and Anja—model wives the three of them. *Why can't you two be more like them?* Of course, Britannia was only a child and cared more to catch flutterbies than husbands.

Across from the girls, the boys did everything but sit— kicking, punching, wrestling, and lobbing insults at one another. There was Borz, proudly showing the stubble of his chin, damning up his energy despite the laughter escaping his lips. Laine and Vaino, the ever-quarrelsome twins were bickering again. Whose head was trapped in whose bony arms was anybody's guess. Lodr and Heimdl, the crafty and tinkering pair, were carving runes into a spear, despite Father having forbidden them from hunting. "Tomorrow we'll bring back a mammoth carcass," they insisted, even though they'd never killed anything larger than a grasshopper, or even knew what a mammoth looked like. Between them, eager to join in whatever anyone was doing, was Baldr, the youngest of the boys, who stood no taller than Father's knee.

The sky, studded with the bright white fires of the gods, was turning azure velvet. In the crisp cool air of dusk, the crickets were starting to wake, singing distantly for lovers. Thelana could see the immense trunk of Old Man Oak, the canopy of branches reaching over their heads, heavenly moonlight gleaming between the foliage. Mother stood in the doorway in petals of orange and violet. Never knowing the touch of a blade, as Ilmar did not cut their hair, her bright red locks flowed over her breasts to her swollen belly. That was how Thelana pictured the Goddess, just like her mother, pregnant with impending life, hair cascading to form all the rivers of the world. If Mother managed to get enough food, she was certain her twelfth sibling would survive. But the fire that raged from the cooking pit burned empty, the rotisserie turning without anything to be cooked. Kettles bubbled and frothed, but none of her siblings, not even Father, managed to bring something to boil.

Looking at herself for the first time, Thelana saw a bony twelve-year-old caked in mud, with twigs and leaves sticking out of her unkempt hair. She was standing before Father, a clean-licked wooden bowl in her outstretched hands. "Baba," she said to him, "Why is there no more food? I'm still hungry."

"Hop," he answered, working his beard into a smile.

"That's silly," she said. "What is that even supposed to mean?"

"It's what my father told us when there wasn't any food," he answered, his face looking suddenly aged. "If you're hungry, hop."

Some of her younger siblings, Nicola and Baldr, were already at it, the leaves crackling under their pounding soles. "I don't think it's helping much, Baba," Thelana admitted.

"Ah, you are the cleverest of us, I fear, too clever for this family." The other children looked on disapprovingly, with envy. Attention from Baba was rarer than fresh meat, but father wielded honesty like a hammer, with no compunction against stating what was, to him at least, obvious.

But Thelana did not care for praise. Her belly was cramping and her older siblings, she was certain, were suffering worse. "You didn't answer my question, Baba," she said, stamping her foot. "Why is there no more food?"

"Thelana, you've had your share for this night. Go to sleep now, as there is much work for you, come morning."

"But Nicola had a full bowl!"

"How stubborn and defiant you are! None of your brothers or sisters speaks to me this way." His voice lost its good humor. "Nicola rarely eats, and she is still a babe. Look how skinny she is. Would you have her become ill?"

She stamped again, quickly working up a rebuttal, but thought better. Father would beat her buttocks red with a switch should she push the matter. Knowing he was right, she looked away, defeated. Rejoining her siblings at the table, she put her weight on her ankles, tucking her soles beneath her. Mother's face showed disapproval. Whether for her daughter's disrespect or her husband's obstinacy, Thelana could not tell. She gazed blankly, as if at nothing, and slipped quietly into the house. Thelana remembered a time when her mother would laugh and take notice of peculiar things, but those days were remote, as when the hills were green.

"This isn't right," said Borz. "Why do they store the food? We could eat today, and for tomorrow I'll bring home boar."

"Or mammoth!" Lodr added, lifting his spear for all to admire.

"Oh, Borz," Amina said, in her imitation of Mother, which annoyed Thelana immensely. "No one has seen any boars around here for cycles, let alone mammoths."

"Mammoths are migratory," Aliaa noted, "and travel in herds. But they prefer arctic to temperate climates. Borz would have to travel far from here, to the North."

"How can you possibly know all that, Aliaa?" Anja asked her.

Thelana leaned forward, coming between them. "Have any of you seen Baba eat this cycle? I haven't."

"Oh, I'm sure he's eating," Anja replied, nervously braiding her hair.

"You're right," Borz said. "He's not been to dinner. He's sparing it for us."

"Why would he do that?" Anja cut in, her brows creasing, rumpling her perfect golden complexion. "Things can't be *that* bad, can they?"

"Surely not," Amina insisted. "I mean . . . things have always been good." Her eldest sister was fully grown, a true woman of the household, and utterly oblivious. She would die of hunger, Thelana thought, should no one warn her of the possibility.

"I've heard that in some families, the parents eat the children!" It was Laine, who delighted in the torment of insects and frogs and rodents, who loved all of life's horrors.

"Ridiculous!" Amina snapped at him. "How dare you say such a thing? Now I'll have nightmares!"

"Oh yes," Britannia added, leaning against the table with a wicked grin. "I heard it, too. They roast them over the fire until good and brown."

"Quiet, all of you!" Amina cried.

"You shut up," Britannia answered. "You're not my mother."

A great deal of yelling ensued, till the smallest of them, who had been quiet till now, pleaded to be heard. They listened because her face was small and her cheeks full of baby fat. "I know what to do!" she exclaimed. "Everyone, lift your bowls up, but don't look at them. I have a surprise."

Borz rolled his eyes, but Amina scolded him with a glance, and the others hesitantly followed Nicola's example.

"I made a stew," she said, sipping the empty wooden bowl. "But you can only taste it if you close your eyes. Isn't it good?"

"Y-Yes," Aliaa agreed. "But it's . . . it's hot. Be careful everyone."

"Hot and salty," Britannia added, licking dry her lips. "Wherever did you find salt?"

"Does it have carrots?" asked Baldr, peeking around the room at his eleven kin. "And ollyps? I love ollyps."

"Oh yes," answered Nicola. "Lots and lots of ollyps, cut thick and juicy."

Thelana could taste it too—feel it warm the walls of her stomach, quiet the groan of hunger where she lay, in the cold and in the darkness of her cell, the best soup she never had.

9

THE GILDED CAGE

With baskets balanced on their heads and along their wrists, slave girls moved in procession, ascending the zigzag of steps to a pillared terrace. Four legions of forty thousand men looked on from below, gathered at tables under the open sky, flaming tripods illuminating their eager faces. Nowhere did the delicacies confound the senses like those found on the commanders' table, where Xandr was seated before piles of assorted breads, bowls of ollyps curled with steam, macadamia-encrusted filets of blabbit simmered in silver pans, deep fried koons in saffron sizzled, grape-sized caviar from rivers of spawning wakefin glistened in fish shaped dishes, ox brains in red-wine sauce, oysters steamed in garlic peppers and couscous alongside horned crustaceans as wide as the table. For dessert, there were honey-dipped dates and cashews and hockenberries. Recipes had been brought in from every niche of the world, making use of meats and spices Xandr could not name. It was an obscene abundance for so few, for the tasting rather than the swallowing. Sarpedon and Aeonus sat beside him, as did the High Priest Urukjinn, who blessed the meal with a prayer and a dash from the waters of the sacred pool.

"You performed your role admirably," the priest said to Xandr. "Your speech. The way you fought and rescued Demacharon. All more than I could have hoped for."

"Bah!" The table shuddered against Sarpedon's heavy hand. In his other hand, he gripped a large chalice of wine. "Wars are won by men," he said with a tinge of envy, "not legends."

"True," Urukjinn replied, "but empires are sustained by those who tell the better story."

Two maids approached the table, an amphora between them as tall as their shoulders. Hoplites in black and gold battled across the curved ceramic surface. With some effort the women tipped the wine, filling Aeonus' kylix. "To Polydorus!" he exclaimed, his lips spilling with laughter.

Sarpedon joined in the toast. "Alas, mighty Polydorus . . . tonight his pyre burns high and bright! Let his enemies tremble at his memory! Many a village did Polydorus raze, and many treasures did he plunder, and barbarians conquer!"

"Let us not forget the women!" bellowed Aeonus. "Can there be any greater spoil? How many brides did Polydorus return with from his campaigns?"

"Were they brides or slaves?" questioned Xandr, swallowing his outrage lest it burst from his mouth.

"Is there any difference?" Sarpedon said with merriment. "Women shuddered before him as did his enemies! Would that I be remembered so—that men would speak with dread at the invocation of my name."

"Surely, good Sarpedon, surely!" said Aeonus, emptying another kylix.

"Why do you not drink?" the burly commander said to Xandr. "Do you mean to offend the memory of Polydorus?"

"I did not know him," said Xandr softly.

"It is no matter!" Sarpedon shouted, forcing a cup into the Ilmarin's hands. The inner rim was painted so that a pentaconter could sail on a sea of wine. "Drink you fool! Drink or I'll run you through here and now!"

"Idle threats," Aeonus cut in. "He is a blathering buffoon when he's drunk."

"Someday . . . someday you'll lose that pretty face," he cried, his cheeks flaring red with drink and anger, his attention now on Aeonus, "What would you do then, if the women did not fancy you?"

"I'd steal them! Just as *you* must," he prodded, and swept a maid into his arms, sending plates and oysters crashing to pieces. "Come," Aeonus said to her, "sit on my lap and show me your barbarian ways!" She pulled instinctively away, but remembering she had little choice in the matter, left him to tug at her chiton, to fondle her exposed breast, to force his lips against hers. It was more of a bite than a kiss. The High Priest looked on with no more expression than the marble faces watching from the corners of the room.

"The whore writhes like a snake," Sarpedon said, tearing the guts from some shelled creature. "They say you're so handsome, that to a woman's eyes no man is your equal, yet still she resists?"

"She was joined, me thinks," laughed Aeonus, trading kisses between gulps of wine and brain meat. "I might have killed her husband, in some god forsaken village in the Korok valley. Many men fell to my sword that day. Fathers, brothers, sons . . . Who can tell who was what to whom?"

Another slave, hardly more than a child, set a trembling dish before the Ilmarin. Myths were told along the border of the plate in gold stencil. The pungent aroma of trubble shrooms—deadly poisonous but for a specific phase of the moons—offended his senses.

"What of Demacharon?" said Xandr. "Where is he?"

"He does not celebrate," answered Aeonus. "Never does. Truly, the man's only mistress is war. No doubt he is in his tower planning a siege."

"I will drink to him then!" Sarpedon muttered, wiping his beard with his forearm. And he summoned a girl to bring a gold-plated horn, which she balanced atop a tripod. "Take it," he said to Xandr, "It is from some beast, a barbarian's cup—is it not?"

"Not of my people," said Xandr, "but it is beautiful."

Urukjinn picked morsels into his small mouth and sipped from his chalice—a relic bejeweled enough to feed a family for years. "There are many such wonders in Hedonia," he said to Xandr, "from all over Aenya."

But Sarpedon would not be interrupted, even by the High Priest, and leaned in so closely that Xandr could smell the fermentation of his meaty lips. "Tell me, did we never subjugate your land? Ilmarinen was it?"

I should kill him. It would be quick and unstoppable— Emmaxis lies waiting at my feet. "No . . . and if you did, you'd find nothing but a barren wasteland. Famine swept through Ilmarinen long ago. When the crops wilted, so did our people. Those that did not flee, starved."

"You left no monuments?" the High Priest inquired. "No idols, or treasures?"

"No," said Xandr. "The Ilmar leave this world as we come into it. It is our way." He smiled at the priest, but was uncertain as to why. Perhaps it was the sustaining power of his people's philosophy, *with nothing to lose, nothing can be lost.* The words remained unspoken, hovering between him and his hosts, unnerving them who obsessed over wealth and power.

Aeonus continued to grope his captive. She was half naked now, her chiton torn to reveal the cleft between her knees. His hand moved down, from her breasts to below her waist, and suddenly, she collapsed forward, knocking a flaming brazier from its chain. It burst with embers, darkening the tile floor with ashes. For a moment she looked to the Ilmarin, but there was no appeal for help, only shame, as hope was long absent from her eyes. Aeonus named the woman by the worst of obscenities, pushing his boot against her buttocks.

"Do I not please you, my Lord?" she said to him, tugging at the tatters of her clothing.

"Meet me tonight in my chamber and we'll see."

"Why do you bother," said Sarpedon, "when so many come willingly?"

"It is the hunt, my dear commander. What is the pleasure of chasing that which does not flee? I bore of easy prey."

"Is it the hunt or the *cunt* that pleases you?" Sarpedon's voice resonated unashamedly, a laugh made by drunkards at foolishness.

Xandr searched the High Priest for disapproval. Finding none, his desire to speak wrestled with his wisdom for prudence. What good could come from ridiculing his hosts? Nothing he could say could help the slave girl or any of the thousand other girls in the city. On the other hand, he was Ilmarin, and watching such injustice without a word tormented him. "Does your god not frown on such depravity?"

"Men willing to die in the name of God are allowed indulgences," he answered. "Besides, these are not proper women, not citizens. They were offered a choice: death or captivity. This is our mercy, a chance we give them to live anew for the good of the Empire."

"Aeonus can have his women," said Sarpedon. "I will indulge in the good grape the gods bestow us. Come now, Ilmarin. You fought like a demigod the other night. I had not believed your people to be so fierce." His voice was beginning to slur. He offered the horn again, having forgotten, in his drunken state, that he'd already done so. "Go on then, give us a toast!"

Xandr lifted the ivory cup warily, watching the deep violet slosh about. The odor offended his nostrils. Wine and mead were strange to him, for the Ilmar did not imbibe fermented drink, or partake in any substance that might alter the clarity of the mind. "To peace," he said finally.

The room grew quiet and somber. Urukjinn stood with his chalice and staff, to defend the honor of his guest. "Yes, to peace, and to you, Batal of Legend, which by the divine right of the priesthood I declare full citizen!" A soft gasp swept through the assembly. "We owe everything to you— our country, our very freedom. The merquid threat is no more. They have fled to the depths of the Sea and there they shall remain, fearing Sargonus and his chosen city!

"All fought bravely . . . Demacharon, Aeonus, Sarpedon, and yes, our fallen commander, Polydorus. May his spirit find rest. But they fought for their people. You, a nomad from a distant land, had no such cause. No reward can fully repay our debt to you. But in my gratitude, I offer you, Xandr of Ilmarinen, a princely dowry, with the hand of my virgin daughter!" Another gasp. "The wedding feast will mark the celebration of our victory!"

There was a roar of hoots and hurrahs and howls, but Urukjinn waved them to silence. A maid fell to her knees before the two men. A sword, ornately patterned in jade and gold, bridged the gap between her outstretched palms. With a ceremonial air, the High Priest took up the sword, placing it into Xandr's hands.

The sword of the Ilmarin girl.

"As you were once barbarian, I offer up this barbarian blade, this treasure of your kind. In taking it, you accept the mantle of regent commander over our newly acquired province in the North. I've no doubt that, with your cunning and courage, we may yet quell the unrest of the northern tribes!" It was the highest possible honor. Forty thousand men looked on with envy.

"Hail Xandr!" Sarpedon exclaimed. "Commander of the North!" He drank again, emptying his kylix. A slave girl bent to refill it.

A circle formed amidst the gathering. Men with lyres, flutes and tambourines spilled into the open space. Music echoed from the terrace to the adjoining walls of the palace as dancers spun in wisps of silk and acrobats tumbled and twirled with batons of flame. Chimes jingled from belts and ankles, from the gold chains in their ears and nostrils. Colors flashed from patterns of inked flesh. Feet stomped in rhythm as voices rose up, and women in skirts of palm fronds tumbled over rings of fire.

To Xandr, it was a mockery—an obscenity—for he saw the performance for what it was, the conquered prostrate before their conquerors. Sacred rituals were turned into amusement, to appease the Hedonians, who devoured without being sated.

"Cast off that somber mask," Aeonus said to him. "Great honors have been given you. Citizenship and command! Wealth and power is yours, more than you can imagine."

"Can I wallow in wealth and power when so many suffer? Is this not the Dark Age of Aenya?"

"I do not see it," said Aeonus icily. Emptying his kylix, he let it crack against the tile as maids hurried to replace it.

"The Dark Age is a name given by the suffering," remarked Sarpedon. "The gods give each man his lot, and with it he takes what he can, kills if he must. You are blessed with strength and resolve, Xandr. What should it matter to you, if the weak are unwilling to rise?"

Shades of cherry red and burgundy streamed from amphora to table to terrace, and sometimes into their cups. "Perhaps we should call this the Age of Wine!" Aeonus exclaimed.

Without ceremony, Sarpedon began to sing. It was an awful sound of drunken exuberance, but the way he carried on waving his hairy arms and slapping his knees, a deaf man might have thought him the greatest showman on Aenya. It was a dirge of two lovers, of a woman in waiting and a man who did not return from battle.

"How is it that all people elsewhere suffer, but you do not?" Xandr said to the priest. "Do not all things in Aenya thrive as one? If no man has a coin for fish, how can the fishmonger prosper?"

"Forgive me for being forthright," the priest said with a gloating grin, "but I assume commerce is not known to your people. I suppose when you want something you simply kill whoever owns it. Am I right?"

"Indeed," Xandr answered, finding the taste of an olive too bitter, "if the man who owned the thing did not deserve it."

"Then allow me to enlighten you. It is known that the lowest class of man is the most common. Upon this base stands a higher rank of men, those who best know to use the world's resources. You see, for a herdsman to be wealthy, he needs many cattle. And for a king to be powerful, he needs many poor in his service. That is why you will find in the darkest of times, the most prosperous of men."

Xandr was prepared to rebuff the priest, when he noticed how the others were growing agitated. "Of course," he answered.

"The same principle applies to fathers with their daughters," Urukjinn added. "Without Merneptes' subservience, how might I barter with the Batal of Legend? But in this case, the arrangement I have made will make us both prosper—you will have rank and influence, and I will rest easy, knowing our northern border is secure. None need suffer."

"About that . . ." Xandr said with hesitation, ". . . might I first speak with her, before the joining ceremony, so that she may know her future husband?"

The priest was taken aback, but Aeonus, his tongue bold with wine, was quick to answer. "Do you wish her to know *you*, or do *you* wish to know her?"

Urukjinn was visibly annoyed, judging his future son-in-law through narrow eyes. "It is highly unorthodox, but if it will settle your mind, you may. Perhaps you will teach her to show respect. I would have beaten her more often, but as I am the mouthpiece of God, I had not the time. A maid will escort you to her bower. And one more thing . . . Grimosse, my guardian, is certain to protect her chastity, so that no man defiles her before the proper time."

This is madness, Xandr thought, as he hurried down the corridor, disorientated, the music and the hoots of frivolity fading to a muddled drone. His fists clenched with anger as he recalled the wisdom of his mentor. He had been played from the beginning, he knew, seeing the pieces come together now. As a barbarian and as Batal of Legend, he became a pawn in Urukjinn's game of faith and politics. No doubt others were seduced to becoming the priest's marionettes. Xandr had only wished to help victims of the merquid onslaught, to defend the downtrodden as he might have battled the bogrens, to do as he was trained. But the Hedonians were no simple people. Only one thing prevented him from fleeing the city, and only one Hedonian, he imagined, might be willing to help her.

The palace was a network of courtyards and colonnades seamlessly extending from one tower to another. Patterns of light and shadow fell across painted walls. Reds, purples and pinks of bougainvillea climbed the rooftops. His guide had yet to speak. Her complexion was like dark honey, her nose broad and flat, unlike the Hedonians he had seen in the agora. Her hair was like cords of black rope, bundled in aristocratic fashion, with hairpins of sea creatures in dull, hammered gold. As they came around a bend of fluted marble, he halted her with an outstretched palm. "Who are you?"

She stared at him blankly.

"What is your name?" he asked again. "What are you called?"

She blinked without reply.

"You do not speak the Hedonian tongue, do you?"

She shook her head slowly.

"Damn. How do they teach you to work?" He did not wait for an answer. Gripping her wrist, he commanded her to go. She obeyed, fear visible in her eyes, and he turned to follow the painted dolphins leaping from room to room.

There were no doors to step through, only avenues of columns, occasional rooftops, and walled partitions suggesting separation from one chamber to the next. Weather-beaten gods watched as Xandr unknowingly entered the court of maidens. He followed the sound of song and trickling water through curtains of silk, and watched her vague form through the translucent divide. She rested in a chaise longue of swirling marble limbs and piles of velvet, singing softly of lost lovers as one servant untangled her hair with tines of alabaster and another painted henna patterns about her wrists and fingers. The monster was there also, motionless as a statue, in stark contrast to the softness and beauty surrounding it.

Xandr pulled the curtain aside, making his presence known, and the women gasped, covered their mouths in shame. But Merneptes was unfazed.

"Leave us," she said to them. "My guardian will protect me."

As they hurried from the room, she neared him with hesitation. He could see her plainly now, beautiful without question, with eyes like the wine dark sea and lips a dull crimson like dying roses. "What brings you to me at this passing?" she said. "Are we not to be joined? We should not be seen together."

"I know," he said, amazed by his loss of words. Forty thousand men did not intimidate like one woman. "I am not here for you," he added, bewildered by their surroundings. Young boys fished from painted piers and long-oared ships sailed from each corner. From the ceiling, loops of gold hanged down, where living ornaments squawked and sang, toucans and parrots and other birds. Fountains sprayed and bubbled and foamed, glittering fish darting and drifting.

Almost imperceptibly, the monster moved over them, its immense bell-shaped hammer suspended inches from the floor. "It's all right, Grimm, let him speak. Speak, barbarian. Say what you are here for."

"There is a prisoner. She is of my people . . . I need to find her."

"And what of me? You would leave me to my fate?"

The antechamber with the painted walls, birds and fish led through another silk veil to an ethereal bed chamber of crystal vials and hammered gold accessories, elaborate armlets, decorative greaves and leafy chokers. But what caught Xandr's eye was the pearl in the seashell-shaped recess in the wall. It was the size of a melon, milky white, and smoother than bamboo against his fingertips.

"You live like a queen," he said at last. "What more could you desire?"

"But I am not free. I am like these birds, you see. Like these fish. It is a beautiful prison, to be sure, but a gilded cage nonetheless."

"I thought you did not wish to be joined."

"I want to be treated with tenderness," she replied, going limp against her chaise. "To be loved, the way bards sing of."

"Such a thing does not exist," he said matter-of-factly. "Love is for singers, and young hearts that do not know the world. There is no place for tenderness in this dark age."

"Just what I expected from a barbarian! I am not so naïve, you know, not as my father thinks. He sees me as a child, but I have my spies. You'd be surprised what secrets a man will divulge in the bedroom. And I know how he plans to use me."

"He is still your father," Xandr tried, despite everything he'd heard the priest say and do. "You must mean something to him—"

Laughter mixed in her throat with a sigh of despair. She threw her head back so that her hair washed ebony against her pillows. "I mean nothing to him."

"If he did not care for you," Xandr objected, "why would he have this . . . this thing protect you?"

"Grimosse?" she said. "He protects my chastity. I am as good as a slave without my chastity. In truth, Urukjinn is not his master—Grimm obeys me. He was found wandering the Endless Plains, killed thirty men before he could be brought to Hedonia. My father wished to harness his strength, to unleash it against his enemies. Nobody could control him, but he proved his worth to me. I was caught in a riot and the mob overcame my guards. Grimm heard my pleas, devastated my attackers, and carried me off in my chariot like a babe in a basket. We still do not know where he came from or why he dotes on me. If I willed it, he could pull the heart from your chest.

"But my father is the only one you should fear. Don't underestimate him. If he had not found a use for Grimm, he would have destroyed him. My mother was the Queen of Tyrill. After the city was ravaged, after he butchered her family, they were joined. I cannot say whether he raped her before or after the ceremony. He needed her to make an heir. She was but a tool to power, and never loved her. He prefers young boys, after all. Urukjinn would have you join me, remain to protect the city, and in ten years you'd end up a lord fighting to take Northendell."

"He has already declared me regent commander," said Xandr. "But I will not accept it."

She sat up suddenly, searched his eyes for deception. "Then you'd just leave, just like that? The dowry, the power, means nothing to you?"

"I am Ilmarin. We do not make gods of such things."

"Forgive me, but I've never known such a man, if you speak truly. Even still, it would insult him. He wouldn't allow it. He'd track you down, have you executed and say you fell in glory in defense of the Empire." Xandr sensed a kind of willful surrender in her voice as her cheek fell slack against her pillow. "Accept it, barbarian—we are prisoners of Fate. There is no recourse for us . . . at least, not in this life."

"Above all things, the Ilmar love freedom," he said. "I will have no part in your father's machinations, let the gods be damned! Now tell me of the girl I seek."

"It is hopeless. The dungeon of Hedonia is not a place one walks into and out of freely. It is a labyrinth of stone and iron. Prisoners are sent there to be forgotten. You would never come across her, unless . . ."

Birds squawked, some imitating human speech, fluttering in dramas of dominion, and fish swam lazily in the pool that was their universe. Grimosse threatened without making a sound, and the priest's daughter studied him, clearly distrustful of words, as hers was a life of truth games and falsities. "There is one man in Hedonia," she said finally, "that may help you."

10

DEMACHARON

War makes monsters of men.

—*Kjus*

"Beautiful night, isn't it?"

Xandr agreed with a nod. The moons hanged heavier and brighter than he remembered. Alashiyan Monks predicted shifts of fate on such nights.

Xandr stood with Demacharon atop the wall. Rooftops clustered beneath them, stretching to the dark lip of the Sea and to the moons beyond. Eon was a tortured rock of luminous violet, like a coin just beyond reach—Xandr could cover it with his thumb. The hazy disc that was Infinity lingered beyond, straddling the horizon with swirls of greens and blues.

"The constellations burn bright tonight," Demacharon continued. "Do you see?" His drew patterns in the sky with his finger, but Xandr could not make them out. "The gods look down upon us, judging us. But we never really look at *them*, do we?"

"I watched the heavens with my mentor," Xandr admitted. "As a boy. For the Ilmar, only the Goddess matters. She is here, within us, surrounding us. The stars are the domains of the others . . ." *of the Wandering God.* "Or so we believe."

Demacharon never turned his attention from the sky, but continued like a lecturer, sometimes like a boy filled with wonder. "Did you know that when Infinity looms large, the tide rises? I once asked the mystics about it . . ." his voice trailed off.

"What did they say?"

"Oh, some nonsense about the will of Sargonus," he half-heartedly replied. "I didn't care for the answer." It was a cold night and a gale was blowing in from the North, tousling the commander's short cropped hair.

"You did not miss the celebration to look at the sky, did you?" he challenged.

Demacharon attempted a smile. "Do you ever wonder, with our wealth and power and wisdom, why none of us are happy? We strut with pride and make bold proclamations, but it all amounts to nothing."

"This is the Dark Age of Aenya," Xandr said quietly.

"No, there is joy to be found in this world. Children, for instance . . . all that they say and do is joy, as if the gods took the very stuff joy is made from and fashioned them. That which we take for granted—the beauty in the moons and stars—the children see it. For them the world is fresh and full of wonders." Demacharon fell into his chair, exhausted. The empire spread across the length of his desk, dotted by little golden weights and colored flags. "My first conquest was twenty years ago. Hedonia gained a new province and a great celebration marked the occasion. I sat through the pomp and ceremony, through the litany of titles and honors bestowed me, but none of it could cleanse the memory of my actions.

"What lands did you lay claim to?"

"It was in Goza. I'd tried everything to stem the bloodshed, tried every damn form of intimidation to force an early surrender. I offered concessions—their king on the throne, their idols unspoiled. They had but to submit to Sargonus—all that meant was gold and soldiers, a trifle really. But they fought on, and on, spouting some patriotic nonsense about liberty and self-determination, love of country. The siege lasted half a year. They fought to the last man—even boys too young to properly hold a sword. We lost many on our side also, friends I knew from birth, whose mothers knew my mother. After that, we were furious, you see. I was enraged by their stubbornness. They allowed it to happen, I told myself. They sacrificed themselves for a banner, for an arbitrary line on a map. What did it matter which king they paid their respects to? What did it matter, tell me?" He cried out, clutching the bell-shaped weight marking Goza on the sheet of vellum. And in that moment, Xandr thought the man would collapse under the weight of his own grief.

"Of course," he continued, lifting himself in his chair, "the High Priest condoned our actions, because we had to set an example, to save others from making the same mistake. After we executed the men, the aged and infirm of Goza, we routed the rest from hiding, the women and the children. Some of them, the younger and prettier ones, were taken as spoils of war, not privately into tents, but on the streets, in sight of all. Mothers were not spared the humiliation, were violated before the eyes of their children, just as their sons and daughters were shackled and marched off to slavery. I took no part in it, but I didn't stop it."

He drew heavy breaths, pained by the words he spoke. "Man is a wretched thing, Xandr. I have yet to attend another ceremony. Or permit myself to be given *honors*."

Xandr digested the images the commander conjured, and in his mind each of the Gozan victims became Ilmarin. "I was made a citizen tonight, and regent commander of the North."

Demacharon eyed him suddenly, as if noticing him for the first time. "When you came to me with your claims, I doubted you. But you proved your mettle on the battlefield. And, someday, you will know the burden that I carry."

"No, commander, the Batal does not lead armies, does not rule provinces."

"Then why did you come here to Hedonia?"

"I am here to . . ." *why am I here, Queffi?* ". . . to champion the downtrodden. But I was mistaken. The Empire is too great to need heroes."

The commander faced the barbarian now, scratching at the stubble of his jaw. "You rebuffed the High Priest?"

Wind whistled between them, made the Ilmarin acutely aware of his bare chest, and how much, by his lack of attire, he differed from the fully suited Hedonian. "No. I merely told him that there was no joy to be found in this Dark Age."

"So you deceived him," said Demacharon. "He does not yet know your desires?"

"The High Priest believes what he wishes to believe," said Xandr. "It is that way with him, I think. The Ilmar know nothing but truth."

His tortured lips managed a bitter chuckle. "Truth!" he echoed, with a mix of sarcasm and longing. "You're bound to get killed telling the truth. People hate it. *We say we love truth, but in truth we lie, and love lies.*"

The barbarian paused at this, contemplated it. His mentor might have said something similar.

"Words of Omeos," Demacharon replied. "Oh, yes, we have our philosophers also, Ilmarin."

"You are nothing like Sarpedon or Aeonus," Xandr said after a moment, "not like any Hedonian I've met."

Demacharon turned to his map, stealing an object from the Sea. "I am not so different, barbarian. As a lad we were purged of compassion, taught it was for the weak. Questions plague me, to be sure, and I am doomed to never having the answers, as all men of rank. Is it right that I slay my enemies? When does warring in defense transition into warring of aggression? When any nation, any people, can become a threat to you, when do you not find the enemy within? There are nights when doubt weighs heavily upon me, when my hands tremble with uncertainty, but when the sun takes its place, I remember that I am a soldier, that I am not meant to question my duty. Leave the moralizing to the priests, for my job is to unleash hell."

"Yet moralizing is what you do now."

"Do not seek in me what is not, barbarian. Leave me to my misery."

"The moons are often said to affect men's minds," Xandr answered him, "and tonight they make you drunk with honesty. Do not begin to lie to me now."

"Go!" Demacharon shouted, and stumbled, and fell after something dropped from his palm. Frantically, he fingered the spaces in the stone floor, until he managed to pull out a piece of driftwood no bigger than his thumb, a toy ship

Xandr knew the moment had passed. How could he ask the man for anything now? How could he have believed that the commander might concern himself over a barbarian thief, when so many innocents perished by his sword? Gradually, Xandr looked out upon the dunes, seeing hundreds of points of light, and understood them as the burning of funeral pyres, and the memory hit him. "Who was that woman who approached you before the battle?"

"She is nothing," he said faintly. "Someone who once existed, but is no more."

"She's your wife," Xandr asserted.

"Her name is Niobe," Demacharon admitted with a nod. "Soon after we were joined, she blessed me with a son. I was called to duty when he was at his mother's teat, and there was not a day I did not ask the gods to let me live, so that I might see them again. The gods shielded me from every spear and arrow, and in my tent I pined for wife and child even as I murdered others'.

"After four hard years in the untamed lands, I came again to the city, into Niobe's waiting arms, and to my son, who could now call me Papa. I had not known joy until that day. But the gods had not spared me out of kindness.

No, their protection was a cruelty, a punishment for my misdeeds. Would that I had died on some foreign soil . . ." He studied the miniature trireme tenderly, brushed its delicate oars.

"What happened to your son, Demacharon?" Xandr could see that the question came at the commander like an arrow.

He steadied himself against the parapet, wrestled himself to regain his voice. "*They* did it," he said at last, softly, quietly. "You can see it in my face, my scar—my sorrow marked for all Aenya to look upon . . .

"I never knew my son, but I loved him," Demacharon went on, his tears trickling freely along the twisting path of his cheek. "The merquid . . . he was playing by the water's edge, with the boat I'd made for him, and for a paltry thing, a mere pearl washed along the shore, they tore him apart . . ." He mangled his words between quivering lips, and only after a great effort could he continue. "I hunted down the fiends, slaughtered them with my bare hands, stabbed out their bulbous eyes even as they clawed away my face! But it was no consolation.

"I'd give all the riches in Hedonia, every honor bestowed me, to see my boy again. Niobe, my poor wife, was lost to me as well. She may walk this earth, but she is a mere specter. And so I am alone in my grief.

"Have no pity for me, Xandr. I am undeserving of it. I've killed children and have watched fathers burned alive with the press of my seal. And for what did I do these things? To bring light and reason to the world? To end human suffering? Suffering will always be with us. It is the natural state of man. I had to return here, to lose my son, to comprehend my folly. Hedonia is doomed, Xandr. So much murder cannot go unpunished. The gods have damned us."

"If you truly believe so," Xandr replied, choosing his words carefully, "then you have no cause for loyalty to this city or its gods. My people have suffered, every one of them, just as you have. We have been driven nearly to extinction. But there is hope for us, for me. The barbarian girl from the temple is of my race. I am going to rescue her with or without your help. If you have wronged barbarians, if it weighs heavily upon your heart, help me now. It is not too late for redemption."

11

THE DOOM THAT CAME TO HEDONIA

Nobody in Hedonia ever called Antigonus pleasing to look upon, and as Xandr waited quietly at the top of the stairs, preparing to approach him, he could see why. The jailer's deformity was such that his shadow was more like an eggplant than a human. He stooped with heavy shoulders, with an eye much larger than the other, and his potato-like head sprouted only a few hairs. Bandages crisscrossed his face from lip to lower eye, yellowed and browned about his mushrooming carbuncle nose.

As the sole keeper of the key for special prisons, Antigonus found solace in the company of a rodent, which made its home in the recesses of the tower. This Xandr had guessed was a cruel rumor, but now, as he watched, he could see that it was true.

"Here, here, Sir Nick," Antigonus affectionately called, fumbling at the bit of brie tucked under his thumb. "Look what uncle has for you. It's good eatin', stole straight from the higher ups' kitchen."

Sir Nick appeared to be listening, occasionally wrinkling his nose so that his whiskers danced, or flattening his upturned ears with spittle. Antigonus visibly bubbled with anticipation for the rat to take the sliver of cheese, until Xandr came out of the shadows, allowing his tall shape to block the little bit of light that spilled down from the stair, casting Sir Nick in darkness. Lurching to his feet, the jailor clutched the heavy chain about his neck as the rat vanished behind a crack in the wall.

"Who goes there?" Antigonus whispered.

"You do not know me," the face in the dark replied, "but I bring urgent orders." Torchlight touched the scroll in Xandr's palm. It was sealed by a red, decorative delta, still warm and bleeding wax.

"The high commander's seal!" the jail keeper exclaimed. "Well I'll be! It's—it's—it's Demacharon's all right. Never seen one o' these before. The warden's seal, sure, but never a legion commander, 'xcept at ceremonies and such, and I been down here forty years."

"You have a prisoner," the man said, the wall of mounted flames casting a lattice of shadow across his blond jaw. "I wish to see her at once."

With trembling fingers, Antigonus plied the scroll apart and mumbled as he read, his asymmetrical eyes scanning the page with appetite. It was remarkable to the Ilmarin that the lowborn man possessed such skill, but he guessed it was part and parcel of the jailer's job. "Says here I'm to let you interrogate the prisoner for security purposes, but I don't see the point as she's here for blasphemy."

"It doesn't say she is to be released?" Xandr could hear the alarm in his own voice, disturbing the dungeon-desolate quiet.

"Oh, no. Never seen release papers for blasphemy before. No, sir. Could only imagine those comin' from the High Priest direct, and even then I can't imagine it, his Eminence being infallible and all. Release papers against charges o' blasphemy would be admittin' his Grace to a mistake, and far as I know, his Grace don't make mistakes. To say so would be . . . would be a . . . well it'd be blasphemy, that's what it'd be!"

"Then I suppose . . ." he murmured, more to himself than to the other, "Demacharon did what he could. Tell me, when is her sentencing to be carried out?"

"What's that now? Sentencing?" Antigonus' smaller, lower eye narrowed to a slit with growing suspicion. "What'd you mean by that?"

"Her death sentence," he replied somberly. "I understand that blasphemy is punished with death."

"Oh, it is, it is!" he said with enthusiasm. "Her sentence is already being carried out."

"Say that again!" Xandr cried, stepping into the light to reveal his intimidating build, the skull face upon the sword reflecting irregular patterns of fire reds and oranges.

"Oh, don't be alarmed, sir!" he said with a startle, groping for the half foot skeleton key attached to his neck chain. "You can still go on about your business. We carry death sentencing real slow in my parts o' the dungeon. No need for firewood n' hangin' ropes, much too wasteful. No, here we lock 'em up without food n' water in the pitch of black. Few days in that and they crack, start jabberin' on to themselves, admittin' to all sorts a guilts. And then they dies. Sargonus be merciful."

"How long has she been down there?" he asked the jailor in a low grumble.

"Three days. Most don't make it much beyond that, and as for the lasses, well, they'll meet the Taker after two. But that sure ain't no woman down there."

"What do you mean?"

"Well, when she were brought in, seeing how she were pretty as a lily, a few of my mates and me tried to have a little fun, you know, feel her up a bit. No harm. I'll admit it—I'm no prince. Dungeon attendees like me-self don't get the ladies much. But the bitch broke two o' my mates' ribs, and sent another to the infirmary! Can you believe that? Cracked 'im upside the neck, she did, and worse . . . she broke me damn nose! See the bandages here?" He gestured to the spots of dried blood. "She did this, ruinin' me perfectly good looks! Like I says, she ain't no woman none but a demon-bitch-whore, wearin' some lass like a pantsuit. S'no wonder she ain't botherin' with a stitch o' clothing like any decent lady—nah—she takes a pleasin' shape to sucker us poor bastards into, you know, what you call a fancy-sense-of-security and all. Don't say I didn't warn you."

"Well then, I'll take my chances," Xandr replied, trying to look concerned. Fortunately for him, Antigonus was tin-eared and unaccustomed to the vagaries of human interaction.

The ladder rattled violently, its metallic echo sounding up and down the narrow shaft. As Xandr descended, he feared the rungs might break from the wall. Years of mold had loosened the mortar around the bolts and surely no one bothered with the upkeep of the dungeons. Despite citizenship, the life of a poor jailor was worth less than a slave in Hedonia. But Xandr had come too far, from across the Potamis River, in search of others like himself, and nothing save for the Taker could turn him away.

He continued on down, through the base level of the tower to the dungeons below. A latch between the rungs released a second ladder running the last ten feet to the bottom. Without it, there was no chance of reaching the hatch above. No hope of escape. Only the worst prisoners were brought here. It was a dank, dark place, devoid of wind or sunlight or earth. For all Xandr could feel, the Goddess may just as well have been dead.

The torch from the opened hatch bathed the cell in fiery orange. She was pressed against the corner like a forgotten doll, knees bent to her bosom, head tilted like a wilting ilm against her kneecaps. Dirt and grime clad her from toe to forehead, so that she nearly vanished, like a chameleon, against the wall. Her auburn hair was a scraggly mess of follicles, loosed from its traditional braid to run across her waist like a makeshift skirt. A still body in the dim orange glow, he could not tell whether the breath of the Goddess remained in her. Muttering to Alashiya, a prayer and a curse, he walked the two steps to her side, parting the hair from her face, wiping a bronze line into her cheek with his forefinger.

"Borz, you've come back?" Her voice was hoarse, trace thin even in the silence.

"No, it's a friend." He tilted her head from the wall as one would a newborn. "I've come to take you from here. Do you remember me, from the temple?"

"I can't see," she answered after a moment, shielding her eyes with her forearm. "The light hurts . . . and my throat. Water would be nice." If she did not look so wretched, he might have thought her beautiful.

In his haste to unfasten it, the knot at his waist proved difficult, but he managed it eventually, letting a few drops onto her tongue. Her lips were bruised purple, cracked and bloody. She convulsed with life at the cool wet touch, bent impulsively at the teat of the waterskin.

"Drink slowly," he murmured.

She shuddered as warmth returned to her body, as the liquid of life filled her mouth. In the dim light he noticed the sickly bluish tone of her skin and cursed under his beard. An Ilmarin so long from the sun was like a caged bird! Why had he not thought to bring covering? He'd planned only for the guard, in the hope of finding her alive, and nothing beyond that. Now he was possessed by the urge to embrace her, to keep her in his arms, but the customs of civilization had diseased his mind, making him doubt his nature, think when he should have acted. "Are you cold?" he said sheepishly. "Can I bring you a tunic?"

"I am Ilmarin, Baba," she said with a forced effort. "I've no need of clothes."

"I am also . . ." he started, *like you*, but the words did not suit the moment. She was still blind, in the shadowy dream realm between waking and death. Without pretense, he pulled her limp form against his, urging the strength of his body into hers. And in that instant, every forgotten desire erupted over the surface of his heart. He had so long to speak with another in his own tongue, to gaze upon clear emerald eyes so like his own. But time was one enemy among many. If Antigonus guessed at his intentions, every prison guard would be upon them. "You must come with me and quickly."

"I've made this my home," she answered. "It's safe here."

"You'll die if you stay," he argued. "If you have strength to walk, come with me now. If not, I'll carry you."

"Let me be," she replied, waving him away, annoyed.

"Wait." He reached over his shoulder, fumbling with his baldric, pulling a smooth length of silver from his back. "I've something for you," he said. "A gilded blade, with a hilt of green stone."

"It's jade," she whispered. "My sword! Oh, how I long for the sense of soft steel." She pushed against the rough masonry, finding her footing more easily than he thought possible. "It's mine!" she cried, staggering forward. "You stole it from me!"

"There's no time for this," he argued, snatching her wrist. "We have to leave here, now! And you can't see to take up a sword! Are you well enough to climb?"

"A ladder?" Flakes of rust broke against her fingertips. She was blind but could still find her way around. The entire loose assemblage rattled with her touch, the metallic echo traveling up the shaft, ringing from the portcullises of other cells, making curious the inhabitants of the underworld beneath the streets of Hedonia. "I can climb anything."

As Xandr came over the lip of the hatch, prepared for dark deeds, he could see the jailer's face contort with fear.

Antigonus backed against the rope hanging in the shadows, a crude blade clutched in his meaty hand. "What you think you're doin' there, friend?"

Xandr came forward, the woman in tow. "I have no quarrel with you," he said, "but I am not leaving without her. Step aside."

"Not without the High Priest's seal," he answered, his dagger wavering in the dim fire. "Me job is keepin' prisoners in their places!"

Carefully, the Ilmarin reached for the glittering pommel behind him. "Don't be a fool! Let us pass!"

"Can't do that," he said. "I got me a firm grip on this here rope, and I'm doubtin' you could strike me down before I pulls it, and should I do that, every guard in this here dungeon will be comin' to bury the both of you. Now you go on and put that girl back, and I'll see about forgettin' all this."

"Look," Xandr pleaded, clenching her wrist more tightly, "I wish no harm upon you, but I will do what I must. Now turn a blind eye. You're job isn't worth your life."

"My job is all I have, sir," the jailer said, and with that his immense shoulders bent to put strength into the rope. Emmaxis was too long for the narrow corridor, but Xandr's ax came up and around in a brilliant arc. A single scream echoed to the pinnacle of the tower and down as blood erupted from the stump that was once Antigonus' elbow. His severed hand and forearm remained, frozen to the rope. Before the jail keeper could think to move, to break from the shock of losing a limb, Xandr pulled him close and with another motion sent him down through the open hatch. Antigonus tumbled like a heavy sack of grain, his screams continuing to rise up the shaft from his newly acquired cell, until Xandr kicked at the hatch. It shut with a resounding clang, and all was silent again.

"Someone will have heard that," she said in a hushed tone.

Xandr did not bother to reply, but with her wrist in one hand and ax in the other, made for the spiral of steps. Up they went, her bare feet falling hard against the cold stone as she blindly groped for a railing that was not there. If not for his lead, she would have needed to cling to the outer wall, take slow, careful steps. Now they were sprinting, to escape notice, for sunlight and freedom.

Occasionally, licks of flame—passing torches— gave fleeting warmth in a place that was otherwise dank and lifeless. There was no sound but the patter of their footfalls, the sound of his desperate breathing in her ears, and the dull clamor of metal against stone.

"Where are we going?" she asked the darkness, but no answer came. She was alone but for his touch, his sweat like a glue, her life literally in his grasp. Finally, there was the unmistakable groan of rusted hinges and the creaking of aged wood.

White light shot through her pupils like arrows, reaching the back of her skull where the pain continued to throb. Her skin picked up where her eyes failed, in the subtle brush of wind against her body hair, in the emerging sun breaking against her cheeks and bosom through the moist fog of night, in the growing moss that grew along the stony rim filling the creases in her feet. The Goddess breathed new life into her body—she was like a wilting ilm, turning imperceptibly to life-giving light. Exploring her guide's hand with nimble fingers, she found his shoulder, his back, the baldric holding her weapon.

"Can you see anything?" he asked her.

"Only shapes," she said. "But that's all I need to hit my target."

As Solos' chariot crept over the horizon, the god painted the world in morning hues. The Sea was at their backs to the west. Before them, a network of arches ran over the rainbow striped tents of the market district, to the city's inner wall. The pyramid temple stood over and beyond it, against the pink and violet of an angry swirl of sky.

Xandr examined her again in the morning light and was dumbfounded. She was no longer a sickly blue, but a golden statue in the sun, her heels raised and ready to explode into motion. Her body was wasted with hunger—he could count her ribs and the many scars made by teeth, by battle, but she was nothing like the feeble village maidens he knew, or the ashen courtesans who lolled about like fattened heifers. The well-defined muscles in her back and thighs attesting to a life of labor, of fighting for survival, a life lived truly. Suddenly he caught himself dwelling too long on her shape, his heart aching, murmuring. He was a boy since last seeing a female of his race, when the girl bathing in the waterfall gave him her lapis lazuli. Now he was with another—a strong, willful woman. But after three days in the dungeons, she should look half-dead. Was it a blessing of the Goddess? Or did she possess some uncanny strength of will? He had known monks with extraordinary mental fortitude, but the Ilmar were still only human.

"Thelana," she intoned.

"Excuse me?" He felt foolish, so like a boy.

"It's my name, should you ever think to ask it."

"I—I'm sorry. I'm Xandr."

"Are you Ilmar?" she asked him coolly.

"You knew I was," he replied.

"Then why are you still dressed like them? Have they shamed you? Have you grown soft like them?"

"This is . . . civilization. They don't understand our ways." He tried to explain, but already he was feeling awkward.

Wearing only a sword, she straightened her shoulders and stood tall and defiant and brazen amidst the sprawling city. "I'll not stay here. We'll go far from men who gather, into the wild, to Alashiya. I am through with civilization and all its hypocrisies!"

She was right and he knew it. A Hedonian kilt tugged at his waist. Sandals of rough leather bound his feet. Why was he still wearing them? An Ilmarin had no need for such trappings, and to the sensibilities of the Hedonian people he cared nothing. Besides, he'd brought nothing for her to wear, and could not allow her to be the only one. The kilt and sandals soon tumbled down to the market below, leaving only his baldric, which weighed him heavily with ax and sword. He longed to free himself of these burdens also, but could not.

She did not need to speak to give approval. She understood the need for weapons beyond Ilmarinen, knew what terrors stalked the untamed lands. With a nimble twist, her sword split open like butterfly wings, revealing an intricate system of strings and pulleys and a compartment of arrows.

"I didn't know your sword could do that. It's not, Ilmarin, is it?"

"There's no time for stories," she replied. "Which way?"

Without another word, he stole her by the wrist, feeling her pulse in his hand. She submitted, following him across the bridge.

Street vendors lifted up their tents, unfurling their most elaborate carpets to hang over stacks of tasseled weaves. Intricately carved lanterns and painted plates and voluptuous pottery were neatly arranged on shelves. Sacks of spices were set down and untied, their enticing aromas attracting the crowds. Fathers tapped bronze dishes with finger-length mallets, instructing their sons in ways of their craft. Children navigated narrow avenues, screaming with delight, lifting kites to the wind. The people were too engrossed in their daily routines and revelries to notice the nude man and woman crossing above them, or the monster that came charging from the opposite direction, the gold of its hammer glinting faintly.

Xandr scarcely saw the flash of teeth, the leathery folds of its hideous camel face, the golden moon expanding toward him. The granite railing crumbled to powder and rubble just as he folded under the hammer, Thelana shooting free of his grasp.

"Grimosse!" he exclaimed, rolling to a crouch. "What are you doing?"

"Grimm crush you!" the monster bellowed, bringing the hammer down again. The floor chipped beneath Xandr's feet, and the foundation upon which they stood swayed and shuddered.

"Why?" Xandr cried, tugging at Emmaxis. "I've done nothing to you!"

"You hurt girl!" the monster answered him. "You say words to her and now she hurt! Now she let blood!"

"I don't understand," said Xandr, recoiling again. "What has happened to Merneptes?" But before he could get an answer, Thelana gave his arm a sharp tug, and pointed. From the other side of the bridge, he could make out a gathering, which, though resembling trees, he surmised to be the Hedonian guard. A voice rang out above the others.

"It's the man from the temple. The one who caught me."

"Stop there, *commander*, you and your naked whore," the Hedonian bellowed, and even the enraged golem gave pause. "I knew no barbarian could be trusted! To think the priest put his faith in your kind makes my blood boil!" He spat. "I would never have agreed to it, not in a thousand years, and now you've given me reason to disobey his Eminence, to rid our ranks of your filth."

"Sarpedon!" Xandr shouted. "Call off your monster! There's no need for blood."

"Ah, but that's the difference between you and I," he said, slowly drawing his sword, "for I believe there is always need for blood. Besides, I have little control over that abomination. I'm just as surprised to find the thing here as you are. I can only hope he'll not take from me the honor of killing you."

"There is no honor among Hedonians!" Xandr shot back, grinding his teeth.

"I suppose it does not matter who does the deed," Sarpedon said, waving his sword dismissively. "The golem is a weapon like any other! Grimosse! He wishes to hurt the princess. Destroy him."

Emmaxis came forward, repelling the hammer as shockwaves coursed through Xandr's fingers, rattling the timbers of his arms. The monster was unstoppable, and on the bridge he could scarcely maneuver, or hope to retreat with Thelana in tow. The hammer rang again and again, every impact pushing him, throwing off his stance, opening his defenses. Before Xandr could close the gap, the bell came around in a golden circle, edging his torso. He crumpled, the skull-faced two-hander shivering like a stringed instrument against the stone, and the golem bent backward for the kill, the round face of his hammer eclipsing the sun. In that same moment Thelana flung herself over Xandr's body, and the monster was taken aback, pulling against tremendous momentum to stop his hammer mid-blow. She did not stir, but remained perfectly still in the shadow of the massive weight, watching as the golem's shoulders grew slack and the angry swelling in its lungs subsided.

"Why do you hesitate?" said Sarpedon. "Go through her. Kill the barbarian girl as well!"

Slowly, the hammer descended, hovering over the cracked and shattered pavers of the floor. "No!" the monster cried. "No kill baby girl! Grimm is to protect girl."

"I . . . I," Sarpedon muttered, clearly dumbfounded, "I didn't say baby. I said barbarian!"

The golem's face contorted, revealing jutting teeth and a white gleam in its pupils. It made its way toward the contingent of guards. They watched apprehensively, awaiting orders from their commander, prepared to defend or flee. But Grimosse moved faster than they could have anticipated. With a single swipe, swords, spears, helmets, bits of shield and the three bodies they belonged to swept over the bridge onto the tents below, scattering the merchants and their patrons. Sarpedon flew into a rage, lashing out with his gladius, shouting for the golem to halt. The hammer came down on him. Thelana looked away as Sarpedon's head popped, shattering into bits of skull like eggshells, his breastplate caving into his ribcage, his limbs twisting up, contorting in each and every direction. The commander was reduced to a pulp of blood and bone and bronze, and Xandr could not look upon him or listen to his final scream without a shudder.

Only three guards remained. Then two met with arrows in their knees.

"I can see much better now," Thelana said, pulling another slender arrow from a compartment in her bow.

Xandr managed to stand, but not without a shock of pain. Breathing was like drawing fire into his lung. A hand's length closer and the blow would have stopped his heart. Without Thelana's boldness, he'd resemble Sarpedon. "Why did you—?"

"They'll live," she replied, "but they'll not follow us."

"No," he said, "you threw yourself over me, you—"

She turned to him, her hair tumbling over her breast and shoulder, the color of redwood. "You are the last Ilmarin. I couldn't let anything happen to you."

"But—" *so are you.* Xandr had only time to think the words, for something was drawing his attention away, an ominous feeling, like an unseen predator waiting to pounce.

A change in the air. He could hear it like a whisper, sense it as the air grew heavy and wet, the wind blowing in from the Sea and playing with his hair and braid like an invisible lover. Across the bridge, the guards were paying Xandr and Thelana no heed. Not even the bloody mass of their commander, or the monster that had murdered him, could steal their attentions away.

Thelana's arrows had failed to penetrate much beyond the bronze joint over their knees—they could run, but instead remained, half-heartedly nursing their wounds, their eyes wide, transfixed to the northwest.

"By all the gods in all the heavens," Thelana murmured. "Are you seeing this?"

Xandr wished to reply, but found that he was unable, his lips paralyzed with wonderment.

All I ask is that you open your eyes. Omens of change abound. Watch the sky.

Under the turquoise moon, a star was falling. It continued down to the earth, dividing the sky with a tail of white fire, and when it struck the crust of Aenya, the earth trembled. Prophecy came to pass as the pyramid quaked, loosening the pearl eyes of Sargonus, which came down like tears. A terrible omen without question, the red mystics ran screaming at the sight, piously plucking out their own eyes with holy relics. Beyond the city wall, piers hung over newly-formed beach. Every vessel lining the coast, from fishing boats to merchant galleys, from fifty-oared pentaconters to triremes, all lay inert, their keels sunk in sand.

The shoreline was gone, retreated, drawn anew.

A white line split the horizon, and the sky tumbled and sloshed and the whole of the Sea rose up to take the shape of a monstrous entity, its tentacles dissolving and reforming in froth. Piers crumbled against the swell and ships were lifted like toys and smashed to timbers. The towers and ramparts of the southern wall toppled, and the Sea came through it, drowning streets and chariots and low-lying homes, sweeping away tents and merchants and patrons alike. When the tide receded, green things sprouted from the foam like blades of grass in a marsh, more in number than the eye could encompass. Amassing through the broken expanse like spawning salmon, they came with stingers and mollusks and other alien devices in their webbed clutches, triumphantly they came, the merquid into the city of Hedonia.

12

THE OMEN

I looked out across the waters
and there came Tsunamis,
mightiest of the depth's demons
that, with flailing arms,
shook the seas,
and split beams of ships,
and made cities fall.

—Omeos, Hedonian poet

The cityscape was transforming before their eyes. Waterfalls found purchase along temple gables and guard towers, forming about Xandr and Thelana in a low muffled roar. Black waves dashed against monuments and the wind carried the spray, turning it to rain. Water snaked through gaps in pavers and shot through walls, cascaded down steps, funneled between columns and windows and archways. The Sea came so powerfully and relentlessly, that bases of columns weathered away instantly, collapsing colonnades into heaps of rings, burying the temples' supplicants under pediments lined with gods. Without prejudice, the current carried away citizens and freemen and slaves, all of whom were tossed together with carts and wares and beasts of burden, battered from crest to crest against structures they and their forefathers had built. People clung with desperate pleas to the feet of gods only to have those bases uprooted and washed off. Fallen architecture, the weight of ten thousand men, toppled, bringing instant death to a fortunate few, whilst burying others between roofs of granite and icy waves.

"We have to get off this bridge!" Xandr exclaimed, tugging at Thelana's wrist.

The prison tower took the brunt of the wave, but as the water coalesced around it, the narrow arches supporting the bridge began to wobble. The opposite side was clear. In the chaos, the golem and the guards had fled, or were claimed by the wave. But the walkway was slick with wet marble dust, and Thelana stumbled as she ran. He yanked her up and pulled her along, just as the bridge came apart in segments and disappeared. She pulled free, scowling at him, unwilling to be handled so. Without a word, he pinned her against a rounded surface as the full height of the next wave came into view. His arms tightened, forcing her body between his and the pillar digging into her spine. The swell pounded them both, the spray prickling like tiny icicles. He shielded her, his back having taken the full impact. The wave rolled over and around, leaving them cold and dripping and disoriented.

The Sea's fury gave pause, and the survivors swam to whatever statues and columns remained standing.

Oarsmen navigated small craft along rivers that were once streets, pulling people from the water. But those who could be counted among the fortunate met with new terrors, invisible beneath the black choppy waters. Things slithered across avenues more swiftly than even the hardiest of citizens could hope to propel themselves with only hands and feet. Teeth and claws came up from unseen places, tugging at flailing limbs, and men and women and children vanished as the swirling water beneath them turned smoky and crimson. The lucky and the strong found footing atop domes and pedestals, the athletes clinging to their stadiums, the wealthy upon palace rooftops. A daring few took up spear and bow and sling, retired soldiers and boys who fancied battle, to meet that which lurked beneath the brine.

Where the land sloped upwards beyond touch of the Sea, aged men watched from afar as merquid spilled through the mouth of the crumbling wall. Fathers stricken with dread barricaded their doors, hiding children too young for understanding into attics or leaky wine cellars. On the hilltops, the priests of the temples and the magistrates of the courthouses joined hands in prayer.

Calamity continued to unfold, and Xandr became unnerved by its familiarity, grew sick with déjà vu. He gazed upon Emmaxis, hating his reflection, and looked out again. Mist sprayed over newly-made ruins. The proud towers of Hedonia no longer scraped the turquoise moon. Only foundations remained, like the roots of cloven sycamores, their masses strewn in segments atop crushed houses and hollowed theaters. Rising from the devastation, a wail came from a multitude of voices. People, clinging to life, looked upon the pyramid for salvation, as if toward Sargonus himself.

His eyes set upon the temple as the inner wall gave way. Unmanned warships sailed through the breach, their rams colliding with the pyramid complex. Sand beneath the southern obelisk turned soft and shifted, and a crack rippled across its base. No longer a silhouette upon the moon, the obelisk broke into three against the pyramid, its peak puncturing the angled wall like a spear in the hand of Sargonus, and the Sea flowed through the opening.

When Xandr and Thelana looked about them again, two new paths had formed, one leading east from the city, the other toward the temple. And as he stood, unblinking before the devastation, his heart turned to those who had helped him, to Demacharon, to Merneptes.

Thelana considered the shrinking ledge at her feet, poking up with sharp, slippery edges. "What are you doing?" she implored. "We must get far from here."

"No. I am going back."

Was he mad? Every passing second, their footing was vanishing under the water—this was no time to ponder. She wanted to scream at him, to argue, but all she could manage was a feeble, "Why?"

"Because," he said, "there are still good people here."

"No," she cried, "they're the enemy. Monsters. They deserve all this!"

She searched his face, through damp golden tangles of hair. His eyes were as grim and blue as the Sea. "You're wrong," he said softly. "They're not so different from us.

They're still human underneath—children of Alashiya. They've only just forgotten."

"Then let the Goddess, or whatever gods they pray to, save them!" she cried. "You owe them nothing! This place is doomed and you can do nothing about it!"

"I have to try, Thelana," he answered, tasting her name on his lips the first time. "If you won't follow, I'll understand."

She sighed. The wind rushed cool and wet into her lungs. "I have a nimble foot," she said, studying the hodge-podge of rooftops thrusting from the spikes and swells of the water. "Let me lead."

Mists broke against them. Wind whistled. Lashing rain threatened their balance. Tiles crinkled and teetered underfoot, breaking off into the tumult below. In the streets, limbs thrashed at life-preserving handholds, at mosaics of chalcedony, beryl and lapis lazuli. Survivors were cast from their perches, drowned by those of power and higher position, just as others sacrificed their place so that the young and meek might live.

As the surge receded and the waters calmed, the next to drown were the soldiers. Encased in bronze, they sank quickly, their armor shackling them below the surface. The highborn citizenry found their richly-embroidered layers of velvet too cumbersome to swim in and followed—drowned with their wealth. But there were greater terrors than the lack of air. Scaly protrusions moved silkily through the waves, emerging and vanishing with the froth. Even the merchants' sons—the strongest swimmers—were taken, quietly plucked from the company of the living.

The ongoing struggle for life tugged at the corners of Thelana's eyes, but she could not look at them, could not hesitate. She chose her passage carefully, where the houses and public edifices clustered closely, leaping from one roof to the other, when suddenly her forefoot slipped against a roof of sliding tiles. Her stomach lurched into her bosom, a muffled splash sounded in her ears, and the water shocked her with its cold embrace. In the murk, she met with dead, round eyes, and wide rows of serrated teeth. Clinging to her breath, she wrestled with the merquid's hooked membranes, but the edges of its gaping maw drew ever nearer. Panic set upon her, pushing out the cold as warm blood filled her veins, but it was quickly fleeting. Without air, her head began to grow light, and every last bit of strength shrank from her. Emptying her lungs, a curtain of bubbles rose up, obscuring the awful sight of the thing taking hold of her. She waited for the sharp pain of its bite, for death, but to her astonishment, its claws grazed away from her skin, drawing faint lines across her shoulders. The merquid was inert, looking somehow deader than before. A hand plunged down, pulling her above water, to an adjacent ledge.

Xandr's locks fell heavily over his brow. He was panting. "Be more careful," he said to her, and she noticed his ax, oozing with the ichor of merquid blood.

She paused to regain strength, seeing that the passage had already changed. Rifts divided the city. The rooftops behind them were gone.

"There's no way back," she murmured.

"Have faith," he said. "Alashiya will show us a way. Take my hand."

Colors nibbled at their ankles and darted away. There were velvety purples and glowing oranges and a splendid array of other hues swimming at their feet, escaping to the outer courtyard, the broken freshwater pool pouring over the briny Sea water, a universe become infinitely larger. Overhead, rainbows of feathers fluttered, liberated from their gilded cages to the open sky, to nest among the hanging gardens of bougainvillea. "Set me free, good dagger," a parrot squawked, over and over. The maidservants were just as lost as the fish and the birds, but there was no joy to be had in their newfound freedom. They wailed and pulled the fasteners from their hair, as makeup streaked across their faces. Even the monster was weeping.

Framed by cascading sheets of water and pastoral depictions of boys with their fishing lines, Grimosse knelt at the body of Merneptes, lifting her ever so slightly from the ankle-deep eddy of rose petals. Tears coursed the strange avenues of its hideous face, and Xandr wondered for what purpose a golem would be created to do so. The tiny dagger still adorned the young girl's hand. Her neck was limp, the head drooping on her shoulders like a scarlet flower languishing when its stem has been cut by the plough.

"Grimm find her this way," he said. "Grimm not know what happened."

"We're too late," Thelana murmured, marveling at the hanging veils and murals, envying the abundance of topaz, pearl, and amber trinkets collected at every corner. "She must have known what was coming."

The monster's giant frame convulsed with sobs. "Grimm made protect girl. Now, what Grimm do?"

"No," Xandr said to Thelana, "this wound is aged more than a passing." He was to blame—he should have given her hope, but instead said nothing.

"She went willingly to the Taker?" she asked. "Why?"

"Only the gods know," he said, "but I believe she wished to be free, of a life not her own. Alas, Merneptes was doomed at birth." And he had failed to see it. "Who mourns for her now? Only a monster . . ."

"You cared for this spoiled princess?" Thelana asked him. "You loved her?" Her voice had a trace of disgust in it.

"No, but without her aid, you would be drowned in your prison. I—*you* owe her."

The water rose up to their knees. It sloshed between rooms and tumbled down stairways. He watched as she squatted, finding a ring of gold and amber and placing it in her palm. "This could have fed my family for a cycle, could have saved Borz," she said softly. The memory of food made her fold over with pain. "Xandr," she said uneasily, "we can do nothing more for her. Let us be gone from this place before *they* come."

"No, there is another we must find."

The monster released the body at last. A gentle tide spread her arms into a cross, and her silks billowed about her, and in this way she drifted with the rose petals from her bower. The slick black eyes, glistening with moisture, turned to the two of them. Grimosse was as tall kneeling as Xandr was standing, but now he towered over, hammer in tow.

"Your words not hurt girl?" he asked the Ilmarin.

Xandr backed away, remembering the position of his sword, prepared to use it if need be. "No, Grimm. I came to save her."

"You protect girl?" he said, gesturing to Thelana with his four-fingered hand.

"Yes," Xandr said carefully, and with slow understanding, added, "but . . . *she* will need you now. You were made to protect, were you not? Here is one needing your protection."

"What?" Thelana said, lifting her head from the fish pool—the first drink she'd had in days. "Are you mad? I don't need this lug tagging behind me everywhere I go! I'm a thief!"

Xandr scolded her with a look. "Would you prefer your cell?"

"What is that thing anyway?" she said, recoiling as the monster drew near.

"It is a guardian," he answered. "They were made to guard. In a moment we'll be neck deep in gill and Grimm can fight."

"Yes," Grimosse agreed, waving his hammer like a toy. "Grimm fight with you. Grimm be you guard-i-an. Grimm must guard. Grimm made to guard."

Thelana nodded assent, her mouth too busy with figs and hockenberries and other fruits to reply. Despite the sharp pang in her shriveled stomach, she forced her innards to accept as much as it could. Only the gods could know when she would be eating again.

"Now," Xandr said to the monster, "tell me where to find Demacharon."

"Blasphemers!"

The High Priest's voice boomed from his gaunt frame but none heeded it. There were no formations, no strategic commands being given. Only desperation. Despite the vastness of the chamber, there was little space for the defenders to maneuver, and the merquid pouring into it were overtaking them. Pikeman bled beside shield-bearing hoplite. Archers desecrated altars seeking positions of advantage even as those positions shrank. Scales and human flesh clashed violently. Swords flailed, broken spears were turned to bludgeoning instruments, screams of rage and despair mixed with equal fervor.

"Blasphemers!" the High Priest shouted to no avail, high upon the sacred pool, clutching the *Ages of Aenya* to his bosom. Behind him, the pinnacle of the obelisk laid in a pile of debris, which archers had taken as a stronghold. From the breach in the pyramid wall, water roared, a fountain of foam radiating from it, running to the alcoves of the eight churches, sloshing about the feet of impassive gods. Already, the statue of Zoë lay in ruin, a terrible omen in the Hedonian's eyes, and the immense life-size wakefins once pulling Sargonus' chariot had come crashing down, their toothy beaks now rubble, the gold chains once linked to their harnesses swaying from the god's outstretched hand.

Aeonus and Demacharon fought before the sacred pool to defend priest and god. As merquid broke through the ranks of lesser men, the two of them turned swords with terrible agility, littering the floor with bodies, turning the white tiles of the temple black with blood.

With the strain of incoming water, worked stone and mortar came raining down, crushing man and merquid alike, and the triumphant arm of Sargonus gave way with a resounding crack. Arm and trident shattered in the watery tumult, despoiling the sacred waters with smoky ash, sending ripples through fin and ankle. Every eye turned upon the idol, hope verses despair, and the whole of Sargonus split, leaving the head to falter between the two halves of the god's torso.

"What shall we do?" Aeonus cried as the clawing throng pressed him against the pool's rim.

Demacharon's gladius punctured the gills of a lunging foe, showering him in gore. "We fight," he said somberly, booting those fixed to his blade to fell another. "We die."

"Keep them from the High Priest!" Aeonus cried, as best he could to reaffirm their waning faith. "All can be rebuilt . . ."

But something strange was happening. Merquid shambled forward, ignoring their attackers, their great bulbous eyes locked as though in a trance. An inhuman drone sounded from their mouths, growing into a croaking like chant, and one by one they began to fall prostrate, webbed fingers reaching, trembling, before the timeworn tentacles of coral beneath the crumbling idol of man—toward Gulgola, the squid god.

Thelana and Xandr had worked their way into the midst of the chamber before Grimosse released his weapon, the loud thunderclap filling the domed space. A wave of gurgling voices radiated from the sound, from the carnage made by a monster with a hammer. Man and non-man alike suffered the blows. Shields failed and Hedonians toppled, one against another, in the cacophony of shattering bronze. Merquid were swept away or made permanent to the floor. As Thelana crouched beside the hammer-wielding monster, a dull twang echoed from her bow, the arrows issuing from the taught string efficiently pinning the flat faces of the merquid with fletching. Opposite her, Xandr with his two-handed sword cut a silver-streaked path through the scaly horde, sending high-flying arcs of blood in their wake, as the three moved steadily and violently toward the altar.

Thelana knew that the Hedonians watching no longer saw two Ilmar, fighting without colors, without armor or defenses of any kind. They saw only the graceful sprays of blood and the lithe bodies responsible for it, bodies like those of their gods.

"Praise Sargonus!" Aeonus shouted. "It is the Batal!"

Thelana could see that Demacharon was too deeply engrossed in the fighting, in the gore and in the awful din of clashing blades and dismemberment and agony, to notice her and Xandr making their way toward him. Nor did he witness it, when a merquid stole a spear from a dead palm, awkwardly lifting, twisting wrist and elbow at inhuman angles against unsuspecting Aeonus. Time enough passed for Demacharon to slay another four, before he caught sight of the spear in his companion's mouth, red draining from the lips, teeth biting down upon the wooden shaft. He reached for his friend just as Aeonus tilted backwards into the sacred pool.

The guardian's frame flew headlong into the swell. Fish heads burst like bubbles against the dome of his hammer. Stingers broke like twigs against his hide. Flying idols and relics-become-missiles did not faze him. Merquid clustered about the monster like termites over a mound, clinging to the golem's immense limbs and shoulders, then BOOM—the hammer cratered the floor and they fell away like dead leaves in a gale. Xandr and Thelana fought within his shadow, the shimmering long tooth of Emmaxis cutting into the merquid two by two, till coming within sight of Demacharon. The commander saluted them with gratitude.

A rumble sounded above the din and Thelana watched as the High Priest looked in horror and dismay, shielding his face with his hands as Sargonus' head nodded like a living thing, rolling from between the broken halves of its collar to the warring multitude, like a boulder, killing dozens before stopping on its ear. And for no other reason, the fighting abated, and men and merquid gathered their ranks to each side of the stone head.

The mortally wounded were beyond counting. The few defenders keeping to their feet possessed a distant look, as though welcoming the Dark God, who was omnipresent, supreme alongside his mistress, Maki, Goddess of War. Other men had grown so weary that their weapons simply slipped from their grasp. The battle was lost, and there was not a one among them who did not know it. A final duty was left to them, to bring whatever merquid they could to the bleak domain of Skullgrin. But even vengeance was denied them as the merquid paused from the slaughter.

An alien throat gave voice, pervading the silence, and the amphibious host parted for one among them to pass through. On the human side, hateful eyes set upon the thing which emerged. It slapped the floor with feet-like appendages, with hips rotating in strange orbits, unaccustomed to walking or bearing the weight of its own body. Yellow shells were fitted to its upper scales, and it held a kind of warped trident fashioned from coral. Xandr rested his sword in the ankle deep flow, staring open-mouthed as the creature shambled forth into the sun. Thelana found the merquid hideous to behold, a sickly-transparent green, giving hints of the workings of organs beneath its scales.

Not a single human dared to accost the creature, save for Xandr. Even Thelana could not bring herself to approach. But Xandr shouldered his weapon and went out amid the invaders' ranks. From three strides distance, the odor assaulted his senses like a rotted fishery, making his eyes water. Was this truly a cousin to man, as his mentor had taught him? A child of Alashiya? Or did the merquid spawn from something other—some strange alien god? Its hideousness, Xandr found, tested the limits of his people's beliefs.

"Why?" he asked. "Why do you come to destroy us? Who are you? Answer me if you have power to speak!"

"This one is," it said, with a voice full of the Sea, "Gol, spawn of Glel, servant of Gulgola." The mouth moved between crystalline teeth, and it appeared strange that words could come from it. "Gill is with human speak, yes? It is as child's babble. But human not with gill tongue. Finding so strange?"

"Yes," Xandr answered after some difficulty. "We did not know you had language. We believed you were . . . like animals."

The creature gasped at breath, from the gelatinous folds in its neck, and spoke, "*You* like animal. Human *do*. Verb is nature. Violence. What named merquid, not know verbs. Learn from human. Gill *not do*. Gill simply *is*."

Now the High Priest descended from the idol, holy book in hand. "Batal," he cried, "how can you stand there conversing with this . . . this thing? It will drive you mad! Don't listen to it!"

Thelana watched as Xandr turned a hard eye upon him. "I've heard enough from you! Let the merquid speak." Urukjinn recoiled, and Xandr again faced that awful face. "Answer me. Why do you wish to destroy us?"

"Answer is," said the merquid, sucking each breath, "eons ago, gill is in great city, Gaglerog, where now is Hedonia. Merquid city it is, human. Merquid city. Then human is, and gill is with human. Gill and human in peace."

"Wait," said Xandr, "there was a merquid city here before, where Hedonia now stands? Is that what you're saying?"

"Yes," Gol answered. "But human is more. Many more. When human many like gill, hate is, and fear is, and envy. One moon, human is with sword and spear, and gill no walls, no weapons. Many gill no longer is then. Much blood, like on this moon."

"When their population grew, they rose up against you," Xandr murmured, "and slaughtered your people?"

"What people!" Urukjinn cried. "They are not people! They're monsters! Kill their ruler and the empire can be saved! Kill him now—it is why you are here. I see it now, your destiny, Batal!"

"Silence!" Xandr barked. "No one dies until I have my answer!"

The merquid seemed to grow weaker and paler as it stood. Each breath came with pain. For every second that it remained above water, it suffered. "Gill learn verbs then. Learn war. Females no longer is. Children no longer is. Priests of gill, no longer is . . ." Even with its garbled, alien tongue, Thelana could sense the sadness behind the words. "Gill city, gill temple, no longer is. Gill under sun, and in fire, much pain. Much pain . . ."

"They tortured you?" Xandr stated. "Left you in the sun?" As his eyes met briefly with Thelana's, she saw what looked like tears forming in his eyes.

"Nothing is of Gaglerog," the merquid continued, "but Gulgola, what named Sargonus, what made human shape."

"The squid idol was your making," Xandr interpreted, "was your god. They used it to mock you, building their god over it."

"Lies!" the priest cried. "All lies!" But none heeded him, not even the Hedonians, who eyed him with suspicion. Thelana turned an arrow toward him and he shrank in silence.

"Gill is in Sea now, and new Gaglerog is. But gill fear human. Far from human is for many eons. Then boat with human is, and human is with eggs—gill eggs—but name pearl. Gill emissary with human, for understanding to human, but not. Not understanding is. And human do. Human *do* to gill."

Xandr looked dumbfounded. "I—I don't understand. You remade your city in the Sea, and then something happened, with an egg?"

Gol gasped for air. Its gills quivered. "See," he said. A low drone spread between the angled walls of the temple and what had been strange and terrible to the human ear was now a melancholy sound. "See," he said again, dipping his hand beneath the water. The eye of Sargonus rested neatly in the membranes of its fingers, and Thelana gasped as that which she had attempted to steal was cracked open against the face of the idol. Her stomach churned. And when she looked at Xandr, she could see the mix of disgust and anger upon his face. It was not so unlike a human fetus when it is removed early from the womb. Images surfaced from the hidden depths of his mind, of human infants, born dead to malnourished mothers. The eye was no pearl, she could see, but an egg. The unborn merquid lay curled within the concave of its shell, a fossil so brittle, it crumbled at his touch.

"By all the gods!" Xandr cried, shaking with rage. "Did you know?" he said, turning savagely to the priest, tugging at the hem of Urukjinn's cope. "Did you know this?"

Brushing the blood from his gladius, Demacharon stepped forward. "He knew," he said softly. "We all knew. But there was a time when we believed—*I* believed—he was the mouthpiece of god."

The High Priest rebuked the commander with a gesture. "Sargonus and I speak as one! It is blasphemy to deny this! Don't you see, Xandr, this is the moment of prophecy. Witness here upon the sacred works of the prophet, truth which cannot be denied." A breeze came in through the cracks of the pyramid, turning the pages of the *Ages of Aenya*. The Batal was depicted again in a vague sketch, his outstretched hand holding Emmaxis, blotches of ink representing the toothy skull. The blade was upright, dividing priest from merquid.

Demacharon turned to Xandr and Thelana with an earnest, imploring look. "Don't listen to him. Kill him before he pollutes your minds."

Urukjinn's pupils became small and pointed, like tips of daggers. "You too, Demacharon, betray me?"

"You are the betrayer, the blasphemer!" he spat. "This whole war is built upon a lie. I'll no longer fight for it."

"What of Astor?" the High Priest implored. "Did I not give him rites of passage? Did I not place obol on his eyelids to ferry the soul?"

"How dare you speak my son's name?" The fury of Demacharon's voice bested the roar of the falling waters at his back. "I should slaughter you myself—"

"Wait!" he said, cowering before the soldier and the barbarian. "Look around you, Xandr. Is this not the destiny you've been seeking? For how long have you wandered the wild, without a home, without a people, or a purpose? With a single stroke of your hand, you can destroy this merquid king, and bring about the Golden Age of Aenya! Only an empire can give you what you most crave, to remake the world—a better world—as it should be. Only an empire can give you back your home, Ilmarinen, just as it was, stone by stone." Thelana could not help listening, wondering, lowering her bow. She was not familiar with how words could be used as weapons, how they could be more powerful than any sword or bow, yet now this very notion played at the back of her mind even as she felt a part of her succumbing to the temptations Urukjinn presented.

"Avenge those fallen here!" Urukjinn preached, "For humanity! It is for what you were born, your fate . . . your destiny. Be the Batal of Legend! Fulfill the prophecy!"

"No," Xandr said, and Thelana felt him tugging her away, waking her as from a trance. "Stones made Hedonia. Ilmarinen was its people. You cannot rebuild it." He pulled Emmaxis up. "But at least we were innocent. You brought this doom upon your own people—you and your hubris."

He forced the priest down by the edge of his sword, toppling the miter into the murky waters of the overflowing pool, jerking the priest's neck around by clumps of gray hair. Gol stood silent as a fish, flapping his gills, no thought or emotion discernible upon his wide, flat face or unblinking bulb eyes.

Urukjinn glared at the carnage that surrounded him, at the bodies of men piled on merquid, but it was clear that he could only see his demise, could only imagine the doom awaiting him. "Spare me, Xandr! Show mercy!"

"You've made me a part of this, a murderer of hundreds, damned me a thousand times over, and I am to spare you?"

Looking on, Thelana cleared her mind of everything but the present, and what she could see was an old man groveling and a murderer with a weapon at his throat, and her heart grew weak and gave way to pity. "No, Xandr, don't do it," she urged. "Let him be. It is not our way."

"Curse you!" the priest spat, quivering with indignation, his gaze wandering between each weary and disillusioned face but lingering on hers. "Curse you all!"

"I was cursed the day my mother bore me," Demacharon answered him, his gladius flying from his hip, and in a flash of red, the priest's body slid softly into the water at the lip of the pool. "Sargonus has forsaken you. All of us."

Thelana watched as Xandr pulled Emmaxis away, from where he had been prepared to kill a defenseless man. She could see that he was still trembling with rage, but Demacharon had saved him from it.

Off in the distance, a contingent of archers emerged from their hiding places. "Traitors! They've killed the mouth of god!" It was a rallying cry from nowhere, and others joined in the chorus. An arrow went flying at a high angle, descending through Gol's neck, and the blood shedding ensued.

Merquid bodies, flaccid as dead fish, flew at them, with nothing but claws and jagged rows of teeth. Xandr, Thelana, Grimosse and Demacharon banded to form a defensive ring. The commander moved his gladius with deadly precision, finding vital organs beneath scales, dropping merquid with every stroke of his arm. Within the circle of devastation forged by Grimosse's hammer, Thelana retreated, folding her bow into a blade, but as the hammer came crashing and the merquid fell into disarray, she emerged, sword in hand. Not a claw or stinger managed to graze her skin, and she relished in the knowledge that her agility protected her more than any armor ever could. She danced in loops, her sword an extension of her arm, and merquid' heads rolled from the collarbone in flashes of gold. Still, she felt comforted by the fact that Xandr never strayed beyond reach of her, bludgeoning the incoming tide by the pommel and crossbeam of his sword, pushing them through the throng to an open space, where Emmaxis came around in his hands, cutting a path of dismemberment. But the merquid continued to press them, growing in number despite their losses.

"They're terribly weak," Thelana said, "like feeble old men."

"Aye," Demacharon replied, "but they're many. Too many."

The battle drew them inward, to where the idol had collapsed. With nowhere left to retreat, they were forced toward higher ground. Xandr and Demacharon clamored over the knuckles and broken fingers of Sargonus as hoplites fell and were devoured behind them. With nothing but the weight of her sword to encumber her, Thelana was first to reach the head of the fallen god. A cluster of webbed hands groped her ankles as she reached for the earlobe, but her sword was quicker, shortening the reach of their arms as she swung herself up and over the idol face to safety.

Gelatinous limbs flailed up, yanking men down from their perches. Merquid were slow to climb and defenseless as they ascended, so Thelana found the killing effortless, but disturbing. Destroying life, even in self-defense, detached her from the world, and made the Goddess feel remote. She would have preferred using her bow so as not to stare into those horrid bulbous eyes, but the compartment that held her arrows was empty, and there were no dead archers around for her to steal from. She alternated between cutting down merquid and reaching for survivors. Most were torn apart before making it to the top, but what of Xandr, she suddenly realized? Her heart throbbed as she dared to glance out across the chaos, where few of the Hedonians' red and gold armor could be counted among the pale green of the merquid. But her dread was short-lived. They were back to back. She could feel him against her, his warm shoulder blades flexing as he fought.

"I rescued you from that pit only to let you die a few passings later," he said, without turning to face her.

"It doesn't matter," she said, finding sanctuary atop the statue's nose, where she stood above the warring masses that moved in patterns demarcated by bloodshed.

Cupping her mouth, she cried out, "We meet Alashiya with courage!"

The Sea continued to rush into the temple and the merquid, weary of battle, found respite at the base of the falls. But the ceiling above was eroded enough for the sky to peer through it, and there the few remaining defenders gathered, under the sunlight, where it pained the merquid to follow. Water tumbled and sloshed in the sun, and the roiling mist obscured sight of all, so that none could say whether the attackers were being repelled, or if the ragtag force of humans was in its death throes.

Over the temple complex a shadow spread like the eclipsing moon, and every eye looked to the gathering darkness. It moved as a single mass, broke into countless pieces and reformed, swarming about the horizon and the moons, flecking the violet sky with gray. Feathers twittered down like snowflakes and the swarm enveloped the temple ruin like a storm.

Thelana's sword was spinning from a severed ear-fin, when she noticed the transformation in the sky. "What's happening?"

A grin cut across Xandr's bearded scowl. "Avians!"

They were not clouds, she could see, but winged men, sweeping down in countless number, snatching up the bewildered human survivors, one by one into the sky. Even the merquid gave pause to this new marvel.

Those that sailed the clouds, the last of Hedonia and Ilmarinen, looked out at what had been. Under a gibbous moon the harbor was reshaped, and the once proud obelisks and idols, theaters and coliseums, temples and libraries and courthouses, the fine pediments and fluted colonnades, all were in ruin, quietly pounded by black waves. The standard of the Empire, the gold trident on blue, was the last to be torn down, not by water, but vengeful hands. And in the pyramid temple, scaly forms not unlike men moved strangely, twisting and writhing in a dance about a single object that stood amidst the rubble and the corpses, the crimson coral idol, Gulgola, the Squid-God.

THE SECOND OMEN

OMEN

The Serpent's Eye

1

CHILDREN OF THE FLOWER

Blooms of orange and purple brushed at her thighs and touched the horizon. It was the time of low moon, the season of color, and Ilmarinen was pregnant with ilms. But Thelana did not bother to guard herself from their thorns, or pause to wonder at their beauty. On she pressed, against the Mother Goddess' breath—the wind—blinking as the swirling petals flew past her eyes. She felt the straightness in her back, the eager bounce in her steps. A rabbit flopped limply over her shoulder, its neck broken and its blood mottled fur tickling her skin. Over the hilltop, she spotted Old Man, the ancient evergreen oak that loomed as a landmark over her house.

At her rear, the tributaries of the Potamis cascaded like a woman's hair, and the land swelled and dipped. She fondly remembered her grandmother, how she would regale them at the ritual of Solstice, with tales of the Goddess, how Alashiya had lain herself across the barren world to become Ilmarinen. But having reached the age of womanhood, Thelana knew to separate fact from folktales.

Trekking homeward, the Goddess lost her shape, separating into formless hills and valleys.

Somewhere in the dense fauna her younger siblings were busy at being children. Heimdl and Lodr and Baldr, Anja, Brittania and Nicola—all of them dodging chores for games of tag and hide and seek, running and climbing, tumbling and collecting bugs. Vaino and Laine, who were older, hammered posts to fence in the hens, complaining of life's various drudgeries, while Aliaa and Amina were turning their feet purple in baskets of mashed blackberries. They would be delighted to know of the meat, even if the rabbit provided only a sliver each. And for a moment, against her heart's desire, Thelana's mind turned to her eldest sibling. Borz loved the taste of rabbit. He would have greeted her with a broad grin, tousling her hair. *Oh, Borz.* A sigh came up from her throat, bringing lumps of pain. *Where are you this moment?*

From within the root folds of Old Man oak, the house rose up like a fallen seedling. Over the years, Baba and his sons had set a myriad of stones and beams—now mired in moss—though the original post and lintel structure had been erected by a much older generation. Built into the side of the house was a silent water wheel, fed by a stony brook that branched from the Potamis. When the climate edged toward cooler winds, bougainvillea speckled the house in icy pinks as though flicked from a paintbrush.

From where she stood, she could see the sharp shadows cast by the ancient tree, and the house felt strangely forlorn, an odd thing for a dwelling of fourteen. Memories beckoned at the gates of her consciousness, but they frightened her, and she pressed on. Remembering her mother's oft-repeated reproach, she scraped the dirt and blades of grass sticking to her soles and pushed against the door. Its hinges creaked, a noise usually lost amid the bustle of work and play. Nicola was at Mother's side, a silhouette of braid and buttocks and jutting spine. She was weeping because a spur had embedded itself in her toe. Thelana frowned—how did Nicola expect to survive, being so weak? Hesitantly, Nicola pulled away from Mother's hair, which was thick with gold braids and flowers and was sometimes all encompassing and could heal bruises of the heart. Mother hushed her younger daughter with a kiss and shooed her from the house, and as the girl moved away, Thelana noticed Baba. They were seated beside one another, Mother and Baba, neither working, which was unusual, for it was midday, and at once Thelana feared them ill.

Whenever Baba was unsettled, he would ring his great hands, as if feelings could be scrubbed off like dirt. When Borz went away, he shed no tears, but there had been much hand scrubbing.

Now he sat still, his hands resting on the table, tightly intertwined.

Thelana slid her bow and quiver against the door, as if slowing her movements could hinder the passage of time. The rabbit carcass, which had carried her home with such swiftness, lay forgotten.

"Baba?" she whispered. "What is it? Has something happened?"

"No, Thelana," he said. "No." Mother sat quietly, dressed in strands of gold hair and petals, with moons and stars of henna about her nipples. Even after twelve children, her body retained its vigor. When Thelana thought of the Mother Goddess, no other came to mind but her own mother. But now, beneath that stoic face, Thelana saw something fragile flickering.

"I brought a rabbit," said Thelana, but the words did not sound right—she'd stressed the wrong syllables.

"We can see, Thelana," said her father, clearing his throat. "Sit down. You must be tired."

Sit down? You must be tired? Her father didn't say things like that. "No, I can stand. I'm strong, Baba."

"Of course," he said. "We know you are." He attempted a smile.

"Is this about Borz?" she asked.

He glanced suddenly to Mother, taking up her hand. She looked strangely detached. Her eyes met his, focusing on him only after a time and lacking consolation. "Not about Borz," he said, but it was a half-truth and Thelana knew it.

"You're going to *sell* me?" Thelana heard herself say.

"No," Mother objected, a bit too loudly, "it's not like that. We made a mistake with your brother."

"You are different," her father said, the words flowing more easily and deliberately. "You are special, like the spirit of the wind. No one place should keep you."

"Like the spirit of the wind?" Thelana echoed. "What does that even mean—?"

"You can no longer stay with us," she heard him say.

This was supposed to be a special day. Mana and Baba were to shower her with praise, spend the day skinning her catch, boiling water to cook the meat. It was not supposed to be like this. "Baba?" she implored. "Mana?" Thelana searched her mother's eyes. They were hazel, sometimes gold. "You're sending me away?"

Father stood and went to her, took her up by the shoulders. How many times had he embraced her so? How many times had he lifted her onto his back or tossed her into the air? "Try to understand. You are not meant to be here— your abilities—the gods have shown us you were meant for greater things. You must go out into the world and do great things."

Thelana was unable to think, unable to digest the words and come to rational thought. She was there with Baba, and then Mother began to sob.

"If this is about food," she started—food was a thing she could understand at least—"I can hunt more, eat less. I can, I can . . ." she stammered.

"No," he whispered at last with a sudden hard edge, his face grown still, impassive. "I have made my decision. It'll do no good to beg. Now be strong, my child. Just as Ilmarinen becomes harsh where the world encroaches— so you must be strong to survive, and shed no tears, nor think on us any longer. Do you understand?"

She took in a deep breath—she could be strong. She'd show him. "When do I leave?"

"Now," he answered her.

"No!" her mother's voice rang out, laden with hysteria. "How can you be so callous? Let her stay a little while—"

Baba scolded her with a glance. "Bryseis," he said, "we've been through this. We've kept this from her for a reason. If the children were to know, it'd make difficulties."

"Wait." Thelana interrupted him, quivering. "I can't say goodbye?"

There was no answer, though she heard her father's voice. "Bryseis, get her things."

"But how will she live?" her mother argued. "You said it yourself—the world beyond is cruel. And she's only a child!"

"Silence yourself, woman!" he cried. "The girl's as strong as she'll ever be. Nothing will happen to her."

"Don't you dare say that!" she contested, throwing her arms up, half in frustration, half in prayer. "You'll give her the bad eye talking like that! You'll bring the gods' envy down upon her. Go knock on wood."

He rolled his eyes and then, thinking better on it, found the lintel of the door to rap his knuckles against it. "There. Now will you go get her things?"

Mother stood mechanically, gathering items into a blanket: a gourd with a cork stopper, an assortment of breads and berries, flint stones for lighting fires, a small paring knife. Her hands shook so violently that her fingers fumbled to knot the four corners. Thelana was quick at her side, adding her fingers to the task.

"Now you remember to keep yourself clean," her mother said as though reciting a verse from the songs, ". . . and making a fire, you know how to do that?"

"Of course, Mana."

"I think that's everything you'll need. I pray the gods I not forget anything. I even made extra *pasteli*. It's still your favorite, isn't it?"

Thelana nodded. Her earliest memories included the chewy mix of sesame seeds and honey. She remembered how her mother used it to soothe her childhood sorrows. Now she was being sent out, like a grown woman, but was she so different from that child?

"Good," said Bryseis. "Remember to eat it sparingly, as it won't spoil." She continued to ramble nervously as her fingers twitched, though the supplies were all packed for the journey. After fastening the bindle to her bow, her mother left the room to return with a long piece of fabric, yellow with patches of brown.

"What is that for, Mana?"

"Something I nearly forgot . . . and I spent weeks at it! Well, it's the best I could do."

"It's a goat," said Thelana, her stomach turning sour. Goats were saved for milk, never for slaughter. Hides stored foodstuffs or were used to make tents. By the pattern of spots, she recognized the young kid. It had been no taller than her kneecaps. She remembered its gentle nature, the way its tongue tickled the straw from her fingers. Now its dead skin was being prepared to cover hers.

Her mother worked up a weak smile, stretching and turning the fabric this way and that. "You remember the soldiers who sought shelter from us? How they were covered?" Spread to its full length, the goatskin tunic dwarfed Thelana's slim frame. With a small knife, Mother cut and rearranged it, imagining how it might go.

"I don't need *that*," said Thelana. "I shall stay as I am, an Ilmarin, no matter where I go."

"That may be," her father answered, "but Alashiya, who protects us, is weak where other gods are strong. In the West, men burn under the sun of Solos, and in the East, cold winds blow from the trumpet of Strom. In other parts of the world, you will learn, *clothing* protects man from these cruelties."

Baba came nearer, embracing her. "But even where the gods are kind, you must be wary of men, for men can be worse than any gods. In the lands far from home, men do not thrive as part of Aenya, but apart from it, seeking to possess every little thing within it. Lust for possession drives men of the outside, causing every evil and misery. If a man should lay eyes upon you, it may drive him to madness, and he will then seek to possess you. From this you must hide yourself, your body."

"I don't understand," said Thelana.

"Trust in our wisdom!" her father said forcefully. "We learned much of the world when the soldiers came. Do you remember how they looked at us, at you? If you reveal yourself, at the very least, they will shun you. Hidden by clothing, they will not know you are Ilmar."

Bryseis pressed her daughter to her bosom, just as Thelana appeared to founder with realization. "You will always be Ilmarin within your heart," she added, "and no one can take that from you."

"Never," Thelana murmured. "I'd never forget you." She grimaced as her mother worked the stiff tunic over her head and down past her knees. But it was a small discomfort amid the uncertainty churning inside of her.

"Where will I go, Baba? What will I do?"

"Follow the river," he said. "Continue until the hills of Ukko become faint, and the ilms sparse. Do you still remember the speech the foreigners taught you?"

Captain Aola. She was the only one kind to me, teaching me the bow, the language of Kratos. Thelana nodded slowly.

"Seek them out, anyone who speaks the same language. Show them what you can do. A skilled bowman has great value in the outside. But do not show fear, or be overly trustful, or let them cow you into service. Promise me never to suffer your brother's fate. And promise one more thing—do not permit yourself to starve. Do what needs be. Understand?"

With a will not her own, Thelana pushed the door open. The tunic, her quiver and bow, and a sack sat heavily upon her. The rabbit lay forgotten in a heap of fur and blood. As the door shut behind her, she slumped onto the porch with great sobs. Faces fluttered in her mind and her heart drained into her stomach. "Why can't I say goodbye!" she cried. Her shoulder fell against the door and it gave with a groan, but her father stood on the opposite side.

Thelana slapped at the door as her father wrestled to shut her out and keep Bryseis away, who sobbed and pleaded for her daughter. "Don't make this harder on your mother!" he shouted. But there was no cruelty in his voice. "Go, child!"

Time lapsed strangely, and when exhaustion set in, her heart toughened and became proud again. She became still, surrendering her struggle to reenter her childhood home.

"I cannot send you away," Baba finally said, his voice muted by the door. He sounded broken, defeated. Finally, he stepped outside, and took Thelana in his arms.

"No," she said softly. "I must go. I'll come back. I'll find gold and jewels, like the men of Kratos had, and there will be food for us always."

"That's my brave girl," he said, stroking her hair as he had when she was a small child. "That's my Thelana."

Her mother remained in the house as her father escorted her to the edge of the porch. At the foot of the steps, an ilm grew from between the floorboards. How many times had her mother made tea from it, for a broken bone, for Vaino or Laine, or even that one time when Lodr attempted to chase Thelana up Old Man's branches? The memory made Thelana smile. Her eyes brimmed with hot tears, the kind that sting—she would never again laugh with her brothers.

"Even here," her father began, thumbing the orange petals, "they grow rarer." With a twist he broke the flower from its stem. The orange blossom filled her cupped hands. "Remember: we are children of the ilm. As long as you keep it close to your heart, this land will never be far behind." The delicate petals trembled, and she forced herself to nod.

With bow-bindle firm in hand and heart lighter than before, Thelana set out across the valley, numb to all but the path ahead. This time she paused at the top of the hill overlooking Old Man oak and the place she once knew of as home, taking care to fill her breath with the intoxicating scent of ilms. Air rushed through the openings in her tunic, knocking orange buds against her thighs. Dying petals swirled around her like fingers holding her back. But it was just the wind escaping to freedom as wind is wont to do.

Her bare feet sank into the rich soil, down hills and up again, coming finally to where the dirt and gravel met hard against her soles. The sounds of the Potamis trickled in her ear, but she had yet to cross it when her sister came trotting up the path. Britannia was a sliver of muscle and bone, thin enough to hide behind a birch, which she made a game of, surprising her siblings by appearing and disappearing from opposite a trunk. Unlike Anja, who was prissy and proper, Britannia never bothered to comb the twigs from her hair or wash the earthy muck from her body, nor did she mind her soles turning to leather against the river rocks. In many ways, Britannia was her mirror image, just two years younger, too young to show any hair about the body but for the chestnut locks that fell over her cheeks and nipples. Now she stood, an accidental flower pattern of mud caked across her, a snog twitching fitfully in her hand.

"What is that?" Britannia asked, eyeing her sister's new garment with fascination.

Thelana worked up a smile. "Something Mana gave me. She called it a *toonik*."

Britannia combed a strand of hair from behind her ear, her face puzzled. "Is it some kind of game?"

"No," Thelana replied, wishing it was. "The outsiders used it to hide their bodies, remember? But I can't really think of any practical use for it."

"It looks scratchy."

Thelana felt her cheeks redden as, for the first time in her life, she avoided her sister's searching stare. Fibers were scraping against her pores, were sticking to her in the sweat of the building heat and stifling her breathing. She tugged at the garment and the sun washed across her shoulders once more. The rush of air was like jumping into a spring on a sultry day. Thelana could not bring herself to understand the ways of outsiders and did not care to. After all, she was who she was, body and all.

Despite her discomfort, Thelana did not wish to disobey her parents so soon after leaving home. Reluctantly, she pulled the sheet around her shoulders again, shutting herself from the touch of the world, and searched her sister's expression.

"Well, you won't catch me in that," Britannia said, rolling off her heels.

Among her sisters and brothers, Thelana would miss Britannia most. Other than Borz, she was her closest friend, the only one of her kin daring enough to venture this far from home.

"I have to go."

Britannia took her by the hand. It felt warm and full of youth. "Come quick. I have to show you something."

Steep and unforgiving earth slashed at their heels and made a staff of Thelana's bow. Memories of past and future floated like petals blooming and decaying. They arrived at a precipice over a broad horizon, but the land beneath was peculiarly absent, only clouds rolling beneath their bare feet.

"Wait. There is no such place as this," Thelana murmured to herself. "This isn't how I remember it. Where are we?"

"Nimbos, I think," Britannia answered.

"Why are we here?" she said, shivering against the cold.

"I'm not here," Britannia said. "Just you. You were brought by the bird people, remember?"

Gradually, Thelana allowed her eyelids to pull apart, and all the warmth went from her. She was without any clothing, curled cat-like into herself, the wind lashing her with icy tendrils. When, at last, the blood ran through her again, she gazed about in wonderment. There was only continuous sky and great swirling shapes vast as mountains—pink and violet clouds gilded with sunlight.

2

HUMANITY ON TRIAL

In mid-sky they stood, no earth or Sea in sight. Distant and engulfing, amorphous clouds towered from unseen depths in oranges and reds, purples to pinks. Wind rattled them in their fine silks and bronze. The air was cold and thin and penetrated their bones. Surely, humans did not belong here.

Blood gushed under her skin, turning her blue and spiky with goose pimples. Her lungs were afire, wrestling with the air. She awoke to many voices, to sounds of panic and dread and swelling sorrow. A single female voice cut through the clamor like a knife. "Has anyone seen my baby?" she howled. "Please, someone tell me if you've seen a little boy. The wave took him from my hands! I couldn't hold on! Gods, have mercy—I couldn't hold on to my child!" Her words slurred into sobs, and then the woman wept, and Thelana knew the sound of that weeping would haunt her ears.

Her first impression was that they were floating in the sky, for there was nothing keeping her from falling towards the clouds below—nothing visible. But with her first step, her plane of view tilted. I'm in a cage, she realized, her fingers brushing against the thread-thin lattice-work, studying it—human hands could never have made anything so fine, yet so strong.

There were countless others above and below her, soldiers and families, cooped like birds. How the cages were suspended, she could not guess. At several paces, Xandr and Demacharon shared a single enclosure, and she grew angry, wondering whether bird men understood the need for warmth between men and women. Alone in her cage, she shrank to a ball, her knees against her chin, but could not keep from shivering. Even her toughened skin could not endure such climates. Home was never this cold. If the outside world was like this, no wonder they found it necessary to cover their bodies. Never before did she feel so exposed, so vulnerable, a fool to be Ilmarin. She wanted to rob the Hedonians now, to tear the long-sleeved djellabahs from their backs.

"The last human empire—lost," Demacharon was saying. "All roads led to it and from it, or so it was said. And now it is gone."

She heard Xandr grumble, even as his teeth clacked together. "Stop saying that, damn you! It does no good to dwell on it."

But the Hedonian was not listening. "Now humanity is fodder for all the sub-species of Aenya, for gill and half-men, and, dare I say, bird men."

"That's not true," Xandr replied. "There are still men in the North, in Northendell and Mythradanaiil."

"Mythradanaiil does not exist," said Demacharon. "Hence its name."

Thelana watched as Xandr grew annoyed, the cage he was locked in beginning to sway. "No! The avians have seen it."

"And you believed them?"

Xandr did not rebut him, for in that moment he noticed she was standing. "You're all right." It was both a question and a statement.

She tried to speak, surprised by the dryness in her throat and the numbness of her lips. "Is this the afterlife?"

Demacharon gazed at her unremarkably. Whether he found her strange or alluring, she could see no trace of it on his scarred face. "No," he said, "but it might as well be. Half of us have died up here. Women and children can't shake the cold. And the troops need their wounds tended to."

"I am to blame," Xandr said almost inaudibly.

Demacharon gave him a puzzled look. "What was that?"

"The blood of these people is on my hands."

"You're talking nonsense," he said. "The thin air is making us all a bit fuzzy."

"If I'm mad," Xandr answered, "it's not the thin air that's making me so. I came to Hedonia not to save it, but to follow my sword." Emmaxis reflected the spectrum of colors from the surrounding cages, but there was no expression on its skull face. It remained inert across his lap, a length of lifeless silver. "It brings death and destruction wherever I take it. A harbinger of ill is all it is."

"But you are the Batal!" Thelana could not help interjecting. "I saw your image in their holy book. The resemblance was uncanny."

"You presume to know who I am," he replied, "when even I do not? I am no hero. And this *damn* thing," he added, lifting the skull to his face, "is my curse."

"You pulled me out of that cell," she answered, blood rushing life to her lips. "Doesn't that count for something? Even if you helped put me there?"

"They would have killed you! I did it to save your life."

"So now you're a hero?" A coy expression came over her face.

"No. I wanted you for me, because . . . because I had no one else," he said softly, finding the words difficult to muster. "You are still Ilmarin, despite killing that mystic in cold blood."

"I didn't kill anyone!" she cried, her cage shuddering.

"Thelana, your arrow was in his body—"

She was too stunned to reply. In the darkness of that night, her heart aflame with fear, even she could not be certain whom she might have killed. Thelana remembered shooting two guards, but it was her life or theirs. She was no cold-blooded murderer. Or was she? The guards were only doing their duty, after all, and she did not belong in the temple. Had she, in her desperation to escape the slums, become a taker of innocent life?

Thelana fingered the smooth jade surface of her bow. "If we're prisoners, why leave us with our weapons?"

"Maybe we're not prisoners," Xandr said, "but only refugees."

"Refugees in cages," Demacharon was quick to respond. "If they had to carry away tens of thousands before getting slaughtered by the gill, they wouldn't have had the time to frisk us."

"But why save us at all?"

Resurgent screams echoed throughout the cages. Demacharon's voice could be heard sharply among the masses. "It's coming back!"

Moving across the horizon was a miniscule thing, as threatening as a gnat. Thelana squinted to get a better look. The thing grew larger as it approached, a vulture hawk of deep purple and crimson with a screech that made the prisoners throw their hands over their ears and buckle onto their knees. Flying between the cages in search of prey, it caused the huddled masses to sway in its wake. With a terrible pounding, the monster bird righted itself, gusts of air spinning like a cyclone from its wing tips, its hooked beak appearing to catch the odor of impending death, until at last crashing against a coop of bloodied soldiers. Despite their thrashing and shouting, the bird shredded the wiry lattice keeping them aloft. Most of the men plummeted into the ether. The less fortunate were snatched up by the monster beak, lashed like worms from side to side, and swallowed whole.

Thelana added her voice to the frightful chorus. "What is that?"

"A very large bird," Demacharon answered.

"Did the avian people save us only to feed us to that *thing*?"

Its hunger sated, the bird soared away, vanishing among the purple shades of cloud. Terror gave way to exhaustion, and the people collapsed against their cages, many in prayer to the Taker for a quick deliverance.

"A worse fate I could never dream of," Demacharon muttered. "Had we only been slain in battle . . . in the Empire."

"If I see that bird coming towards me," Thelana remarked, brandishing her gold blade, "I'll make it pay for lunch with an eye."

A lamentable sound rose up again. People spoke of loved ones they had lost, or still hoped to find. The mother's weeping was answered in kind by others with missing children.

"Do not despair!" Xandr shouted over them. "All of you! Listen to me! I know these bird men. They will not leave us to die." But his voice was lost to the wind and the sorrow, and those few that could hear him did not appear to take courage.

When an avian finally arrived, few of the caged survivors were conscious to take notice. And it was not, to Xandr's expectation, the face of Ouranos that came, but a younger creature. Thelana had never seen an avian before and looked on with wonder, mouth agape. If merquid were the embodiment of all that was grotesque and ungainly, the avian was its opposite, beautiful and elegant. He floated in the air with only the slightest effort, as if immersed in water, a willowy being with long, loose limbs and blue-gray wings that extended seamlessly from his arms. His helmet, arm bands and greaves were of swirling patterns, fitting like part of his body.

"I am Pteros," he said, "ambassador from Nimbos." His voice was sharp as a violin. "We apologize for the great caw—that was a mistake, but it has been contained and shan't return."

"By what right do you hold us captive?" Demacharon barked at him. "We didn't ask for your aid. We were holding our own against the merquid!"

"Oh," said Pteros, raising a feathered eyebrow, "you misunderstand. You have violated the laws of the Ascendency. You are here to plead your case before our most high, King Azrael."

"What of the rest of us?" Xandr demanded. "Our females and our nestlings cannot survive at this altitude. The air's too thin and much too cold. Humans do not possess the anatomy of bird men."

The feminine features of Pteros' face seemed a stranger to sorrow. "Our apologies, but outsiders are forbidden within the city, and we had no place else to keep you. However, I will bring the knowledge of your hardships to my superiors. In the meantime, I am to deliver three of you to represent humanity."

Mount Nimbos thrust from the clouds like spearheads, snow breaking from silver peaks into fingers of cascading rivers, pooling into basins. White trees, alien to Thelana's eyes, branched from the steep face, and vegetation abounded from under craggy overhangs. In the spaces between the mountains, towers of alabaster rose from every precarious niche.

Birds littered the azure sky, and avian children twirled and made light of gravity, as the more mature of the species commanded great birds from saddleback, or from the seat of airborne skiffs.

Rolling over their human eyes was the strange and wondrous. Every time Thelana wanted to point and call out, some new wonder snared her gaze and froze her tongue. It was like a dream.

Wings thundered above them as the world passed below, curls of wind lashing their cages, icing the marrow of their bones. From the talons of two dove-like creatures, they toured the kingdom of clouds and mountains. Pteros called them *ibs*. They could be fierce predators, he explained. "They obey the sound of my whistle. Without blinders, they'd likely tear you to shreds."

The avian led the two ibs and the cages strung beneath them around another dagger-sharp peak, breaking through a veil of mist into the cityscape of Nimbos.

Like an ivory rose about to blossom, the Tower of Heaven stood above all, its spade archways leading into it from every angle. Upon command, the ibs set down upon an elliptical platform suspended by no visible means, and the latticed framework of their cages became brittle, disintegrating like webbing.

Thelana longed to rush out to Xandr, to feel his warm embrace, but she stopped herself short. Was it his body heat she needed or him?

"Are you all right?" he asked her.

She was numb beyond sensation, but could feel the blood surge to her wrist as he took it. *I don't need you.* It was the voice of the hunter within, the one she called upon in battle, that had helped her to survive since leaving home. There was another, smaller voice, however, saying, *Hold me.* But all she could muster was a feeble, "Fine."

In that alien landscape, she could see that even the
Ilmar and the Hedonian found comfort in each other's
presence, drifting closely together as they followed their
avian guide.

In Nimbos, there were no straight lines, nor edges or
corners, only curving shapes. Their feet and hands met
impossible angles, challenging their concepts of architecture. Where there would be doors or windows were rounded absences, and where there should be walls there was
open sky. Thelana ran her fingertips against a wall etched
with swirling, interlacing patterns. It was a pearly texture
unlike stone or wood, or any building material known to
her. The floor was like a warm eggshell against her bare
soles. It pulsed under and through her with a life-like energy, like something she might feel atop a camphor tree.

Pteros led them to the Rotunda of Aza, where the
city's swirling lines converged to form a flowering pattern inlaid with gold, silver, and ivory. A dizzying array of
spade-shaped archways spiraled above and below them.
Elliptical platforms stemmed like giant leaves from the
curving walls, vanishing into white depths. The space was
devoid of ladders, stairs, or bridges, and it became un-
nervingly evident that this was no place for a species that
could not fly.

The rotunda filled quickly with every imaginable hue.
They perched at all angles, young specimens in short gray
feathers, and older, more revered avians, flaunting tall
crests in vibrant colors. To Thelana they looked like parrots or toucans, some like the phoenix. Their attire was of
exceeding sophistication, accentuating their plumage and
elegant bodies, with form-fitting designs and the same

ever-present swirling patterns found in their architecture. They did not possess actual bird faces, but it was the custom of many to don masks—bronze abstracts of bird species—to complement the likeness. Unlike the civilized peoples she knew, the avian concept of clothing differed significantly, in that they did not care to hide their genitals, which were only partly obscured by feathers. What bird men chose to cover was subject to individual preference, and the coverings purely ornamental. She wondered whether they saw a marked difference between herself and Xandr and the heavily decorated Hedonian. But unlike the Ilmar, they were a vain species, moving about their perches with a pompous air, making grand gestures with wings extended to their fullest.

Thelana huddled more closely to Xandr now, squeezing his forearm with quivering fingers. "Don't be afraid," he whispered. "I have a friend among them. He should be along . . . soon."

When the avian host was assembled, many thousands above and below them, Xandr witnessed what he could only imagine to be a religious ritual. The females made pleasing, almost musical chirping noises, while the males expelled angry, frightfully loud screeches. Despite his inability to understand the avian language, it sounded to Xandr that an argument of historic magnitude was taking place.

"What's going on?" he asked.

Pteros did not look his way. "They are calling for Azael," he said with resignation, making a sound like a sigh. "It's always this way, it seems—they want always the highest, never the lower, never Azrael or Azraendel, who would do just as well, I think."

As Xandr continued to listen, he could almost make out the call. "Give us Azael!" they shouted in turn, over and over. Something peculiar happened then. A formless stone was lowered, from an invisible thread, onto a central platform. It was an ancient limestone, pitted with moss, with a vague impression on its surface like that of a bunched up bird, most of the image worn away by time. At the sight of the relic, the bird men quieted, a number clucking with contentment.

"There's been appeasement," Pteros explained. "Azael will preside."

Xandr considered asking more about the ritual, but without extensive knowledge of avian culture and history, he knew that he would never make sense of it.

The top of the dome diminished like the iris of a great eye, and a shaft of light streamed from the aperture, turning the three humans a ghostly white. Avian warriors descended in spiral formation, clad in gleaming silver, carrying long trumpets and wing-shaped swords with blades for feathers. Gravity held no sway over them, it seemed, as they gracefully lowered to the central platform, blaring their trumpets.

A winged throne descended from the iris opening. The king's raiment was far more intricate than of those assembled. Xandr guessed him to be eight or nine feet tall, but thinner than Demacharon, with plumage that shimmered green, then violet, depending on the angle. Pteros chirped something to him, crisscrossed his wings to form an X, and bowed.

With an awkward high-stepping gait, the avian king accosted the human captives. As he stooped to address them, his gold hawk mask opened from the beak to reveal his aged, feather-bearded face. "I am Azrael," he said, at once beautiful and imposing as he spread his wings across them. "Who are you?"

He opened his mouth to speak, his voice echoing loudly from the rotunda walls, catching him by surprise. "Xandr of Ilmarinen."

"And who are you?" the king asked, waving a long knobby finger at the Hedonian.

"First Commander of the Hedonian Legion," was his reply, "Centurion of the Empire, Defender of the People, Regent of the Southern Provinces."

Azrael grew suddenly tall, appearing to ponder the answer for some time. "A long name you have, do you not think, human?"

Demacharon's face was impenetrable. "Is there a point to that question?"

The king ignored the quip, taking the time to admire his wing instead. Like most avians, Azrael was overly conscious of his appearance, strutting and posing as he spoke. "And who are you?" he inquired, his taloned finger nearly poking Thelana in the eye.

"I'm Thelana," she answered. "Just Thelana."

"A strange name it is, Just Thelana," the bird man replied.

She was doing her best to show a brave face. But was it the cold making her shiver so? Or fear? Xandr could not tell.

"And do you three represent humanity?"

"No one can speak for an entire species," Xandr objected. "We are many different people, with many cultures, many—"

"Please," Demacharon said, setting his hand on Xandr's shoulder, "your truth is not looked for here, my friend. Let me speak."

Azrael's high voice sounded from above. "We understand that you are plentiful, just as are we of diverse plumage. I see that two of you are featherless, while one has fashioned coverings from the plants of the earth and the metals of the mountains. But you are also of a kind, cursed to walk without wings, *groundlings*. We have watched you—groundlings—commit atrocities against the waterlings. We have seen this from the high places of Mount Nimbos! Avian eyes are far keener than your own. These crimes cannot go unanswered. So I ask again, which one of you shall speak for your race?"

Xandr opened his mouth, but Demacharon spoke first. "I will. But first," he said, with a strength defying the situation, "if I am to take part in this so-called trial, you must swear to release our survivors, starting with the women and children."

"Of course," the king said with a nod, "if we were without compassion, we would have allowed your people to perish by the Sea. The survivors of Hedonia will be relocated to where they can do the least harm, far from waterling establishments, and this mountain, beginning, of course, with your females and your hatchlings."

"In that case," Demacharon replied, "let judgment come swiftly, for my people cannot remain any longer at this altitude."

"Then let it be known, in the presence of the Ascendency and all-seeing Azael, the trial commences!" The avian king lifted his scepter, an iron moon gripped in the talon of a phoenix, and waved it over the three of them. "The charges are stacked against you, First Commander of the Hedonian Legions. We have watched, for over one thousand years, and dislike what we have seen. You are mindlessly devoted to lowly causes, blind of lofty perspective, oblivious to the needs of the lower, and thus your kind cannot exist peaceably. Even amongst yourselves, you commit war, the greatest of offences. Greed, deceit, hatred. Are these not the ways of man?"

"Surely there are worse creatures on Aenya!" Xandr interjected. "What of the halfmen? They are cannibals!"

"That is true," the king replied, "but halfmen are little more than beasts. They do not gather, like you do, to build great cities from which to launch armies, to make siege engines of war. Their population is small and poses little threat to Aenya."

"But there are others!" Xandr cried out. "Bogren armies, and horg. Why not put them on trial?"

Azrael strutted forward, bending at the waist to meet his gaze. "And what would a trial mean to a mindless bogren? They cannot be reasoned with."

The commander put a fist under his nose, clinking in his bronze as he paced the alabaster platform. "While I cannot speak for my friends," he began, "much less for humanity, I agree these traits you speak of are common to man, but not to all men. If you would watch us more closely, your Highness, you would see that there is goodness among us. But if you would put the question to me alone, whether war, and all its ills, is a part of me, I can only plead guilty."

"Guilty!" a squawking voice sounded, followed by many others from above and below.

"Wait!" Xandr protested. "Most High One, let me speak in defense of this man. It is true that he is a warrior among his people . . . but I have known him to be honorable and just."

Demacharon hushed him with an outstretched hand. "Quiet, you fool! Can't you see this is a charade? If they want to crucify someone, better me than the innocents outside!" King Azrael studied his feathers once more, looking uninterested. His judgment, Xandr knew, had been decided long before.

"The verdict is determined by admission." With an ominous mechanical whirr and a click, his mask closed into a hawk's head again, glinting in the shaft of light. Standing to eight feet, with shoulders thrown back and wings spread nearly twice that of his height, King Azrael loomed like a god. His voice blared from the sculpted hawk beak like a trumpet. It carried to the farthest reaches of the rotunda, terrible and commanding. "For millennia we've waited, hoping that humanity might evolve to become lofty, but this did not happen.

"From the time of the coming of the greater moon, Aza the Almighty charged us to observe his progeny, but forbade us to intervene. But when a daughter of Aza chooses to eradicate her sister, our sister, we may not sit idle, cooped in our mountain. For such offense, three representing humanity shall face the final judgment. As Supreme High One of Nimbos, I do sentence you: If innocent, you shall ascend, but should the guilt of your crimes weigh your spirit, you shall know death."

Xandr offered no plea, accepting what the Hedonian had told him. The trial was a charade, the grand rotunda a theater for birds.

3

BATTLE IN THE CLOUDS

"It's not the fall that kills you but the sudden stop at the end."

Thelana fixed her gaze on him. His smirk showed even beneath his brutal scar. "How can you be so glib at a time like this?"

Another poke from the silver feather cut between her shoulder blades. Blood trickled down her spine, burning against her frozen skin, but she could not scratch it. The metallic thread binding her wrists was smooth and slender, like something for a wealthy woman's neck. It was known as *whisper chain*, forged from an element known only to the avians, and was said to be unbreakable.

"These *bird* men don't impress me," Demacharon said loudly, for everyone to hear. "Their bones are hollow. Snap like twigs. If only my hands were free . . . I'd show you."

"You are not permitted to speak!" It was one of the avian warriors behind them, unable to resist the Hedonian's incessant goading.

After the trial, Demacharon had spat and cursed, and argued in vain for the life of his Ilmarin comrades. Xandr did not blink at the verdict, but Thelana could see he was reluctant to give up Emmaxis, chanting over the weapon as it was wrestled from his grasp.

The air hit them like ice water as they moved from the rotunda to the walkway under the sky. Bands of pink swirled within and without, through and around them. The cloud was so heavy, Thelana felt she could ball it up in her hands and throw it. Occasionally, gusts of wind punched pockets in the haze, offering her a view of their avian captors and the godlike King Azrael.

Thelana's brothers used to marvel at how daringly she navigated the branches of Old Man oak. She could reach the highest twig without it breaking under her weight, and she was never afraid. Even when she scaled the pyramidal walls of Sargonus' Temple and descended to its idol, there had been no fear. But then, she had never entertained the thought of falling. Only once, when she was being chased by a halfman, had she lost concentration and lost her hold, but even then she was unhurt. Death by sudden impact with the ground was an alien concept to her, but was growing uneasily in the pit of her stomach. At least she no longer sensed the cold. Terror was better at keeping her warm than any piece of clothing.

She turned to Xandr in search of hope. He looked solemn but unafraid. "You do have a plan, don't you?"

"Not really."

"What about your friend? Your bird man friend?"

"I haven't seen him," he said.

"Well . . . where is he?" she cried.

"Silence, you two!" The avian prodded her again, adding another small cut to her back.

"I suppose he's busy," Xandr answered her, ignoring the bird man's warning.

She wanted to argue, to scream at him as though the whole situation was his fault, but decided it was better to follow his example to escape further mutilation.

The blue-green shimmer of the king's wing spread across their field of view. They halted. From this vantage, the pink haze surrounding them coalesced into thin bands of cirrus clouds. Looking back, the cloud washed over the walkway, making it sometimes vanish. A sky away, the Tower of Heaven stood upon empty air, an ivory flower appearing and disappearing as bands of cirrus flowed like rivers of froth around it. Directly ahead, Thelana could see what she had been avoiding—the edge of the platform, the sky yawning fatefully below.

This was no way to die. Without a fight. Forced to jump to their deaths.

"We are not without respect for your customs." It was the booming voice of Azrael, greatly amplified by his hawk mask. "We will allow you a brief moment to carry out whatever rituals you may have, to prepare for rebirth or afterlife, or make peace with your gods."

Avian warriors surrounded them, forcing them into a tight circle. She could feel Xandr's breath on her cheeks—all the warmth they would ever share.

"When we die . . ." she said softly, with realization as the words came out, "our race will become extinct."

"No," said Xandr. "There are others." His tender tone greatly contrasted with his brooding visage.

"Well, that is a small comfort, at least." She searched him deeply. His dark pupils swam in a calm lake of blue, quivering only as he was made to look upon her. But she could find no betrayal of emotion—his eyes were like shields over his soul.

"Xandr, there is something that . . . that I think I want to tell you."

"What is it, Thelana?"

You make me weak. You make me tremble . . . Damn it, why must Demacharon stand so close!

Thelana suddenly wished to be more eloquent, to make some brilliant declaration for poets to recount for generations. But she was not like him. When she opened her mouth only her poverty, her lack of wit and education, spilled forth. But it probably didn't matter. No avian would take the time to record their last words. No human would even remember them. It would be as if the Ilmar never existed at all.

"Thank you for saving me." It was the best she could do. At least it was honest.

"Enough," said the king. "Wingmen, carry out the sentencing."

The bird men formed an arch of swords that stretched from one end of the platform to the other. The only escape was down. One grabbed Demacharon by the chains, towing him to the edge.

"Wait!" he cried. "There is something I need to say to the Ilmarin." His scarred eye focused on Xandr.

Azrael nodded and his wingmen gave retreat. "Well, get on with it. I have other duties to attend to."

The two men huddled closely so the others could not hear. "I don't know what I believe about your being the

Batal," he began, "but a light has gone out from the world where Hedonia once stood. I've seen you fight with more than courage—with conviction of purpose—and I've seen you inspire hope in men. Don't become a jaded old fool like me. Aenya needs its heroes, you and Thelana both, you . . . *skyclad warriors.*"

"Demacharon what are you talking about? They're going to kill us all."

"No," he said. "You will break free of those chains."

"I—I can't," Xandr grumbled, the muscles in his arms stiffening at freedom, "it's like iron."

"*You* may not be able to," he replied, "but the Batal can. You have only to believe. I'll give them what they want. I'll jump, and when I do, they'll be distracted long enough for you and Thelana to flee." A smile cut across his tortured face, joining his scar to form a crude angle.

"Don't be foolish!" Xandr protested, clasping him arm to arm, wrist to elbow. "There's no sense in martyrdom! There's nobody here to witness it. Let us fight together."

"No," Demacharon murmured, "I've fought enough battles. This old warrior has nothing left, nothing left to fight for. So I'll go to *them* . . ." His voice failed, a broken man with a broken tongue. "I go to Niobe's waiting arms . . . I go to my son Astor."

As the Hedonian ran across the platform, Thelana could not suppress the scream that came from deep within her throat. He made no sound as he fell.

"Bravely done," said the king, studying the way the sunlight colored his plumage a more vivid shade of green and violet. "No attempt at bribery. No pleading for mercy. Unexpected from one of your race. As for you, who is known as Xandr, you may, if you so desire, be spared from seeing the female fall, and follow the male."

The point of the wing-sword dug into his back, but Xandr did not take another step. He fell, instead, to his knees. "Azrael," he growled, "this has gone far enough. My hands have enough innocent blood on them. Spare us and save your people."

Wind swirled about them, ruffled hair and feathers alike. Sunlight cut like a spear through the clouds revealing the ghostly lip of the turquoise moon.

"An empty threat!" the king replied, before stepping away. "Well-acted. But it will not avail you."

"Azrael!" he shouted behind him, "you're making a mistake." The Batal's chains snapped tight, groaning with the intense strain. Only Thelana was close enough to see the slender links separating.

"If you will not jump willingly," the trumpet-like voice blared, "we will kill you where you remain!" As if to emphasize the threat, the hawk beak opened to show the avian king's determined scowl.

Xandr did not stir.

Taking a deep breath, Azrael's massive torso expanded like a balloon. "And I had so hoped to avoid putting a stain upon my city. No matter. Wingmen, kill them both."

As the arch of swords closed to form a ring, the avian closest to Thelana threw off his helmet, directing it at the enclosing flock. Feathers flew as one helmet collided with another, resounding with a GONG, toppling one of the wingmen. Azrael stood motionless, a bewildered expression upon his face. The sword at Xandr's back was now in his hands, a string of glittering links were now scattered at his feet, and the avian beside him lay flat.

Moonlight glinted off his borrowed blade as Xandr crossed the platform with a tremendous leap to join the bareheaded avian. "Ouranos!" he cried. "It's about damn time!" The others faltered, unsettled by the emergence of a traitor and the threat of resistance.

"I am your king!" Azrael exclaimed, closing his mask again as he took to the sky. "Fear me, not him!"

Thelana's wrists ached from trying, to be free of the whisper chain, for she longed to join Xandr in the fight. Suddenly, the floor disappeared and her feet were dangling, and she had to look down to the shrinking platform to believe it. She was airborne, suspended by the waist on Ouranos' arm, ascending uneasily into the air.

The avian wingmen spread their arms to give pursuit, when a large shadow fell across the platform. It was the giant pigeon form of the ib, tearing at the air with its hooked talons, its head bobbing loosely without blinders to shield its eyes. Another being soared beside it, and Thelana marveled at her snowy plumage and long, willowy figure, her waist no thicker than Xandr's thigh.

"Avia!" Azrael screeched. "What are you doing?"

"I follow my nest mate, Father," she said, her vocal cords like a harp, her words ringing like music.

"Ouranos?" the king called out. "He is of lowly plumage! I shan't allow it! Come down here at once, young chick!"

But she, possessing the unruliness of youth, did not obey. "Away, Flick Flack," she crowed, snapping at the reins about the bird's bridle, just as Thelana was tossed upon its saddle behind her.

As the ferocious ib fended off the frightened wingmen, Ouranos nosedived to the platform and with a tilt of his wings lifted across its flooring, sweeping Xandr over the edge and into the sky.

The scene of battle shrank as Flick Flack distanced itself from Nimbos with a speed, power, and grace that bellied its size. Xandr and Thelana, knees bent at the wing, clawed at the stems of its feathers to keep in their seats. All too quickly Thelana learned that a giant bird was unlike any mount of the land. Keeping aloft its back was a necessary skill and she had little time to master it.

Bird man and bird coasted apart and then drifted together again. Ouranos stretched over the sky, toes to fingertips, effortlessly navigating the upward drafts, a master of the wind.

Xandr shouted over the rushing air and drumming of wings. "Demacharon! What of Demacharon?"

"He is gone, my friend. Perhaps, if he had not encased himself in bronze, we could have caught him."

"You came too late."

"After relocating the survivors, I was sent as part of a delegation to meet with Gol, the merquid king, to inquire after the star that fell from the heavens."

"What of it?" Xandr shouted in reply, remembering the streak that rent the sky and the flash on the horizon heralding the doom of that city by the sea.

"The merquid claim no responsibility, but regard it as an act of Gulgola. I believed them. It's not in their nature to speak untruths, unless they learned it from their recent contact with humans."

"And all this time you knew nothing, nothing of our plight in the cages, of the trial?"

"I was watching, biding my time. How could I have known the Hedonian would jump? And I could not very well break you out of the tower now, could I? Besides, I had to procure your weapons."

Where the air grew thin, Flick Flack batted its wings in violent rebellion of gravity, rattling the riders' bones, and then catching a rising gale, glided, without a single flex of muscle. Avia turned her head almost completely backwards. Her eyes were nothing like a human's, but massive almond shapes, blue as the sky, glittering with colors like diamonds in sunlight. Adding to her alien beauty, red feathers curved from her eyebrows in a crest over her head. "You're too stiff," she cawed to the two of them. "Loosen your grip."

Ignoring her, Xandr called back to his avian friend. "You have it? My sword?"

"Look there," Ouranos gestured.

In a bundle beside his saddle, Xandr freed the gleaming shaft, along with Thelana's gold and jade bow-sword. He held the two weapons, one in each hand, as their blunt surfaces wavered against the air. With some effort, he pressed the jade handle into her palm.

Wind whistled through Thelana's hair, snapping her braid like a whip. Growing bolder, she let go of the reins enough to turn around and look. Mount Nimbos and its flowering spires were diminishing into silhouettes, becoming indistinguishable from the clouds. Freedom beckoned ahead out of the wide blue horizon, and the moons were still and distant, giving the impression that they were free-wheeling in space.

"Won't they come after us?" she asked Avia.

"No avian can fly faster than an ib," she replied, "and my Flick Flack is a swift one. By the time they wrangle other ibs, we'll be far gone."

The bird pitched suddenly into the wind, and the world teetered on its side. Fortunately for Thelana, she could not remember the last time she'd eaten a proper meal, and figured she had no food in her stomach to lose.

Ouranos shifted his glide to within reach of Xandr. "Why didn't you tell the king that you were the Batal? That I sent you to Hedonia? He might have spared your life."

"Because," he said, eyeing his sword, "I chose to go, and I am not the Batal."

"But you have the sword," Ouranos replied at last.

"This?" said Xandr, "it is nothing, nothing but the taker of lives."

"If you hate it so, why don't you just drop it? Let it go."

Xandr glanced at the bird man and then at the blade. "I can't . . ."

At that moment, a terrible screeching interrupted his thoughts. Flick Flack bobbed her head around, frantically flapping. Looking back, they could see the long, narrow silhouette that followed, wings encompassing their plane of sight, growing larger with each passing second.

"Almighty Aza!" As if forgetting to fly, Ouranos zig-zagged erratically. "They've sent the caw after us!"

Thelana's fingers tightened round her bow-sword. "You mean that other giant bird? That eats people!"

"Yes!" Avia answered her.

"I thought ibs were vicious. Can't it defend us?"

"Ibs are a caw's favorite prey," Avia remarked. "Don't worry though. We'll try to lose it in the storm cloud."

They dived, Xandr and Thelana flailing and nearly falling from the bird's sides. Ahead of them, the sky turned gray, heavy, and wet. A deep rumble rolled underfoot, popped and cracked in their ears—it was deafening. Hair Thelana did not know she possessed grew long and straight out from her body and then everything turned white. She was blind. Pellets of water were pounding her, beading across her bosom, rolling over her every limb. As her eyes refocused, she could make out the jagged blazing tendrils cutting through the haze. A second pair of wings sounded behind them. Its screech was still terrifying, despite the thunderclap that dulled her ears. Looking over her shoulder, the gray void was thick but empty. Her hairs pricked up again and she slammed her eyes shut against the light. A second bolt split the sky. She could see it through her eyelids, and when she looked again, the long purple form of the vulture hawk loomed above, vanishing and reemerging with every flash. Suddenly the caw was at the ib's tail. Its vulture-like head was bigger than Thelana could have imagined, its beak snapping wildly at anything within reach. When it screeched, the sound came in waves so powerful she thought she could see them, shaking her so violently the noise remained like a poison in her ears.

"Can you hit it?" said a voice, the syllables blown by wind and rain, by the thunder and that awful screeching. "Can you hit it?" Xandr shouted again, "With your arrows?"

"I never miss," she replied, snapping her sword apart. The presence of arrows, concealed within the blade's shaft, surprised her as she remembered the battle atop Sargonus' head, when she was left to fend off merquid with nothing but her sword. Had Ouranos been so thorough in regaining their arms? Had he expected a struggle? With no time to think, she slipped a strange-looking arrow between her fingers, avian in design, as Flick Flack banked in a sharp angle and the caw spun from view. Avia wrestled with the reins, but the bird was terrified beyond her control.

Distance, direction, and wind—every factor amounted to total chaos. The ib buffeted with frantic strokes, making her aim impossibly unsteady, but her target was huge. The arrow escaped into a cloud. Again the ib banked, and Xandr and Thelana were thrown sideways, struggling to maintain balance.

"It disappeared," Thelana remarked, re-nocking her bow.

"Do you think it's gone?" Xandr asked.

In answer, the caw's great beak broke from the clouds, stealing feathers from the giant pigeon, snapping at Thelana's foot. Now Avia lost all control, and predator and prey fell into a spiraling dive. The surface of Aenya emerged clumsily, rolling overhead. Everything turned sideways, upside down, and right again. Thelana let out another shot to no avail and it came closer, too close, the gold edge of her blade ricocheting off its beak as if hacking at a chunk of iron. At any moment, that beak would clamp down and their mount would be devoured, and then they'd be fodder for the caw. There was no recourse but to do something bold, desperate. Cold dread turned to fire in her veins, when she threw herself headlong at the caw, bridging the gap between the two birds, the mountains like crumpled bedding underfoot. All her weight was in her hands as she came down, her steel breaking through the shell, sinking to the hilt into the monster's beak.

"Thelana!" Xandr cried. "Where is she?"

Wounded, the caw sailed backwards. Thelana's feet slipped from its rounded beak, but she was still hanging on, clutching the hilt of her embedded sword.

"I'll get her!" Ouranos said, twirling back around.

But the caw was already upon them. Its talons cut like a scythe across the bird man's back and he fell away with a shriek. The second talon hooked through its prey and Thelana tumbled down against the ib. Xandr caught her by the ankle, but the violence between the tangled birds loosed even his powerful grip. Everything was spinning. There was no way to make sense of direction and Avia, their only guide, was nowhere to be seen. Thelana managed to bend into a C-shape before flopping earthbound, her braid a four-foot jumble of movement below her.

Hold me. Xandr.

Without a sound, Thelana slid away from him and into the ether.

4

FERAL CHILD

The bud of the Ilm was shriveled and brittle and dull brown. Occasionally, she looked at it to remember what was past, careful to keep it in one piece, but it was so misshapen and colorless that it hardly brought thoughts of home anymore. At least they managed to find it, at her insistence, but her bow and quiver were lost to the woods.

Wrapped in a cloak, she dragged her feet alongside the scouting party, the worked soil cool and damp against her soles. The garment belonged to the captain—the handsome one they called Dantes. The camp was down a slope by the edge of the woods, overlooking a wide plain, not far from where they'd found her. Threads of smoke wafted up from chimneys and campfires. Walls meandered along the perimeter without doors or rooftops.

To her Ilmarin eyes, the humans residing at the camp scurried like ants, one person atop another, too many to be sustained by the shelters provided. She marveled at the infinite variety of fabrics and trinkets adorning their bodies, at the young and old, stout and feeble, and those like the three who escorted her. Soldiers wandered in arrangements of bronze and leather, some clean-shaven, others scarred, hobbling on crutches, missing limbs.

Wherever they went, others pressed about her, made curious by her mud-caked face. She buried herself in her cloak to shield from their stares. And then she felt a tug at her hem. An ancient woman held fast to it—she looked to have at least sixty years, but there was something else wrong with her, beyond old age. Her face was sallow and shriveled and pox-ridden.

"Dying!" the haggard woman cried. "Soon, yes, very soon I'll be dying!"

"Come on," he said to her, "don't look at them. You'll only give them hope."

But Thelana could not help herself, and stood listening to the woman rant on about sickness, poverty, and impending death.

"Haven't you seen a leper before?" He tugged at her arm but she kept staring even as she was led away.

When Thelana opened her eyes, the memories flooded back: the woods, the halfman, the old leper woman, Captain Dantes. She remembered devouring wafers of bread and clumps of meat. And she remembered being admonished by the 'obscene' way in which she sat and ate, though the captain had again come to her rescue, justifying her 'feral' ways as common for one born of the woods. Some other women took her away after that, scrubbing her down like a hog while dumping buckets of cold water over her head. And then, before being brought to her cot, she was inspected by an old hairless man—a healer—who declared that her arm was dislocated, as though she could not figure that out herself.

Sitting upright, Thelana ran long fingers across the soft linen where she lay. It eased her aches and sores, but she hated the feel of it—it was numbing, like a blindfold over her sense of touch. The dim light and quiet were also unnerving. Hanging from the chair where the healer had sat was now a length of cloth white as a cloud on a clear day. Her whole being throbbed as she got to her feet but, remembering she was Ilmarin, she shrugged it off, unfurling the brilliant cloth as she stood.

Gold thread embroidered the hem, the cuffs of the sleeves, and U-shaped neckline. As she turned and stretched it in her hands, the sight of a girl startled her: bronze skin, jutting ribs, underdeveloped breasts, rivets of muscle about the calves and forearms.

It's me.

Her fingers met the cold surface of her reflection. It was like still water, only she had never seen herself so clearly. *I don't look womanly at all. Why couldn't I be more like Anja?*

"Try it on," said a voice. "It's a k'shaba. I got it at the bazaar this morning. Had to haggle for a fair price, and that's not my strong suit. Nothing fancy, but it's the best I could afford."

She stared at him awkwardly, studied her reflection again, and then looked back at the garment. She held it in her fingers like a dead animal. If she were to put it on, her body would disappear from the mirror, and she would no longer recognize herself.

"What's the matter? Haven't you seen anything like it before?"

She continued to stare at him without uttering a word. He was as handsome as she remembered—but it was a strange thing, knowing only his face, his dark hair and short cut beard, and she was forced to wonder about the rest of him. Beneath all that bronze and leather, was he the same as her father? Her brothers? Could she even be certain he was a male?

"Come now . . . your people must wear clothing sometimes. When it's cold?"

We sit by the fire.

"Or when it's very hot?"

We lay in the river.

He mimed shivering with cold, then wiping away imaginary sweat. He seemed desperate to communicate, to escape the bewilderment in her emerald eyes, and Thelana suppressed an urge to laugh.

"I suppose it was stupid of me to assume things about you. But you can't just walk around naked . . ."

Why not?

"The people—the men especially, my men especially—they won't understand . . ."

Oh. And suddenly she remembered Brutus, how he used to stare at her, and then she watched her reflection slip the garment overhead. The material still grated uncomfortably against her skin, but it made all the difference in the mirror. She spun giddily. The hem swirled about her knees in a way that made her smile.

"Do you like it? I hope you do." Hearing his voice was like sitting by the hearth on a cold day.

It's beautiful.

"Oh," he said, "how very foolish of me. I keep forgetting you don't speak."

But I do.

"You can think of it . . . as a parting gift. I had hoped to defend your honor against these aristocratic snobs, but our troop is on the move again. I spoke to the servants of the household. They promised they'd not put you out."

He's leaving. The only person who shows me any kindness and he's leaving. And then she remembered what her Baba had said and why she had been chosen to leave Ilmarinen. *Show them what you can do.*

"Shoot," she called out.

He left the door, turned halfway back. "You can talk? I—I assumed, hoped, you understood me, but not that you could talk!"

"Shoot," she repeated.

"Shoes?" he replied. "Of course, you'll need shoes. How foolish of me—"

"No!" she said, stamping her foot. "Shoot! You fight. I can fight too. Take me with you."

He let slip a grin, but the certainty and eagerness in her face was unmistakable. "Wait. You want to be recruited? Into the Kratan army?"

"Yes."

"This is crazy. Who are you? How do you even know our language?"

"Aola."

"What does that mean?"

"She was kind to me. Taught me the bow."

"You're an archer?"

"Yes."

He paused, rubbing the stubble of his jaw with a gloved knuckle. "Most of our force has been snowballed from other races, societies, less to our liking . . . but you have no society. Do you even know what we're up against? What we fight for?"

"I'll fight for you. For whatever you fight for."

"We are desperate for numbers," he murmured, stepping into her shadow, "but you're hardly a grown woman. You wouldn't last a day. Better you stay here."

"No," she said. "I won't become like them. Not a servant."

"You'll die."

"I'll die *here*," she whispered. "Maybe not today, but someday."

"How good are you?" His face showed intrigue but skepticism. His glare was penetrating.

I can hit a sparrow in flight. I can hit a hare darting through the bush. And she spoke the words she'd long rehearsed. "I am Thelana, child of the flower."

"The recruitment tent is being packed up already. We'll be shoving off by midday. We'd best hurry."

The area was strewn with grass and gravel, crisscrossed by streets of overturned soil and feces. Tent poles were already being fastened to mules and war chests shouldered onto wagons. Of the dozens of straw men painted with bull's-eyes, only a couple remained still posted to the ground.

A curious few descended to the clearing, having heard rumor of the wild child born of the forest that bested a halfman with her dagger. The army physician examined her tongue and pulse, declaring her "fit as a horse." She was then escorted by a man with a shaggy beard and a lazy eye, who went by the name of Torgin, to a table of bows. There was the short bow, the longbow, and the double-bent composite bow. They were straight as arrows, so her first test was to bend and string them. She rubbed the sore spot in her shoulder, where her arm had been dislocated the day before, and took up the longbow. It was nearly as tall as she was, and the pattern of its grain showed it to be of cedar, a sturdy yet flexible wood. Between her hands, however, it wobbled every which way, resisting her efforts to slip the loop around either tip. As she struggled, she could hear the jeers behind her—the shouts of "whore" and "dirty girl"—the impoverished and disease-ridden directing their hatreds at her.

"Enough!" Captain Dantes commanded. "Stringing bows is a task for those with brawn but not brain. We are in desperate need of recruits. If she can pull an arrow and hit a target, that's all I care for." He handed her the short bow, taut and ready.

She chose her arrow carefully, what most resembled the kind she could make, though their points were heavier, of bronze, rather than obsidian.

The straw man's limp body, with its oversized head and sagging arms, was posted thirty paces from where she stood. She adjusted the height and angle of her aim to compensate for wind and distance, and let it slip. Gasps of anticipation came from the gathering, followed by a collective groan. Many were already choosing to return to their daily routine.

"If she had been aiming for a giant to the far right of the straw man," said Torgin, "she would have hit him square in the head."

The Captain's face showed disappointment, but for reasons he could not quite grasp, he remained faithful. "All right, give the girl another chance, will you, Torgin, you fluffy bastard? Don't forget I knew your father."

Torgin's eye went everywhere. He sighed. "I'll do this for you, Captain, because I love you so, but if the girl ain't no good, you can't just lug her along, no matter how much you fancy her. Wouldn't be right."

"Let's get one thing straight here. My only concern is for the well-being of my troop. Understood, corporal?"

"Sure thing, sure, no need to pull rank on me. Give it another go, my dear."

Her second arrow went into the straw, but not the straw man. Her third arrow somehow flew sideways, nearly killing a passer-by, who sped along with his wagon cursing. Nobody was quite sure where the fourth went.

"All right, then," said Torgin, rubbing his hands together. "I have enough to do today without having to go chasing god-knows-where for arrows that, might I remind you, we only have a finite few of."

The captain turned to the Ilmarin girl. She was unable to look at him. "We found you in the wood with a knife, trying to fend off a halfman, perhaps a short sword would be a better match for you. I could teach you—"

She didn't speak. The bow was too powerful. It needed less pull, less compensation than hers did. She marched angrily from the clearing, not knowing where to go or what she would do. And then, strapped to a mule among a bundle of kindling, she found it. It was rough to the touch, with all the twists and knobs of a branch cut from the tree—she had even chosen to leave a single leaf where it sprouted. It was her bow. The gathering was mostly dispersed now, and few eyes were upon her. As one of the soldiers packed up his quiver, she ducked behind him with a stealthy foot, snatching up a fistful of arrows.

At sixty paces they went flying. Torgin ducked with dread, believing they were under attack. The straw man appeared to be sprouting tail feathers. Arrows marked its hands and feet as though she were decorating. The bull's-eye had a neat grouping of arrows within it, as though placed by hand. She walked and fired, letting each one go until her hand was empty.

"By Strom's surly beard!" Torgin exclaimed.

"Did I do good?" Thelana asked. Captain Dantes simply smiled.

5

THE GREAT WHITE FLAT

The phoenix dipped for a second pass, its multi-hued feathers flashing against the white backdrop. Popping from the sand to meet its hooked talons were the milky fangs of a serpent. Coiled into an S, the serpent repelled the flurry of attacks with whip-like lunges. But the bird was the aggressor, its beak a snapping blur over the shifting sands, picking off scales where it could.

After repeated attempts of one to kill the other, the dance between earth and sky came to an end, as the phoenix, fatigued with hunger and from battle, ascended to the sky, perhaps to safer prey. Before disappearing under the sand, the serpent gave a final hiss.

The scene played out as if nothing else in the universe existed. Serpent and phoenix and white sands were everything, before there was such a thing as an *I*.

Standing brought pain, and pain brought a torrent of memories, most of them unwelcome. For a time he tried not to think, because thinking also brought pain. Instead, he simply looked. But there was nothing to look at but the flat white surface of the world, extending in all directions to meet the pale horizon. The vast emptiness gave him some sense of peace. He was alone in his mind, and he closed his eyes and breathed deep the hot air, longing to return to unconsciousness, to forget. But there were things he had to do. Memories—a single memory—brought him back.

Thelana.

He sifted the sand between his fingers. It was white and thick as crystal, caking his lips, covering his arms and sticking to his hair and flaking from his brows. If he had been wearing any article of clothing, he was certain it would be full of the stuff. *Salt!* Nothing but salt. He spit out a mouthful—it had lined the inside of his throat, making him gag.

Dusting himself was a futile task. Wind continually resettled the salt-sands, and he could only hope to unearth himself enough to not resemble a creature made entirely of white granules.

When he was satisfied with his relative cleanliness, he made out in a random direction, for he had no marker to indicate which way to go. The sun was directly overhead, which was too bright to look at, and a pale outline hinted at the greater moon to the east. His eyes sought anything that stood out, for evidence that he was not alone in this universe. Then he remembered the serpent and phoenix.

Was it a dream? No, he decided not. Their battle had awakened him from his stupor. He'd watched them for a long while. If they could survive here, so could he.

He continued on, his despair growing as his ankles sank further beneath the surface, until he noticed, or thought he noticed, an inkling of purple. He rubbed the salt from the pits of his tear ducts and looked again. It was no trick of the imagination. There was clearly color in this world. He rushed toward it, finding a hard stem, like a curved broomstick handle poking through the ground. Digging with his hands, he found a single purple feather, as long as he was tall. It was from the giant caw. *This is where we fell. But where is Thelana?*

With new understanding, he set out looking for the body of a girl. She was tough, a warrior and Ilmarin-born like himself. But she could not have survived such a fall—then again—why was *he* still alive?

More feathers, strewn for passings' walking, and then something caught the light of the sun, glinting from afar. He followed it like a ship to a beacon. It was gold, the edge of something more massive, half-buried like everything else, a crumpled velvety fabric all around it. With frantic strokes, he dove under the sand, unearthing rich blues and hard bronze surfaces, the colors of Hedonia.

Demacharon? Could it be? He tried to shout the commander's name but only a thirsty sound came from his throat.

He dug deeper, but the form was strangely off, too massive to be the commander, or any human for that matter. At last, a hideous face emerged. The long snout and leathery folds and black olive eyes were unmistakable.

He tried to speak, but the dry air caught in his throat. He tried again and a hoarse choking noise broke through his bloodied lips. "Grimosse?"

The monster stood abruptly as if it had been sleeping. Salt rained down from its immense frame. "Master?"

"Where did you come from?"

"Grimm come from sand," he answered without a trace of irony.

"Yes, but how did you make it here, to this place?"

"Grimm fell."

"It's pointless speaking to you!" The peace he'd felt was gone, his blood running hot under the skin. Why this monster? Why not Thelana? Or Demacharon? Or any human companion?

He continued searching, time drawn out by his sense of fatigue. A dark spot appeared on the horizon like a pepper seed in milk. Xandr squinted through the heat, and the spot turned into a fuzzy blotch, which turned into the slender silhouette of a body. His heart thundered in his ears as he raced toward the vision, the soles of his feet rising with effort above the sinking surface.

"Thelana!" He shouted her name before knowing she was there. Who else could it be? Her form emerged out of the flatness like a sand sculpture, a rough nude shape. She collapsed in his arms, Emmaxis and her bow dropping to her heels.

Words were insufficient. He stared at her freckled cheeks, her bow-line lips split and bloodied and clinging to the crystalline gravel. Despite her buried-alive appearance, he wanted nothing more than to embrace her—to shout to the Goddess for joy. But they were no better off than in the hands of the merquid or the avians. What good would it do, to let hope rise in his bosom, when they were without a crumb of food or a drop of water? If there was joy in seeing her alive, he would bury the feeling, like everything else in the desert.

"You look horrible," he said.

"Nice seeing you too," she managed between cracked lips.

He did not reply, but moved past her, snatching up the sword, running a finger along the milk-silver blade. There was not a grain on it. "How did you find this?"

"I don't know," she said. "I didn't care to look for it, but it just . . . called to me. And when I found it I couldn't let go."

She was visibly shaken by its presence, relieved to have passed it on. He had studied the weapon for years, could handle it like no one else alive, yet it never ceased to unnerve him. If the skull face moved, he never saw it, but at times the eye sockets appeared to shrink, or the teeth would rearrange or go missing, or the metallic hilt form an expression. Tricks of light and shadow, he supposed.

"How is it we're alive?" she asked him.

"The Taker must not want us."

"Really?" she said, revealing herself, piece by piece, as she brushed away the sand.

"Cyclones," he replied. "We were over it when we fell. They've been known to carry entire caravans over fields and set them down undamaged."

"Caught by a cyclone? That's the best you can come up with?"

"You have a better answer?"

"The gods," she affirmed. "They've other things planned for the Batal."

226

He rolled his eyes heavenward. If she believed in the legend of Batal, he was too tired to argue. But the mention of gods made him angry. "Where were the gods in Hedonia? Or Ilmarinen? What of Ouranos and Avia? And Demacharon?"

"I—I wish I knew," she said softly.

"Your lips," he noted, gently wiping her mouth with his fingers.

"Ouch!" She pulled away, licking the blood. "Cuts and salt . . . not my favorite mix."

"We'd best get moving," he said. "We can't remain here, with our bare backs to the sun."

She walked alongside him, back the way he came. The flat surface of the desert met the horizon with perfect symmetry. The sky, in its vast emptiness, mirrored the world below. They scanned their surroundings, but could find nothing to break the flatness, not the silhouette of human occupation, not distant hills, not a lone rock.

"The outside is an awful place," she grumbled. "In Nimbos, I thought the cold unbearable, but this, this heat . . ."

"Don't talk—you're wasting water. And if we don't find any soon, we won't survive."

"There isn't a river or a lake anywhere around here," she answered drearily. "Maybe some supplies fell off the ib?"

He watched her stumble, dragging her only possession, the gold and jade sword, along the ground. She was right about the world beyond the Potamis river valley. Ilmar were not meant to survive such harsh climates. Without clothing, they were like ilm flowers planted in the desert. If they didn't cover soon, the sun would roast their exposed skin like meat on a skewer. Perhaps he could fashion a shade from the caw's feathers, or clothing from what the golem was wearing.

With Thelana in tow, he raced back to where he remembered leaving the golem. Despite the surrounding emptiness, the shimmering waves of heat coming off the ground made the monster a challenge to find.

Lugging his massive bell-shaped hammer, Grimosse approached them, as if he could do battle against necessity. "Masters!" he bellowed. "You come back to Grimm? Let Grimm guard you?"

"Is this talking monster still following us?" she said with a smirk.

"Grimm not monster!" he said. "Grimm is guardian."

"We were in such a hurry before, I didn't really look at him," she admitted. "He's like no creature I've ever seen, and I've seen my share of strange species."

"He is not of the Goddess," Xandr replied, "but a thing made of dead flesh, brought to life by arcane and forbidden knowledge, by knowledge not tempered by wisdom. He was made to protect, apparently."

Thelana moved to examine him, and the golem followed in step. His shadow gave her some respite from the sun. "He . . . seems to be following me."

"That is odd," Xandr mused. "When I went to find you, he didn't show such devotion to me. Perhaps it has something to do with your *sex*."

"She glared at him. "What you're suggesting is . . . I mean, does it even have a—"

"No, Thelana, it's not like that. Merneptes, the High Priest's daughter, was his master before. Now that she's gone," he added, careful not to mention her suicide, "he thinks *you* are his master. You must remind him of the princess."

She approached cautiously, daring to stand beneath the golem, craning her neck up to its pitted eyes. "Are you sure he's safe?"

"I've heard tales of guardians going insane, killing their masters. But he seems harmless."

"Harmless? Did you see what he did to those gill? To Sarpedon?"

"I saw what you did to those gill," he answered. "You're menacing with that bow."

"But what makes him different? How do we know he won't go insane and kill us too?"

Xandr was unable to reply, and in that gap of silence, the monster answered, "*He* good to Grimm."

"Who?" Xandr asked. "Who was good to you? Urukjinn?"

"No!" his voice rumbled. "First master. Give life to Grimm. Give name to Grimm. Grimm made for girl. Little girl. Hold in hand." The monster looked wistfully into his empty, four-fingered palm.

"She was an infant?" Thelana murmured.

The guardian grew suddenly intimidating, his leafy ears contorting and stubby teeth flashing, his brow folding over his beady eyes. "Men came," he said, "bad men, not like us. They say master no good. They say girl is witch." Now the hand became a fist. "Grimm want bash them! But master say run, hide girl, take to doorstep. Grimm runs from bad men, to big walls, to Sea."

"To Hedonia," Thelana murmured. "If he was made to protect an infant, he must know to be gentle."

"As long as we don't anger him we'll be safe," said Xandr, "till we can find a place to leave him."

"You intend to abandon him?" she cried. "He has no one! Who will take care of him?"

"He's eight feet tall! He can take care of himself."

"Are you going to ditch me, too," she cried, wiping the blood from her lips, "when you've no need of me? As soon as you find somewhere to lose me?"

"Thelana. Please—stop talking, you're making it worse."

"Don't tell me what to do!"

"You've suffered greatly," he said. "Delirium is setting in."

"You're right, why waste my spit on you?" she cried. "You don't care about me—or anyone. Why did you even bother saving me that night? You should have left me to rot."

Emotion was brewing under her eyes. Only Ilmarin women possessed such clear irises, such vivid, intense hues—hers were so much like an emerald lagoon. He seized her by the shoulders suddenly and shook her. "Thelana, shut up."

She wrestled in his arms, half-willing to be held.

He kissed her.

The tangle of his mustache must be paining her, he knew, where the dry air had split the rim of her mouth. He tasted the blood on her lips, but her tongue was like a dead leaf.

"What was that for?" she asked, looking stunned.

"Listen," he said to her, "you have no idea what's out there. Where I'm going, you can't—" A distant rumble cut him short. It was like a herd of charging aurochs. Their eyes turned to the horizon, to the rising cloud of dust. The desert was no longer flat, but rounded and fuzzy, like a long narrow roll of moving cotton. Visible chunks pelted them like hail, stinging like angry insects. Xandr winced as salt hit him in his eyes, blinding him with pain. The storm swallowed them whole, depositing into the open cracks of his lips, into every niche in his body. He reached for Thelana, who was vanishing in the haze, and pulled her tight. And together they collapsed under Grimosse.

The sun was obscured, its light filtered and separated into bands of color. A striped tent swayed softly in the breeze above him.

Xandr marveled at the power of the sandstorm as he worked his arm above his shoulder. His other hand still held tight to hers. She was still breathing. Somehow she managed to keep half of her face aboveground. With the little strength remaining in him, he pulled the rest of her free.

From under Grimosse's plated knees, he could see the colorful tent, rising on four poles from a scaly green hill. The head of the creature turned casually to regard him, spittle drawing webs of foam in the sand beneath its curving beak, hot vapors expelling from nostrils he could reach an arm into. It was an elder tri-horn, grown to full size. As he brushed the crust from his eyes to take a better look, Thelana's nervous fingers tugged on the crook of his elbow.

"That's the biggest trike I've ever seen!" he heard her say.

"I call him *Rurk*, for the sound that he makes when he croons." The man was seated under the striped awning of the howdah fastened to the shoulders and fan-shaped plate extending from the saurian's skull. "And you may call me Nesper." His eyes were dark, nearly absent of white about the pupils. By the fit of his djellabah and the rolls of skins fastened to the beast's hide, Xandr guessed that he was a nomad merchant. "What in Solos are you three doing out here? Without supplies? Without a saurian of any sort?" His voice was gravelly, unaccustomed to use, muffled in part by the scarf about his face. "Were you dropped by a bird, or something?"

"Actually," Thelana began, shooting a bemused glance at Xandr, "we were—"

"Wait," said the nomad, "don't tell me. You're runaway slaves, of course! Sex slaves no doubt. Why else would you be standing in the middle of nowhere without a stitch? And from the looks of you, you must have escaped some time ago. She looks like she hasn't eaten for a cycle."

"I've forgotten what hunger is," she admitted.

"You're . . . very astute," Xandr replied. "And what of this one?" he added, gesturing to Grimosse. "You're not afraid of him?"

"Nesper has seen many strange things in his travels," he said, stepping down from his trike's horn, "and I am no stranger to golems and their like. No doubt he was to be sold by your *slaver* and seeks freedom also." He spoke as though unconvinced, as one liar to another. "With a golem in your power, escape must have been easy, no?

Even procuring weapons," he added, eyeing Emmaxis with intense curiosity. "No doubt your slavers ran for their lives . . . leaving you to die of the elements."

"You weave a convincing tale," Xandr said.

"I can think of no other story better fitting your situation," he answered. "And if I'm wrong, you can tell it along the way! Nesper loves a good tale! After all, we have some days ahead of us." He loosened a knot from one of his bundles, tossing a sheet of cloth their way. Rurk trumpeted through its nostrils and shook its head. "Now then, you'd best put that on, my dear, or the Eye of Solos will cook the skin off your back. You can pay Nesper later."

Thelana caught the djellabah by the sleeve, studied it curiously. "Is there a town nearby?" she asked, clumsily pulling the garment overhead.

"Was a town, once," Nesper said. "Baartook, a trading post, a stop for merchants like me. But the sands moved in on it, year after year, wiping out more settlers. Population dipped to, oh, about forty, when the big storm came. All that was left was the signpost, where Baartook once was. I sold it for a copper. Not many towns survive these lands."

"And just what lands are these?" Xandr asked him.

"You're off the map, my friend," he said, his tone growing dark. "You're *nowhere*. But those in my work, well, we call this the *Great White Flat*. Only experienced nomads travel through here. You wouldn't survive it even with the proper supplies. The gods certainly smile on you today, I must say, in that you've found a friend in Nesper."

"Why help us?" Xandr asked him.

"Why not?" said the merchant. "You believe greed rules everything on Aenya? I'm no slaver. Besides, Nesper could use a few strong hands. The Flat is not an easy place to live and it's hard finding anyone willing to go as far west as I."

Xandr cupped a hand over his brow. Nothing could be seen but white, meeting the horizon in all directions, and the faint tint of turquoise from the greater moon in the east. The emergence of the nomad was uncanny, almost too much of a coincidence. "You are headed east, then?"

"No," Nesper replied, climbing back up the horns of his trike to sit under the makeshift shade.

"No?" Xandr echoed. "Only a madman would venture further west. The Dead Zones—"

"Nesper knows too well of what you speak. I alone have laid eyes upon it, a hellish place—the Dead Zones—where no man can step foot, where the Eye of Solos does not blink, where molten rock and fire spits from the earth and sand turns to roiling glass. But there is an expanse that comes before, called Ocean, where the salt of the Flat gives way to rock. There, known to few men, a wondrous ancient city waits. Many artifacts and riches have I procured from it. I go to the Lost City of Shess, and if you hope to live, you have little choice but to come with me."

6

TWILIGHT IN MONOLITH VALLEY

Rurk was a gentle creature, obeying the nomad's odd vocal clicks as it lumbered forward. But it was so much more massive than any horse or hippocampus and Thelana did not imagine the trike would notice a tug on the reins of its horns. Its rounded spine sat the four of them. She could feel the saurian's muscles contracting beneath her, the steady rise and fall of its movement like the subtle undulation of a boat in the Potamis. Like tiny birds atop a herbivore, they found safe haven from the terrors rumored to lurk in the wastelands of the Dead Zones. Aside from the occasional tongue-click command, their guide kept eerily silent. Xandr and Grimosse remained quiet also, leaving Thelana to her thoughts, to the creak and sway of the teetering howdah, to the sound of shifting sands and guttural braying of the trike's nostrils.

Many moons passed as they moved into the sun, what Nesper called the *Eye of Solos*, the face of Infinity a green-blue rim on the eastern horizon. Under the striped shade, her skin no longer burning, Thelana welcomed the warmth. For too long she'd suffered the cold, from the deathly chill of a prison cell to the icy waves that toppled Hedonia to the unwelcoming mountain winds of Nimbos. By midday, the sun had reached its zenith, washing the colors from their tent to blinding white. Heat pummeled her djellabah, and she found herself all the more thankful for it, hiding more deeply in its folds, tugging at her veil to keep the moisture from escaping with each breath. Nesper had been kind enough to offer a water gourd, but she resisted the urge to drain the last drop from it. "Only taste the water," she remembered Nesper saying to them. "Do not drink or you will forever want of thirst."

The white of the Great White Flat thinned away, revealing uneven sheets of rock beneath, till all that remained of the endless expanse were narrow dunes reaching like piers of salt across the rugged landscape. Where land met sky, the horizon shimmered, the red-orange surface cascading upwards in waves of heat.

Thelana had known nomadic merchants from the far eastern nation of Shemselinihar, having set their tents beyond the walls of Hedonia. She knew them to wear modest clothing—long striped djellabahs similar to what she now wore—and in their business dealings they chose their words carefully. Insulting a desert nomad's parentage was tantamount to a death challenge. Revealing a bare ankle was a sexual lure. She was long puzzled by such people, but if the western nations were like this, she could no longer find fault in their customs. The heat sapped her will to speak, even to think of what to say. To waste words on idle chatter, for a desert people, was foolish—and making the effort to speak only to insult someone made the insult all the more potent.

As for her nakedness, to someone like Nesper, it must have seemed absurd at best, perverse at worst.

After a time, Thelana could feel the pinch in her neck where it bent to meet Xandr's shoulder. At their backs, the sun moved to eclipse with the greater moon, and the change in the air revived her from the heat-induced trance she had fallen into. Rock formations towered around them now. "Monolith Valley," Nesper called it, the first he had spoken since the onset of travel.

Thelana watched the earthen shapes go by. They were like sculptures left by gods, twisting, weather-beaten bodies. One of the spires reminded her of a lean man bent by age. Another was stooped in contemplation. She was soon inventing names for them, as she did for the trees in Ilmarinen. *Hunchback. Gaping Mouth. Mother with Child.* Twilight had cooled the air to a comfortable degree and Thelana unfastened the belts of her garment. Ahead of them, the ground disappeared, as if they'd come to the edge of the world. Nesper made a shrill clucking sound and stepped down from his bone seat, tethering the reins to a stake in the ground. Thelana did not know how such a massive creature could be contained by a single piece of wood, but Nesper explained how when Rurk was born, it learned that it was unable to break its post. Its peanut-sized brain could never think otherwise. She wondered whether humans could be made the same way, incapable of changing beliefs held from birth, no matter the evidence to the contrary.

After setting up their tents, which were in great supply, as Nesper was a vendor of hard fabrics, he led them to the edge of Monolith Valley, gesturing toward the rocky vista.

"This is the desert called Ocean," he said. "Once, it was filled with life. Before the Great Cataclysm."

Xandr stood looking unimpressed. "How far to the city?"

"Not far, friend," Nesper said. "Not far."

Thelana squatted over the edge, tossing a stone into the canyon. It twirled as it dropped, skipping several steps before disappearing into the shadows below, a good long while passing before a faint clickity-clack came up from the bottom. She flung another into the twilight, telling herself there was some logic to it, but it was more childlike curiosity than anything else. She was an innocent from Ilmarinen and the world was still teeming with marvels.

What power could have wounded the Goddess so deeply to make the world so barren? What colors once grew here? What beasts shook the ground in search of prey? Or did only the small scamper here? Whether enormous as a long-necked saurian or as tiny as a hop mouse, the living could not have known of their impending oblivion. After all, what had her family foreseen of the drought that drove their people to extinction?

Sunlight receded from the crags of the canyon like a great sheet pulled away to reveal the darkness. Her joints were stiff and her thighs ached as she stood. On the back of Nesper's saurian, the day had been long. Another journey awaited them in the morning and she did not have long to sleep. Close to the western hemisphere, nights grew shorter as the greater moon became more distant and low in the sky. But sleep was an unwelcome thought. She looked out over the last stretch of Ocean visible in the waning light and saw in its vast emptiness a mirror of herself.

With the Sun God surrendering the heavens, the glittering images of the more remote gods took shape. The valley was so flat and the darkness so complete, stars moved across her field of vision like fireflies, leaving her to drift among them, to walk through space between the constellations. Skullgrin grinned toothily from above, and Alashiya across from him, the Goddess' phoenix' wings spread over the velvet sky.

With nothing but a dark void where Ocean had been, she returned to camp, to a circle of fire, the ground blue and cool beneath her soles. Grimosse stood in constant vigilance, silent as the myriad monoliths. She caught herself wondering whether the monster slept, or slept standing, and whether a sleepless guardian was comforting or disturbing. Across from the golem, a muscular silhouette showed through the opposite side of the tent canvas. She walked around it. Xandr sat by the fire, his clothing removed. Flat across his knees, Emmaxis mirrored the dancing reds and yellows of the flame. His eyes were half-closed, trance-like, his mane falling like gold reeds against his beard. Without a word, she folded her legs, dropping into a heap of fabric. Even in her djellabah, she could not help shivering. It was far colder upon Mount Nimbos, but nothing was out to kill her now.

Xandr leaned into the fire—the mangled corpse of a chameleon was on a stick in his hand.

"You have food!" she cried, lifting to her knees. The smell of burning flesh poked her insides and she nearly bent double with the pain.

"You can have it," he said, roasting the narrow sliver over the flame. It did not take long to blacken the legs and tail.

Thelana did not argue, snatching the lizard from the skewer, but found her ability to eat lessened. She broke the tail and nibbled. It was dry and bony, like an over-cooked fish. There was little meat to be had and the scales tasted of paper. But she was surprised by the subtle flavor. Hunger is the best chef, she remembered her mother saying. Nor did she mind the tiny organs, the parts of the head that might have disgusted civilized people. By the time the lizard was half gone, she remembered Xandr, who lay on his elbows, watching her intently.

"I'm sorry. I didn't offer . . ."

"I'm not hungry."

"Where did you get this?" she asked, sucking the bones clean. "I'm starved!"

"Nesper gave it to me."

She trembled in her clothes, her skin prickling against the cool night air. Something about their guide, even the mention of him, unnerved her. Or was it merely getting colder? "Where is he?"

He glanced over his shoulder. Three tents stood in stark contrast to the surrounding gloom, the towering spires a deeper black in the distance. "He's gone to his tent."

"Without a word? He just up and went to sleep?"

"What would you have him do?"

"Did he tell you anything? I might have . . . fallen asleep along the way."

"I asked him how long to Shess, but he would only say that it was not far."

A sound broke the silence, from a hilly silhouette, the long trumpet-like bray of the trike. It did sound like it was speaking its name. "So what of you?" Thelana asked him. "Can't sleep?"

"I don't care for it." His face gave no hint of emotion. "With sleep come dreams."

"I used to like to dream. To feel far and away," she explained. "But when I close my eyes, I go to my family. There is no pathway to the future. The dream wood is deep and has many forks, but whichever one I take, it leads home."

"Dreams are meaningless," he said. "Things the mind cannot let go of."

"Oh," she murmured, disheartened. "I always thought dreams are journeys for the soul. You can visit other worlds even, if you know the way. Didn't your father teach you that?"

"I never had—never mind!"

"But you are Ilmarin . . ."

"I am," he affirmed, "without believing as you do."

"Are you?" she replied, a bit sharply. "It did not look that way in Hedonia. You fought with the foreigners, took their counsel—you even dressed like them."

"Watch what you say! I am and ever shall be of the Ilmar. And from what I know, theft and murder have never been our way."

"I did what I had to!" She gazed at the campfire, smothering the hurt in the flames. "Would you have me starve so the wealthy might keep their golden spoons?"

"And in the temple?" he asked. "What happened to the red mystic?"

"Alright." She sighed. "I did not intend to kill anyone—except they would have seen me, alerted more guards, and you know what they do to their prisoners."

"So you killed a sentry?"

"Only," she answered, "when the mystic found the body, he thought it some kind of terrible omen, and dragged it to an altar to perform a ritual. Words were spoken I'd never heard before. And then he used the guard's blood to write that message on the wall. It was awful and it scared me."

"Doom," Xandr remembered, "a sacrifice to divine the future."

"The mystic was so distraught by it, that he turned the arrow on himself. I didn't kill him. All I wanted was enough to never beg again." She wondered whether he ever had to beg or steal to abate hunger, or if his heart ever ached for his family, as hers did, making him act against his nature.

"I do not judge you," he replied. "These are dark days indeed. We cannot expect to keep to our ways in this world."

Darkness enveloped them like a shroud as the ring of firelight gave way to embers that shone like gold. The world was vast and empty, and they were alone in it—in the darkness—the last two Ilmar, two people, in the universe.

"Why Hedonia?" she asked, pulling her knees against her bosom.

"What do you mean?"

"Of all Aenya, why go there?"

"The sword led me," he replied. "I did not wish to go there."

"Your sword?" she echoed. "I don't understand . . . it's a lifeless thing."

"You know that's not true. You've touched it. You've felt it."

"I have," she admitted, balling up into her robes, "but—"

"Upon its steel, I see myself—trapped by the reflection—but also, the faces of the lives I've taken. Every time it kills," he added, the waning light masking him in shadow, "it grows heavier." He gazed long upon the lurid skull-faced hilt. "I long to be free of the sword, but must endure."

"Why not cast it away? Be done with it? Are we not Ilmar? *We keep nothing but the bodies we are born into. We carry nothing but the sky on our shoulders.*"

"You sound like Ouranos." He laughed bitterly. "And you quote from Kjus beautifully, but you were born in the lowlands, and I the mountains. Many mysteries were taught to me and I was given purpose, to wield this weapon against the darkness or to guard it from evil—I know not which. Besides, you hold fast to that jade and gold sword, or is it a bow? Ilmar have no need of such fineries, I thought. It'd have brought a hefty sum, kept you from the alleys."

"I suppose you're right." She looked down, unable to meet his eyes. "I suppose the outside changes us. I was convinced that a good weapon is invaluable, for hunting and defense. Truth be told, I found it pretty, and I've never owned anything pretty."

"Two weapons in one? It *is* remarkable. How did you come by it?"

"I robbed a man," she said quietly, "before coming to Hedonia. He found me in the slums, dirty, bone-thin, and smelling of aurochs' dung. He took me in, fed and bathed me, taught me to take what I wanted. And then, well . . . he thought I owed him more than I could repay, and that I—*we* were good as whores. So many Ilmarin women have starved, I don't doubt the truth of it. So I left him in an alley, bleeding his last drop. This," she added, fingering the ornate jade pattern on the bow, "was his making. He was cunning and brilliant, and a bastard."

"You've quite a story," he replied. "Worthy of the songs."

"I've a talent for survival is all," she murmured. "Not like you. A hero. A legend. Everyone says those things about you. They call you the Batal. Is it true?"

He looked away. In the East, tall silhouettes of monoliths stood like men, watching, listening. "I . . . No," he said with finality. "There was a time when Ouranos and I roamed the lands to fight any man or monster that might challenge us. We were little more than children reveling in battle, proud as fools, mistaking our passion for truth. We'd save a village from a horg, stave off hordes of nerquii, quell the ravages of an angered god. But to what end, when a thousand other villages smoldered around us, when in time all our heroism came to naught? Maki, Mother Goddess of Battle, has a way of robbing a man of his ideals. When you watch a man die, well . . . the Batal is just a myth."

"Demacharon believed in you," she said quietly.

"It pleased him to think so, before ending his own life. Faith is for the dying."

She searched hard for a reply, and was surprised by the anger swelling in her throat. "Well, you're a miserable brooding bastard—you know that? I'm galled to think I ever looked up to you. If you want to know what I believe . . . I believe *belief* is all we have, to hold onto in these dark times. And if you're not Batal, then what in the gods' names are we doing out here? We could have abandoned Hedonia to its fate. But you chose to stay and fight, for outsiders, for people who scorn and hate us."

"I don't know. It felt like the right thing to do. I suppose it was more than just the sword that led me to the city." He let the silence sit between them as he looked for the truth within himself. "It was also the *why*," he added quietly. "It is said we live in a dark age, but why is that so, Thelana? Why do gods look upon men with such enmity? Why do they take from us that which is most dear? Learned men lived in Hedonia, I'd heard, priests and mystics with great libraries. If they could not answer me—who then? That is what I sought."

"You seek mysteries no mortal can know."

He stared at her meaningfully, but gave no reply.

"All the gods ask is that we endure."

"I know the adage," he said.

"Words of my Baba," she replied softly. "And it wasn't just a saying for us. He repeated it during the worst of times, when we hadn't a grain to eat, when the pain in our bellies was insufferable."

Embers turned to ash, to sinews of black, and it was not long before they existed by the bright glow of the moons and the flicker of stars. His intense pale topaz eyes returned her gaze. "What of your father?" he asked. "Does he still live?"

"It is what *I* sought in Hedonia." She shuddered again. "I was told it was a place of many peoples, of refugees without home, and also, a place of slaves. I hoped to find my family begging, or laboring under the lash at some monument. I did not find them and was again driven to theft. It was easy to take from the hardworking merchants. But I could see how it hurt them. The wealthy were well-guarded and invited death, but with the years I became more daring, so much so, that when I learned of the temple's treasures, I thought it could be done. With such wealth, nothing was beyond reach, even my family.

"My father wanted me to be strong, but at times, I fear, I am becoming like a stone, unfeeling." Her voice fell to a whisper. "Once I used to see my brothers and sisters, in my mind's eye. But I do not see them anymore. Even in my dreams, they are like phantoms." Despite her reluctance to show weakness, her words came in great heaping sobs, shaking her.

"Thelana," he murmured, pressing against her, stilling her heaving breast.

"Have I forgotten, Xandr?" she asked, facing him, her hands no longer hiding her streaming cheeks. "Have I forgotten them completely?"

"No," he said, and his rough edges dissolved in that moment, his eyes growing tender. "You have only to speak of them to remember." Ever so gently, he pulled her closer. "It's cold outside. Let us move into the tent."

7

THELANA'S TALE

"It's been so long since I've spoken of this," she began, her thin body lost in the folds of her djellabah, "actually, I've never spoken about these things to anyone. Where to begin?"

"At the beginning," he suggested. "Tell me of your childhood, so that I might also remember mine."

"The magnificent oaks and camphors and sycamores, and the colors of the ilms—by the Goddess—they were everywhere! They linger in my mind, yet it's been so long since I've laid eyes on them, on such trees, on such flowers. Our home was built from an oak. Old Man oak, we called it, and it'd stood for generations. How I loved to run its boughs, climb till the branches bent under my weight. The whole valley would open before me. Baba would yell for me to come down. Sometimes, I'd hide in the trees to escape his beatings." A smile crossed her lips and Xandr caught himself sharing it. "Other times, I'd stay up there, watching the stars and the moons dance across the sky.

"My brothers couldn't catch me either. I even bested them at wrestling, except for Borz. He was the oldest and showed little sympathy for my being a girl. Once I broke his arm. Baba gave me the worst beating for that. He used a switch and turned my butt red. I never shed a tear, though I felt so badly for Borz.

"I loved to follow Baba and the older boys, when they went hunting at dawn. Thanking the animal for the sustenance it provided, apologizing for its pain, the rites of passage into manhood—I also did those things, despite my brothers' protests. I even wore my braid to the side, till mother redid it in my sleep. My sisters helped with sweeping and milking and feeding, braiding hair and doing henna, all except me, and Britannia, the fifth born. We didn't care to take after the women. I wanted to matter, to be more than one of twelve."

"You had eleven siblings?" Xandr asked her.

"Five sisters, six brothers," she said without pause. "Even with all those children, mother never lacked for strength. And I helped her with the births." She laughed. "My brothers couldn't be in the same room with her on those days.

"Xandr," she said abruptly, "do you remember the days of the Solstice, when the moons and the sun became one? Do you remember the dancing and singing and the jumping of bonfires? When we joined hands, our family with others from across the valley, river and hill folk and mountain folk, we were one . . . one people."

"Thelana," he murmured. Buried under innumerable horrors, a faint tune played in his mind. "I was taken from the lowlands to live with the keepers. If I did witness the Solstice Night, I was too young to remember it."

"You were a keeper?"

"I was *supposed* to be."

"Oh." She was quiet, her eyes searching his. "Earlier, when you spoke of the Zo and of the forbidden knowledge, I didn't know what to think. We were simple farmers and knew little of that. The Mountain People were always strange to us. They talked funny—not that you do, I mean—"

"Your family," he interrupted, closing his eyes to dream her dreams, "can you show them to me?"

"Yes," she exclaimed. "I can see them now." She breathed deeply from her recollections, from joy and from despair. "For a time, a golden time, we were happy . . . I can't remember when or how things turned. We were always hearing about these terrible things happening in faraway places, rumors whispered at bedtime, stories told around the hearth, but Baba denied it all, and by sunrise all seemed well. I used to think . . ." and she laughed at herself, embarrassed by the admission, ". . . that the whole world was the valley and the hills and the surrounding mountains. Life was simpler when the world was small, when you could walk from one end of it to the other. Ilmarinen was the only thing we knew. We never imagined any evil befalling us. We were among the fortunate, perhaps the last of the families affected. Our house was built a days' hike from any other. Our remoteness kept us safe.

"Then things began to change. We no longer met others in the woods when we went hunting, and the ilms bloomed later in the year, covering less and less of the countryside. Clothed outsiders started to appear, which we'd never seen before. As hard as we worked, the land would not yield, not nearly enough. We had to sell the live-stock. I remember being angry at Baba for having nothing but potatoes. I blamed them.

Here she paused, and Xandr could see her fists at her sides, clenched.

"I remember the hunger. There were days when nothing else mattered, when food was everything. You could see it in my ribs, and in my knees. I think it's why I never grew ample breasts. Baba decided that he could not watch us starve. So he made the only choice left to him . . ." Her voice failed. "I—Xandr, I'm sorry. I thought I could be—*should* be—stronger."

He took her hand in his. "You see, Thelana," he said, "you are not a stone."

"Borz had twenty-two years," she murmured. "I remember the strangers that came asking for men with strong backs, offering food for children. Mana begged Baba not to do it. Bur Borz, he understood the sacrifice needed of him. He did it for us . . ." Her voice trailed off at the memory, soft as a falling petal. "We had grain for three cycles."

"Baba was never the same. He used to lift our spirits during the worst of times, make jokes. But after Borz was taken he became quiet. He would sit on the edge of the porch just rubbing his hands together. I remember his hands—they were always black from the hoeing and weeding. As for Mana, she became a shadow. I think she loved Borz most.

"With my eldest brother gone, I took it upon myself to do his duties. Baba didn't think much of it. He knew I was strong, but farm work is hard even for boys. I dug the trenches, turned the soil, and battled weeds till my hands were bloody. And I never let on how much I ached. He never gave me a kind word, but the way he looked at me, I knew.

"In my fourteenth year, soldiers came to our home. We didn't know anything about their war or the country their banner stood for, but they were wounded, some dying. Baba feared trouble would follow them, but he could not turn them away. They were children of the Goddess, he explained, as human as we, though I had my doubts.

"No enemies came to our door, but Baba still fretted. We were not to speak to them. Their ideas would sicken our minds, he told us, like the white weevils that eat of the trees and cause them to die from within. At first, I hated the outsiders. They laughed and pointed and leered at my sisters. Brutus was the worst, always trying to get one of us alone with him—I think he wanted to mate, like we were herd animals, without ceremony, without the bonding between families, without the rites accorded to the gods. Their captain, Aola, gave us protection. Even when she proved to me that, beneath all of that armor, we were no different, she was still more than human, so tall and mighty with her boots and her jerkin and that fine silk cape. I wondered why we didn't have such things. For a time, I started to feel . . . *naked* . . . and I hated myself. That other feeling, envy, poisoned my mind also, just as Baba had warned us it would.

"Aola taught me the common tongue, of places and things I'd never dreamed of, and of the bow and sword, which killed more easily than the spear or the atlatl. Later that year, I whittled my first bow from one of Old Man's branches, and used it to bring in more food. It was well and good, for a while."

Thelana paused, her face pained, contorted. She shuddered again, ruffling the folds of her covering. Xandr moved closer, feeling her breath on his face. "What happened after?"

"It doesn't matter," she answered. She looked with distant, wistful eyes, fixed to the past that played before her, and then her eyes glistened over. "I only wanted to remember my family. And I do." She sighed heavily, showing regret for the memories she had conjured.

"You haven't seen them since leaving home?"

She shook her head.

"Thelana," he murmured, "you're still shaking. But we can be warm." His tenderness caught her off-guard, made her suddenly aware that her oversized robe revealed a bare shoulder. As she fumbled nervously to find her hands within the sleeves, she could feel his warmth fall upon the round bare spot.

Xandr could no longer ignore the primal truth, the way her neckline curved into her chin, her braid falling like a silk rope against her freckles, her eyes made more dazzling emeralds by their wetness. She was nothing like the civilized women he knew, but raw as an uncut jewel, the hardship of battle and loss and hunger having beaten her face into sharp, elegant angles.

I love her.

But was it his loneliness, his lust, or the opportunity of the moment that made him feel so? "You have my mother's eyes," he murmured. "I don't know how I know this, but I do." His hands were rough, but she did not seem to mind his touch.

"If you're trying to give me a compliment, you're doing a terrible job." She shivered, and he wondered if it was because of the cold wafting through their tent, or something more. "Xandr, when you kissed me before, did you do it because, because I was . . . bleeding?"

"No," he said.

She scurried away, less than an arm's length. "I'm filthy. And I must smell like a goat . . ."

He smiled. Her face was in need of a good washing, but the tears and blood and dirt made her more striking, more alive.

"Then do it again," she whispered. "Kiss me this time like you mean it."

She could feel his finger under the supple flesh of her chin, tilting her face upwards. Her lips motioned to catch his, her eyelids closing mechanically, but in that instant a violent force sent her reeling. There had been no kiss. Light-headedness gave way to stiff rage, but what she saw when she looked again cut her breath short. Xandr was on one knee, Emmaxis fast in his palm, his pupils focused. He was no longer looking in her direction but at the opening, where a serpentine shape was skulking. A white blade poked through the small space, rending it apart, and all was concealed.

Crawling from beneath the collapsed tent, she could hear his anger.

"Villain!" he cried, wrestling the milky white blade from his face.

Frantic, Thelana looked for her bow-sword, but she could do nothing but stare, frozen, split between aiding him bare fisted or searching for her weapon.

Under the dim light of the gods, Xandr grappled with the ghostly hooded form, the milk-white blade, long and curved like a serpent's fang, emerging from his attacker's flowing sleeve.

"You shall not have it!" It was a strange voice, full of rolling 'R's' and throaty 'S's', but unmistakably familiar.

"Nesper!" Xandr cried, throwing him to the ground to reveal, by the light of the dying embers, the shadowy face of the nomad.

"It shall be mine!" Nesper cried, snatching his blade from the sand and lunging again with unnatural speed.

Xandr recoiled. Blood ran down his cheek.

"Away from him, monster!" Thelana was upon the assassin now, pinning his throat with her wrist, but he shrugged her off, smacking her across the face with a leathery fist. Xandr watched as she hit the ground with her shoulders, but he could not reach for her. Nesper stood between them.

"Why?" Xandr cried. His voice sounded far away, as if coming from someone else. Wiping his cheek, his hand felt heavy, slow. "Why do you betray us?"

"You feel it already, don't you, Xandr?" Nesper hissed. "The bile of my ancestors, coursing through you? It works quickly, does it not? It is the *purple death* you feel, and it awaits you all!"

Something was happening to him, she could see. He moved clumsily, as though the ground was teetering under his feet, where he looked for his sword under layers of canvas.

The nomad leapt into the air, djellabah fluttering, dagger curved down against Xandr's throat, but his body smacked hard against a round object and the impact sent Nesper back into the circle of embers. The ground quaked under Grimosse's hammer, but Nesper crawled, lizard-like, along the golem's arm, stabbing repeatedly.

The silence of the valley was disturbed with grunts and hisses and braying. "You shall not have it!" Nesper kept saying, in a voice that became less human with each passing syllable.

Grimosse replied, in kind, "You not hurt masters!"

Realizing the futility of holding onto his hammer, Grimosse let it drop, to crush Nesper in his arms. The dagger sank once more into the guardian's shoulder, breaking at the hilt, but the golem did not show pain. The nomad thrashed, limbs bending freely of joints, pupils growing to fill the whites of his eyes to black, until finally his hood fell away to reveal a face of scales.

"No!" the creature cried. "How is it you still live? Nothing survives the *purple death*! The Serpent's Eye, rod of my kings—it is to be mine." A snaking tongue, forked at the tip, smacked against Grimosse's toothy maw, waggling with desperation, then falling limp and lifeless.

Nesper's body remained still where Grimosse dropped it. Thelana turned from the spectacle to find Xandr. He was pale and stumbling, and she was unnerved by the sense of having witnessed the same event before, déjà vu, prickling the small hairs of her body.

"Are you all right?" she asked, knowing he was not.

"Only a scratch," he said, but it was much worse. Purple spots, thick as blood drops, were filling his eyes.

Rushing under him, catching him, she let out a cry. "What was he talking about? The purple death?"

"Poison . . ." he whispered hoarsely, and he became too heavy for her to lift.

The world spun around her as she bent over him, pounding her fists angrily, lovingly, against his breast. She swallowed her screams. The monoliths stood watching, ever silent and indifferent. Over the plain, the sun began to rise, giving dimension to the emptiness surrounding her, and the western hemisphere kept quiet its promise of a city, of any shelter beyond.

The desert was so vast. And she was alone in it.

8

THE CIRCLES

The madman sat against the concavity, drawing circles and mumbling. A few wisps of hair fought for dominance over his scalp, and his right eye was larger than his left, bulging over the red, watery lip that contained it. He smiled often, his brow folding into further creases, his mouth opening to reveal the many gaps between his teeth, and it only made him look the more insane.

Markings surrounded the two men. Walls and floor were covered white with chalk or dull crimson blood or etchings in mildew. Some of it was made with broad strokes. In other places, the writing was so minute as to be illegible, as if the man had overestimated the space given to complete his work. Writing overlapped other writing. Numbers and letters interwove without prejudice, often without spaces to separate one from the other. Lines connected script to circles and to circles within circles.

None of it made any sense, and the way in which he went about his work, as though his life depended on his efforts, confirmed that the man was without reason.

The blocks of stone against his back were unforgiving to the touch, poking out as though crudely constructed or dilapidated by centuries of neglect. Only the mildew offered comfort, which was slick and fetid and grown so thick that the color of the masonry, whether green or black, was difficult to discern. Stretching his legs, he stood to follow the wall with his fingertips, but nowhere could a straight angle be found. The only light was of a dull, distant source, filtering down from a circular opening. His eyes had taken a long time to adjust to the dimness, and the air was heavy with wetness, almost unbearably so, but he was thankful for it, for the moisture that managed to settle on his tongue. It was the only welcoming sensation. Everything else felt strangely unfamiliar.

Finally, the madman's incessant rambling broke his nerves. "What in the Mother Goddess' name are you going on about?"

"Oh," he replied, without lifting his finger, "not quite finished yet. Please, don't bother me."

"I'll bother you if I choose. Now turn your eyes upon me and give me an answer!"

"Great," the stranger intoned, exasperated, "you've gone and ruined my concentration! You think this is easy? That I can just up and do this stuff in my head?"

"All these . . . these damned circles! How does it help any?"

"They're ellipses," the man corrected, bent at his work.

"Be glib with me, will you?" Stomping forward, he erased the edge of the diagram with his feet.

"What did you have to go and do that for? Are you crazy?"

"Me? I'm not the one drooling over nonsense."

"Oh . . . why bother with explanations. Your feeble mind wouldn't get it. I think I preferred being alone."

"I did not ask to be imprisoned with a lunatic."

"Please, if you would be so kind, just leave me to my . . . as you like to call them, my circles. They are very important."

"How?" he screamed. "How can this be important? You're wasting time. How high are these walls? Maybe if you stand on my shoulders, I can lift you—"

"Impossible," he said without looking. "It's too high."

"How do you know? Have you tried? What if—"

"Sixteen feet, three inches," the madman cut in, "and our combined height is eleven feet, two inches. Even with my arm outstretched, assuming I had the strength to pull myself up, which I do not, I'd never make it. Now quit your rambling and leave me to my work, please."

"Is there no other way out? Are we trapped in here?"

"No and yes, in order of your questions—now leave me in peace."

"But what if I—"

"Aht, aht! The circles!" The man turned his back, pressed a finger against the wall, and continued to work.

"Those circles will never help us get out of here."

"Oh? Are you always so sure of everything? If only I had your assuredness."

Sarcasm? Really? He reached out in anger, before a bolt of agony shot up his arm, and he was forced to recoil. "Why am I . . . why does it hurt so?"

"They've been trying to break your spirit," said the madman, his finger rounding a perfect elliptical shape, "on the rack. But it's good to see you still have that spark of insolence, what got you here to begin with."

"Who are *they?*"

"You know . . . the ones who put us here."

"I don't know what you mean. I don't remember anything."

"Head banged up?" the madman questioned, then replied as if some third person had answered, "but not on purpose, I'm sure. Torture is more effective if you remember it."

"I've been tortured?" He looked at his hand again. It trembled.

"Aye," the madman said casually, "you lay there three days before waking to bother me."

"No, wait. I do remember." *Thelana.* "I was in the desert. I was attacked by a chameleon, a monster pretending to be a man, and then, all's black."

"The last thing you remember is the part of your brain that didn't get damaged. Could be what you remember happening was years, maybe decades ago. Everything between that time and now," and he made a *whoosh* sound with his lips, "gone."

Feeling suddenly humbled, Xandr sat back down before knowing he wanted to. "How much do you know about what's happened to me?"

"Not much," he said. "I first saw you when they brought you in. You put up quite a fight. But they're stronger than men."

"Who? Who are *they?*"

"Why, snake men, of course!" the man replied, his brow going smooth, "*Septhera.* And if you've forgotten them, I can hardly imagine how you can remember anything else."

"Septhera?" Xandr echoed. "But they went extinct ages ago, before the Great Cataclysm. Before the greater moon."

With an abrupt, jerky motion, the madman pulled away from his circles, mildew falling in clumps from his fingertip. He turned to Xandr, his face growing even paler, like the color of eggshells. "You know? You know of the Great Cataclysm?"

"Of course. I was trained by the Monks of Alashiya."

"This can't be!" the madman exclaimed. "Only I can divine such things. Unless you . . . did you by chance come across any strange angles, or curves?"

"Enough with your damn circles!"

"Ellipses," he corrected again. "Now listen to me—listen carefully." He gestured for Xandr to sit down, and leaned in, close enough for Xandr to smell the rotting of his gums. "I came here to study you, Batal."

"Why do you call me Batal?"

"That is your name, is it not?"

"I am Xandr of Ilmarinen," he answered. "The Batal is just a myth."

"No!" the madman protested, "the Batal is a man, the name your parents, *his parents*, gave him. The first of a kind, you see, a great ancestor of Xandr's. After centuries, the name became synonymous with many things. Champion, hero, martyr. It became an adjective—*he who stands up*. Or a verb—*to stand up*. Do you understand?"

Xandr searched the man's face for meaning, but could find little.

"Let me put it this way. Among other roles—that of mathematician, astronomer, philosopher, prophet—if there is such a thing—I am first and foremost a historian. You see, I am writing a book . . ." He hurried to a part of the wall, like a child eager to show off a drawing, loosening a block from its place. It fell with a thud in a cloud of dust. From the newly-made aperture, he produced a leather-bound tome. The face of the book startled Xandr—the skull depicted on the cover was an exact match of Emmaxis. "My life's work! I have come to this time to document your historic act. But already I've said too much! If I should reveal to you your future, you might not proceed accordingly, and then the universe might be destroyed!"

"I know you," Xandr said hazily. "You're Eldin, the First Prophet, founder of the Hedonian's religion."

The madman swatted the air in front of his nose, as if to disperse some stench. "I may be many things, but I am no founder of religions! Those small-minded fools will turn faith out of anything they don't understand."

"But you wrote of the gods, of Sargonus and Gulgola—"

"Gross poetic license," he replied. "You must understand that after a thousand generations of translations and interpretations, the original meaning is bound to get lost. Only this book, this book here, possesses a true record of Aenya."

"But that book of the High Priest . . . it predicted that doom would come to Hedonia, and that I would arrive to save the empire."

"No, no, no," Eldin exclaimed. "They got it wrong. Urukjinn had it all wrong. Don't forget that they called you a naked barbarian! It was the only way they knew to identify your people. But I never wrote that you, an Ilmarin, would save the empire. In the eyes of the priesthood, the empire and Aenya are synonymous. The truth is, you are meant to—" He gasped, twisting his lips around as if to lock up his mouth. "Shut up, Eldin! At this rate, I'll doom both this time stream and your own . . ."

Xandr took a step back and shook his head as though he'd walked into a cobweb. "Wait . . . the prophet Eldin died ages ago. Either the snake men shattered my brains, or your madness is infectious, that I could think you were the same man."

"Death is a moment," he answered, "but time is eternal."

"No more nonsense!" Xandr cried. "Tell me plainly, if you have power of reason—who are you and how came you by my name?"

"As you surmised, I am Eldin, and I've known you, at least the *you* you think you are, since Hedonia. Remember the sketch I made of you, the one Urukjinn was so fond of? I was there to see it, which is why I drew it here, from memory. How else can that be explained?"

"Damn you! You lure me into your web of insanity like a spider her prey."

"Is it truly so hard to believe? Look around you, Batal! Look where we are, a Septheran prison. You will cross their scaly hides soon, yet you know them to be extinct."

"But how can that be? None of this makes sense."

"When I was a younger man, just a few centuries from now, in the days of the Zo, whom you call the Ancients, I discovered certain angles in my studies that caused me to slip through the back doors of time. Since then, I've been lost. Lost in time." With his finger he drew a single long line in the muck on the floor. "You believe that time is linear and intangible, but that is only due to your limited perception. Suppose you were a two-dimensional being, possessing only length and width, you would perceive every sphere as a circle and every cube as a square. Just as you would be ignorant of the third dimension, you are ignorant of the fourth: time.

"Time is not linear, Batal. Nothing is. If you walk far enough down one path, it loops back around. Past, present, and future exist simultaneously like a never-ending labyrinth. Each choice takes us down a different passage in that labyrinth. My past may very well be your future, and my future your past."

Xandr stood, a little too quickly, sending reams of pain through his nervous system. "I won't listen to more of this," he managed, his voice turning to a low growl. "You're nothing but a simple prisoner, kept too long from the light of day. You must have heard my secrets in my sleep. I'd wager your name isn't Eldin."

"Do you not dream?" the man replied. "In dreams, the consciousness escapes the body. Free of dimension, your consciousness can go anywhere, revisit any time."

They shared a quiet moment, when all that could be heard was the patter of distant water against the rock, and as Xandr mused over the vividness of his dreams, he reconsidered the man's words. "There may be some method to your madness, some seed of truth to it. So what of me, then? How did I come to be here?"

"I do not know," he replied, peeling his scalp with black fingernails. "You obviously possess the body of your ancestor, the first Batal. But how this happened, I do not know. When I slip through angles, my physical being does not go with me. Matter is too big to fit through a wormhole!" He laughed uneasily to himself, at a joke Xandr could make no sense of. "I must leap into another's life, see through another's eyes. Before leaving this prisoner's body, I will meditate, still my heart below that of deep slumber, near death."

"I remember that I was," Xandr said quietly, "poisoned."

The man calling himself Eldin shook his head. "But that wouldn't have been enough. Could you imagine if, whenever someone went drinking hemlock, they'd end up in another time? The universe would be riddled with wormholes! No—there's more to it than that. You must have come across some very acute angles, a device of some sort that can warp . . . The *Serpent's Eye!*" he added with realization. "Yes! The Septhera used it as the source of power in their ship. It has the power to bend space-time, you see—"

Xandr clenched his fists, fearing for his sanity as he caught himself nodding in agreement. Why did he listen? Soon, he too would be rambling and drawing circles! He wanted to beat the man's wispy head against the wall, but willed himself against it.

"Look, it doesn't matter what you believe, only that you not change course from what you are to do tomorrow. If this time is altered, if you do not do what you were meant to do, all will be lost, and Xandr of Ilmarinen, possibly even Ilmarinen itself, may never even exist."

"You urge me to heroics, prophesy great things to come, yet all you do is scrawl gibberish on walls and draw . . . *el-lipses*. If you are indeed Eldin then Eldin is mad, and his prophecies ramblings."

With a sigh whistling through the gaps of his teeth, Eldin surrendered, combing the top of his head though his hair refused to straighten. "Of course, there is also the trouble of getting you back to your own age. If you should fail to return, there is no less at stake. I have been to your future. I have seen the *thing* with my own eyes, high in the mountain, the terror that has fallen to your world, your time, the darkness that walks . . ."

Xandr grimaced, as though someone had given him something sour to eat. *By the gods, there is no end to this!*

"All right," Xandr said, taking a long, deep breath, "but tell me one last thing. Why? I did not ask for this fate. Why was I chosen to be the Batal?"

"What was that?" Eldin's face turned shades of green as the dim light reflected from the grime-covered walls. "What makes you say you were chosen? The Batal is not chosen—it is a *choice*. You embody your great ancestor now, perhaps, because he made that choice, and his qualities reside in you. But nothing is preordained. There is no divine intervention. The gods, if they exist at all, are remote, impersonal energies. But when a great number of people suffer, they cry out, that a man might rise. Ultimately, the choice to rise is in the man who does or doesn't. Time could not exist without choice."

"But I'm just one man!"

Eldin's brow creased into thin layers like crumpled parchment. "The Batal is a star in the darkness. All the darkness in the universe cannot extinguish the light of a single star."

9

RACING SOLOS

Her unbraided hair spread across his face and torso like chestnut roots. Heavy tears ran the course from her eyes to the tip of her nose, pooling between his muscled breast, try as she might to withhold them.

Everything appeared more sharp and vivid in the morning thin air. Beyond the drop, the western expanse possessed a desolate beauty. The rising sun touched the surface, unveiling more of the land, boulders and gorges and far-off pinnacles in ruddy shades of gold. But no sounds of life came from it.

Grimosse seemed to think his master asleep, making no sounds of sorrow, and as he was not a creature of nature, no breathing came from his camel-like nostrils. Occasionally, Rurk made itself known, but otherwise the silence was pervasive, magnifying her isolation. Even the wind was deathly quiet, though she could feel its occasional stir.

Lowering her ear to his breast, she sensed the rhythm of his heart, the slow rise and fall of his torso. Pulling away, her hair cascaded over her face, veiling her grief, clinging to the wetness of her cheeks.

"Xandr," she whispered, "don't leave me just yet. There's so much I do not know. What is this weakness I feel when you are near me? Is this what they call love? How can I know for certain, without the bonfires of the Solstice Night and the gods in the stars to tell us so?

"You see," she said, leaning in as if to share a secret, "I returned to find my family but—I didn't find them, or anyone else, and I thought myself the last of the Ilmar, alone in this entire world. I never knew a man's touch, only loneliness, like no other has ever known, but then you came to me in my cell, at my darkest moment.

"Perhaps I am foolish, or naïve, but I do believe there's more meaning to this life than we know . . . and let gods be damned if in this dark age, if in this short existence, all we have that matters isn't love. We can have that. Please, you cannot go, for the gods cannot have smiled on you so often, just to let you die."

A chill came over her, and suddenly she saw the Taker, standing there in all his awfulness, in long tapering robes and with a grinning gleaming skull face.

She screamed. "Away from us, devil! You can't take him! I won't let you!"

But the Taker was quiet as death.

Finding her sword, she rushed headlong into the waiting arms of the Dark God. The blade slashed through the robes, cutting it to threads, but there was no flesh underneath to take wounding. Thelana battled with him, but he

merely stood and did not move against her, and she came
to understand the reason. The Taker had not come for
her. Shockwaves moved through her limbs and the sword
grew heavy. She collapsed, lifting wet eyes upon the Dark
God, and with broken whispers pleaded, "Away, away . . . I
beg you. Please."

The chilling presence was gone. As the sun's rays enveloped her, Thelana looked again to where the Taker had
stood, but did not see him, only the tent, cut to shreds.
The skull face had been no more than Xandr's sword,
dressed in canvas billowing in the wind.

What a fool she'd been! *Gather yourself, Thelana! Baba
would not wish you to act this way.* Her tears spent, she wiped
her cheeks with her knuckles, and looked out across the
desolate landscape as a fighter would an opponent.

If she was to survive this, and save him, she would have
to somehow reach Shess. But how far would she have to
travel? And in which direction? All she knew was that the
fabled city was in the West. She lifted herself, sheathed her
weapon, and carefully wrapped Emmaxis in the tent cloth.
She then approached the trike, carefully lest the beast become startled. It was still tethered to the small stake in the
ground. Fastened to its lizard belly were bundles of rolled
tents, kindling, salted meats, water filled gourds, a tinderbox, and a shovel. The trike had everything they might
need, and she could not hope to carry Xandr without it.
But could she command such a creature? As she pondered
this, she remembered the one monster who did obey her.

"Grimosse!" she called. "Am I not your master?"

He stood over her, shading her completely. His brut-
ish posture and the toothy grin cutting his face were

intimidating. At any moment, she knew, he might have squashed her like a beetle, but he replied, without pause, "Thelana Grimm's master. Grimm guardian. Grimm made to guard."

"Good," she said, putting every ounce of power into her voice. "I command you then: pull up that stake to release the trike, and if you can, subdue him."

The golem did as he was told. But restraining the saurian was not an easy task. With Nesper dead, Rurk awoke to confusion, tilting its enormous three-horned head to consider her, and then stumbling like a four-legged drunk in a cloud of rusty hues. Its thundering hooves and trumpet-like bray echoed over the canyon. Despite the golem's inhuman strength, Rurk tossed him like a child. Stubbornly holding to the saurian's reins, Grimosse twirled along the ground, and then became enraged. Hoisting his hammer up, he charged at the horn-plated head.

"No!" Thelana shouted. "Stop! I command you!"

The golem stumbled to a halt an arm's length from the trike's nose horn. Surging with power, Grimosse's shoulders rose and fell heavily. Reluctantly, slowly, he lowered his hammer. With little understanding, Rurk blinked and twitched its ears.

This won't do, the trike will kill him. She ordered Grimosse away, choosing gentleness over force. Calmly she approached, cupping her palms over the saurian's eyelids.

No reason to fear. It's just a big dumb ox. If you can plow an ox, you can ride this . . .

Rurk let out a terrifying bray that left a sharp ringing in her ears, but she did not flinch, and when she could hear again she moved to its side, unhooking an oversized gourd. Its mouth was hard, like a bird's beak, so that most of the water she tried to give it spilled to the ground. But its tongue was long and agile, lapping the pooling water like a mop.

"Grimosse, help me with Xandr. Set him on the trike, but be gentle."

"Master sleeps?" he said, draping the limp body over the beast like a fresh kill.

"Yes," she answered. "He's only *sleeping*." It was not entirely untrue.

"What Grimm do with snake man?"

"Leave him to rot," she said.

Already, Nesper's not-quite-human corpse was decomposing, turning black and leathery like a dead lizard on a paved road. "Grimm help rot!" the golem said, pounding the corpse to dust.

Having tamed Rurk, Thelana started preparations for their journey, finding a gourd small enough for her hands and extra clothing to shield from the sun. Amidst these items, there was a narrow tube containing a scroll. The papyrus was so aged and weather-beaten, it ripped even as she unrolled it. More carefully now, she smoothed its edges against the ground, discovering, in a crude hand, the relative positions of the moons and sun, various rifts and gorges and mountainous shapes. At the bottom of the scroll, far to the west, there was a word squeezed into a square in long, narrow, curving strokes, unlike any writing she had ever seen. But it was the sketch beside it that captured her fancy, a snake's head biting a gem. If it was a scepter, as it appeared to be, and not some smaller article of jewelry, the jewel would be as large as her fist.

Could this be what Nesper was after? What he attacked them for? The Serpent's Eye? Or was it some lost relic that even the people of Shess did not know of? A thought crossed her mind, conjuring a tiny smile—the map might lead her to the gem, and surely the people of Shess could work some magic to save Xandr, for a fraction of its price. And then they could live together like kings . . . if only there was enough time. Her thoughts turned grim again. Xandr's unconscious body still stirred, roped above the trike's rear legs. How long did she have before the poison set in? Could he still be saved? She watched him breathe and fretted.

Securing the bridle about the trike's front horn, Thelana managed her way onto the beast's neck behind its shell. Overhead, the striped tent posted to its shoulders swayed. Grimosse sat behind her, above Rurk's squat, front legs. Wrapping a scarf about her lips and nose, Thelana looked out across the Ocean once more and snapped the reins.

The trike felt large and clumsy under her control, but she managed to steer it toward the cliff's edge. It found footing, a narrow outcropping broad enough for it to descend, and continued downward. As the land passed far beneath her feet, Thelana watched with anxiety. Occasionally, a rock broke under the trike's hooves and plummeted. The cliff was as steep as a wall, the ledge cutting across it in a zigzag pattern, and she could not be certain whether at some point the trail would narrow to nothing, leaving them no choice but to go on foot and abandon Xandr.

The surface of the Ocean was baked to ceramic, forming a landscape of broken tiles. Waves of heat came off of it, making her feel like she was riding through shimmering waters. It was still early morning.

As the sun started to rise, the heat was like a fire, burning through her tent and the layers of her djellabah. Every now and then, gusts of air broke across her face like a blast from a furnace when coal is added to it. Breathing became painful and drinking an act of desperation that grew more frequent with time. The supply of water seemed sufficient for their journey, but her gourd became hotter with each moon passing and she was forced to bury it beneath rolls of carpet to keep it from boiling. Whether Grimosse suffered as she did, or had want of water, he did not say, and she was too feeble to turn and look at him, so feeble that a number of times she caught herself slipping off the trike's neck. Rurk never wavered. The shell over its head remained cool to the touch, and its scales seemed to deflect rather than absorb heat. Layers of fat as thick as a hundred-year oak tree, she surmised, protected the saurian's organs from roasting. One thing was certain—Nesper's saurian was indispensable. It not only carried much needed supplies, but kept her and Grimosse a good six to eight feet from the ground, which simmered as it cooked in the sun.

When the Eye of Solos ascended to its zenith, her fingers and the spaces around her lips began to blister, and she knew she had made a grave mistake, that she should have awaited nightfall. But if she had, could Xandr have survived the day?

To look across the tortured landscape was to suffer the hot air against her eyeballs. Each and every time she lifted her head, there was never any sign of Shess, and the same questions battered her mind, filling her with a current of dread. Was she going the right way? Would Xandr make it alive to Shess? How far now? There was also the inescapable thought that Nesper had lied, that there was no such city in the Dead Zones, that he'd led them, knowingly, to their deaths. If that were so, she and Xandr were finished, perhaps to leave Rurk and Grimosse to wander in search of new masters. But what choice did she have? There was no other direction she knew to go. And if Nesper had deceived· them, what of the map? Could that have been part of some elaborate ruse? No, she thought not. There was something out there, beyond the vale of fire, and she would find it.

She reached across Rurk's side to examine the scroll again. Whether any of the rock formations resembled those on Nesper's map, she could not see well enough to tell. The sun was too bright and the heat played tricks with her vision. Touching the cracked papyrus brought lumps to her throat. She swallowed dryly and it was like drinking sand. In a frantic attempt for relief, she spilled the gourd out onto her face, pulled extra garments over her head, and folded herself under Rurk's shell. But the sun was everywhere, burning through her concealed eyelids, blinding her white. She was riding into the sun itself, watching from without as her flesh burned away to reveal raw muscle and smoking bone.

She decided she could not go on, that she would die. Tugging at the reins, she brought Rurk to a halt and in that moment of uncertainty, something fluttered across her path. It came and went so quickly, she thought it a manifestation, but then it crossed again, with bright, flashing wings the color of fire. It perched atop the rim of the trike's shell, spreading its wings before the sun, and burst into flame. Even as it burned, the bird did not smolder. And Thelana remembered the phoenix from her homeland. It was the herald of Alashiya, a symbol of the nature of life. *When the ilm wilts, another takes it place. Out of death comes rebirth.*

The bird spun its head this way and that, seemingly indifferent to her, and squawked. It lifted with flaming wings and dove back down, poking its talons between the plates in the ground to fish out a serpent. With its prey squirming in its clutches, the phoenix vanished into the sun, leaving a small hole where the serpent had been.

If a snake could survive out here, so could they. "Grimosse!" she cried, eyeing the shovel fastened to Rurk's hide. "Dig us a hole! Quickly!"

The golem did as he was told, either unaffected by or shrugging off the effects of the surface. As if doing battle with Aenya, shards of ceramic flew from his hammer to reveal a soft layer of earth and clay. Against the clay, Grimosse found his hammer less useful, and started at it with his hands, before Thelana suggested the shovel. When the ground was cool enough for her to stand on, she dropped to her knees and aided in the digging, though the golem did the bulk of the work.

In a pocket beneath the surface, the three found shelter, Xandr flat on his back, Grimosse helping support the walls of their hollow, and Thelana snug between them. It was an uncomfortable arrangement, and when the ground shifted, clumps of earth fell in her eyes and mixed into her hair. From above, the dull thump of Rurk's hooves assured her that their mount was still there, without which they could not hope to journey forward or backward. But it was also unnerving that a stray step might bring the whole weight of the trike upon them.

Among Nesper's belongings, she found long strips of cloth to bandage her hands. Her lips fared no better, swollen and tender with blisters, which she had also been foolish enough to leave uncovered. In Ilmarinen, there was a leaf her mother knew to make into a medicine for just such an occasion, but she could not imagine such a plant existing anywhere anymore. Remembering the serpent, Thelana did not sleep easily, checking and rechecking the ground for holes. She found none, but what she did find, digging deeper with her fingernails, were curved bits of gravel, white and soft as bone, some lined with grooves, others in swirling patterns.

Seashells.

What were shells doing here, when there was but one Sea? Could a river have cut through here once? Could there be water somewhere in this hellish place?

In this way she continued, hiding in holes during the day, running from the sun at night. When the sun began its descent into eclipse and the heat came within her tolerance to endure, the race against Solos began. But the further she moved into the West, the lower the moons dipped on the horizon and the shorter the nights. Thelana did not know how much time she had between sunrise and sunset, only that it lessened with each outing, giving her fewer passings to travel. Sometimes, the phoenix circled overhead, or soared ahead as if leading them.

The shells, she discovered, were not an anomaly. She found them in every hole, in a layer beneath the Ocean, as numerous as the pebbles on the Bay of Sarnath.

Even in his unconscious state, Thelana drew strength from Xandr, knowing he could not survive if she were to fail to reach the city. It was her purpose. His face, despite his beard and hair and her best efforts to conceal it, was turning red with white, thumb-sized blisters. She was no more attractive, she knew, but made light of his appearance anyway, during the night as he slept beside her. As Grimosse was little better at conversation than her unconscious partner, Thelana told Xandr of her hopes and fears and dreams, as he lay motionless and unresponsive. She described Shess as she imagined it, with great fountain pools and towering structures built to resist the sun's devastating rays, and comfortable rooms with servants and fruits piled on silver dishes. She came to expect that her brothers and sisters awaited them, as if she had set out to meet them. They would greet her with smiles and open arms, and there would be dancing and a feast to last the whole of the night, and Borz would make some boorish jest as he often did, making her and her sisters blush—and her mother would be there also, and her father to admonish him.

Many nights came and went and Thelana's spirits lifted. In the clear light of morning, horse-shaped pinnacles could be seen like those on the map, a ring of mountains resembling a chariot with six drowning horses, or so she imagined it, perhaps from something she'd witnessed in Hedonia, though she could not place the memory. She made for them with renewed fervor, but the nights were shorter than ever and the distance greater than she estimated. After digging half a dozen holes and half a dozen nights of sleeping, or waiting sleeplessly under clay and rubble, she reached the foothills of the horse-headed mountains. In a grotto beneath a hill she dubbed *Drowning Chariot,* she found shelter without having to bury herself, for which she duly thanked the Goddess. From that point onward, the once-empty country unfolded, revealing other formations identifiable on her map.

A number of days passed before she could bring herself to abandon the mountain shade. She navigated by the various landmarks until coming to a gorge, and a bridge she supposed was placed by the gods. The gorge rent the desert in half and dropped to depths beyond the sun's reach. With no way around it, she drove Rurk across, walking beside the saurian to lessen their combined weight. Distant winds sang to her from below, forcing her to look down, to contemplate collapse. Who would ever find her body, should she fall? She would decompose in the sun, never to nourish new life, for nothing could thrive in such a place.

For a half-passing before reaching the opposite side, she prayed that the land bridge hold the saurian's weight. She went no further, camping along the ridge without having to dig a hollow, as the gorge provided a refreshing updraft of cooler air. That night she dreamed there were ten suns in the sky, bearing down on her like evil, sentient things. Not one of her arrows missed their mark as each sun burst into showers of glass. When all ten were gone, her djellabah fell away, and she stood naked in the cool blackness of night, and like a goddess she walked among the cold constellations, hand-in-hand with Alashiya.

In the light of dawn that followed, she saw it, a broken line etched across the horizon. She'd seen it a thousand times in her mind, but now it was there, in the real. She might have wept if she had the capacity.

"We made it, Xandr! It's the city, thank the gods!" She whipped the saurian vigorously, unwilling to suffer another night buried under rubble. Rurk could not move quickly enough.

The closer she came to it, the more beautiful it seemed. The city stood against the sun in a halo of color, a fiery aurora of reds and oranges and violets. As the moons swam across the sky, with each of Rurk's stomping hoof falls, the city became better defined, its structures more distinct and recognizable. Homes were built in clusters like bricks, piled one atop the other, single and double rooms of clay and rock. Leading into its center, were remnants of paving, from what had once been roads, and there were taller buildings beyond with multiple sections, with balconies and arched causeways, and hexagonal towers with stepped walls leaning into the sun. But something was amiss. In all her excitement, she did not see, or to hold to that moment of hope, had blinded herself from seeing.

There were no doors in Shess, nor shutters, only open spaces in walls. Any wood framing that might have existed had rotted to nothing ages ago. Any plants that once flourished left no trace of ever having been. There was none of the sound of a bustling, thriving populace, nothing but the murmur of shifting sand in the wind. An eerie, dead calm pervaded everything.

As if sitting on the trike was somehow clouding her vision, Thelana dismounted and continued on foot. Grimosse called to her, but she dismissed him with a wave. She wandered streets, searched in doorways, shaken by an awful sense of déjà vu. She was alone, but some growing sense of dread kept her from uttering a word. At last, her mind succumbed to the reality.

Nobody's lived here for over a thousand years.

Shess was a dead city.

10

ESCAPE FROM THE SNAKE PITS

Separated from the light of the sun and moons, in the long stretches of inactivity, time became a stranger, and Xandr found himself welcoming the bizarre notions suggested by his prison mate. Whether passings came and went, or days, or cycles, neither of them could tell. It was not long before the revulsion he felt for his companion changed to affection. He asked many things of Eldin, sometimes repeatedly, of the meaning of the ellipses, of time and space, and of the history of their predicament. He asked about the Septhera, about their height and how well they could see in darkness. And when Xandr was satisfied with the answers, he would sit quietly and let his mind travel.

There was nothing to entertain his senses but the slight dimming or brightening of their hollow and sounds made faint by the masonry around them. What little could be heard only served to stifle his hopes—the rattle of chains, the groan of portcullises, and screams of such pitiable nature as to turn his blood to ice.

Mind, body, and spirit began to atrophy. Panic set in as he realized what was happening to him and Xandr did what little he could to fight it. He ran in tight circles as much as he was able, punched walls until his knuckles turned tender, jumped, clawed, and thought up designs for climbing devices.

Darkness and silence swallowed him whole. He felt himself descending into a serene nothingness. Piece by piece, he felt his sanity slip away, and he welcomed the sensation. There was comfort to be found in madness, a barrier against misery. And in the realm of memory, Xandr found escape, and there was also the joy of having known another, a strong woman born of the Ilmar. He traced her every line and curve in his mind's eye, and those lines held firm against the lure of oblivion.

He awoke with a start to the nearby clank of iron. A pair of lights emerged from the gloom above, shifting over him, and a chain came down against the wall. Without hesitation, his fingers hooked through the links, and though slick with blood and grime, he managed to climb it and roll over the lip of the pit. As the space spread about him, he followed the chain to its source, discovering that it was not tied to any object, as he at first imagined, but to a leathery fist.

The creature was crimson, with yellow diamonds bands, a head taller than Xandr and broader in torso. Its body was more angular than any human, with bones nearly poking through it, and its inverted ankles gave the impression that it might pounce at any moment. The tail, which made for half its length, swayed and coiled like an enormous serpent, and Xandr did not doubt what Eldin had told him, seeing with his own eyes the race that held them captive. But the Septheran was nothing like the nomad who had betrayed him. The thing that stood before him was more monstrous. Nesper was but a distant cousin.

Unflinching, Xandr accosted the creature, though he found it difficult looking into the black reflective orbs that were its eyes. "What do you want from me?"

It gave no answer, but quivered with violent energy, peeling back its muzzle to reveal fangs like daggers. Its hand fell like a mailed glove across Xandr's face and his back hit the ground. Pink blood oozed from his lips and a pair of teeth tumbled from his mouth and onto the cold stone flooring like dice. The Septheran's stance was unchanged and Xandr understood that he, a human, was something inferior to those serpentine eyes, that he was not one with whom to do battle, but punish, like a child controlled by an abusive parent.

"Do not bother reasoning with him," came a voice from below. "The Septhera have no ears!"

As the spool of iron unraveled between the snake man's hands, Xandr realized that he was to be taken, to be tortured again or executed. But he would not go willingly. Finding strength in his limbs, he flew up, shoulder and fists against the monster. Its scales were like worked leather, impervious to his pounding. When his blows failed, he continued with a grapple, pushing the snake man toward the pit. Limbs intertwined, muscles strained, and a horrible hissing and rattling echoed throughout. Soon, Xandr found himself pinned between its arms and chest, gums folding about his skull, milk-white fangs dripping onto his cheek. The Septheran's deep-set eyes gleamed like a predator's before the kill and then Xandr could feel it—the chain still dangling beside his fingertips. He grabbed it, looping its links around the monster's neck, wrestling to turn his weight into the chain. The Septheran thrashed, clawing, biting, tearing ribbons from his skin, but Xandr did not loosen his hold. The forked tongue lashed from side to side and straight up, quivering like a fishing reel, until, eventually, it lolled lifelessly against its maw.

Assuring himself that the creature no longer stirred, Xandr let the spool through his palms and the snake man dropped with a thud. He shuddered, looking over what he had killed, and beat the body with his fists until his blood-lust was spent, letting the snake man tip into the pit in a mass of broken scales.

"The Batal triumphant!" Eldin exclaimed. "Now be gone before more of them arrive!"

Xandr crouched by the edge overlooking the old man. "Wait, I'll lower the chain to you—"

"No," said Eldin, "let me be."

"There's no time for your madness," Xandr replied. "Take it and climb."

"I am not built like you, Batal—my arms are feeble."

"Then I'll carry you!" Xandr asserted.

"No," said Eldin again, "flee while you can!"

"You old bastard . . . you'll rot in there!"

"We will both rot if you do not go! Besides, I have my own exit planned—my ellipses, remember? Now go. History awaits you. Do not fail us!"

If the madman was insistent to remain, Xandr could not save him. Perhaps it was best, as he did not wish to be hobbled by the old man's emaciated limbs.

"I will return to you," he called down at last.

With the chain heavy about his shoulders, Xandr tried to regain his bearings, but his mind was numb, fragile. The whole of the chamber reeked of decay and the air was stale and thick. Rows of pits spread before his feet. Walls faded in and out of the charcoal darkness.

No exit made itself apparent. There was but a faint glow, emanating from his left, and in this direction he started out, hammering the numbness out of his feet as his soles struck the slick floor. Images assaulted his eyes, things he wished to keep from seeing but could not. Within each of the hollows, like the one he had abandoned Eldin to, there were men, or pieces of men: bloody, deformed, dismembered. As Xandr moved past the pits of the living, those that were able lifted their voices, but their words, unused for so long, failed to form coherently. Against the urging of his compassion, he moved beyond them, abandoning them to their misery. Wails of desperation followed him, each voice rising to form a symphony in his ears. He shut his eyes, steeled himself, and fled away from the pleas and the sounds of suffering, toward the light and quiet.

He stopped for a moment, cupping his knees, breathing hard, shaking the eeriness from his limbs. And there, directly below his feet, he could see the most fortunate among the prisoners—corpses with festering flesh, feasted on by maggots, or white-boned with hollowed eye sockets still looking upwards for salvation. The natural torments of aging were unfolding in succession, as if the Septhera had arrayed their prisoners to make some sort of morbid statement, beginning with the height of vitality and youth—himself—to the aged and infirm, Eldin, to the final pits ending in death and decay. Where was the sacred spark of the Goddess? Existence did not end in death, he knew, but in the Goddess, in rebirth. The faith of his people gave him courage as he moved further toward the light.

An arch met him where the dungeon came to an end, opening to a tunnel through which the light that had guided Xandr had emanated. He paused to find his breath, and to thank the Mother Goddess. No sooner than when he did so, a pair of shadows crept along the open passage. In the gloom, Xandr mistook them for women. They were as short and slender as Thelana, but in the light he could see they were not human, but serpentine creatures with breasts and human-like hips, their hides glistening in crimson, yellow ovals lining their tails. Their bobbing heads paused sharply upon him, and with a hiss and a rattle, they brandished their elegant, sickle-like swords.

Instinctively, Xandr reached for Emmaxis, but its hilt no longer straddled his shoulder. With his sword, he could do away with the Septheran women, but armed only with a chain, he became fearful. He stepped away as they slinked closer, corralling him as if he were a dangerous animal, and forcing him back into the dungeon. At his heels, an empty pit waited. Their broad swords were at the ready, one high at the shoulder, the other low at the waist. Their mouths cut seamlessly through their round heads and their eyes were mere absences. Without faces, he could not read their intentions, determine whether they were angered by his escape, or as fearful of him as he was of them. All he could do was watch for sudden movement and try and calm his heart. They hissed threateningly and their limbs

swayed, their movement like silk in the wind, their inverted ankles creeping closer to him. Xandr remained steadfast, the rusty chain spooled about his knuckles. He knew
they had every advantage—full bellies, armor-like scales,
and the reach of their sickle-like swords—and the thought
occurred to him that they may not wish to kill him, but to
keep him imprisoned, that to fight would mean his doom.
But one thing was certain in his mind—let the Taker claim
him, he would not go back to the pits! His only chance was
to hold against them, so he waited until, in an explosive
blur, the more forward of the two went flying at him. With
little room to maneuver, he moved to her flank, raising
the chain over his face. The iron links snapped tight between his fists, directing the blade away from his nose, the
sword's momentum carrying it downward to spark against
the rim of the pit. Dashing past her, he ran into the arms
of the second Septheran, who guarded the exit. Her sword
slashed the air between them and Xandr saw that he was
trapped between the two.

In his other hand, the chain spun like a mace, clashing
with the sword, wrapping around the blade. With a tug,
Xandr sent the sword across the floor. It teetered over the
pit, its curved point tilting to and fro. As she clambered
to retrieve it, Xandr hurled atop her bulbous spine, forcing all his weight upon her. She convulsed, twisting and
writhing in ways impossible for a human, her scaly touch
making him shudder. Her tail snaked about his thigh, his
waist, his throat. Her claws raked his chest as her head
throbbed and her mouth snapped between his hands. It
was a grotesque match of strengths and wills. And yet, he
managed to distance himself from her fangs, battering

the floor with her skull. Then the sickle, balanced over
the edge, circled around, so that the pommel now dangled
over the pit, and on the blade's surface he saw himself. For
the first time.

He recoiled.

It's not me! By all the gods, I am not me!

Stunned by his reflection, the snake woman wrestled
free, but the sword was lost to the pit. He heard the chink
of the second sickle strike the floor beside his head. It was
the other of the two. Her blade was lodged in the stone,
and as she tugged at it, his elbow fell hard and fast against
her face, and her sword was his. In a flash of silver, her
small round head rolled away in a spray of blood.

Only one female remained, and she was without a
weapon.

He stared her down and spat, brandishing his chain in
one hand and the sickle-blade, still oozing with the blood
of her fallen comrade, in the other.

Undeterred, she launched herself at him, fangs gleaming and claws hooked, but he was ready, pounding her
with a fistful of chain. She fell to the floor and sprang up
again, only to be shouldered into the pit.

With the threat of the Septheran females gone, Xandr
surrendered to his exhaustion, letting the chain uncoil.
But the sword he kept, lifting it hesitantly to his face. Had
he seen what he thought he had seen?

His reflection was a stranger, but not terribly unfamiliar to him. The basic features of his face were similar—
cheekbones, lips, hair, beard—and yet, it was not the face
he knew. It was almost as if he had changed appearances
with a close relative, a brother or a father. As he strained

to recall Eldin's words, a whoosh came from behind and his insides erupted. He stumbled forward in agony, the sword slipping from his fingertips to crash and wobble on the floor. Even as he turned to see what had hit him, his vision was failing. But he could still hear her, that awful hissing.

She jumped. The Septhera can jump higher than a man, you fool!

It was his only thought before succumbing to the pain.

He was not meant to die, that much he knew. The blade had cut between his organs with surgical precision, to maim him. But to what end, he did not know—perhaps, he thought, to further torment and humiliate him. As the strength drained from his body, he resolved to steel his mind against them, to remain defiant in word and spirit for however long he could. He accepted that somehow he was living as an ancestor and was supposed to do great things. But what could be done to better such a world?

Gravel tore his knees as he was dragged from chamber to chamber. He shut his eyes tightly, as if the horrors might seep under his eyelids, but he was also seized with a compulsion to face those same horrors. He came upon bodies, rows and rows of them, hanging without discrimination for age or gender, on hooks from chains, the flesh loose and shriveled like animal hides. The images invaded his consciousness, and the walls of hatred and anger he had built to shield himself from despair began to founder.

As daylight pained his eyes, he came to know how deeply he had been imprisoned. Forced to his feet, he was made to stumble along, blind to all but a white glow. His other senses made up for what he could not see. The air was heavy, warm and wet, which he found pleasing despite the circumstances, and the aroma of rain filled his lungs.

Gradually, his eyes adjusted to the brightness. A vast network of plants and masonry surrounded him. Leaves laden with dew sprouted between paving stones, and roots spread over the floor, and the trunks of strange trees grew through spaces in the roof. Vines hung from walls like curtains, heavy with mammoth-eared fronds. Corridors moved through an overgrowth of greenery, bridging inner and outer courtyards, and great arches opened to the sky, to sharp hills and sloping valleys.

He was being led through an area of collapsed architecture, a place where lizards crossed freely at their feet and bird-sized dragonflies buzzed lazily overhead. A recollection of joy surfaced at the sight of such abundant life, but none of the plants were familiar to him, and even the trees he thought he could name appeared alien upon closer inspection. Even the sun glowed with a strange, whitish hue, and the greater moon, ever present in his world, was nowhere to be seen, which only served to confirm the impossible, that he was not in his own time, but in the distant past, in the age of the Septhera.

Further ahead, the walls joined to form a single chamber, dimly lit by beams of sunlight cutting through the mist. Every surface was painted with glyphs, but the vines made them difficult to read, and Xandr wondered whether the complex had been built by the Septhera or if it was some ruin from an even earlier civilization. Heavy columns led toward a congregation. There must be hundreds of them, Xandr thought dreadfully, as varied in length and in color as the snakes of his time. Some were as colorful as the striped coral, others spotted with diamonds or ovals. Most lacked attire, but some, in particular the females, ornamented themselves in dull gold armlets, wristbands and pendants. The warriors were armed with curved swords and daggers, sickles and short throwing axes. Pressing closer, he could discern nothing from their inexpressive faces, even as they continued to direct their slick, colorless eyes at him, the lone human in the room.

Above him there was a dais and a throne. The creature sitting upon it was of such elegant shape and color, Xandr thought him perversely beautiful. His scales—like tiles of ivory and gold—were artfully arrayed, and his head was broad and flat and framed by an elliptical membrane— a cobra's hood. In the king's hand was a serpent-shaped scepter and in the serpent's mouth was a fist-sized jewel, blood red, and glowing like a kerosene lamp, bending light in seemingly impossible directions. Objects surrounding the jewel were made to appear at odd angles, like reflections in a broken mirror.

Before the king, the Septhera stood deathly still, but for the undulating motion of their tails. Xandr could feel a point enter his back, forcing him to the center. Remembering Eldin's prophecy, that he was to do great things—historic things—it occurred to him that his destiny had come at last. With a few leaps, he could be at the king's throat, but would the strength of his hands be enough? How could he do such a thing, without a weapon, amid so many? And was it even what he was supposed to do?

They tugged at his hair, forcing his eyes upon the cobra king. The scepter's glow cast swirling glimmers about the Septheran's pupils, which were round and black like beads dipped in ink, and Xandr was powerless to avoid them. In that moment, something clammy began slithering around in his head and he could feel a voice enter it, as if by force.

You've killed two of my children and maimed another. This is curious.

Even though the king's mouth did not move, he could hear him. The voice was flat and calculating, each syllable stabbing his brain like needles.

Xandr wrestled with his weakened body, forcing himself to an upright posture. "Who are you? Why have you imprisoned and tortured us?"

By humans, I am called Pharaoh. You may also. But I do not understand your question. We do not imprison or torture—you are herded and maintained. You are livestock. It is the way of things. The stronger species feed upon the weaker.

Though it explained everything he had seen Xandr recoiled at the revelation, doubling over to vomit, though nothing but spittle came from his lips. Regaining his composure, he continued, "How can you call us livestock? Are we not thinking, feeling?"

The cattle you slaughter also think. Also feel. But you are deaf to their thoughts. It is true that you are more evolved than simple beasts—humans that show intellect live as slaves. You have shown great promise for your cunning and strength, so you shall be taken to stud with the females of your species.

Memories of Thelana flickered in his mind. He thrust his body toward the dais, bounding for the throne, and was struck down. The blow came to his abdomen so swiftly he did not even see which of the snake men had struck him. As he collapsed against the steps, he knew there was no plan of attack he could devise that would go unforeseen. They could sense his every intention. Only his disgust and rage, his compassion, the Septhera seemed to have no comprehension of.

"No!" Xandr cried, beating his bosom. "You are history. I have seen it! Such cruelty cannot be endured!"

You think us cruel? When we arrived on this planet, we had never before encountered a species so bent on self-destruction. It is a trait absent in our people. Septhera do not slaughter each other for want of territory. We are not the cause of your suffering. Rather, we've quelled it, directing your efforts toward productive labor. Those who would have died wastefully in war are now made to supply our *need for food.*

Too weak to lift himself, Xandr planted his arm down, the weather-beaten stonework coarse and hard against his palm. "We have the right to kill each other! You . . . pernicious devil . . . do not! I choose self-destruction over slavery. I choose freedom!"

This is unfortunate. Despite your physical qualities, your rebellious nature cannot be allowed to be passed to future generations. No matter, I have chosen for you a nobler fate. You shall be used for sport in the Arena, where you shall meet my brother and have the honor to die the purple death by his venom.

So he was to be taken away, he realized.

Is this what you intended for me, Eldin? If so, I have failed you. And mankind. Xandr's mind chased answers that were not there. Even with Emmaxis, he could not fight so many. "I may die," he said, "but the gods hear men's prayers. So may the gods damn you— damn you to forever crawl the earth!" It was an empty threat, but he could do no better.

A boy approached the dais. He was so skeletal, Xandr hardly recognized him as human. With a tremble, the boy set a bronze dish on the arm of the throne. The dish kicked as if alive, writhing with fur and tails, and the Pharaoh lifted a rat from it, feeding its whole squirming body into his mouth.

Your species is young, human, and you still cling to false theories. There is no justice in this universe but that which is set by the natural laws of chance. There are no gods. You pray to no one.

11

SANCTUARY

First came the Xexaz
And the Quid bowed to them
And the Ilman bowed to them
And the Septs bowed to them
But with Time the Septs envied
And stole the fire of the stars
And stole the words from the minds
And the Life from the Xexaz
Now the Quid hid in the waters
And the Ilman of the mountains in the clouds
And the Ilman of the woods in the woods
But the Ilman of the land hid in himself
And became Man
Then was the Septs
And Man bowed to them.

—From Glyphs on a Septheran wall

L ooking back across the Ocean, Thelana could see further than before. Monoliths from days past emerged in the morning light as distant silhouettes. The city was on high ground, the elevation increasing so gradually that she had not noticed it until now.

Seeing Rurk shake its head gave her comfort in that something other than herself and Grimosse possessed breath—if the constructed mass of flesh, in fact, did breathe. She tethered the saurian under the shade of what remained of a fortification wall and commanded the golem to bring Xandr down.

"Soon, my love, we will find sanctuary." But she feared it would not matter. She had no knowledge of poisons and he could not survive without an apothecary. It was enough of a miracle that his heart still made a faint sound against her ear.

With Xandr's swaddled body slung over his shoulder, the golem followed her around the barren streets of Shess. She no longer expected to find any living person, but hoped that a temple of some sort might serve as better shelter than a hole and a mound of dirt. Most of the structures were four-walled and rectangular, but these were of the rural outskirts. Towards the city center, the streets broadened and walls became higher, and evidence appeared of a more sophisticated civilization. Having become nearly indistinct by the decay of time, Thelana thought the lumps of limestone scattered here and there to be collapsed architecture or rocks quarried from the surrounding mountains. Upon closer inspection shapes emerged: fragments of an obelisk, saurian sphinxes turned half to sand, giant feet cloven at the ankle. Her curiosity piqued, she followed the path made by the strewn pieces of statue, here a kilt the size of a house, there part of a fist clenching a bit of staff. But the body had inhuman qualities to it. Its ankles were backwards, its hand covered in scales, and its nails looked to have once been pointed. She resisted coming to the dreadful conclusion that lurked at the recesses of her mind, and assumed that the ancient people of Shess had been a strange race of men who preferred to depict their gods as monsters.

An avenue of sphinxes led toward the central square and to a domed structure, the largest to be found in the city. She headed towards it, passing marbled corners suggesting magnificent temples, and gates opening to nothing, and columns supporting empty sky. Soon, dirt gave way to paved road. On her left, a wall of massive proportions rose, its far end fading in the distance. If she had never been witness to the monuments of Hedonia, she might have thought it built by giants. What the wall was for, she could not guess, but it curved as she moved along it. Through its broken façade, rows of steps could be seen, spanning the entirety of the circular structure. It was a coliseum. Games were played in such places.

Thoughts of play eased her apprehension. Sport was something familiar, pleasant, reminding her of home. She remembered beating her brothers in foot races, and in swimming contests, and in climbing. The Ilmar were fond of athletics, believing it strengthened the body, which was sacred. Surely, something similar took place here, ages ago. But as the great monument at the city center came into view, she took a step back. Though scored by winds and heat for untold centuries, its likeness was unmistakable.

The head of a cobra rose like a mountain from the desert. Its shadow fell on her from more than a hundred paces, the sun lingering over it like a fiery crown.

The sun!

It was high. Too high. Captivated by the ruins, and with the city walls shielding much of the heat, she had not noticed the sun creep along the sky. In a fraction of a moon passing, the sun would reach its zenith, and no shade would suffice enough for survival.

"Grimosse!" she cried. "Run!"

She sprinted and stumbled, her feet catching in her flowing robes, and just as quickly lifted herself and took off again. She was unaccustomed to running in anything but bare feet, but the ground was still too hot for her soles. Dust billowed up around her, obscuring her vision. Whether Grimosse followed with Xandr's body, she could only listen and hope for. Slamming into the wall under the mouth of the cobra, she came to a stop, breathing hard. The jaw of the idol, or monument, or whatever it was, loomed high above her, and the air was cool as the sunlight had yet to reach the tiles below. She searched for an opening, an arch or entryway of any kind, finding none. She wrapped her knuckles against the stone, but it was of solid granite and returned no sound. Could the structure be nothing more than a hill, cut into the form of a snake's head? If that were so, she had no time to seek another place of shelter. As Grimosse approached, she bid he place Xandr against the wall, and searched the golem in a panic.

"The shovel? Where's the shovel!"

The monster gazed at her with a puzzled expression. "Master did not say to bring shovel."

"You idiot! You should always have the shovel!" she scolded him. "You brought your hammer, why not the shovel?"

"Grimm always has hammer," he replied. "Grimm made to guard."

Her hands clenched to fists, but he did not blink even as she pounded him. "There's nothing to defend against here! Solos is our enemy, Grimm. We can't fight the sun with a hammer . . ." But there was nobody to be angry with. The golem could not be expected to think—the fault was entirely hers and she knew it.

"Grimm bring shovel now?"

No, she thought without answering, *there's no time.* She studied the ground at their feet. It was worked tile and as tough as granite. "No way to dig through this," she murmured. "We're going to die . . . Xandr's going to die. Unless . . . Grimm, help me search for an entrance!"

A ring of sweat formed across her brow. As her fingers brushed centuries from the wall, a bas-relief came into view, of men and snake-headed gods, of trikes and other saurians. She paid the images little heed, her only concern in finding shelter, but she could not help but notice the details as they were revealed.

Why were there so many gods? Gods everywhere? It couldn't be. No, not gods, a race—a race of snake men, like Nesper. He was one of them.

The sun's growing intensity illuminated the stone, and she stepped back into the cascading fire to behold the story in its entirety. Armies of snake men clashed with armies of mankind. Humans were kneeling, being hacked to pieces, their limbs being devoured. Further along the wall, skeletons—no, she'd seen herself like that before, emaciated by hunger, bone skinny—people were forced into pits and made to carry stones on their backs. And there was more to the story, much more. But Thelana had no time to study it. As the heat continued to rise, she felt her strength slip away, each inhale becoming short and sharp. She decided to search another part of the wall. Here was an array of precious stones, round and small as her thumb, of beryl and lapis lazuli. Brushed clean of sand, the glittering stones formed circles and ellipses both intersecting and concentric, and there was something familiar in the way they were arranged. She had spent enough nights on the limbs of Old Man to recognize their various patterns—they were the constellations. Nothing in Shess was made at whimsy, she surmised. Perhaps, if she could find some meaning among the constellations, the entrance would present itself. She shoved one circle inward and the shape gave way, receding into the wall. "The moon," she muttered.

The little bit of shade that remained was diminishing and her time nearly spent. She found Grimosse, who appeared to be loafing, and screamed. "Grimm, help me push these circles."

One by one, two by two, the circles were pressed. But nothing was happening. She knew that given the correct combination something would trigger, but whoever built the lock would not have made it easy. They were scratching at a secret that would take days to discover. Days she did not have.

Her sweat-tipped fingers slipped from the moon's impression, her cheek grazing the wall with her weight, her brain rolling freely about her skull. She could smell the flames from Grimosse's cloak, the golem's white hot boots having ignited the velvety fabric. At her knees, Xandr remained quiet, like a shrouded corpse waiting to be buried. With her last bit of strength, she pulled herself away from the wall and screamed. "Grimm! Make us a door! Now!"

His hammer struck moons and stars like thunder, and the wall turned to rubble at her fingertips. Darkness swallowed her as she fell, her stomach lurching into her throat. Where she landed, she remained. The air was cool and wonderful then, filtering through the layers of her djellabah, and the cold stone floor was as comfortable as any bed. It was, she decided, a good place to let her eyes rest.

She was considering lying on the floor a little while longer, but a fear that she might never rise again gave her the strength to lift herself, to disregard the soreness in her wrists and knees and ankles. Grimosse stood like a silhouette in the dark and she wondered for how long he had watched her, waited for her, and what thoughts, if any, passed through his artificial mind. If she were to die, what would he do without her? Could he survive without any purpose?

"Grimm," she groaned, "is Xandr alright? Do you have him?"

"Grimm protect sleeping master," he replied. "No have fear."

She crawled to the bundle of fabric lying at the golem's feet, peeling the shroud from his face. He was deathly pale, stiff, the hairs of his beard white and brittle. At a glance, he looked dead, but somehow his bosom, ever so perceptibly, swelled with life. "Thank the Mother Goddess," she murmured. "You must have some incredible fortitude. Or, truly, you are loved by the gods."

The golem helped her to stand, kept her steady in his massive arms as she worked the ache from her joints. After making certain that none of her bones were broken, she lifted her eyes to his. The deep shadows made the folds of his muzzle more pronounced, rendering him more hideous than ever. "Grimm, where are we?"

"In room," he answered, without a trace of sarcasm.

"I keep forgetting not to ask you questions."

Darkness stretched above them, impenetrable, and there was no way to tell how far they had fallen, but given the relative cool of the room, she knew they were deep beneath the surface. Only a faint red glow gave any sense of shape or dimension to their surroundings. She focused on the light, moving carefully forward. An iron torch was fitted to the wall. Whatever fuel there had been was long turned to ash, so she made a knot from her sleeve and stuffed it inside and, with a flint stone from her pack, the torch blazed anew.

"By the gods!"

Gold glittered across her field of vision. Despite the dust and decay and webs thick as ropes, the firelight reflected on the various hard surfaces with a dazzling brilliance. So many wonders enamored her senses that she did not know where to turn, and whenever she reached for one thing, some greater wonder pulled her gaze away. Obol and drachmae coins littered the shelves amid bejeweled amphoras and silver goblets. Coffers brimmed with rubies and sapphires, jade and lapis lazuli. Urns of ivory and obsidian abounded, their lids fashioned into trike and dragon heads and other beasts unfamiliar to her. Even the tables and chairs were gilded. A whole chariot stood in a dark corner, preserved in gold leaf.

She scooped up handfuls of jewels, let them spill like pebbles between her fingers, only to scoop them up and drop them again. She loved how they captured the light, the sound they made, like tinkling raindrops, even the cold, hard feel of them. For the first time in her life, she knew what it meant to possess beyond what was necessary, to be truly, decadently wealthy. She was ankle-deep in gold, in ornaments most people could never hope to own. A dazzling dragonfly necklace adorned her neck, its gold wings spread across her collarbone. A gold serpent with ruby eyes coiled about her forearm, from her wrist all the way up to her elbow, and her mind flooded with possibilities. It was enough to never go hungry, to have servants, if she so wished! No one would dare imprison her, or look down upon her, or mistake her for a harlot. Princess Thelana, they might call her. No, Empress Thelana! She was giddy as she pictured herself in her own palace, surrounded by family and a cornucopia of food . . . but the reality of her current situation was not far behind. How would she transport such wealth? And could she even find her way back from the Dead Zones? She quickly chased from her mind the memory of trekking back across that sun-scorched wasteland. There had to be another way.

Next she moved to examine the chariot. An assortment of shields, swords and bows leaned up against the wheel, and it reminded her that she was not a princess, but a hunter and a wanderer, that she was free of the trappings and hypocrisies of civilization. The longbow was of dull gold, shaped like two serpents joined at the tail. The craftsmanship was exquisite, perhaps superior to her jade bow, though the pull string was missing. Slinging the serpent bow over her shoulder, she was overcome by a new sense of prosperity, and she could not recall when last she was happy. It was so long and forgotten a feeling that it gave her pause. The gods were cruel, she knew, and no fortune came without sacrifice.

Taking greater precaution, she continued to explore the room, finding things that spoke of ancient evil. With meticulous detail, the legs of the furniture were carved to resemble men, but in a kind of deformed mockery of the human body. Bent at the task of supporting seats and tabletops, the slave's limbs were spidery, and their ribs jutted out over stomachs that held the appearance of hollowed out pits. Anguish was cut into every ivory face. Bringing the torch to the wall, the fire revealed a mural, a golden city of obelisks, statues, and sphinxes. Massive saurians were driven along paved streets, but never by humans. Men and women were depicted laboring under the whip, burdened under slabs of rock, leashed to wagons. Every human figure was emaciated, deformed, wincing. Shuddering with disgust and horror, she reconsidered adorning herself in the accouterments of that evil race. She let the coiled snake bracelet slip to the ground and cast away the dragonfly necklace, not even bothering to unhook it from its chain.

But just a handful could buy back her family's freedom, if she should find them, or Borz's, at the very least.

The torchlight indicated a passageway, but she could not leave the room without securing some of the treasure, enough to never want from hunger, for herself and for her brothers and sisters. Coins and jewels filled her sack and she stuffed the gourd with gems until the water began to leak out. A few rubies, the size of grapes, would not fit through the opening and she considered swallowing them. It pained her to let them go, imagining what they could buy, perhaps a plot of land with good soil, but her sack was heavy with jewels already and that, she decided, would have to be enough.

Translucent webs impeded the passageway like silk curtains, thick and white and sticky about the edges. Air flowed from beyond, causing the loose threads to flutter and the veil to swell and retract as if the passage was alive and breathing. Touched by the flame, the webbing disintegrated in a flash of orange and red, illuminating her way. She moved forward, the glow of her torch chasing shadows on the wall, revealing splashes of color from the continuing mural. She had no knowledge of archaeology, but knew enough to understand that the images told a story.

In simple lines etched into the limestone, there were a number of figures, the first of which were neither human nor snake man, or any other race she knew, and yet their distinct shapes were familiar. They were wide-bodied creatures, with rounded, dome-like heads and enormous hands. Ultimately, she recognized them, and shivered.

Golems.

Like the boulders littering Ilmarinen, like the faceless statues in the ruins in the woods, the resemblance was unmistakable. But who or what were they? By the pictographs on the wall, she could see that snake men and humans, even the people with fish-heads that could only be merquid, knelt beneath the golem-like race, perhaps as subjects. Her curiosity piqued, she followed the story with her fingertips, commanding Grimosse to bring the torch closer to the wall. In the following panel, the golem and snake race stood alone under a strange moon, surrounded by exotic, leafy plants. But their moon, or perhaps it was their sun—it was difficult to tell as it was nothing more than a simple circle—expanded, filling the sky, and the plants of their world were no more, and the golem race vanished also, or so she figured, since they were never shown again. There was a cobra-headed king then, who directed his subjects to build galleys without sails or oars, and in his hand was a scepter, its red jewel radiating lines like the sun. The galleys were set to sail without water, amid the stars, and many things happened after involving ellipses she could only guess at, but there was no doubting the basics of the history. The king reemerged from his galley and the three simple shapes representing mankind were shown to be kneeling, just as the other races had knelt before the golems.

They came from another world to enslave us. But this is ancient history. The snake men are no more.

Where the mural ended, there was a wall, engraved with stars of rubies and sapphires. A reddish glow radiated from behind it in vertical, parallel ridges. She could feel the sizzle of power against her probing fingers. Scrubbing the surface, the reddish light formed into the shape of a door. She called to Grimosse, who had to crouch to advance, and with a gesture from her he brought his door-making hammer to the wall.

Thoom!

Her ears quaked at the sound, but the wall did not surrender access. As rubble rained down on them, she squatted under his kneecap, fearing that the centuries-old architecture might fail atop them.

On the third attempt, a cloud of glittering vapors swallowed the hallway. She rushed blindly through the opening, under falling rubble, coughing, rubbing the haze from her eyes. A cavernous chamber spread before her. It reminded her of a mausoleum, dank with the musky odor of things long dead. The walls and ceiling, if any existed, vanished in the gloom. Moss and lichen covered every surface. Weeds split the floor, bulging under paving stones, and thorny vines came down from the shadows to weave across the floor.

Further on, a crimson sphere beckoned from a dais. For how long it shed its light, like a beacon summoning a ship to shore, she could scarcely imagine, though she knew no eyes had lain upon the chamber for untold ages. She moved toward the glow as long-tailed creatures with flipper-like appendages slithered across her path, mutations of a forgotten history, things like serpents but not.

As she approached the pedestal, Thelana could see that wherever the light of the sphere touched, the room was fractured, like a shattered mirror. Each fragment seemed to exist separately from the others adjacent to it, in its own light, in differing states of decay. One piece of the room was dimly lit, gray and lifeless, while another was green and vivid and bright. How was such architecture possible? She moved into the lighted area, fascinated by how sharply it divided from the rest of the room, and as she stood over it she was startled by the sudden warmth washing over her, and by the surprising echo of birdsong. Stepping backward into silence, she passed her arm through the space again, feeling the soft sudden rays of sunshine. When pulling away, the dank atmosphere gripped her arm and the skin prickled with gooseflesh. With great difficulty, she accepted what she was seeing was no clever trick of masonry, that somehow, beyond compression, where the sun appeared to touch her was an actual place, existing within the room but only occupying a part of it.

Many of the fragments were similar in size, while most varied greatly in proportion, either large enough for her to stand in or no bigger than the width of her finger. The break lines converged to a single point, a shatter point upon the pedestal, the red glow. It was the fire from within a gem fixed to the mouth of a scepter. It was the Serpent's Eye.

The decrepit steps chipped under her weight as she climbed the dais. She did not know the reason, but her heart quaked as she neared the source. Something about the gem unnerved her, and yet its strangeness possessed her with a yearning to know its secrets.

As she reached the top, the jewel's radiance enveloped her. A fine white ash, like powdered bone, covered the floor of the dais. The pedestal was a simple granite slab tinted red by the Eye's glow, but as she moved closer, its timeworn features became defined, revealing a great sarcophagus in the semblance of a hooded snake man, the scepter protruding from its stone claws. There she froze, marveling at it, losing any hesitation she might have had for stealing it. The gem was the size of her fist, its thousand glassy facets multiplying her reflection in a kaleidoscope of reddish hues.

She could buy the entire world with this stone. No wonder Nesper was after it. No wonder he would have killed them for it.

As she reached for the scepter, her arm bent like a broken stick and her fingers became elongated. She moved her hand through many odd, distorted angles, the air around the gem bending the light like still water—at least, *still water* was the only way her mind could process it. Shrugging off her sense of unease, she closed her hand about the scepter and it came loose without resistance. The Serpent's Eye was lighter than she expected, and turning it in her hand, she noticed that the Eye itself was not set between the serpent's fangs, as she had thought, but held by some invisible thread. She'd never seen any such thing, but it reminded her, for reasons she did not fully comprehend, of Emmaxis, of something otherworldly.

She returned from the dais briskly, skipping down the steps like a child late to supper, in her heart a mix of guilt and relief. Thelana could not remember being so fortunate. Such a treasure would be easy to carry and was no doubt equal to all the valuables in the other room combined. And then, as she lifted her eyes to look for Grimosse, her heart lost its rhythm, forgetting for a moment to beat.

Another person was in the room with her and it was clearly not Grimosse. It could not be a native, she told herself—there was not a trace of life in Shess. Was it a wanderer like herself? No—that was impossible, for who else could survive the journey here and arrive at the same exact moment? Yet there it was, standing between the dais and the door she'd come through, an apparition in

sun-tortured and eroded garments, with deep folds suggesting a woman or a young boy, a body emaciated by hunger like her own.

"Wh-Who are you?" Thelana asked, despite the sinking suspicion that she knew the answer already.

The other girl stared, just as wide-eyed, just as frightened. "Who am I? I am Thelana."

"No, you can't be Thelana," Thelana said, feeling her
lips quivering as she spoke the words. "I am."

12

THE PRINCE OF SERPENTS

Xandr was in a dark place. It was not the cage he had been placed into or the walls beyond, but the dungeon of the self, the light of reason and hope having gone from him. Such darkness could not be abated, even by the noonday sun. It was the place he came to in the deep valleys of sleep, where he would question the Mother Goddess and doubt his purpose, when he feared his existence, all existence, possessed no grand design, but was little more than a succession of happenstance, misery and fortune being two sides of the same coin. After wandering through labyrinths of doubt, Xandr often found escape in the ghostly memory of QuasiI, or by the guiding hand of the Mother Goddess, or in Thelana's loving eyes. Where were they now? Was the Mother Goddess too remote in this bleak fragment of history to hear him? Only one thing was certain. He was alone.

The grinding of chains lifting him into the open sky roused him from his stupor. He did not have the will to wrestle with the cage, though he could now, in the light, make out its crude construction, the rust flaking from the bars. He sat there for a moment, squinting under the intense blaze of sun, and then the sound of human voices brought strength back into his limbs. He tore the cage from its hinges and crawled into a standing position. Light percolated through a grated wall, casting hexagonal shadows across his face and body. The grate was on one side, adjacent to three walls streaked with blood, and the ceiling was low, barely enough to accommodate his height. Eldin was there, looking more animated than usual, as were two other men far younger than Eldin, with skin like deep copper and stomachs hollowed for want of food. But like his ancestor whose body he occupied, they were corded with muscle throughout, their limbs like entwined ropes. And like him, they were both naked, and seemed commonly so, but he could only guess whether clothing was denied them or if, being in the distant past, man had yet to adopt a concept of shame. Either way, hope arose in his heart, however small, for under inhuman rule all humanity was as one brotherhood, and he rushed to Eldin's side, stopping short of an embrace.

"Batal," the old man addressed him, "it is good you are here. I wished to document this most historic of days to complete my book, that is, of course, if I survive to write about it."

"No," said Xandr solemnly, "I have already failed you. I was within reach of the pharaoh, but could not lay a hand on him."

Eldin's face bunched into a ball of hair and wrinkles. "And what makes you think killing the pharaoh would have made any difference?"

"Wouldn't it?" The other two men were watching, and Xandr could see the surrender in their haggard faces. He wondered if he looked as awful.

"No," Eldin replied, "of course not! Kings are deposed throughout history, quite frequently I might add, and never has a nation fallen because of it. Nations are made by its people, not its rulers. Our fight is with the Septhera."

"Enough of your lessons!" Xandr cried, taking the old man by the shoulders. "Tell me what I'm supposed to do!"

"I cannot!"

"And why not?"

"Because," he gasped, "I don't know!"

Xandr released him and fell against the wall, clutching his throat. "How could you not know? I thought you were a historian. I thought you knew these events. Understood them."

"History is a mosaic, Xandr, which historians are always assembling and rearranging. We make conjectures. We make guesses on what the mosaic might look like if completed, but we never have all the pieces! We possess a mere handful, when there exist perhaps tens of thousands."

"Then how do you know I will do anything at all today?"

"Because your name is Batal, and your descendants would not have immortalized the name, if you did not do great things. Shortly after this day, the revolution will begin to end Septheran domination over this planet, to bring the snake men to extinction! But alas, I've said too much!"

"No, tell me more. Tell me everything you know."

The larger of the two prisoners turned from Xandr to Eldin, saying, "Yes, tell us more about this revolution, if you are a prophet, for we are in need of good tidings."

"No, no, no!" Eldin exclaimed, "Me and my big mouth! I fear I am not well-suited to be a time traveling historian. My presence here, meeting you, which may or may not be part of the original time-line, might alter things, might prevent you from acting in the intended way. It is already disconcerting that you have taken the place of your ancestor. Will you be as driven as he, without his experiences, without his particular losses to strengthen your resolve to fight?"

"I have my own loss," Xandr said quietly. "The Septhera have done enough to warrant my hate."

"How could anyone not hate them?" the more robust of the two prisoners replied. "There are many, it is true, who have come to accept their fate—who believe abject obedience is the wiser course . . . There are even those who ally themselves with the snakes, worshipping the pharaoh as a god, preaching that submission is to guarantee life. But I say such men are traitors. Any man who does not lift his hand against a snake is no better than they."

Xandr looked at him with renewed interest. He had spoken with a dignity that came unexpectedly, given his appearance. "Who are you and how did you get here?"

"I am known as Tellhus. Before the serpents came to our village in Ilithia, I was a proud father and mason. They forced my people into the mines to look for metals, murdered those too weak for labor. They . . . they ate my wife and children," he added, devoid of feeling. "I rallied men to fight them . . . our pickaxes and shovels broke their leathery scales."

"But you did not succeed," Xandr affirmed.

"We did not know it at the time, but our battle was with *slavers*, a lesser caste. After killing a good number of them, they sent for their warriors." His voice grew frail, exacting, as though reading the words from a scroll with difficulty. "We were fifty strong, strong with hate and anger and vengeance, and they were three, only three, cold and calculating and . . . fast . . . and we were slaughtered like swine. I alone survived, prepared to meet god with my pick in my hand, but they ensnared me, sent me to rot in their prison."

"But we are no longer in the pits. Where are we now?"

"This is the arena," Tellhus answered. "We are here, I suppose, because of our willingness to fight."

"They make sport of suffering!" the lesser man chimed in, his voice full of dust and sorrow.

Tellhus silenced him with a stare. "We make things more entertaining for them. Since snake men do not work, and can spend cycles digesting, they bore easily. They like to watch things die, pitting beast against beast, man against man. And rarely, man against one of their own. But no single human can stand up to them and live. More than seventy went up against their slavers, the weakest of their race, and we killed four, maybe five, before we lost twenty to the Taker. Against three from the warrior caste, the fifty that remained stood no chance. They are superior to us, far superior. To fight them is to die."

"That's not true." It was the other prisoner again. "I was in the pits and I heard the talk, that the Batal alone killed two of them! Warriors as well, and with his bare hands."

"Impossible," said Tellhus. "Tell him the truth, if you are the one called Batal."

"He speaks truly," said Xandr. "But I only started out bare-handed. I later acquired a chain, and then a sword.

They are not unbeatable, they . . ." *By the Mother Goddess, is this it? Is this why I am here? To inspire hope?*

Eldin smiled as understanding dawned on Xandr's face. And though Tellhus appeared doubtful, the other prisoner looked on, unblinking.

"You may have been fortunate, if what you say is true, Batal—and some of us may break loose from time to time, but humans will never be free of the yoke. When they came to Ilithia, our greatest hunters resisted them, but quickly we understood that they were the hunters, and we, the prey. Their first commandment was to forbid us our weapons—for without them we are powerless. Even in their digestive slumber, they are protected by the scales they are born with. Truth be told, man is the most pathetic of creatures. Should we fall upon rock, we bruise—we bleed. Long ago, man thought himself first among predators, because of his reason. But against those who think like men but fight like animals, we are no match."

Xandr thought long on these words, knowing it was his duty to convince him otherwise. "If the snake men can think, then we must outthink them. If they have weapons, we must make superior ones. If they have scales, we must do better, with armor of bronze."

"Armor? Bronze?" Tellhus echoed. "I know not what you mean."

"Wait, you don't have—" Xandr started, but cut himself short, considering how it might impact the future. He looked to Eldin, who nodded approval. "Armor is used to protect the body, like clothing—"

"Clothing?" Tellhus remarked. "We have nothing like that in Ilithia. Is it customary in your village?"

By Alashiya! Xandr fell speechless with the realization, that in this forgotten past his people's customs were not taboo, that as an Ilmar he was no stranger. The words of his mentor came back to him. *Since time immemorial when men became men, before the greater moon loomed in the heavens, we were all Ilmar. For hundreds of millennia, humanity knew nothing of want or possessions.*

His heart swelled at the notion. Before the Septhera, all of Aenya could be called Ilmarinen. But after the revolution, when the snake men were forced to extinction, mankind—the world itself—was irrevocably changed. Subjugation and war must have taught man to fear, and that fear must have bred desire for power to overcome those fears. Somehow, through the millennia, Ilmarinen remained the last bastion of a simpler age, of an innocent humanity. Perhaps, even now, hidden in the river valleys between the Mountains of Ukko, the Ilmar were living free and prosperous, oblivious to the plight of the rest of mankind. But there was more to the story, he knew—for the world in which he was born was a ruined one, was divided into two hemispheres, where life could scarcely hope to thrive. Such questions had tormented him since childhood, and now the only man who might have the answers was standing before him. But time did not favor his curiosity, for already he could see the serpentine shapes casting long shadows across their cell. The mechanism holding the gate in place was undone and the five men, led by Xandr, wandered out into the haze. The earth was coarse, the sharp red-orange rock uninviting to human soles. Through a distant arch in the surrounding wall, the sun glared, giving form and color to the tapestry of men and snake men seated along the perimeter. Most were slaves, but

NICK ALIMONOS

many thousands were snake-headed, their elongated faces trained on the five men.

So many humans. And yet, no one dares to challenge them.

Somewhere a snare drum rattled and a portcullis began lifting. The squeal of a winch and chain sounded for eternity. And then, an eerie chant of throaty S's and rolling R's swept through the masses, a long strain of repeated syllables impossible for the human tongue to approximate.

"What are they saying?" Xandr asked Eldin.

"It is the prince," Tellhus interjected. "They chant his name. When we sing our woes in Ilithia, he is called *Purple Death Adder*, or simply, the *Adder*. I am surprised that your people know not of him. The name alone inspires dread. Workers show greater fear of his mention than of the lash. Our masters must think quite highly of us, or of you, if we are to face him. For some it is considered an honor."

"Can he be killed?" Xandr asked.

"He is a pureblood," Tellhus explained, "of the royal caste. Pray we die quickly. Avoid the bite. Avoid the purple death."

"What is the purple death?"

"The venom of the pure bloods," he said. "Death comes quickly, but is exceedingly painful. For some less fortunate, the venom can linger for days, even cycles, during which time the victim lives out dreams of unspeakable terror, as vivid as life itself."

Xandr's skin crawled with the possibility. Could he be dreaming, he wondered, lying in the cold grip of the Taker all this time, dying slowly as Thelana watched and waited? It certainly made more sense than any of Eldin's explanations.

"Dreams?" the lesser man murmured. "Did you say dreams?" But the question was drowned out by the rising cacophony of hissing and rattling as a pair of hoofed saurians emerged from the open portcullis in a cloud of orange.

Tellhus did not shrink at the sight, but the other man shook with fear. Xandr put a hand on his shoulder to calm him. "Tell me your name?"

"My name, most regrettably, is Soog."

"And how is that regrettable?"

"How can it not be, as it is a man with my name that must die a gruesome and untimely death? Surely, yours cannot be a more fortunate name, as you stand here with me."

"Courage, Soog! Don't let them see your fear. Stand behind me and believe."

"Believe?" he repeated, the word sounding strangely from his tongue. "What is there to believe in? Nothing but death awaits us. I don't want to die. I am afraid! I'll admit it. I'm no hunter . . . I was but a simple fisherman before this." And he continued to sob and tremble, despite his efforts to restrain himself.

"Sometimes," Xandr replied, "belief is all we have. I'll not deceive you, Soog. It is unlikely you will see another dawn, but all men must face the Taker. It is only how one faces him that matters. And we shall not be killed to amuse these monsters. Our deaths will have a nobler meaning."

"Such heroic words!" Eldin exclaimed. "If only I remember them! Historians rarely have the opportunity to observe, firsthand, such great events!"

Xandr scowled. "Fool! What do your writings matter at a time like this? Do you not stand here with us? Will you not share our fate?"

"Perhaps," he said, "but perhaps not. You see, Xandr, I also was not born into this body. I found myself here the same way you did. I followed the *wormhole* made by the Serpent's Eye. They are very tiny, you see, these *wormholes*, so tiny, in fact, that even light cannot fit through it. But something that does not possess matter, a soul, perhaps, consciousness—"

"Still your rambling tongue," Xandr replied. "The prince is here."

Having circled the arena, the saurian pair came to a stop, the dust still billowing like orange smoke from their hooves, and a cloaked figure dismounted, closing the distance between them with unnatural movements. Shining blades appeared from the hems of its sleeves and a snake's tail drew hypnotic patterns in the air. As the cloak slipped from its scaly body, Soog let out a shriek, but his objections quickly went unnoticed amid the cheers, not from the Septheran's throats—to Xandr's confusion and dismay—but from the human onlookers in the rafters.

"Wait, Xandr!" Eldin cried, his eyes turning white. "Hear me out! If you manage to find your way back to your time, you must seek out the book, the one written by my hand, in the original language of the Zo. By then, I will have pieced together the complete history of Aenya and you will be prepared to learn the truth."

"What truth?" he asked.

"The truth you have been seeking, about the Great Cataclysm, about the Dark Age, and what has been kept secret from you since birth . . . the thing you've been raised to face as the *Batal* of your age!"

"How can you know all this?" Xandr exclaimed.

"I have seen it. Your future is my past and my past your future! I've lived events you have not yet reached, like on the mountain top, yes!" he added with a maniacal grin. "I will see you again on the mountain, but I won't remember you!"

"In the face of the Taker, your madness knows no bounds!" Xandr admitted.

"Just remember the book, damn you. It will be no easy task, but I will try to place it somewhere so that it ends up in your hands."

Wind blasted the ground, etching away the hard-edged shapes at their feet. Swords and axes appeared as if molded from the earth. Stepping forward, Tellhus lifted a sickle-like sword to his face. There was no blood on its cutting edge, even after he ran his thumb hard against it.

"Khopesh," he said. "A guard's sword, albeit an old one. At least they offer weapons."

"What good are these!" cried Soog, considering the small ax. "They're rusted beyond use! We might as well go bare-handed."

"It is all for show," Tellhus replied. "But if I can get in one good blow—just one—if I could but cripple the bastard, aye, I'd meet death with contentment."

Standing over the weapons, Xandr counted one for each, but did not choose. "Your heart is full of hate, vengeance, but that will do us no good, Tellhus."

"And what would you suggest, Batal?"

"Let me handle this prince of serpents. I believe that I can best him, and that it may inspire others to rise against their masters. Think only of the men and women who are watching us. Our fight is for their eyes, not for the Septhera's."

"Mankind is doomed, Batal. Nothing will change after this day," he added, dashing off and shouting, "but my honor, when I twist this blade into that monster's bowels!"

"No, Tellhus!" Xandr howled after him. "Let's face him together—don't throw your life away!"

Sunlight reflected off the Septheran's body, tinting him violet, but where the sun did not touch directly, his scales were as black and shiny as volcanic glass. Like his brother, the Pharaoh, the creature named Purple Death Adder possessed the cobra-like membrane connecting the top of his head to his shoulders. With his approach, his awfulness became more intimidating. He was much taller than any human, with sinewy arms that reached to his knees and talons that snatched at the air, and in each hand was a long dagger in the shape of a crescent moon. Tellhus charged with a lame leg and a desperate cry, his khopesh thrust at its gut, but the prince of serpents did not stir. Whether staring down his attacker or sleeping, the creature's eyes showed no sign. But as the sun moved across his pointed face, his pinpoint eyes flickered from black to white and his head pivoted like a predator before a kill. In the instant of impact, the Adder became a torrent of motion, slashing at Tellhus' sword arm. Blood gushed from the limb, cleanly cut from the elbow, but Tellhus simply stared where that part of him had been, the pain having yet to reach his senses. Retracting the scarlet blade, the Septheran crawled, lizard like, along the man's body, biting deep into the shoulder. As the venom took hold, he became rigid, and even from a distance Xandr could see the discoloration—the subtle purple tint in the veins beneath the skin. Tellhus fell, shriveled to the bone, like a preserved corpse dead a dozen or more years.

A wretched sound circled the arena, filling the ears with dread, hisses and snare drums and human cheer. It wasn't a battle they had been anticipating, but a slaughter. And they approved, Xandr realized with disgust. Even the human slaves accompanying their masters were too cowed, too complacent in their misery, to think otherwise.

As the spectators grew silent again, Purple Death Adder turned his attention to the three remaining humans. At this, Soog keeled over, his vomit pooling between his knees.

"Up!" Xandr commanded him. "Do not show them any weakness!"

"But we are weak!" Soog admitted. "Haven't you figured that out yet? Tellhus is dead! Dead! And we'll soon be with him!"

"We'll all be dead someday," Xandr replied softly, "but few men die with purpose."

"*Few men die with purpose!*" Eldin repeated excitedly. "It's a popular saying of yours, you know." Xandr gave him an annoyed look, but he went on. "Come to think of it, I *must* live through this day, either me or Soog, or who else will have recorded it? You don't happen to be a bard or historian, Soog?"

"No . . ." Soog replied timidly, "but I could start."

"You're mistaken," Xandr said to him. "I learned the saying from my mentor."

"Precisely," Eldin agreed, "but it was passed down from you, from the Batal, which means—by the gods!—you were meant to embody your ancestor!"

Ever so gradually, the Septheran prince was making his way toward them, to prolong the kill for the crowds, and to torment his victims with impending death. In his periphery, Xandr could see Eldin retreat behind him. "If you're so certain about all this, why do you tremble?"

"I —um—am only human," he admitted, "and my calculations may be off!"

"The two of you stay here," Xandr said finally, taking the least beaten sword from the ground and the small ax from Soog's bumbling fingers.

Compared to the weight of his two-hander, carrying the khopesh was like going into battle empty-handed. The sickle-like blade twirled in Xandr's palm as he rummaged through his memory for the techniques his mentor taught him for small swords. It was too dull to chop, that much he knew, but the Septheran's armor-like hide made that a moot point. Any sword could do the deed if one were to simply *push*. The ax was a distraction, so he tossed it, marking the divide between him and the prince.

Purple Death Adder's crescent blades silvered in the noonday sun. His neck stretched, accordion like, making him a head taller. His eyes rolled over Xandr's body, studying his build, his demeanor. Caution showed in the snake man's coiled posture.

You do not fear me.

The voice was thick and venomous, rattling his brain, but Xandr resisted the instinct to step away from it. "No."

Even while standing, the prince was all motion, every limb writhing, its head bobbing, its tail curling and snapping and recoiling. *Why not?* he asked simply.

"Because my loved ones have already gone to the Taker," Xandr answered, "and you cannot harm them."

Do you not value your own life?

"I do," he said, digging his fingers into the khopesh' rusty hilt. "But I value the lives of others more."

That is folly, the snake man communicated telepathically, his head agitated from side to side. *Compassion is for the weak!* All the while, the chatter from the wall intensified, the masses having never witnessed such an exchange between a man and a Septheran.

"You cannot understand because you are coldblooded," Xandr said, his heart quickening, watching for any sign of attack, though the snake man's posture and constant motion was utterly alien, mesmerizing. "Your cruelty is your weakness. No species can thrive on the suffering of another. The day will come when humankind shall triumph over you."

That day is not today!

Xandr's head screamed, the voice in it shaking him to his knees, as the prince's scales quivered, his mouth gaping wide enough to swallow a man whole, his fangs milky white, dripping with ichor. Anticipating the attack, Xandr bent at the ankle, but he was already too late, the moon blades crossing his throat, grazing the stubble of his chin. He had never seen anything, beast or man, move so swiftly. In retreating, Xandr made a slashing shield with the dull edge of his sword, but the tail came out of nowhere, cutting his brow like a whip. The snake man was less limited by tendons, moving more fluidly than any man could, attacking from the side as readily as from the front. Xandr was outmatched and he knew it. Without thinking, his hand went to his breast, clutching his heart as if it might jump out, but the familiar scar crossing his torso was not there, and he remembered that he was not himself. He was Batal, and somehow . . . somehow the Batal had managed to make history. If he were to die at the hands of this monster, before so many witnesses, what difference could he make?

I must not lose. I must move faster.

But the Septheran was everywhere at once. Silver clashed with dull iron, pelting him with rust. Attacks came so suddenly and in such succession that Xandr could not hope to use his khopesh but to defend, and he realized with some horror that he was fighting only to survive. The tail, though it could not kill him, flayed his skin to ribbons, cut slices from his body piece-by-piece. The mouth lunged, flashing fangs, but they came too quickly for Xandr to contemplate—only some primal terror distanced him from their venom.

The crescent moons crossed again, the black-purple maw snapping between flashes of silver. As the first blade whizzed past his nose, the rusted sickle caught against the second. But Xandr's weapon was wearing thin, each deflected blow adding a notch to the blade.

As hopeless as things seemed to him, he knew that from the walls above, the spectators could see the defiance, courage, and strength of a human slave, a sight never before witnessed in that arena. To Xandr, their faces were stony abstracts, too distant to distinguish, yet he could see the turmoil on their brows, in the sunken ridges of their eyes. Despite their masters' angry lashing tongues, one-by-one, from the lowest to the highest tier, slaves began to rise from their seats.

The onslaught was unrelenting. And the day was sweltering hot, sapping the fight from him. Blinking the sweat from his eyes, he did not see the blade until it was too late, until he felt it tear across his liver. He watched his blood speckle the orange rock, the curved edge turn red as if dipped in paint. The arena was spinning, Eldin and Soog and Tellhus, and shadowy faces far and wide dashed with hopelessness, all spinning. Without any sense of falling, he was on the ground—there was no pain, only cold and numbness.

Where is my sword?

It was gone. Knocked somewhere out of his hand. He tried to regain control of his feet but they would not obey. He'd done all he could do.

The roar of thousands hushed to a whisper, and Xandr wondered why Purple Death Adder had not yet killed him. His only desire, his only regret in that instant, was that he would not see Thelana again. It was a selfish impulse and he knew it.

Out of the orange haze, a female shape was walking toward him, her hair like the tributaries in the valleys of Ilmarinen, and at first it was Thelana, but somehow she was more, was Alashiya also, for he remembered that the Goddess was in him, and all things of Aenya, and her skin glowed gold like the sun, became the sun.

You are not alone. Xandr. Her voice was a song, a mother's coo.

When Alashiya reached down to him, and her hand was clasped in his, he was no longer in a place of darkness. Xandr stood to face Purple Death Adder again, sword at his side. The Septheran took a step back. The human spectators began shouting with fervor. Looking around him, at every hopeful face, he understood what he had to do. The fight was not his to win—it was theirs, and the Batal would not fail them.

"You wish to cow them?" Xandr cried, waving his sword over the masses, "then show them what they most fear . . . Bite me! I welcome the purple death!"

The prince was quick to the bait, leaving his moon blades in the dust. *You do not know for what you ask . . . it is not a good death. It will avail your species nothing!*

"Enough!" Xandr screamed, dashing forward. "Show me!"

Purple Death Adder leapt, his pink glossy gums agape. But Xandr drew him in with a *delayed counter,* the tactic taught to him by his mentor, giving the attacker what he thought he wanted. Rather than bite throat and shoulder, as the Adder intended, Xandr offered up his forearm. The fang cut deep, through to the other side, and as Xandr tore himself free the venom started to fill, coursing through his veins like searing needles. His hand was a bloody pulp. His forearm dangled from the elbow in meaty tatters. But the prince of serpents staggered back, the elongated neck stretched to its breaking point. With frantic strokes, it clawed at its mouth, desperate to remove the sliver of iron from its throat. Xandr moved slowly, weakly, despite his urgency and the short time he had in which to live. With his one remaining hand, he retrieved the ax, bringing it down upon the serpent prince, in a wedge though its slender face and head. Purple Death Adder flailed backward without so much as a hiss, now groping blindly at the ax handle jutting from its face, and hit the ground writhing.

Cheers sounded above panicked hisses. He had defeated the Septheran champion at the cost of his own life, but would it be enough to inspire men's hearts to revolution? The poison was setting in. Each heartbeat was a dagger twisting in his chest. But they would not be wasted. Raising the ax overhead, wet with blood of the fallen champion, Xandr turned toward the stepped walls, to man and snake man alike. "I am a man . . . and I have beaten you!" Even as he spoke, the venom continued to cripple him, his fingers growing icy, his legs giving way.

"Men of Aenya!" he gasped. "You lose no freedom . . . when you are free to fight!" Those were his last words before he dropped to his knees, toppling forward to join Tellhus.

It would have to do, he decided, confident that the name would live on to inspire hope, to become part of folksongs, to pass through history and be recalled by generations, in cities by the sea, and by the simple people of the Goddess, those untouched by civilization. One name.

Batal.

13

REDUX

*She exists in the long memory of shadows. In
the coming light she is gone—she is never been.*

—Ilmarin folksong

Thelana was looking straight at herself, at the same
emerald eyes, the same freckled cheeks and ruddy hair. She was even wearing an identical djellabah, the creases and worn edges and sun-scorched discoloration unmistakable. Thelana had seen herself before,
in mirrors, in the still waters of her native country, on
the polished surface of Emmaxis. But the Thelana standing before her looked older than she remembered. Her
skin was a burnt sienna, her hair a tangled mess of fading
strands, and she was so terribly thin that the bones showed
from beneath her cheeks.

"I know who I am," said the second Thelana. "And you .
. . you're an illusion, something to confuse me."

The other woman sounded sincere, even afraid. But Thelana held fast to her trophy, to the Serpent's Eye bathing the two in its crimson glow. "Let me pass," she said, a chill running through her that forced her to look away.

"No," said the other. "I've come too far for that scepter. I won't leave without it."

"I rightly stole this," Thelana argued, "and there's more than enough treasure for you in the other room, whoever you are." But her assertions sounded hollow. Each passing second was like an echo.

"This must be a trick!" she cried, "but I'm no fool! Give me the *Eye* or I'll pry it from your dead hands!" A jade and gold sword emerged from under a flap at her side. It was identical in every way to Thelana's sword, down to the nicks and scratches it had received in past battles.

Clinking against the stone floor, the Serpent's Eye rolled away as the two women wrestled for control of the sword. Having dropped the scepter, Thelana gripped her other self by the wrist, bringing her elbow down on her opposite's eye. As the other reeled from the blow, Thelana felt a dull pain in her own eye and a raw feeling around it, like an injury suffered earlier.

It's the same eye.

She felt her skin turn to gooseflesh as new memories flooded her brain—a meeting with a woman who appeared and claimed to be Thelana already in possession of the Serpent's Eye, a fight with herself, and the awful realization of having lived the same moment infinite times before. The understanding that came to her was so profound and improbable that it bent her mind to the breaking point.

Thelana let loose a scream, shielding herself from herself just as the other's sword came around. "Truce!"

The other scowled, lowering her attack, her eye socket a bruised shade of purple. "What is it?"

"If you kill me . . . you'll be committing suicide."

"Is that some kind of threat?"

"No, not at all. Look at me. At my eye. Do you see it? You don't remember me because you're from before . . . but I remember you. I stood there, where you are, because I'm from later . . . I'm you."

"You're not making sense."

"I'm you!" Thelana cried. "I am your future."

"No," her past self murmured. "That can't be . . . Grimosse!"

The guardian came out of the shadows and kept still, shifting his stare between the one and the other. But before he could think of something to say, a second Grimosse appeared out of the gloom.

The Thelana blocking the doorway screamed.

"Listen to me—it's the only thing that makes sense. If I am an imposter, how would I know about Borz, the brother closest to your, I mean . . . our heart, or Britannia, the last person to see us leave home?"

"This . . . this is wrong," she said in a frightful whisper, "not natural."

"It's the *Eye*," Thelana remarked, lifting the scepter. "There is no other explanation I can think of."

"So what do we do now?" the other replied.

"Destroy it," said Thelana, finding it again, the jewel's fire rotating continuously, forming ever more mesmerizing patterns. "It's an evil thing. Evil must be destroyed."

"But how can you be sure that's the right thing to do? What if it—what if we perish? If things become as they should be, one of us will cease to exist . . ."

"Better that than live on like this."

Thelana felt herself beyond the boundaries of creation, in the white spaces where even the gods did not hear or see. It was an ugly, sick sensation, of something perverse and unnatural eating her from within. "I know you feel it too."

"You're right. There is a wrongness here I can't even describe, a thing that should not be." With a sigh, her past self nodded in agreement.

Thelana placed the scepter in a bald spot on the ground. Moss formed where it lay and decayed and formed again. "Grimosse, smite this with your hammer, as hard as you can."

Both guardians hobbled forth, not bothering to question the existence of the other, and then the more forward of the two raised his arms over the scepter.

"A shame," said the one Thelana. "It was so beautiful."

The gold bell landed on the gem, and as glass facets exploded around them, its fire rose up, blinding them with crimson.

Thelana could hear herself screaming. But her words were muffled by the surrounding blaze of light—as if, in the dimension she'd stepped through, light and sound were one. She was being pulled in all directions at once, sickened with vertigo, and then the ground was beneath her feet again. When the light receded and balled up into the sun, her screaming escaped into the present and she came rushing after it.

Nesper's body collapsed in a heap. Thelana turned from the spectacle to find Xandr, pale and stumbling. There was a sense of having witnessed the same event before, and her skin prickled her from brow to toe.

"Are you all right?"

"Only a scratch," he said.

Rushing under him, catching him, she let out a cry. "What was he talking about? The purple death?"

"Poison," he admitted, and he became too heavy for her to lift.

The world spun around her as she bent over him, pounding her fists angrily, lovingly, against his breast. She swallowed hard her screams. The monoliths stood ever silent, watching, indifferent. Over the plain, the sun began to rise, giving texture and dimension to the emptiness surrounding her. Towards the East, the *Great White Flat* waited, and the western hemisphere kept quiet its promise of shelter.

The desert was so vast.

Wait. Not again. I've done this. I've been here . . . No!

Images deposited like sediments in her mind's eye. Days transpired in seconds. She remembered descending the cliffs atop Rurk to the scorched surface of the Ocean, remembered the digging, the sleeping underground, the abandoned ruins of Shess, the lurid glow of the Serpent's Eye. She would not, could not, live it again.

Then there was a touch, the warm brush of another's skin against her.

He's alive.

His shoulders lifted with great effort. His eyes were reddened with fatigue, with miseries, but there was no purple-like dye filling his retinas as before. She frisked his body but could find no mark of entry. "Nesper's dagger?"

"You were screaming," he said sleepily. "*The dagger, poison*, you kept saying. I nearly threw myself the other way . . ."

"But you said it was only a scratch, like before, remember?" She was frantic, confused. "What did you mean?"

He placed a shaky hand over his brow, where Purple Death Adder's tail had made its mark. His flesh was clean now, only the memory of the pain remaining. A moment ago was ancient history. Another man had fought and died in that arena, Xandr's great ancestor, the first to carry the name Batal.

"Xandr," she murmured, "you look at me as if you've not seen me in ages."

"It's . . ." he started, blinking with confusion, "it's *been* ages, truly. Tellhus!" he called. "Eldin! Mother Goddess, the people in the pits . . . they're still down there . . . fodder for snake men, they're—"

She nudged him onto his back. "It's over," she whispered, her understanding becoming as keen as her dagger. "There's nothing but dust in those pits. The snake men are no more."

"Thelana." He reached for her cheek, his limbs moving heavily, like a newborn unaccustomed to its body. "What a dream I've had! You wouldn't believe how real—"

"I'd believe it," she answered sharply. "Believe me I'd believe it. It is just as the Ilmar say: a dream is a journey."

His smile was barely discernible beneath the bristles of his lip, and tears formed in the ducts of his eyes. "You've never looked so beautiful, Thelana."

"Me?" The remark caught her off guard. "I must look a wretch." She fumbled a moment with her locks, but braiding was never her forte and the desert only served to fray her hair. But despite her effort, he did not see her, since he was again asleep. For a moment she feared he was succumbing to the venom, that she'd overlooked a razor-thin scratch somewhere. But his color was not as she remembered it in the desert. His breast expanded and contracted with the might of his strong, slumbering body.

If not for Xandr's recollections, Thelana was certain she would be questioning her sanity. After talking to the guardian, she realized Grimosse was oblivious to their journey across the Ocean. Perhaps his minute brain rejected the paradox. She had found him where he stood before, pounding Nesper's corpse into the dust. With the golem's aid, she moved Xandr into the newly propped tent, and waited, wanting nothing more than to lay her arms about his rising bosom and be comforted by his embrace. But she was still feeling dizzy. Simply thinking about the last few days was tying her mind into a knot.

Does the Serpent's Eye still exist now that things have gone back? Does Shess remain undisturbed? Did anything I do even happen? Absently, she rummaged through her garments, but there was no trace of the Septheran treasure.

As her mind wandered, it turned at last to Nesper's map. The map was the pivot point between past and future. Before finding it, she was where she now stood. Afterwards, she'd gone into the desert to find Shess. If the map was still there, she could trust everything else to exist: the seashells, the ruined city, and the *Serpent's Eye.*

Rurk stood patiently as ever, the massive saurian's freedom impeded by a single stake. Searching among the tools and rolled canvases along its side, she found no funnel, no map. But in its place was a book. She set it down against the flat of a rock. The binding was scaly and wrinkled. Turning her head sideways, she could see its creases rising to form a broad, toothy skull. It looked trapped, as if forcing its bony face through the binding. It was eerily familiar.

The contradiction between what was and what should be set her mind spinning. Had she remembered correctly? Was there a map or a book before, or was she truly going insane? *The heat has been said to drive men mad, hasn't it?*

Exhausted, she followed her body into Xandr's tent and laid herself down beside him.

The orange expanse of the Ocean beckoned with seductive twists of barren riverbeds, horizon-hugging gorges, a towering architecture of rock. Every silhouette, every crevice hiding unseen wonders, was like a lover longing to be explored. It was difficult to sit over the drop and not wonder at it. But his mind was engrossed by greater mysteries, by the open tome in his lap, by the symbols on the page.

It was the language of the Zo, its meaning lost to the centuries. The calligraphy was mesmerizing. It was difficult to believe the crazy old man could have achieved it, that any mortal hand could have produced such elegant angles, line after line, page after page without error, but there it was, the *Ages of Aenya*. Major events were fully revealed in oils, including his ancestor's battle with the snake prince. Thousands of pages separated the first Batal from the last, from the time of the human rebellion to the fall of Hedonia. But it was the final few pages, the prophecies of things to come after Hedonia, which troubled him. The paintings were done in a hurried hand, in dark shades of olive greens and charcoal grays. In some places, the ink spilled in splotches or in ribbons of black. It was strangely unlike Eldin and the perfectionist hand that came before. Did the old man finally lose his mind or did some other take his place to complete the work?

"The falling star . . ." Thelana intoned. He could feel her palm rest on his shoulder as she knelt beside him. "And is that, the Pewter Mountains?"

"It is," he replied, "more specifically, the Absent Mountain." Identical peaks reached into a white sky split by the fiery trail of a falling star. "Do you see it? From this angle, the space between the mountains forms an inverted third mountain, but it's an illusion. There is only one place where this can be seen, the Endless Plain. That is where the star has fallen."

"We saw it just before Hedonia was destroyed. It was a terrible omen."

"Indeed," he said. "But did we misinterpret the omen? The Hedonian priesthood took it to mean the end of the empire—after all, their entire world *was* the empire. But could the omen have portended something much worse?"

"What could be worse than the deaths of all those—"

"The death of all people," he said matter-of-factly, and turned the page. "The destruction of Aenya."

The final page in the *Ages of Aenya* was frayed at the edges, brittle like a dead leaf. There was the outline of a jagged mountain rim and a human-like silhouette painted in a hurried, frightened hand.

"I've seen something like that before," she murmured, "when I first left Ilmarinen, when I was being chased by a halfman. Many of them, in a ruined city in the woods—they were terribly ancient, long forgotten. *Golems.*" The unmistakable shapes etched into the walls at Shess were etched into her memory also, broad-bodied beings who stood over the Septhera, but she did not tell him of it. Her story was a long and difficult one she could hardly explain to herself. "What does it mean? Golems are just statues. They're not, alive, are they?"

Xandr lifted his eyes toward their encampment. Grimosse stood beside the tethered Rurk, vigilant as ever. "Is he alive?"

Thelana wanted to smack herself for never having made the connection. "All right . . . so what does it mean?"

"When I was a child, when I first noticed the shapes in the boulders—when I realized they couldn't have been made by erosion, I asked my mentor about them. He called them *Xexaz*, a word that means *forgotten*. I assumed, at the time, that what he meant was that he didn't know, that they were so ancient as to have become forgotten. Now I am not so sure. The man who wrote this . . . knew of them." His finger lingered over the page. "It would seem they are an ancient race, and that they—at least this one—is returning."

"Returning from where?" Thelana murmured, a slight shiver running down her spine. "And . . . what does that mean exactly?"

"In my dream . . . I witnessed a world of unimaginable evils, all humanity in subservience to another race. Those people could not imagine a world different from the one they knew. The legend of the Batal was born in such times. When a people suffer, Thelana, they cry for a man to rise up, to inspire hope in them. I did not dream in vain."

"And you believe that such a time has come again?"

"I was raised in the Mountains of Ukko, under the guidance of the Alashiyan Monks, taught in the ways of Kjus. The monks believed I was destined for something important. I was a child then. My mentor tried to explain, to teach me that compassion makes a man what he is. I didn't understand. I was trying to right all the wrongs of this world by the sword I was given. You were right, Thelana—a dream is a journey, and it takes a man a journey to find true understanding."

"And now," she said. "What are you going to do? Where are we going to go?"

"Not west," he replied.

She stole a chance to smile despite the somber occasion.

"To the northeast, to find this star, to find what I was meant for. Eldin was trying to warn me of something, something he has seen but that hasn't yet happened. On a mountaintop . . . we must go there."

"Who's Eldin?"

"It doesn't matter," he said, letting the book fall shut, its skull face scowling up at them. "And this . . ." he began, fingering the raised image.

"It's like your sword," she admitted. "The resemblance is uncanny."

"Is it? I don't know what it means. I can't see the connection. Before he died, my master told me to retrieve the sword. It was kept in a room with many strange things—things we Ilmar could not have possibly made, but how or what they were I never learned. The monastery burned before I could discern its mysteries. The sword is the only link I have to my past, to who I am, or who I'm supposed to be. If this book can answer those questions, then I must seek those who can interpret it. The book and the star is everything."

"This is too much for me," she replied, as if to herself, stepping away from the ledge. "All I ever wanted was to find my family, not save the world."

"You're right," he said, meeting her gaze. "You should not be involved in this. When we reach the forest, you can go where you will."

"No," she exclaimed, "that's not what I meant, I—"

He hushed her. "Thelana, I know what you meant, but I have seen the sacrifices required of Batal, of me. My eyes have been opened. My mentor raised me for this, and I can no longer dishonor him by running from my fate."

"I am not telling you to turn from it," she said. "I only want to be a part of it, to fight for what you fight."

"You don't know what you ask," he answered. "My ancestor, the Batal before me, gave his life for Aenya. And so did his friends."

"That doesn't have to happen," she argued. "The past doesn't dictate the future . . . and if you'd be Batal, I'd have my bow ready at his side."

"Thelana," he implored, "everyone I've ever cared about is gone. I won't ask you to risk yourself—"

"After all the trike-dung we've been through," she cried, her words coming through angry quivering lips. "Nearly drowning in Hedonia, falling out of the sky, being tossed around by birds only to land in gods' forsaken nowhere, and then nearly being burned alive, sleeping in dirt and starving half to death . . ." She paused to breathe. "Did you think that was fun for me? I've risked myself a thousand times over already for you! Do you even know that I dragged your carcass halfway across this sun-scorched hell just to revive you? You'd have no future without me! And now you ask me to step aside, to forget everything and go along my merry way? Well, I think not! You're stuck with me, *Batal*, destiny be damned!"

As the green fire of her eyes subsided, she shrank, her sharp shoulders pulling close to her sides, their shape disappearing beneath the folds of her djellabah. Her outburst left her drained, and Xandr noticed how terribly frail she looked, as if she were held together by twine. He wondered when last she ate. For a long time he noticed her. The silence between them spoke more truths than any declarations could. Sunlight made her eyes glitter like emeralds, painted freckles onto her cheeks like constellations. The top of her lip curved when she pouted, dipping in the middle, so much like a bow. And he could not wait. There was a primal thing inside of him, too long subdued. He attacked her with a kiss. But there were still remnants of anger, of resentment in her. She shrugged him away.

"Get off!" she managed, her lips muffled by his. "I hate you!" *I love you.*

They worked their way backward, toward the tent, littering the Ocean shelf with clothing. Soon they were in the tent, as free of clothing as Ilmar are wont to be. The sudden freedom from fabric, the loose, open, smooth sensation of every element against her skin, a feeling so long unremembered, was exhilarating. But she was not free, because he was with her, everywhere she was. His hand was full of her buttocks and the fingers of his other stroked her locks.

"Take me," she huffed. "I want you. *Inside.*" She arched her spine to meet him, driving her belly against his muscled abdomen, and he knew that she needed him urgently, that she would die without it. Sweat formed along her extremities, pooling in the pit of her neck, trickling between her breasts and down her ribs like a stairwell. She spread for him, her copper thighs tight about his hips. He descended, breaking her like a peach, and she cried out, wept as pleasure lapped against her, drowned her in sensation. Every pretense melted away, every defense tumbled down. He gave in, surrendering to her entirely, and he saw that selfsame instinct reflected in her eyes.

As the light pulled away like a canvas from the hills, Thelana gazed once more over the precipice. A cool wind was blowing and she held tight to her djellabah. Xandr still slept, but soon she would rouse him, to follow the waning sun and under the cover of night trek toward more hospitable lands in the East. It would be a long journey, perhaps cycles, and it would be hard. After all she'd seen and done, she did not doubt they would survive it. But she feared the awkward silences to come. Thelana was a simple farm girl, and simple farm girls found mates with whom to build homes and make children. That was and always had been the Ilmarin way. But whatever was meant to be, her way of life, her traditions, all was dashed the day she left home. She listened to him snore and wondered what he would be to her. Without a land to call their own, could two Ilmar find a place to begin anew? Could the Batal be expected to be husband, father, or even a lover? Could he belong to her or would Aenya claim him? Joining to his flesh did not bring the bliss she anticipated. Rather, her heart was in turmoil, with the same lingering loneliness. Xandr's presence did not erase her pining for her loved ones, nor alleviate the questions that left her mind bruised with repetition, the questions she could never hope to escape unanswered—were they out there, somewhere, wondering about her also? Or had they gone to the Taker? She looked out over the last lighted remains of the Ocean as though she might see some face emerge from the cliffs, leaving whispered names for the desert.

14

NO ONE

Under an orange sky choked by fumes, the din of battle died away over the Plains of Narth. Most of the bodies were human, but the little ones, with their bony frames and taut gray skin and cruel etched faces, were not. Vulture spiders roamed among them, their elongated legs picking among the carrion, carrying the bodies away in web cocoons. Further in the distance, the hills were moving—or things that looked like hills—bashing anything that stirred. Since the dead did not stir, they crossed over to the dying, occasionally crushing the skulls of allies as they went. Thelana knew she was the only one that remained—neither horg nor bogren nor corpse—a small figure flitting swiftly through the haze. It was difficult for her to run without broken arrowheads digging into her soles—they clustered like weeds—but she managed her way back, vaulting herself over the makeshift ramp of sludge and dead and supplies.

"Torgin is down," she said calmly, pressing her back against the rampart beside him.

"Are you sure?" Dantes said uneasily. "Did you see the body?"

She wanted to tell him how she'd found him, how his brains were splattered against a horg's iron, how his lazy eye was as still as any other, but she answered simply, "Yes. I'm sorry."

Usually, Dantes would say something to stir the soul, or mutter some prayer to his gods. But this time, he cursed. Dantes loved Torgin as a brother. "What about the lines? Are they intact?" There was real desperation in his voice, unlike anything she had ever heard.

"I . . . didn't find anyone out there, Captain. I believe they're all—"

"Damn it to Skullgrin, Thelana!" he screamed.

Even after cycles of fighting, he had called her, 'new girl'. 'Come here, new girl,' he would say, or, 'What did you find out, new girl?' She hated it at first, but gradually came to think of it as a sign of his affection for her. After all, much to the irritation of the others in her company, he made tactical decisions that, one way or the other, put her out of harm's way, using her swift footing, for instance, for scouting out the enemy. Only recently, when their numbers began to dwindle and her bow came into play more frequently, did he begin calling her by name.

"It's over, isn't it?" she asked.

Dantes was never known to admit defeat. Most often, as in the case of recruiting his youngest and best archer, he would get his way. It was what Thelana loved about him. But now his pride, his refusal to retreat, had led his friends and comrades to their deaths. "It's over for us," he said quietly, "but we've done our duty. That is all the gods can ask of us. We've slowed their advance, that much is certain, and the city guard will be waiting."

"But what will *we* do? Where we will go?" She was frightened of the answer even as she asked.

"We will stay," he replied, without a trace of hesitation. "We will fight to the end."

Having lost so many lives, to flee could only bring him shame. Men of honor could not live with shame, yet she pressed him. "But what good will it do? Let's leave this place. Together. Begin a new life somewhere far away."

"No," he said, without argument, without explanation of any kind.

"But—"

"Am I still not your Captain?" he shouted. "Every second we delay those monsters, every second they spend fighting us, is another second we give to the people of Kratos."

"I'm sorry," she said softly, her hand moving close enough for him to feel it. "I was being selfish. But—but if we are to die," she started, surprised by her nervousness even in the face of the Taker, "at least tell me what I mean to you."

His gaze fell hard on her, as if suddenly realizing that a woman was fighting alongside him and an uncomfortable space started to form between them. "I don't know what you're trying to . . ."

She had always believed, or was it mere hope, that he would be expecting such a query. *Is it too soon? How can it be? Unless he doesn't know . . . unless he feels nothing.* "I thought you cared about me. You always sent me on those scouting missions, and in battle you kept me close to you—"

"Thelana," he said, his face souring, "of course I care about you. You're a great archer, a loyal ally—"

She cupped his hand with her own. His knuckles were hard, her palm scabrous—their scars fit together in places. "Dantes, that's not what I meant."

The words froze between them. She searched his face for any sign of affection amid the anguish for his men. He averted her gaze, focused on her as he would any soldier. But he understood the meaning in her questing eyes, saw the love he could not return. And suddenly she felt ashamed, wanting to take back even those simple words.

"Thelana, you're a very young girl and I have, well . . . I have a wife waiting for me."

"You're joined?" Her heart tightened against the pain, but the revelation kept digging deeper like a bogren's spear. "I've never seen her! You've never mentioned her!"

"And I have daughters as well. One of them is your age."

She wanted to cry out, to weep, but amid so many dead and dying, love seemed like a foolish thing to weep for.

"Now you know why I can't retreat," he said. "My wife and children are in the city. I need to give them time. It is for the families of Kratos that we face the Taker." As he finished speaking, a terrible groan echoed across the plain, making them rattle in their armor.

"It's close," he said.

She pulled herself over the heap of dirt and broken bodies. It was there at thirty paces, a grotesque heap of fat. Boils popped from its folds, sizzling on the ground. The blood of its victims gleamed from a gargantuan battle-ax. Its skull was cut open like a melon, revealing a brain and the cords stretching out from it. A little gray creature sat on its shoulders, massaging the brain into submission, manipulating the strings with its other hand to move the horg's massive limbs like a marionette.

Thelana ducked back under. "It's a smart one."

"Can you take it down?"

"Do you have to ask?" Peering over the mound, she surveyed the broken landscape for unseen dangers, but there were none she could see. She slipped her longbow from her shoulder, nocked an arrow in it, and waited for the monster to turn her way. Horgs were nigh invincible, could take dozens of arrows in their leathery folds and keep coming. But they were also as stupid as herd animals. Without their bogren masters, they were easily trapped and killed. Her arrow went soaring just as the gray one's eyes narrowed in her direction. The bogren shrieked and tumbled from its perch—the cords attached to the horg's brain pulled tight and went slack. Without a creature to control it, the horg shambled toward her, bellowing in agony, swinging its enormous ax at invisible enemies.

"Dantes!" she cried. "It's coming straight for us. Run!"

"No," he said, hiding his dark brows beneath his helmet. "We must meet the enemy head on. There's no other way."

"We'll be killed."

"One less horg for the city guard to worry about!" he cried, less to her than to himself. With shield and sword high, he rushed at the monster, without strategy, without an ally with whom to organize an effectual assault.

No, Dantes, this isn't like you . . . this isn't like you at all . . .

He ran into the arms of the Taker as he ran into the monster's ax. Thelana shouted after him, but turned away at the final moment. Suddenly, all her years of daydreaming came to nothing. A thick lump welled up from the base of her being, up into her throat, choked her.

He was gone. The man she had loved.

No one stood alive on the Plains of Narth, no other human but her. The emptiness was overwhelming, but such emotions were a luxury afforded to mothers and wives and to those wealthy enough to purchase walls. The world stood vast and barren all around her, but the weight of its people still pressed her. Broken swords, clutched by inert fingers, spread like blades of grass. The horror of it—so remote from the simple world she was brought into—shattered something inside her and she ran screaming, clumsily in her boots, into the midst of the dead.

Unsatisfied by Dantes' blood, the horg lumbered for another kill, braying like a bull. She tugged at her beloved's shield until his body surrendered just as the ax came crashing against it, laying her flat. She fumbled for a sword—any sword—and sprang back to her feet. The ax came around again, splintering the wood from the boss and tearing it from her arms. With the shield in pieces and her shoulder aching from the impact, she stumbled over the fallen bodies of her regiment, knowing that soon the horg would cut her down and all her pain would be over. But a distant memory was teasing her—she had to keep moving. Against the overwhelming force of the horg's ax, her leather bindings were inconsequential, a hindrance that weighed and constrained her motion. This was not the way that Ilmar fought. Dantes had given strict orders that she keep her clothes on. *You'll lose face,* he'd said. *You will not look a soldier and the men will think you're available.* But Dantes was gone and every eye that might have shamed her was closed forever. In their armor, she was a prisoner, her breeches shackles of shame from a world she scarcely understood. She rounded the monster, keeping safely from its whizzing ax, and piece by piece, the accouterments of the Kratan soldier dropped like empty shells, the horrors of war peeling away with her chain greaves and belt, her brassiere and boots. She tore at the stitching as if burned by it. Even the fine muslin tunic Dantes had given her, the only article of clothing she had loved, crumpled in the dirt.

Wearing nothing but a sword, she stood under the sky, the Goddess a river surging through her. She closed her eyes to the enveloping touch of the battlefield, the shift in the ground as the horg stomped in blind circles, the small hairs of her body prickling as the ax came around and around.

He was twice her height. Ten times her weight. One blow and she was pulp. But having lost everything, she faced him. The horg charged, and she met him first, clambering up his rolls of fat, crossing his arm like the bough of a tree. Before his dimwitted mind could work out where she'd gone to, she was riding his back, plunging her sword into his exposed brain. The horg gave a confused groan and toppled like a column as Thelana rolled from his shoulders.

For a long while she stood, staring at the grotesque thing she had killed. Dantes was avenged, but there was no joy to be found in the slaying. For the Ilmar, every life was a part of the Goddess. To pull even a flower from its root was a moment for lamentation. But there were more like the one she killed. She could hear the monsters now, breaking through the trees. She could outrun them with ease, but would she dishonor those who had fallen?

The world was cold and crisp. Wind nymphs teased her body, filling her pores, waking her to sensations long forgotten. Dantes died for his family, but hers was not in Kratos.

She ran. Further and further her legs carried her, away from the plains of Narth, away from all things having to do with the people of Kratos, or war, or civilizations, or things not of Ilmarinen. She ran as though she could out-run the pain of losing him. When her calves finally gave in to exhaustion, she looked up from the ground in a daze, without a notion of where she was or how much time had passed. But the pain was still there, having followed her from the battlefield. Dantes' death had not the power to extinguish her affection for him. Rather, it burrowed in, festering in her heart. .

And she decided then that she never loved Dantes. She stood anew under the turquoise glow of the greater moon, drawing strength from the Goddess, the wooded hilltop to the north calling her to freedom, to home.

What mountains rolled beneath her soles, what grasses broke to her passage, what heavy rains pounded clean her lithe frame as she searched for shelter among fallen civilizations? For Thelana, it was of no consequence. The moons and sun waltzed across the sky uncounted times, for each step northward brought her closer to home, strengthening her will, adding swiftness to her thighs. All the while, she banished from her mind every evil she had been witness to, even the memory of her beloved Dantes. Over the following hill, her sisters would greet her with giggles and her brothers with cruel games of jest, and Mother and Baba would open their arms and never let her go. Any day now it would happen. Just over the next hill she would see it, beyond a waving sea of purple and orange, Old Man oak with its ancient boughs, and her home, built to shelter all of them, by her father's hands.

Just one more hill, and she would be there.

Through a winding path of dense foliage, she came in sight of the mountains of Ukko. They stood like fossilized sentinels guarding the horizon. She climbed gray sheets of granite, pulling herself by slender tree limbs that found perch in the mountainside, until the valley spread before her with its semblance of womanly hips and tributaries like cascading hair. But it was not as Thelana imagined. She did not feel the elation she had expected, but rather, a reserved sense of joy, a doubt guarding her heart. She feared what old warriors would often say in the trenches, that home was not a place one could return to, but a place in memory. After all she had seen and done, was it possible to go back to a simple life? *No*, she assured herself, *I will not be spoiled by war*. She raced downward, never minding the dangerously steep and rocky terrain—she had no time to bother with it, for her family was waiting, and she only hoped the sun would last so she might sleep in her cot come nightfall.

There was no color in the valley but ash grays and browns. The orange petals and violet stamens were no more, and the ilms that remained drooped from their stems, their buds curled and brittle. Other plants, the likes she had never seen, had taken their place, with flowers like teeth and leaves with sharp edges. When Thelana tried to pass between them, they drew blood across her sides, and unseen weeds stabbed at her from below, making her wish for shoes. Reluctantly, she followed her knife's edge forward, but deep in the valley the weeds closed above her, making it difficult to know in which direction she was moving.

Old Man's fingers were thin and spidery, reaching out like a drowning man in the gray haze of sky. Under the shadow of the oak, her house stood quietly in a shroud of fallen leaves. Her hands found purchase in the gnarled roots that formed the base of her home and she clambered onto the porch. The dinner table, sitting under the shade of the branches in the patterns of sunlight, was gray and lifeless. She brushed a hand across the tabletop, removing leaves and dust. Every bump and crevice conjured memories of mealtime, of father's booming laughter and her brothers' antics, of days when food became a matter of difficult division and decision.

The front door swung open suddenly, and she imagined someone noticing her, rushing to greet her. But it was only the whim of the wind.

The air within was thick and reeked of age, and the main room with its cooking hearth and washbasin and the stool where Mother so often could be found spinning pottery was dreamy and pallid, at once familiar and strange. The pot was cracked and mice feasted on the grain that spilled from it. Mother's stool had fallen over, its edges frayed by vermin. She returned it to its place.

How can Mana leave the house this way? It must be Britannia, shirking her duties again. Mana should beat her butt raw for this . . .

The house looked awful. But it only needed attending to. Sweeping and sanding, she assured herself.

But the weeds! By the gods, what were the boys doing? It would take cycles, perhaps even years, to pull every one, but she'd help out. She was stronger than ever now. She drifted to the pantry, searching for breads or sticks of pasteli, but there was neither grain nor her favorite honey-sesame seed treat. She found only a pot of honey. A diorama of insects was trapped in it, but she scraped at the ceramic eagerly, and when she was done her fingertips were stuck together.

It was then she heard a distinctive snap.

The noise came from the bedroom, shaking her from her stupor, and Thelana rushed through the doorway. A crow was at the windowsill, buffeting its wings, and seeing her it disappeared. Twigs sprouted from the floorboards and roots were making way through the walls and ceiling. She knelt down, feeling suddenly ill. The room was in disarray. Sunlight shone through a seam in the ceiling, and the cots were scattered, layered with balls of dust, crawling with mites. With a troubled smile, she conjured Baba's stern face as he demanded that the twelve of them lie quietly. But the giddy faces of her brothers and sisters were as vague as shadows, and the decaying walls trapped the echo of their laughter.

Thelana moved from room to room, went outside to the porch and back again.

For too long she wandered, rejecting her senses, seeing only memories. Occasionally, she shouted a name, in hopes that some voice might answer, knowing none would. At last, she came to the rear of the house, noticing the small stone mounds. She pulled at the weeds surrounding them until her fingers became slick with blood, finding the choked and withered remains of the ilms planted to mark the graves. All of her ancestors were buried under Old Man oak. Most became flowers. Some, like her grand-mother, became trees. The mounds were markers for mourners who did not wish the deceased to pass quickly from memory. Which of her loved ones lay buried at her feet? Was it Baba, Mana? If not them, how could they have endured it, to bury their children after losing Borz, after losing her? Mother was a woman born for child-rearing— it was her purpose for being. Thelana hoped her mother to have perished before suffering such a loss. But if her parents had gone to the Taker, who would have cared for the others? Without Borz, who possessed the strength? Amina? Laine? Vaino?

How did it happen? There was little food in the house and the land was barren. Could they have become sick with starvation? Most likely, her youngest sister, Nicola, who was sickly, would have gone first.

I should have never left.

Which of her loved ones lay buried at her feet? Again the question tormented her. She could dig up the bodies. Assuming the worms had not eaten them beyond recogni-tion, it could resolve a lifetime of wondering, but the idea made her shudder, and she resolved, albeit with great dif-ficulty, to never knowing.

One thing was certain, they were not killed. There were no blade marks on the house, or broken arrows or footprints. Most of the farm tools and grain stores were taken. Ilmarinen was abandoned, she imagined, as food became scarce. But where had her family gone to? Was it a forced exodus? Had strangers taken them into slavery?

Shriveled ilm petals swirled about her like spirits of the dead, landing where she knelt beside the stones. Unwilling to think, too exhausted to feel, she dreaded a return to the house, with its quiet walls. She decided that home existed in some other place, in some other Ilmarinen. But for now, she would remain under Old Man oak's familiar branches. And as day rolled into night, she laid herself down in darkness, in the damp, chill air, comforted in knowing her loved ones rested closely beneath her.

THE THIRD OMEN

OMEN

Flesh and Steel

1

DONKEY FACE

The only thing Emmalina longed for was to be loved, but she felt certain that nobody cared for her. Of friends, she had none, nor did she understand how other people came to have friends, when she did not. Only one person occupied any space in her life—the man she called, albeit with little affection, father. Between his strange comings and goings, Emma possessed passings with only herself to talk to, or sing to, and as the years went by she found a kind of solace in loneliness. She became her own friend and sister, and parent. And who better to understand her than Emma? She felt safe in the cloak that had belonged to her mother and was black as a moonless night. Since her mother had been a tall woman, the sleeves drooped well past Emma's fingers, and often wrapped protectively around her waist.

The world Emmalina knew was gray and cold and hard. But sometimes, after the Thunder God shook the world and split the sky and loosed rain that fell like pebbles, a band of colors would appear bridging the sky.

Delians called it *Strom's Bow* and it was a good omen, a sign that the god's anger had abated. Such explanations didn't satisfy Emma, and she would sit in wonderment, watching as the last hint of violet faded, dreaming of places strange and ancient and faraway. Occasionally, orchids sprouted between the cracks of the Wall, with blue and red and orange, but this color did not last long either, wilting quickly in the cold.

As far as she knew, there were two seasons in Aenya: high moon and low moon. During high moon, the people of Northendell huddled inside their houses to watch fireballs rain down on them, and men-at-arms returned from the Wall bloodied or broken or carried on the bier. In the peace that followed, the streets became slick with ice, and clumps of frozen sky dropped out of the ether to shatter shingles from rooftops. Delians did not venture out on such days, but year after year there were those too stubborn for caution, who were sometimes later found with their skulls caved in.

When the snow flowed out of the city, the second season began, and the people felt safe enough to set up tents in the market square, to barter, haggle and gossip. In the alleyways, boys played at war as girls hopscotched, or together they went into hiding and seeking, an ideal game in the labyrinthine city. When the snows came down softly to cover the streets like white linen, the children found joy in it, all except Emma. For years she'd watched from her tower window, pining to explore the city with the other children. But the door to the tower was locked from the inside. Father was fond of keys. The iron ring at his belt chimed heavily wherever he went, so Emma could hear him marching downstairs to his study, or out the front door in the pitch of night. By her ninth year, her father relented and Emma came into possession of her own key.

Emma was now ten. She turned the key in the lock twice, put her weight into the door, and looked up. Was it morning or late afternoon? The sky gave no indication, looking gray and bleak and ready to crush her under its weight. There was no horizon in Emma's world, only a distant haze and the silver outline of the Pewter Mountains poking through it.

She started down the cobblestone path, fingering the gaps in the Wall. Fig trees ripped through the masonry, which no one ever bothered to repair. Her father had forgotten the ritual of breakfast years ago, so Emma was fortunate when the fruit was in season. Drop fruit, as Delians called it, littered the cobblestones, dappling the ice and rock with purple splotches. The fuzzy brown ones split into soft sweet clovers like honey. She ate until she was no longer hungry, filling her satchel with as many as she could, and continued down.

She moved sideways where the houses were built too closely together and walked with the aid of her palms where the streets tilted. The edges with missing cobblestones sometimes bloodied her feet. But such unforgiving passages were advantageous to one who longed to be lost and who, unlike most children, was never missed. Scrawny enough to disappear beneath her robes, Emma was able to slip through alleyways too narrow for grown women, finding alcoves that even the lords of the city could not lay claim to, discovering mysteries she was certain no one knew existed.

Though she had never seen beyond the Wall, Northendell, she knew, was built into the mountain. Where the natural rock tapered off and hand-worked stone began was difficult to discern. Finding remnants of a home or church in what was once believed a boulder was not uncommon. Behind the city, the caves went on forever, or so Emma, unnoticed in the niches above the people's homes, heard people say. Adventuring locals who went into them were said to be there still, navigating the remainder of their lives to get home. Such stories were enough to frighten children, even many adults, from becoming lost. But Emma was undeterred.

In walls within walls, Emma found her place. She came to poke and prod at life's queries, to wonder and hear her own voice and feed crumbs to her friends, the ravens perched in the niches above. On one such occasion, she became absorbed watching a copper line of ants marching off to battle a horned beetle, their mandibles clamping against its armored shell fruitlessly as the unfazed beetle kept plodded along. She had never seen such a resilient creature among the insect world, and as the ants continued to scurry and fight with increasing urgency, she devised a new story and became a goddess, swooping down to the ant world in an act of divine providence. The horned beetle kicked pairs of chubby thighs helplessly between her fingers, where the birds hovered, crowding about her arm and shoulders. In a snapping of beak too swift to be seen, the beetle's armor cracked like a walnut. Part of her was saddened by its demise, but the ravens were growing bored with bread. Other Delians shunned the black birds, viewed them as heralds of the

Taker. A flock of milling ravens was a sign of imminent death. Families with elders or sick children watched fretfully as the birds lingered about. But Emma was skeptical, having spent entire days in their company, without either herself or her father falling dead. Besides, ravens were beautiful. Their sleek, black feathers shimmered in the moons, much like her hair, contrasting sharply against the pallid backdrop of broken masonry. And like her, they were reclusive, unloved.

"But you can fly above these walls," she murmured. "Above the city. High above the world . . ."

Snickering sounded behind her, and she turned, her heart leaping into her throat. No adult could hope to fit between the narrow passages to her secret place, but she was not the only child in Northendell. The bemused, snearing faces confronting her were not unfamiliar. "Look at her going on like that," said the roundest of the three boys. "By Strom, she's downright loony!"

Emma knew him as Bood, the one whom other boys listened to, who made friends . . . managed somehow to earn respect. Like a dog at his heel was Deed. He was not as well-fed and his clothing was always too tight or loose, which was not uncommon for a bastard, a whoreson, as she once heard someone say. The third boy, Obi, was younger than the two and finely tailored. Emma did not see him often, knowing only that he fidgeted a lot and spoke rarely and with a stammer.

Deed approached her with an accusing look. "Were you talking to yourself this time or to the birds?"

"I wasn't—" she started, searching for a believable justification.

"She talks to both," Bood answered for her. "I would too if I was as *ugly* as she was."

Deed gave a nervous chuckle. "Hey, that's a good point!" Obi stood in their shadows, trying to look large and important.

"You know crows can't talk, don't you?" Bood asked her.

"They're ravens," she corrected.

"Crows, ravens . . . who cares? They're just stupid, ugly birds. Obi, your father's a knight, right? He kills dragons, right? Show us how he does it." He presented the boy with a smooth rock, about the size of his fist, as if it were a fine sword.

"I c-c-can do it," he stammered, squinting at the perches overhead.

Emma followed his aim and her sleeves came up like banners, to shield the birds from harm. "Don't!"

"What do you care?" said Bood. "Oh, I forgot. They're your friends, aren't they?"

"Why won't you leave me alone?" she replied. "This is my place."

"*Your* place? How is it *your* place? You don't own the city. You're *not* royalty. You're *not* even high born. You're just a *wall-born* girl with a *donkey face* that nobody can stand to look at, which is why you talk to birds . . . isn't that right, Obi?" It wasn't just the words, but the inflection of his voice, the emphasis on this or that word, the contortion of his face that twisted in her gut. When the tears ran from her eyes at the threshold of her father's study, she never managed to recreate the scene. She could recite the words verbatim, but from her mouth Bood's insults fell flat.

Deed was nowhere near as clever, but no less cruel, mimicking Bood's every action. "Donkey face!" he half cried, half laughed.

"Stop it!" she insisted, as if they could be reasoned with. "Stop saying that!" Each outburst brought lumps of sorrow to her throat. She wanted to say more, but found that she couldn't.

Obi's rock missed its mark, clacking against a third floor parapet. Dozens of ravens spread wing, abandoning their perches to circle above. Deed picked up another rock.

"Stop it!" she cried. "Leave them alone!"

"Or you'll what?" Bood threatened. "What are you going to do to me, princess?"

"More like princess of donkeys," Deed added, throwing and missing.

All three boys were focused on the birds now, on their aim, not seeing the slender stone slip beneath her sleeve. She eyed Bood's forehead with intense hatred, but Emma lived in the mind, in a world of imagined feats, and she drew first blood, instead, across Obi's eyebrow. The youngest of the three boys, who'd never spoken unkindly to her, crumpled against the wall and started weeping.

"Dammit!" Bood cried. "His father's gonna thrash us!"

"Get her!" Deed shouted.

Emma dashed between the walls as the rocks began to fly. She could hear them cracking against the buildings, heavy enough to open her skull. Bood squeezed through the passage in pursuit, his gut flattening, with Deed close behind, leaving Obi alone with his tears.

The panic went to her limbs as Emma pulled herself around corners, clamored up sloping streets, tripping over the hem of her robes and bruising her palms, on her feet again and running blindly, things catching and tearing at her sleeves, shouts and the clack-clack-clack of stones following her. Walls came at her like battering rams, every which way, leading her, pressing her to the shoulder, twisting her heels, expanding onto courtyards in a kaleidoscope of possible directions. Her thoughts came in fragmented bursts. Which way? Not a creature of instinct, she hesitated, without knowing how closely the boys followed. Should she hide? Slip into a side passage in the hope they not see her?

No.

In a dead-end alcove, she would be trapped and they would kill her. What she wanted more than anything was to be home. Father would know what to do with these bullies, she assured herself. *He can't be too busy to help you at a time like this, can he?* But Northendell was a mountain city, built in levels, and her tower was on the highest tier, on the outer edges of the Wall. The steps, having become uneven over the centuries, grew higher and further apart, and her legs began to ache. Exhaustion drove her to her knees. As she gathered up her robes to lift herself again, she wondered why Bood and Deed were not yet upon her, and then something white whizzed past her cheek. They had been stupid enough to stop and scoop up stones, and it had given her the advantage. A second stone ruffled her cloak, but the third crashed under her knee. She managed to limp to a courtyard where the cobblestones formed a circular pattern about an olive tree, just as Bood overtook her, knocking her onto the rough pavement. Despite his rotund belly, the boy moved quickly, at least more quickly than his waif partner, who caught up to them, panting.

No amount of imagination could help Emma escape her impending reality. She could only watch, bruised by the city's hard edges, her breathing sharp, a mix of exhaustion and fear rooting her to the spot. Bood tugged at the olive tree where she lay, littering the ground with dark green leaves. The makeshift sword in his meaty fingers swished to and fro.

Her eyes darted between the two boys, desperately seeking a passerby. Even her father would suffice. Homes scattered around them, in tiers above and below, but no one would hear her screams but the ravens perched at the windowsills and banner masts.

"Please!" She was trembling, her sleeve masking her like a veil. "I didn't mean to hurt Obi—honest!"

"What was that?" Bood cried, brandishing his stick. "Did you hear something, Deed?"

The boy shrugged, not catching on to the joke. "Uh ... no?"

"Well *I* heard something," said Bood, "and it went *hee-haw, hee-haw!*"

Deed shared a chuckle with his friend, adding his own, albeit poorly imitated, donkey sounds. Emma's vision swam and, as the tears made their way to her cheeks, she knew she would have preferred the beating to their mockery.

"Let me the stick," Deed blurted, "and I'll teach this donkey some obedience!" Deed's cruelty was blunt, more brutal than his friend's. She shut her eyes as something hard splintered against her lips and chin. It was like nothing she had felt before, a lightning bolt in the face, followed by throbbing and stinging. She awaited a successive blow, all quivering, but it did not come. A heavy voice rang in the air and, when she dared to look, a copper helm shone in her eyes. She could hear the marching boots, their orange breast plates clanking atop their shoulders. The stick spotted with her blood was in the hands of a man-at-arms, a *copperhead*, whose lip and jaw were squarely framed by the thick hairs of his mustache.

"Bohemond," the man-at-arms admonished, his face-plate retracting into his armored collar, "you're the butcher's boy, aren't you?"

"Yes, sir," Bood answered, trying his best to look mature, though his voice was that of a frightened boy.

"And you," he said, directing a furrowed eyebrow toward Obi, whom Emma had not noticed arrive, "I know your father. You're Ovulus' youngest, aren't you?"

"Ovulus j-j-junior, sir," he admitted. "Ovulus the s-s-second."

"Explain yourselves." His words and his looks were like the blows of a hammer on an anvil.

"W-W-Well, sir," Ovulus said with his usual stammer, "I—we—I mean my friends and I, well we—"

"Out with it, boy, or I'll beat it of you."

"Well, we met this g-g-girl, you see, and then she hit me, so we ch-chased her, and now we're here and . . ."

"I can see that!" the soldier replied. "By Strom's surly beard, they'll be calling you Ovulus the Obvious someday! But what I don't understand is what you're doing here with this riff-raff. Your father is a knight. Someday you will be a knight. You'd best start acting like one. Understood?"

"Y-Yes, sir."

"Now run off and tell your father what you've been doing. Or I will. And as for you boys," he said, turning to Bood and Deed, "I don't want you crossing my sight again."

Both saluted him, Bood showing a modicum of sincerity, but Emma saw nothing but spite in Deed's eyes. The man-at-arms glared back, his eyes an icy blue, and he sent them scurrying with a smack to their behinds.

Emma tried to speak, finding it painful, feeling her lip doubled in size.

"You, girl," said the man-at-arms. "Don't think I've seen you around."

She was afraid to answer, as if she might get a beating for saying the wrong thing, but seeing she was without choice in the matter, broke the silence at last. "People usually . . . don't see me, sir," she said, searching for patterns in the cobblestones, unable to look at him.

"Well, you must have somewhere better to be than here. Where's your mother?"

"Dead, sir," she answered.

"I see," he said. "And your father, what of him?"

"Don't know," she replied.

"You're no vagabond?" he half asked, studying the cut of her robes.

"No—no. He's busy. He has . . . important work."

"I see," he said, working his mustache. "I take it you live somewhere, then?"

"Oh, yes, sir. I live up there, on the Wall." She considered pointing it out, but worried she might look foolish.

"Wall-born, eh?" he replied. "No shame in that. I know plenty of good men born on the Wall. And you'd best get back there and stay put. Streets are no place for a girl your age."

"Truly, sir, and I thank you . . ."

"Duncan," he grumbled. "My name's Duncan. Now see to it we never meet again."

"Yes, sir. Of course."

Strolling away, the man-at-arms noted the black feathers littering the stones under his boots. "Damn birds," he grumbled, "worst omen I've ever seen!" She looked up and took them in. They were everywhere, perched all along the rooftops, some circling, others waiting.

2

THROUGH THE GATES OF
THE SILVER KEY

The tower rose out of the northeast portion of the Wall, a simple cylindrical shape of mossy uneven stones with narrow archery windows. In centuries past, when the city was little more than a castle, it would have defended against an armies' easterly advance. But now, the tower was a curious relic overlooking a crowded neighborhood, a throwback to days long gone. Children never visited Emma's home—to them, it was a ghastly and foreboding place, something to conjure tales of ghosts and witches and dark rituals.

With her shoulder against it, Emma forced open the tower's wood and iron door. The inside was no more pleasing to look upon than the out. Sunbeams crisscrossed from high windows, forming strange patterns of light and dark, illuminating objects in unnatural ways. Each room was sparsely furnished, with the occasional rug or tapestry, though the scenes upon their fibers had long faded.

But despite its forlorn appearance, Emma was relieved to be home, to be anywhere far from Bood and Deed.

The base floor split at the entrance into the upper and lower levels. The stair leading up to her bedchamber was steep and without a handrail, with steps less than the width of her foot, so that going to and from her room was fraught with the possibility of tumbling to one's death. But it was the lower, broader stair that frightened her. Even to look in that direction caused her palms to sweat, and she had, in recent years, learned to not look there, to forget even that that section of her home existed. The reason for her fear was a mystery, an indistinct memory on a distant shore.

Sometimes, when examining some artifact in her home, or when her thoughts turned to some oddity, hazy images would inexplicably surface and then vanish like a stagecoach passing in the night. Whenever she attempted to focus on these memories, they became even less defined. She held fast, however, to one recollection in particular, from when she first walked on shaky legs unaccustomed to bipedal movement. She was looking for her father, wanted to show him how well she could manage the stairs without his hand or the wall to balance. He was, she knew, in the same place as always. She made her way down to the open doorway, anticipating being lifted into his arms, being showered with adulation. But there was only screaming. And a fear that gripped her heart and never let go. Forever afterwards, the door remained shut.

Once, when the world was still new for her, in that age when children begin to voice their wonders, she dared to question him about the door beyond the stair. It was his private study, he explained, and she was never to go down there, never to ask of the happenings within. If she was ever to disobey, she would regret it. He was never explicit in his threats, but his tone was firm, and her vague memories served as enough of a deterrent.

Now Emma was possessed by more urgent troubles. Her knee ached from the stoning. Her lip had grown fatter and more tender. But it was her heart that pained her most. Bood and Deed's words had struck like arrows and remained festering deep between her ribs, forcing her to scrutinize herself in the tall mirror beside the stair. A featureless girl stared back, looking so unremarkable that she might as well have not existed. Her face belonged to a porcelain doll, framed by long flat strands as black as pitch, which made her all the whiter, almost translucent to look upon. Making matters worse, the recent swelling of her lip had turned her mouth into a snout.

"You *do* look like a donkey," she said to the mirror, lifting her sleeves to dry her eyes. "You're so ugly! So very ugly!"

She balled her hands into fists, raised them against herself. She wanted to smash the image, but resisted the urge. Father would be furious should she break his mirror, no doubt an heirloom. Instead, she retreated, watching her reflection diminish, her limbs recede into the folds of her robes. At a distance, she could make out a dark shape, a raven. She flapped her arms and the sleeves transformed into wings.

"Not a donkey. If you were a raven . . . You'd make a beautiful raven. Your feathers would be blacker than all the others', and the raven king would choose you for his bride. You'd soar above the city, and poop on everybody's heads, and fly south, to the Sea. Oh, to look upon the Sea and the splendors of the southern kingdoms! What a sight that would be!"

Round and round the tower she spun, fluttering in her robes, her cloak flowing and rippling like a banner and, when she was quite dizzy, she collapsed into a heap of cloth.

It was then that she felt very alone. She lifted herself and tiptoed about the tower. Where was Father? Beyond the windows, the sun was retreating, stretching red-orange-yellow fingers across the pale moiré sky.

It occurred to her that Father should have been finished with his afternoon duties.

Every morning he would leave, and before eclipse return, if only to lock himself in his study. She never knew where he went, or for what purpose, but he always came and went with urgency. When asked, he would say that he had important work and nothing more. It was in those brief in-between moments that Emma hoped to see her father.

In the golden dawn of youth, Emma loved him as any daughter, when he fed and clothed and bathed her. No matter the substance of her meals or the quality of her garments, to her they were treasures fit for a princess. He even shared, with particular enthusiasm, knowledge of symbols, giving her books of faerie-tales and adventures, which she devoured more readily than the food she was given. But as the sun and moons went about their motions, she saw less and less of him, and by the time her skirt covered little of her thighs, her father took to half-measures, leaving her cold dishes at breakfast and garments at her bedside, without a thought given to her shape or size. Her heart pined in his absence until it could pine no more, and like a flower that shrivels as it goes untended, so did her love for him. And yet, she never lost the seed of affection planted in her since infanthood, and still cherished the rare moments spent with him.

Now more than ever, she needed him. This was not her first tussle with bullies, nor her first encounter with Bood and Deed, but in the past Father had dismissed her tears, accusing her of being soft-hearted or—what angered her most—exaggerating in order to win undue attention. But now she could show him. Her broken face did not pain her nearly as much as their jeers, but it was something he could at least see. She could only pray he not return, as he so often did, in a foul mood.

She looked in each and every room, including her own sparse bedchamber, but he was nowhere to be found. Could he have returned earlier? Or was he just late? She rounded the stairs again, between the upper and lower floors, when something caught the light, and her eye like a fishhook. She tiptoed toward the little rounded table, its back cut to the shape of the concave wall. To anyone else, it would appear unremarkable—a key of the simple skeleton variety, with an oval loop and three simple tines—but Emma could not keep from shuddering at the sight of it. Her father was never without his silver key. Before leaving the tower, he would touch his breast pocket again and again, to assure himself, sometimes removing it to make certain that the thing he was touching was, in fact, the key. Now it was lying, unceremoniously, on the half table. Had he actually forgotten it? Should she take it, to keep safe, or would that anger him? After much contemplation, she found the key balanced on the tips of her quivering fingers, gyrating slowly from side to side. There was nothing special about it. But she knew what it did. She knew where the key could take her.

For what seemed like eternity, Emma stood at the topmost step of the lower stairwell, trembling with doubt, the key in her palm cold and slick with perspiration. The door was set into an arched frame at the base of the stair and was split down the middle like a gate. The oak grain was bare and rough, with minimal patterning. No Delian would pause at such a door.

The power of her uncertainty was equally matched by curiosity. For as long as she could remember, she had possessed a voracious appetite for knowledge. It was what drove her to becoming lost in the forgotten niches of Northendell, why she wondered at the ravens that followed her and the rainbows coloring the sky. But what was greater than simple curiosity was her desire to know her father's business, to learn what consumed him and forced him into a prison of his own making. Something beyond the door had made her father a stranger to her, when she had no one else to love. The more she thought on it, the more her heart turned from fear to anger, and it gave her the strength to confront the door. She would know her father's secrets, consequences be damned!

Emma fumbled with the silver key. It was slippery and unwieldy, like a captive mouse, but she managed, with both hands, to direct it toward the door. The stair led to a space below the street, lit by a single brassiere set into an alcove. Her shadow blacked out the lock, but after a bit of blind prodding she found the aperture. The locking mechanism was long rusted, resisting her efforts to open it, and a dreadful thought occurred to her then, that it might not work, that perhaps she had the wrong key. More fidgeting and the key started to turn in the lock, erasing such fears just as her mind conjured new ones.

What if Father returns now? And finds you here at his door?

"No," she whispered, though she could feel her heart rummaging under her robes. "Don't think like that, Emma. You're his only child, after all, and he should not keep anything from you . . ." But what if it was some evil she was not meant to see? That no mortal should ever see? Rich with imagination, her mind summoned all possible horrors, But again, her resolve overcame her paralysis, driving her hand, and the tumblers of the lock thundered, one by one, into place.

"It's open," she informed herself, and with her hem in her fist, Emma entered through the gates of the silver key.

3

FABULOUS SECRETS

The way forward was darker than Emma expected, and so she turned back to the brassiere, removed it from the wall and, listening once more for her father, continued on. Centuries-worn masonry hugged her shoulders, leading down another set of steps to a sharp turn. The swinging glow from the brassiere gave glimpses of unlit candelabras, rising like stalks of corn from many tables. Others came up from the floor—elaborate crowns of candles tall as a man. She proceeded to touch flame to wick, though much of the wax was short and fat with tears and would not last the passing. In due course, her father's study emerged amid the flickering light in wisps of smoke. Whether grand as a ballroom or small as a war closet, Emma could not determine the size of the space. Everywhere she looked, there were things in great heaping piles. Books stacked like twisting minarets above her head. Shelves lined every wall, buckling under the weight of countless pages, a few coming unchained from the mooring. Some shelves had collapsed upon others to form sloping hills of paper. If there was any passage behind the books, she could not have known it lest she tunnel through.

With caution, Emma made herself part of the mess, venturing deeper amid the tomes until she could no longer see her way out.

She was not only taken aback by the sheer volume of books in her father's collection, but by the number of books in existence. Who could have penned so many pages? And could there truly be so many tales, so many subjects in the entire world to write about? Was that what her father was doing, trying to read every book ever written? To what end?

And why keep it all secret? No . . . this couldn't be all there was.

But the secret, if one existed, she could not see, even as she stood in the midst of her father's most private sanctuary. And it made her angry.

Her eyes began to crawl along leather bound covers and spines, picking out words. Most were without titles, but many she found intriguing. She recognized her favorite story, *The Epic of Thangar and Sint*, and wondered how it had left from under her bed. Two heroes crossed many lands in search of a princess, to do battle against the three-headed dragon, *Polykefalos*. When Sint died in Thangar's arms, Emma mourned him for days. She did not, however, recognize any other title. *On the Origin of Monsters. The Ancient Zo: Masters of the Universe, a History. The Great Cataclysm: Contemplations on Planetary Geology in Relation to the Decline of Giant Species. A History of the Great Aean Migration to the Founding of the Sea Kingdoms, a Translation of Eldin. Lost Expeditions: From Mythradanaiil to Baartook.*

She tugged her eyes away. The words were befuddling her brain. What did *contemplations on planetary geology* mean? It sounded like gibberish. Nobody she knew, even those well-to-do aristocrats she loved to spy upon, talked like that. And she could not stretch her imagination enough to guess what sorts of tales those books might contain. Even still, she felt a longing to keep searching, to keep reading. If she only had more time!

Without warning, a monstrous, human shape jumped at her, and she nearly tripped over the hem of her robe with fright. It was snarling, with eyes glazed in fury, mouth agape, threatening her with its finger-length, pointed canines. But it was not moving—it never had. Her hand worked under her robes to still her heart. The other reached out with trepidation, to touch its eerily real, blood red fur.

"It isn't alive, Emma," she assured herself. Hearing her voice, her own name, had a calming effect. She stepped back to examine the figure in its entirety. Stuffed. Like the trophy kills in the tavern. What was the word? Taxonomy? Taxidermy? That's it.

But Emma had never seen such a creature. It was very clearly a beast, neither bogren nor horg, and yet, it was so remarkably human. She could almost read the expression of rage on its face. It could not have been native to the Pewter Mountains. What was it? A placard beside the creature gave the answer: *Eastern Halfman, Forest of Narth.*

Despite her realization that the halfman was filled with sawdust, the very sight of it unnerved her. Surely, if she came across such a thing in the woods, she would die of fright. It made her appreciate the thick city walls which kept out the wild. *But why would Father bother to keep such a dreadful thing in his study?*

Segmenting the labyrinth of books, she came upon other, equally curious objects. There were collections of bones in varying stages of decay, some yellowed with age, others black as obsidian and just as hard. One set was arranged into the nearly complete skeleton of a saurian-like creature, with branching, finger-like joints forming what looked like wings. A fractured, humanoid cranium fit neatly in her hand. She pondered it a moment before replacing it, exactly as before. In another corner of the room, a large skull served as the base of a table.

Amid the clutter, there was an empty space, like a clearing in a forest. It was her father's desk. His chair. She shuddered, suddenly remembering him in his most foul moments, even as she was drawn forward like a needle to a loadstone. It was not, as she would have expected, a clean work surface. There was more parchment, more lines of books, so much so that the underlying wood grain was impossible to make out. Beneath the loose pages was another layer of ink outlines, the dark eastern hemisphere and the bright western Dead Zones, the borders of kingdoms clustered about a solitary Sea—configurations she recognized from the tapestries hanging in wealthy peoples' gardens. Her hands quivered from object to object. She considered opening the compass, an object she recognized from one of her faerie tales, but thought better on it. Her fingerprints could mar the immaculate gold surface. There was also a quill and an inkwell, but she did not touch these either. And then she came across an open journal, freshly inked. Leaning eagerly over the desk, she recognized her father's hand-writing and, for a moment, forgot her apprehension. Should she be flogged for this, it would be worth it. She thumbed through the pages, with great care not to tear the edges, until stopping upon a passage.

> 411213
>
> *After considerable contemplation and research, considerable, I might add, and far beyond the scope of any detractors who might doubt me or call me mad, I am become determined, that my work, however misunderstood, however abominable it may be deemed, continue. Why should it be, after all, for a man, any man, of any society, to consider madness what I seek? Why should it be thought insanity, to be unwilling to preserve that which we, as a species, hold, or declare to hold, most precious? If such a quest as mine be called folly, or madness, then it is only from doubting and fearful minded fools, who cow before remote and dispassionate gods and reject the reasoning that is the natural fruit of man's brain, that which is man's heritage . . .*

She halted mid-sentence, thinking hard upon the words, but was left with only impressions. She was desperate to absorb as much as possible, but all she knew was that her father wanted something very badly, and was angry that others did not approve of it. *Too many words.* She thumbed forward through the years, pausing before a charcoal sketch of two skulls, one smaller than the other, with a heading that read:

BOGREN = HUMAN?
417540

It is not beyond my comprehension how such an inference may be made, though blasphemous, some might even say, an abomination of reason. And yet, with reason and evidence as my guides, I have, inescapably, arrived at just such a conclusion. There is little difference between these two specimens, though we know with certainty that one is human and the other is not. What is the significance of this? This transmogrification over the aeons? What is the mechanism at work? And what natural purpose is served, by the one becoming the other? More importantly still, how then does "the theory" shed light on our most recent history, with regards to our endless struggle, which we find, myself included, as natives of Northendell, threatening us yearly at the very gates of our fair city, which, without the good graces and sacrifices of our men-at-arms, I would never chance to live enough to discover the objective of my research?

Emma wanted to scream. None of it made sense. None of his words could explain why he had chosen this room, these books, over her, or even more curiously, why he was unable to share with her these obsessions. *One more try . . .*

423966

. . . *we see them everywhere. Why are the people
of this world so blind? Or do they not wish to see?
Though I have not laid my own eyes upon them,
men have testified to the mysteries abundant in
this world, returning from long exploits with tales
of things beyond our imagining. What is, for instance, the secret of the Golden Halo, which rises
high as a hilltop in the midst of the Endless Plains?
Or the Pyramid in Ossea, made entirely of glass,
which men have sworn possesses no entrance, and
yet is centered by a single, solitary throne? Who
sits there, or sat therein, I wonder? And what of
the stone golems that litter the countryside, from
the mountains to the valleys? There is not a child
in all Aenya that does not know of them, and yet
the eldest among us are utterly ignorant as to their
origin and purpose, despite my own theory. These
wonders were left to us by the Ancients, which, I
cannot refrain from repeating, is a misnomer, as
the documents I have procured has revealed to me
their true name, as that of the Zo.*

*What is it of these marvels, these Ancients, if you
must, that my countrymen so fear? Why can we
not speak of them plainly? And not be subjected
to the torch, or imprisonment? Magic is a word
spoken in ignorance. Magic is whatever is not
understood. If we should banish magic, let us do
so by demystifying it, by understanding it . . .*

Emma abandoned the nonsensical script, drifting deeper into the study, as if digging to the core of her father's brain. She felt oddly buoyant, as if her feet did not touch the floor. There were many more skeletons to be found, most incomplete, held together by pins, and more stacks of books, and loose papers, and hurried charcoal sketches. Despite her care not to disturb anything, her arm bumped against some object, and it teetered to the edge of the table before her eyes could pick it out from the clutter. It was a rectangular box of fine wood, as smooth as brass. Her fingertips brushed over the flower pattern etched onto its surface. The dust made her eyes water. Years of neglect kept the box tightly closed, but with some effort the hinges cracked apart. A small paper floated free, its folded halves catching the air like the wings of a moth. It was a note, written in a hand different from her father's:

My Dearest Mattathias,

You have always been a great contributor to our cause and, more importantly, I would like to think, a faithful friend to Ilsa and me. Do not torment yourself any further. You did all that could be done.

As for my gift, I pray you not refuse it. I considered safeguarding it for when the little one comes of age, but I am too stricken with grief and cannot bear the sight of it any longer. It

*never strayed far from Ilsa's lips. You will find
it possesses some remarkable qualities, as it is
made from a rare, possibly extinct, Ilmarin
oak.*

Your friend,
Dak

Mattathias? She knew her father's name as Mathias, but
who was Mattathias? Could they be one and the same?
Emma lowered the paper, folded it nervously and tucked it
into her pocket. Dak's gift was a wooden tube pitted with
holes, engraved with swirling lines, a short flute, or piccolo. It was fixed in a bed of silk, and though Emma feared
to disturb anything, she figured her father would not notice its absence. Besides, it was beautifully made, and she
possessed so few beautiful things. She propped the flute
from its bed and slipped it under her sleeve, then proceeded to align the empty box with the dust-vacant rectangle
on the table.

Emma continued to search, but everything she came
across left her with questions, and she was beginning to
feel like a fool. *What did you expect to find, a book clearly stating the reasons for Father's neglect?*

The back wall curved into a circular alcove. A series of glass spheres, stained in varying colors, were suspended from struts in the floor. Emma was mesmerized,
never having seen a contraption so strange, ornaments
so perfectly round. The central orb—about which every
other emanated—was the circumference of their dinner
table, and was composed of clusters of kerosene lamps.

The outer spheres were smaller, their supporting rods linked to an intricate apparatus of toothed wheels which allowed the spheres to move about one another. It was a delicate arrangement that Father could not help but notice should it be moved, yet Emma was compelled to toy with it, her daring bolstered by what she had so far discovered. Stepping over cogs and ducking under struts, she slinked her way toward a triad of spheres. One was violet, no bigger than a drachma coin. Another was the size of a pumpkin and turquoise as the moon. But what caught her fancy was a ball of exceeding complexity, like a gaudy piece of jewelry. It was the size of a pomegranate, consisting of a transparent outer shell of silver dots— constellations. Looking deeper, in a plethora of earthy hues, she could make out the familiar outlines of mountain ranges, and a solitary Sea made of lapis lazuli, and a great rift—looking like someone had thrown the sphere and cracked it—marking the divide between the eastern hemisphere and middle Aenya . . .

"Step away from that!"

Emma was crippled. With moist palms, she caught her surroundings to keep from falling, turning on her knee-cap, which still ached where the stone had hit her earlier that day. His eyes were round and silver, like coins, staring so intently she could feel his pupils stabbing through her. Mathias was an unassuming man, with tufts of gray at the temples. He looked prematurely aged, as if he'd worn his young face too long. But when enraged, he only resembled the person she knew. He became something else entirely, the creature that lived beneath her father's skin.

"What are you doing here?"

All she wanted was to confess the hurt that lived within her, to let him know how much she needed him. But she could not seem to open her mouth.

"Come here!" he barked. "What did you see?"

Her legs shook as she stepped away from the spheres, so dreading to damage anything that she had to hold herself from swooning.

"Answer me!"

"I don't know," she managed, in a barely audible whisper.

"What do you mean, 'you don't know'? How can you not know? Or are you afraid to tell me?"

She didn't look at him. She couldn't. Rather, she studied the cracks in the masonry, so much like riverbeds that could carry her to faraway lands, to better, freer places, where every parent loved and listened to his child. He snatched her arm and shook her violently. Robes fluttered like a sail in a storm. The silver key sprang from her pocket, ringing upon the stone floor.

"Please," she said, wincing, "don't hurt me!"

"All this time . . . I thought I could trust you to obey me!"

"I'm sorry."

He tugged her out of the room, knocking pages into the air, showing little concern for the position of his belongings. Passing from the astrolabes to his desk to the candles to the entryway, she was amazed by how short the distance was, by how vast curiosity and dread had made his study seem. Her arm contorted painfully in his grip, but she did not resist as he dragged her up the stairs.

"This will not go . . . unpunished!" he roared, breathless with rage. "You'll learn . . . I will teach you . . . I will teach you to respect your elders."

She found herself facing her bed. The door slammed and a lock clicked into place.

He's locking you in!

"You want to explore, do you? Wander all about, do you?" His voice sounded clearly through the timbers of the door. "Well, I'll teach you a lesson you'll not soon forget! You will learn your place, young one. Or you'll stay in your room forever!"

Her knees buckled at the doorframe, and she collapsed into a heap. Her entire body convulsed, ached with silent tears. "No, Father, forgive me. Father . . ."

But he did not give her time for explanations, or plea bargains. She could already hear his footfalls falling stiffly against the steps below. She waited, steadying her sobbing, until the silence came again—pervasive, cold, and much too familiar. Her bedchamber was sparse, lonely. The empty aching in her bosom continued anew.

Certain he was out of earshot, she reached for the shaft hidden under her sleeve, lifting it to her lips. A sharp stinging sensation reminded her of Bood and Deed, though her encounter with the two boys already seemed to have happened ages ago. And then it occurred to her that he had not even noticed, that her father—no, she would never call him that again—that *Mathias* did not even notice her swollen lip. She brought the piccolo to the corner of her mouth where the flesh was less tender and forced her breath through the wood, until a single lonesome note floated from her window, carried in the wind like a raven's feather.

Ilsa.

4

INQUISITION

One whole year she spent in solitude, as she had in her younger days, which was all the more cruel after having tasted freedom. When Mathias decided her sentence was met, whatever joy she found in liberty was mixed with bitterness. She spent the remainder of her childhood far from home, fearing and detesting the man she once called father, stealing silently through her tower door in the dark of eclipse and praying never to cross paths with him again. In this way she came into womanhood, from an imaginative and reclusive street orphan roaming the inner walls, to a seemingly crazed young woman dancing and playing the piccolo and babbling to herself. It was enough to draw the suspicion of superstition folk, and the ire of the king's men.

The steps cut into the hillside followed a winding course. Men-at-arms were posted at every turn. They were like statues, Emma thought, with narrow slits for eyes between helmet and breastplate. Like a lonesome sentry, Hoarfrost stood at the peak of the hill overlooking the snow-covered sprawl of rooftops.

Hoarfrost was the modest crown of Northendell, a simple rectangle of pinewood beams with a gabled roof resembling a capsized galleon. Little more than a glorified mead hall, it nonetheless served as the seat of power. Over the ages, as stone and mortar cropped about its wooden facade, Hoarfrost remained, far from the largest structure in the city, unchanged, a straggler from a bygone era, which better suited its occupants, Emma figured, who were just as stubborn and resistant to change.

Little of Hoarfrost's history was known, as the craft of writing was a lowly pursuit, a trade for slim-wristed men too dainty to hold a weapon. Bards sang of Hoarfrost's proud origins, however, how it was made by Strom the Thunderer himself after the god's longboat ran aground upon the Pewter Mountains. In days of old, only the strongest of the strong and the bravest of the brave could dwell in its high halls. These founding heroes tamed the harsh wilderness and defended against the evils that crept nightly from the East, making possible the settlement of merchants and laborers. Hoarfrost later became home to Northendell's first king—the *Batal*—who slew a dozen giants in single combat and stole the *Ice Crown* from the giant who ruled the mountain. These tales were recited and embellished in taverns throughout the land, but Emma found them tedious, despite her fondness for books of epic adventure.

What appeared to be a featureless box beyond the traverse of wind and snow proved elaborate at arm's length. Beneath a glaze of hoarfrost, in patterns in the wood, she could see dragons, griffons, bogrens, horgs and giants, all in battle against men-at-arms, and heroes, and gods. In a perimeter lining the structure, round shields that had taken one too many blows made for gruesome decor, as did the fractured helmets of the fallen. In Northendell, no device of war was ever discarded. Delians were frugal to the point of unreason. As for the door, Emma could see none. It was not hidden, only unnecessarily massive, much more like a wall. Exposing iron rings from the snow, two men-at-arms heaved backward, and the mouth of Hoarfrost split open.

Tall windows crossed beams of ashen light from opposite sides. Antlered chandeliers swayed from the ceiling, which was like the ribbed spine of some immense fish. And yet, no amount of light could lift the gloom. The design embodied the ethos of its builders: simple and functional. Its solitary feature was a rectangle of dark mahogany, a table for more than a hundred people, too broad for anyone to reach across.

King Frederick Frizzbeard's buttocks filled a throne of oak and furs. Displayed prominently behind him were trophies from his days as prince, when, as he never let anyone forget, he slew a horg with his own hand, and a dragon, and a giant, and a whole host of bogrens. Emma could see the dragon's claw over his left shoulder, and the giant's giant ear above him, and a horg's black-as-pitch eyeball to his right. The decades following his youth, however, had been less than flattering. The king's face was pudgy and reddish, like a half-year-old, and the hairs on his head and chin grew pointed and divergent, as if each of his follicles was frightened of the one next to it. Despite his great girth, he still fit into the silver and gold of his better days, the mammoth lining showing between the plates, though his fat pushed the armor out on all sides, where it threatened to pop loose from his body. Seated around him were a host

of men-at-arms, whom he admired, and highborn aristocrats, whom he openly despised, and members of the royal
family, whom he barely tolerated. His son, Aldric Fairhair,
was lanky, fair-haired, and beardless, and the only one in
attendance who felt armor excessive at the dinner table.
Or so Emma surmised, as only the king's son was decked
in so little garb, a simple tunic and furs. Even his sister, Sif
Redhair, known also as Sif, *Daughter of Thunder*, stood to
the right of her father's throne in a chain corset, in brac-
ers and greaves, with a gilded scabbard at her hip.

"Bring forth the accused!" the king's voice erupted,
much more loudly than was necessary, though no one,
aside from Emma, was startled by it.

She stepped into the ashen cascade of light, eyes down-
cast, watching the sway of her black-on-black robes. She
said nothing, not daring to look up from the floor. An
older woman in peasant's rags also emerged.

"Let us be forthright and not waste words, as our forefathers were men of action," the king began, and then, for
no apparent reason, he simply stared at the two women,
without a further word. It was an awkward moment, with
nothing but the occasional cough breaking the silence.
Then his daughter leaned into his ear. He jerked in his seat
like a puppet brought to life, downed a swig of mead, and
continued as if nothing strange had happened. "Ah, yes,
quite right! We are here in response to the recent goings-
on, as surely everybody here must know: the falling of the
Taker's tooth, the ruin of our fair neighbor, Kiathos, the
drowning of Hedonia—though the sodomites were not
undeserving of it—and the quake that shook our proud
walls . . . I have decreed that we are to purge our city of

sorcery, and all forbidden arts, as my father so decreed before me and his father before him, so that we not suffer more the wrath of the gods." His daughter leaned down again, but he waved her off like a gnat, his face flushed with annoyance. "You, there—Emmalina Wallborn, is it?"

She nodded hesitantly, peering through a tangle of raven-colored locks. With sudden interest, Aldric straightened off his elbows. "Show us your face, girl! You disrespect the king!"

She attempted a makeshift bun, but her hair did not cooperate, leaving her in a more haggard state than before.

Frizzbeard did not share his son's concern, saying nothing of the matter. "You are accused of witchery most foul. How do you plead?"

She tried to give answer, but made unintelligible sounds instead, then shrank like a shadow within the black of her clothes.

"Eh? What was that? I cannot hear you too well. You see, I lost part of my hearing fighting a dragon, fire-breathing and all that . . . Did I ever tell you how I killed it, with only a jawbone?"

Sif was quick to whisper in his good ear, though it was obvious to Emma that everyone at the table could hear her. "Now is not the time, your Majesty."

"Oh? It isn't, is it," he agreed, with a bit of sadness. "Quite right! Anyway, *girl*, speak up and let us all hear how you plead."

"I didn't do anything." Her small voice carried awkwardly about the chamber, sounding insincere even when she was speaking the truth—a quality she hated in herself.

"Did you not, now?" He scratched under his chin aggressively, as if riddled with parasites. "Very well, then." He sighed with boredom, having hoped for a confession, or better yet, a story of interest. "Let us hear from the accuser."

The other woman was prodded into speaking. "That girl there," she said, bending a finger at Emma, "is a wicked sorceress! I've known her since she was a child. Always acting strange, always wandering about alone where she doesn't belong. I never thought her any harm, though, or I would have reported her. But then, when I was with child, I saw her looking straight at me, giving me the *evil eye*. Then, the day after . . ." Her words hung heavily in the air. She cupped her fallen belly tenderly, her crooked face frayed by malice and heartache. "She killed my baby! I swear by all the gods above and below, let them strike me down if I be telling lies! *She* did it! What's more, your Majesty, she talks to ravens! Those dark devils act upon her evil whims! Just ask anyone—they follow wherever she goes!"

"It's not true!" Emma protested. "I never looked at her that way . . . I mean, I don't even know what *that way* is . . . or anything about *evil* eyes."

"And the ravens?" said the king. "Do you deny this as well?"

"Well," she said, "they're not all evil . . ."

A wave of murmuring came and went like a gust of wind. Eyes fixed on her sharply, and she wanted to disappear into her clothes like she used to when she was a child, but her robes were no longer too big for her, and everyone expected her to make an argument.

"They're not evil," she declared again, with less confidence.

Frizzbeard ran his meaty fingers through his beard. And his hairs tried, albeit unsuccessfully, to escape. "Hrrrm." It was a sound midway between a word and clearing phlegm from his throat, and the court reacted as though the king had made a solemn decree. Nervously, Emma snuck a bit of her hair into her mouth and started to eat it.

"This talking to ravens business," he began, "hrrm . . . does not speak well of you. Ravens are harbingers of ill, messengers of the Horned God." He gulped another flagon of mead, wiped the foam from his mustache and shouted for the errand boy. "Oh, how these troubled times bring me to thirst. Now where was I?" His daughter motioned to speak, but he waved her off with a frustrated look. "Also, what I wished to say was, ravens and such wicked fowl serve as the eyes and ears of the East. There can be no trusting such birds!" Everyone in the room, except one, nodded in agreement.

Emma listened until she could no more, erupting like a kettle brought to boil. "That's not true!" she shouted. "They're hungry is all, and I bring them things to eat, sometimes bugs—" A gasp spread among the common folk, and the king's face swelled, looking like strawberries. Knowing she had made an awful mistake in manners, she broke the silence softly, apologetically, "—they're my friends, after all."

Frederick Frizzbeard looked to be stunned by her audacity, not knowing how to respond. She envisioned nobles and visiting monarchs, kowtowing to his nonsense, and here she was, little more than a child, daring to challenge him. But he did not shout. Did not appear angry in the least. He must be sick of all the weaklings filling his mead hall, she told herself, of everyone cringing before his every utterance, without a story to boast of.

But it was Prince Aldric, who had been dozing till now, who decided the matter. "Execute her," he said calmly. "Clearly, she's a witch and in league with the East. She shall be burned at dawn. Men-at-arms, take her away—"

Unseen hands tightened about her shoulders, pulling her from the table. She did not resist, but inside her head was screaming. She wanted to explain to them the loneliness that preceded her talking to birds, to tell them of the day Mathias locked in her room for a year, to explain how the ravens at her windowsill kept her sane. And where was Mathias, anyway? Surely, he understood matters of law. Surely, he could better argue on her behalf. But the men of the mead hall cared only for matters of war. They had clearly decided her fate before she had arrived. Everything after was a formality.

Opposite the table, the other woman was led away more gently. Her head was bowed, but Emma could feel her hate, burning like a cold flame. And when no one was looking, she shot Emma a triumphant smile.

By the gods, does she actually think you caused her to lose her baby? Do you even know her? She could not remember ever having seen the woman's face.

"Hold." The voice of the king's daughter rang powerfully. Her boots thudded against the wooden floor as she stepped forward, her jewel-encrusted scabbard glittering in the sun, her crimson hair spilling to her waist. Emma decided, in that moment, that she was the most beautiful woman in the world. "Sir Duncan Greyoak wishes to speak on the behalf of the accused."

A feeling of recognition filled her like a cup of warm milk. Duncan had not changed in the past ten years since rescuing her from the bullies, save for the gray follicles about his temples and mustache.

The king addressed him as he made his presence known. "Are you sure of this, Duncan?"

"With all due respect, your Mightiness," he said, removing his helmet, "is it not by decree of the king, and king only, that executions be carried out?" Aldric glowered in Duncan's direction, but the man-at-arms paid him no attention.

"Quite right, Duncan, quite right!" the king bellowed. "So then, what do you suggest we do with the witch?"

"I've known this girl many years. She's a street urchin where my men patrol. I do not believe her to be evil. And if she were in league with our enemies, what vital secret could they learn from her? That our walls are impregnable, as we have proven for centuries? If she speaks to birds, then she is simply mad, and if the ravens follow her, then she is to be pitied for her ill fortune."

The prince stood abruptly, slamming his fist on the table. "Such ill fortune, as you say, may come down upon us! Do not forget what happened to Hedonia! And Kiathos!"

Duncan nodded, and then added, "Remember that I am in charge of defending these walls, and was killing bogrens when you were at your mother's teat. I know what is best for our security, and have no fear of maidens in bloom."

Aldric pulled a dagger, drawing shapes into the table. "How dare you defy me? Make a fool of me!"

With a face as determined as a stone, the man-at-arms acknowledged him, saying, "Do you wish to settle this the old way?"

Suddenly, a musical chorus filled their ears, as if a choir of boys went singing into the room. From the source of the sound—the scabbard at Sif's waist—a bluish glow flowered, emanated.

"Lady Sif." With a sincere bow, Duncan bid her to speak.

She sheathed her sword and the harmonic light parade subsided to a single high-pitched note. "Let the gods decide," she said. "As we are not of one mind, let her be banished. If the gods pity her, she'll not perish."

Emma glared from her curtain of hair. Sif, it seemed, was no longer so beautiful.

A smile crept over Aldric's face just as a scowl came over Duncan's. Protest piled in the old man-at-arms' throat, but his reverence for the princess stayed his lips. "A grim decree," he said quietly. "It is high moon, when the cold blows in from the East and the denizens of the Dark Hemisphere follow. Sending her out there is tantamount to a burning at the stake. Might you not consider a payment of *wergild*, for loss of child—?"

"That woman's unborn child is not the issue!" Aldric objected. "We are here to purge the kingdom of witchcraft, per the king's decree!"

Princess Redhair weighed both arguments and looked away. "I defer to the king."

Frizzbeard awoke with a shout. "What now? What was that you suggested?"

"Banishment—" Aldric started.

"Wonderful idea!" he said. "Now I tire of this matter. And I'm hungry. Who likes pheasant?"

The prince shot Duncan a final, condescending look before shuffling away. But the man-at-arms was too busy to notice. He called for Ovulus, pulling the boy aside.

"She is to be banished," he said in a hushed tone, "but I'll not have the cold take her. Find her an escort."

Ovulus lowered his visor. It squeaked, drawing disinterested faces. When the attention was no longer on them, he asked, "B-But who, sir?"

"Doesn't matter. A tradesman. A hunting party. Any southbound caravan. But be sure they have a wagon of some sort."

"V-Very good, sir. That would k-keep the cold off her, wouldn't it?"

"Ah, Ovulus," he said, his mustache pinching at the corners, "you're as bright as ever."

"Thank you, sir."

"And one more thing. Make haste."

Emma was beginning to feel the strain of being pulled around like a dog, the chains forming crosshatch patterns across her wrists. Events were unfolding too rapidly. One moment she was alone, rearranging the notes of a popular ditty, and the next a host of men-at-arms was leading her away. Now her captor, who was barely old enough to shave, whom she knew from childhood, was taking her outside the city wall, in the middle of high moon. It was a cruel irony, for she had longed for many years to journey beyond the city's limits—but alone, in the cold, she could never survive it.

Ovulus continued down a spiral of steps beneath Hoarfrost, which connected to a passage within the outer wall. She could only assume it would lead them to one of the many guard towers that surrounded Northendell.

"Obi."

Either the clanking of his armor was drowning out her voice or he did not wish to respond.

"Obi," she tried again, more forcefully.

His voice echoed weirdly from his helmet. "What d-do you want?"

"Obi," she repeated, with greater affection, "I knew it was you. Do you remember me?"

"I do," he said, but his pace did not slow.

"Why are you doing this? You're not like them—they were unkind to you, forced you to do things."

"We were n-n-never friends," he said. "And I was a kid then. Now, I'm just doing my d-duty."

They moved further from Hoarfrost, from the hill at the center of the city. Despite the warmth from his torch, she could feel the cold from the outside, penetrating the masonry. It was as if someone was packing her robe with snow. "Is this what you wanted?" she asked, quivering. "To be a knight, a man-at-arms, like your father?"

"I'm only a s-s-squire. Duncan's squire. Someday, maybe. Now be q-q-q—stop talking!"

"But are you happy?" she pressed him, the "H" sound appearing in the air. "Or are you doing it because it's what's expected of you—what your father expected of you?"

He pivoted on his heel. She could make out only part of his face through the grill of his helm, the torchlight making the copper glitter. "Shut up! You know n-n-n—you don't know me! It's true what they say about you."

"What's that?"

"You're a witch. And you're t-t-trying to bewitch me now, but I won't listen."

"Nobody ever listens," she replied softly, more for her ears than his. "Can I say farewell to my father at least? Even witches deserve some small kindness—"

"No. Sir Duncan told me to m-make haste. That's what I'm g-going to do."

"At least let me put on a thicker robe," she stammered, careful not to mimic his speech impediment lest he think she was mocking him.

"No. Shut up."

Emma began to realize that if she were to survive, she would have to elude her captor. Pieces of a plan formed in her mind. Obi was feeble and easily intimidated. She could use this to her advantage, to escape, then bide her time among the forgotten alcoves of the city—places only she knew about—until warmer days, until she could make her way to the southern kingdoms, perhaps to lay eyes upon the Sea . . .

Her daydreaming was squashed as she was thrown into an adjoining room. They were in the guard tower. An open shaft loomed many floors above, with a network of supporting buttresses creaking from the weight and pressure of the outer walls, and stations for archers interspersed at differing heights. Facing her from across the room, there was a single, solitary door of solid iron too narrow for an invading party to rush through, but broad enough for a passing trader. From where she stood, Emma could hear the wind howling. This was the end. Just beyond the door, a vast frozen wasteland awaited her—tundra to the south and an impassible mountain range of icy rocks and Sea-deep snow drifts to the north. Even if she were to somehow survive hypothermia, there were monsters—bogrens and horgs—and nameless, inconceivable horrors that came out of the dark forest of Gloomwood during high moon. But it was not the sight of the door that so suddenly dashed her hopes of escape. She was certain she could outsmart Obi, appeal to his better nature if need be. But the two men blocking the door, she knew, could not be persuaded. They were not knights. She could tell by the way they slouched against the wall. Their attire consisted of animal skins, teeth, and horns. If Emma had not known better, she might have thought the fat-bellied man a giant. Black, bramble-like hairs grew from his cheeks and ears, and he carried a crude ax. His companion was like a pine tree, tall and lanky, with stem like appendages and gnarled fingers. A hood partly concealed his leprous face, and the little that showed was tomato-red with rash. Boils the size of peas masked him from neck to forehead.

"What have we here?" said the hooded, lanky figure, fondling Emma's hair like a merchant appraising a spool of silk. He reeked of mead and fetid gums.

She recoiled with disgust and recognition. "Deed?"

His small mouth broadened, but a boil on his lip found the movement disagreeable, popping into puss. "They call me Dagger, now."

She moved backward into the wall. In her youth, he was known as Deed Whoreson. Whatever remnant of childhood, of innocence, might have existed within him was long dead. She knew the gossip, had seen the posters that spoke of his profession. He was a dagger for little coin, a poor man's assassin, who took any job no matter how brutal or heinous.

He rushed forward, pinning her by the shoulders, and ever so slowly, slipped a jagged-toothed dirk from a sheath at his side. Her eyes flashed around the room, fixing on Obi. The boy was a man-at-arms, after all—he had given an oath to Strom, to the gods, to live with honor.

"D-D-Don't do that," said Ovulus.

"Shut up, *Obvious*," Deed said, licking at the grape-sized boil in the corner of his mouth. "I just want to take a little look—underneath." He worked his dirk under her breeches, cutting at the fabric between her thighs.

"Deed!" she screamed. "Don't! It's me . . ." She said it as if it would matter, as if their shared childhood might conjure some measure of compassion. Still, she was unable to look at him. He was too hideous.

Drunk with lust, he stumbled off of her, as if to see her for the first time. "My," he said, "it is you, isn't it! You've really . . . grown out!" He groped her breast like a ball of dough. Knowing his victim made him all the bolder.

"Still a donkey," she spat, using every effort to relax her heart. "You said so yourself."

But Deed Whoreson, otherwise known as Dagger, wasn't listening. Finding a path under her garments, his fingers made their way to her nipples. She could feel the heat of his nostrils on her neck, his hooked nose flattening against her lips, his chin stubble roving her face with small kisses. Despite her growing nausea, she could only turn away so far, pinned as she was to the wall, her other cheek blocked, buried in the lichen in the cracks of the masonry. Fear spread through her body, making her spine quiver and ache, making her limbs loose, doll-like. She caught a glimpse of the young man-at-arms as he looked on, clearly tormented by his lack of courage.

In that moment, deep within her being, something strange was starting to happen, a thing only she could feel. Her fingers were curling, stiffening like branches, her hair bristling, as if full of tiny, stiff stems. This had to be more than a reaction to fear—it was painful and surreal, more frightening even than her rapist. *What's happening to you, Emma?*

And then a memory came to her, followed by an idea.

"I knew you were a whore's son," she managed, "but I didn't think you so lowly as to lay with a donkey—"

He snapped away, nearly taking her robe off, and swung around again, bringing the point of the blade under the soft part of her chin.

"Let her go." Her salvation came from an unexpected place. It was the broad, ax wielding brute. Bood. "She's worth a lot of coin."

"I'd rather leave her in a ditch," Deed said, his dirk quivering with anticipation, "after I fill her up, of course."

"She's unspoiled goods," Bood argued. "Leave her alone."

"What makes you think that?" he said. "The way she turns those hips, like a demure little girl?" His pimpled lips dripped with sarcasm.

"No, you idiot—it's the way she cringes, more from your touch than your blade."

With a smug expression, Deed exposed his teeth, pitted and yellowed, each tooth disagreeing with the other as to direction. "I just have that effect on women. Give me a quarter passing alone with her—"

Bood stared him down like a dog, overpowering his friend's will, despite Deed's profession. "Do that and she'll not be worth a tenth what she is! That's what unspoiled means, you moron." As if regretting the rebuke, Bood added, more tactfully, "After we sell her, I'll buy you a whole harem, a whore for each appendage."

The blade slipped uneasily into its sheath as Deed motioned Emma to the door. The cold wind on the other side of the tower made it difficult to open. Frost sealed the hinges. But Bood managed the exit with a broad stroke of his shoulder.

Emma stood trembling between the two men. A woolly mammoth stamped the snow outside. Had the occasion been different, she would have delighted in seeing such a creature. Instead, she looked back through the doorway, at her last sight of home, and found Obi's eyes. And for a brief moment she forgot her troubles and pitied him.

5

A MONSTER AT THE DOOR

Somewhere between wakefulness and
sleep is the fountain of the real.

—Kjus

Wheels churned beneath her feet, squealing like tormented rodents. Tumbling over snow and rock, her cell dipped and rattled and tossed her from wall to wall. Thoughts of escape came and went. The door was barred by a beam from the outside. Beyond it lay a cold, slow death. A narrow window opened west, its bars glazed with ice and painfully cold to the touch. She looked out. Her eyelids clenched shut, watering against the air wafting from between the bars. There was nothing to see but a white shifting haze and the jagged ridge of the Pewter Mountains. The cart never strayed from its southerly course, much to her dismay, so she never saw the city as it diminished, could make no final farewells to what had been her home since birth.

Another window faced east and the tall silhouette of trees that was Gloomwood. Hunting parties went into the forest but rarely returned with all of their limbs, or lives. It was the gate through which the denizens of the dark hemisphere emerged with awful regularity. The coldest days of the year, the season of high moon, were almost upon them, and Emma knew that, if she were to somehow escape the prison wagon, she would be but fodder for whatever nightmare crept from Gloomwood.

Navigating the cart's unceasing sway, Emma moved to the front, the floor groaning with each step. She placed an ear to the partition and listened for Bood or Deed, for any clue as to where they might be taking her. But if they spoke at all, she would not have known. The beams were too thick and the howling winds swallowed voices like wolves preying on sound. With little to do, she slumped into a corner. It was too cold not to ball herself up into the folds of her robes, the layers of her hair keeping her cheekbones from icing. The wind continued to murmur beyond the cart, occasionally stirring into an argument. With that, and the rhythmic thumping of mammoth feet, Emma felt herself being lulled into unconsciousness.

Her waking sensation was of thirst and, to a lesser degree, hunger. She could not remember when last she ate, but the grumble in her stomach informed her it was long ago. Her joints were stiff and pained and slow to movement. Her hands opened like decayed blossoms and she worried over the numbness, over whether she would lose her ability to pluck at her piccolo, knowing so many men-at-arms who, venturing out during high-moon, had lost many of their fingers. Frantically, she waved and kicked and balled her hands into fists, pumping enough blood through her limbs to stand and steady herself against the window. She considered the noise of the stomping beast, hearing it as for the first time. They were still moving. The outside air was dull with cold, but the iron bars no longer burned her fingertips. Icicles came down across the window like glassy teeth, dripping with the rocking of the wheels. Blinded by thirst, she caught each drop on her tongue, and when the water stopped falling, she snapped the icy stalactite from the window, revealing, behind a crystalline curtain, a changed world. She took a step away, to better frame the landscape of glacial blues, marveling.

How long has it been? Did you miss nightfall? Did we camp?

At the other window, the turquoise moon and its small violet partner colored the horizon so vividly, she could make out their cracked and pockmarked surfaces like never before. Reaching between the bars, she weighed the celestial bodies like fruits, one in each palm. More remarkable still, there was not a hill or mountain anywhere, only the undulating tundra, infinite on the horizon, a frozen blue-white sheet broken here and there by pockets of bare gray rock. Before now, such a landscape existed only in her mind. If a mere flat terrain of ice and snow could stir her heart so, how great a wonder might the sight of endless water be? How unbelievable the Sea and its fabled kingdoms? If sold as a slave in the South, in the coastal cities of Thetis or Thalassar, she would soon know, perhaps living close enough to a beach—*a beach!*—for even the Sea to become commonplace.

Suddenly, the wagon dipped, jerking her away from the window, turning her eyes toward the walls of her prison. *You're so naïve, Emma. What do your infantile fantasies matter now? You'll be a slave.* She would never again wander the avenues of her beloved city or peruse the secrets of Mathias' study. Collapsing once again into a heap, she focused again on the window, recalling her yearlong isolation, when she was nine, when Mathias turned her bedchamber into a prison.

For countless days, she had suffered unbearable boredom, with nothing but a bed and a chest and a number of story books memorized word for word, and the thing that would come to give her the most comfort, the item she'd stolen from Mathias' study. As in the wagon, a lone archery window had been her only glimpse of freedom, teasing her with all the games a girl might hope to play. She screamed, begged, and wept until her voice left her, pounded the door until her fists ached, but the only mercy he ever showed was to deliver food and water. The door opened widely enough for a plate and cup and was just as quickly shut. At nine years of age and thin as a strut, Emma was too feeble to force her way past him, and the few times she attempted it, food deprivation became the punishment. In time, she came to accept her new life—a life lived within a room—and whatever affection she might have had for the man she called Father wilted to nothing.

For nine-year-old Emma, time moved strangely, becoming vague, the present indistinguishable from the future, the veil between the real and fantasy world less pronounced, translucent. She learned to see through the illusion of existence, learned escape through the vessel of the mind, found solace in the self. Only the world that busied itself beneath her windowsill, and the visits by her raven friends, tethered her. When the greater moon loomed wide, the birds would entreat her, *Come fly with us! Don't be afraid*, but she would always refuse them, ever so politely, as she could never fit her human body through the strip of open space where the ravens gathered. In the light of morning, Emma would shrug off the memory of talking birds, figuring it little more than a dream. Her stolen piccolo gave her purpose. She practiced whenever Mathias was out, or deep in his study. She found power in the long stretches of isolation, the power to focus all of one's mental faculties to the mastery of a single skill. By her tenth birthday, the persistence of time lost all meaning. It was on that day that Emma found her door unlocked, and she emerged from her room a master musician. If her father ever did discover her talent, he did not say a word about it, nor did he mention the piccolo taken from his study. In a pocket on the underside of her sleeve, she kept it hidden from him, and the world.

Emma's new prison was much smaller and colder, but it could not last, she told herself. Bood and Deed would take her someplace sunny, to a better life, even if it entailed an existence as a slave. The chances of a master as cruel and callous as her father were slim. She rubbed and clenched and interlocked her hands, working the numbness from her fingers. Out of her sleeve, the piccolo slid into her palm, and she was tempted to lift it to her lips.

But what if they hear? And take it? It was more than her most precious possession. The piccolo kept a faint but distinct aroma, like sweet gardenia perfume, which caused her to ache deep in her heart. Sometimes, with her piccolo laying quietly across her lap, Emma watched young girls cling to their mothers' bosoms, frolic in the strands of their mothers' hair, and she would experience the same aching, the same deep longing. When she found courage enough to accost Mathias about her mother, he answered her dismissively, saying, "Oh, she was good woman," and nothing more.

Emma's darkest dread was that she had no mother at all, that she was some creature of dead flesh brought to life through alchemy, through the forbidden arts that only her father knew of, that that was the awful secret kept from her all these years. It would certainly explain why she was so strange, why she spooked people, and why nobody loved her—for an unnatural creature, she knew, was not to be loved. But the faint aroma emanating from her piccolo, and the name, *Ilsa*, gave doubts to such dread. Though she did not know how she knew, the piccolo represented a key to her past, a past locked up in her father's study.

Lowering the instrument, Emma lifted her voice instead, in song. Music was a thing nobody could steal from her. The day she first pressed lips to her piccolo, she discovered it—a sweet, angelic voice. Her shyness did not matter when she was alone. After all, it was the only form of talking to oneself acceptable to Delian society. But singing always made her sad, perhaps because she chose the most tragic of dirges, like the *Ballad of Titian and Midiana*.

Her song did not last to the end of the story. As the wheels began to lurch over stones, she was shaken into silence, into the reality of captivity. The terrain was growing harsher, making it difficult to hold a tune.

"No point singing tragedies now, Emma," she muttered to herself. "You're in one yourself."

She looked through the window again, seeing nothing but the vast spread of the plain and a receding line of snow. The wait, the uncertainty, was becoming unbearable, and she almost wished Bood had not kept Deed from gutting her. If only she could breathe her music, her spirits might be lifted, but for now the notes would remain trapped in her head. All she could do was ball against the corner of the wagon and watch the sky change from pastel blues to purple darkness, to glittering constellations.

In the dimension of the subconscious, the door to her father's study was wide open, and the books and artifacts free for her to peruse. The myriad of unfamiliar artifacts was too specific, too unlike the vagueness of dream to be unreal. She recalled the words on the pages, with enough accuracy to write them down, had she wanted to. But just as she reached for the one volume on the shelf that would reveal everything she wanted to know, she was pulled back into the waking world. Every night, Emma mined her memory, forcing the vessel of her brain to return to the study, to the mysterious volume she could scarcely recall. But more often than not, her mind followed different, unwanted courses. In darker moods, her dream self wandered to times and places that frightened her, to where a young Mathias sat scribbling feverishly.

> *The construct cannot survive the horrific rigors of interstellar travel lest the body be fashioned from firmer stuff, something as hard as steel and yet, to permit sentience, supple as flesh, an amalgam of both, perhaps—flesh and steel.*

Mathias leaned in his chair, alleviating the soreness in his spine, his eyes making love to the words still wet and glossy on the page. *Yes! That's good. A bit of conjecture, but it should suffice.* The feather of his quill tickled the creases of his lips as he pondered the next sentence, and then, with a sigh like a man set before some arduous task, he bent over his desk again.

Bock! Bock! Bock!

The sudden knocking came like dragon mosquitoes in his ears. Mathias had always been comforted by the dim solace of his study, had come to revel in the nuanced sounds of pen scraping paper and the flickering of candle flame. Even the occasional scamper of rat feet did not lift him from his writing. He pretended he did not hear the knocking, but it came again, resonating through the mahogany entry to the tower, down the steps and through the door of his study.

Mathias did not rise to the sound. He waved it off, assuming the trespasser had come to the wrong house and would soon, realizing his error, be off. He put one fist into another, using the interruption to rest his strained hands, and waited for peace to return again. At length, the knocking stopped, and quiet fell over him like a warm blanket. He sighed contentedly. *Now where was I?*

BOCK! BOCK! BOCK!

Rows of candelabras flickered. Shadows jolted out of place, and his hand twitched, tipping an inkwell. Blackness spread across a collage of pages, continued along the desk toward a timeglass.

Despite his best efforts to wait it out, the sound did not cease. Rather, it intensified, rattling the delicate equilibrium of his mind. On the rare occasion when visitors came to his home, Mathias was ever certain to sit quietly until they went away. Not only did he not wish to be disturbed, he hoped for nobody to know that anyone lived in the decrepit old tower. After all, he made his best effort to make his comings and goings discreet, leaving in the pitch of night to fetch whatever sustenance was needed to survive and whatever artifacts were required to continue his research.

BOCK! BOCK! BOCK!

He sighed. The person at the door was either very stupid or terribly stubborn. Who could it be, anyhow? There was no one whom Mathias could honestly call friend, and the few surviving members of his family had not spoken to him in decades. He listened again, unwilling to return to his work until he was certain the intruder was gone. When, finally, there was only the scratching of the mice in the walls, a satisfied smile spread across his cheeks— stretching his face into unaccustomed angles. He had won. His stubbornness had outlasted the other's stubbornness. With a sense of triumph, he bent over his desk again, paying little heed to the ache in his spine, and dipped his quill.

BOCK! BOCK! BOCK!

Ink speckled the page. *Ruined it!* He tossed the quill and ran black fingers through his diminishing hair. Mathias hated minor flaws—a wrinkle, an errant stain, a tiny tear—they would make him think and think incessantly until he would destroy the paper himself and start over.

BOCK! BOCK! BOCK!

Will this racket never cease! Is this man mad? Doesn't he know that nobody is home? Mathias tried again to turn his mind to the topic of his research, but every theory and conjecture fled from his mind. Perhaps, if he answered the door and demanded that the man leave, he might attain the peace he so cherished. As he managed himself to his feet, the knocking resumed and he loosed a myriad of obscenities. It was a cold, high-moon night, and as he hobbled over to his study door, he tugged at the sleeve of his coat and snatched up one of many oil lamps. The door boomed more loudly. "I'm coming!" Mathias shouted and slipped through the dark hallway to the stair.

As he climbed, the whole of the tower shuddered, every crossbeam groaning in rhythm. By the time Mathias made his way to the door, the continuous THOOM! resonated more deeply than he believed possible. The three-finger thick mahogany coughed up decades of dust as it rattled, and Mathias realized, with horror, that no human hand could be pounding on the door. It was more like a battering ram in sound, but the regularity with which it sounded gave the distinct impression of someone knocking.

As his mind turned to the possibilities, he chewed his fingernails, considering that his time had come at last, his punishment for questing too deeply into matters of nature. The door resonated again, lurching at him as he stepped away in horror. He tried to raise his voice above the clamor, but the air was too thick. He swallowed dryly and tried again. "Eh . . . ahem," he managed. "Who—who's there?"

No answer came. Only more knocking.

His knees quaked, and he considered fleeing back to his study, to hide among his books. But there was no escaping the sound. Somehow he knew it would continue, on through the night, tormenting him. There was no choice but to address it, to answer the door.

A blast of cold cut through him, clamped down on his bones. Snowflakes performed careful routines across a vacant sky, gathering along a wall of naked muscle, over shoulders and clefts of muscle. Mathias strained his neck to look up to the toothy muzzle. He could see his own terror-stricken face in the black orbs that were its eyes. The monster retreated from the doorway then, and Mathias felt an inkling of optimism. If the thing had come to harm him, he would be dead already.

"Wait," Mathias murmured. "I know you! You're Dak's construct. But if you're here, that means, that means—" *Dak is dead.* He did not dare utter it. He could not. It was not for his love of the man, for Mathias truly loved no one, but what such news could mean for him. *Does the king know? Am I next?*

The monster hardly moved. The only indication that it was not some crime of sculpture, some composition of dead mass, was its slow, steady breathing. Snowflakes continued to speckle its arms, its shoulders, clothing it in white. Otherwise, the monster was a patchwork of naked earthy hues. Its forearms were as thick as a man's thighs, gashed with dull shades of scarlet. Gashes also ran across its underbelly, the cuts of many desperate swords, but its flesh was like clay, and did not take to wounding as anything of nature might.

In the crook of the monster's arm, in a bundle of cloth, another life made itself known. Part of the bundle came loose, revealing an elfish face, too young to stretch into a smile. It squirmed against the elements, its stubby limbs testing its abilities, looking frail and helpless against the icy chill and wind. With barely a flex, Mathias knew, the monster could crush the bundle like a grape, but the infant looked secure, even cozy. Its hair was black as ink, its cheeks red as ripe tomatoes. With dark, knowing eyes, the infant stared at Mathias.

Mathias hesitated, his eyes altercating between the monster and the infant. The contrast could not have been more extreme. The monster exuded power, threatening by its mere presence, its face hideous to look upon, and its body an affront to nature. The infant was in every way its opposite, frail enough to be stolen by the wind, with a face softening even Mathias' hard resolve.

"What is this?" he said at last. "What am I—?"

Sensing rejection, the monster flared its nostrils in retort, and proceeded to position the infant under the lintel of the door.

"No!" Mathias growled, unable to meet the child's needful gaze.

The monster made no reply.

Mathias peeked across the intersecting avenues. The sun was deep in its ecliptic cycle. No one was about and the windows across from his were shut up for the night. Northendell slept on, oblivious. "I have important work to do!" he argued, as if the monster might understand. "Am I to be saddled with this . . . this thing?"

And then the construct uttered two syllables. It was a long dead voice, sounding dry and hollow from its long snout, like stones dropping into a cavern. "Em-ma."

With trembling fingers, pained by the cold, Mathias reached out. The swaddling unspooled from around the monster's arms. The infant was lighter than expected. He pulled her against his breast, startled by the stirring in his heart, but was quick to quell the sensation. *I am not suited for this. I'll take her for now, just until I find a nursemaid.*

From across the alley, Mathias could hear the clomping of boots. The infant crowed like a bird, as if to signal the approaching men-at-arms. *If they find me with the construct, I'll be implicated! I'll lose everything!* "Construct!" he cried, "you must be gone from here! Quick!"

"Grimm is guardian. Grimm is made to guard."

"No time for that!" he shouted, waving his free arm. "Leave from here! Make haste!" Mathias considered shutting the door and leaving the monster outside. But the thing would not budge and there would be questions. "Wait," he muttered, mostly to his own ears. "Constructs exist for a single purpose. You have relinquished the babe to me, and your master is dead . . ."

"Grimm is guardian. Grimm is made to guard."

Boots echoed. At any moment the street patrol would be upon them and Mathias would have much to answer for. "You are awaiting new commands," he said with realization. "Very well then. Grimm, I command you to go south, as far as you can, to the Sea if need be. Seek out a new master and let me alone!"

"But," the monster said, its voice like sandpaper, "Grimm is made to guard," and Mathias thought he heard a note of sadness in its voice, which, from everything he had read of constructs, was not possible.

"Go then and find another to guard! Anyone will do! Someone in need of guarding! Just make it far from here! Go now! Go!"

Shadows of soldiers grew long against the tower wall, and Mathias did not wait to see whether the construct would obey. He yanked the door shut, the infant in the crook of his other arm, and listened intently to the clamor of armor and crunching snow, until the marching grew faint. There were no shouted commands. No sounds of pursuit. Pressing his ear to the door, Mathias heard only the whisper of the wind, the shrinking of wood fibers against the budding ice. The infant was oddly calm in the dimness of his home. But already his feeble arms were tiring. He fumbled with the oblong bundle, the child like a new specimen he did not know to handle. And then, placing a finger over her lips, he let a sliver of moonlight through the door to take another look. There was no evidence the monster had ever been there, but for the impression of giant feet, already disappearing under the falling snow, and the tiny girl now peacefully slumbering in his arms.

6

WILD HUMANS

Fly with us, fly with us . . .
Come be a bird with us . . .

As the whispers died away, she squinted, blinking at her surroundings. It took time to process the sheets of sun percolating through the wooden beams and the barred windows, to trace back the events that put her there. She felt oddly disconnected from her body, as if her spirit had had difficulty finding its way and was only now aligning itself to her bones. After regaining some sensation in her limbs, she managed to stand. Her tailbone was sore. She shifted pressure from thigh to calf, steadying herself against the rocking compartment. She felt twice as heavy, needed twice the effort to reach the window.

The wheels were complaining more than usual as they were forced over the soil. After two days of travel by cart, Emma took pride in her ability to determine the terrain by feel. So far, they had made their way over dense ice, sped up and around hills of sheet rock, and quietly rolled across dirt. Whenever the wagon met wet soil, however, the wheels turned up mud, which made for a jarring ride of backward dips and forward bursts.

Her ears now met a thrashing sound amid the thump of mammoth hooves and squealing axles, a sound she could not place. She looked out the window and could not understand the image flitting across it. Recognition came, at last, from its amber sway, from the way the slender forms were clustered. Emma had seen bundles of the stuff carted through the city streets. She knew it came from the ground, that it was used to make food, but what she never imagined was how they could grow so densely packed, so far and wide.

Wheat.

Streaks of gold thrashed against the prison wagon, snapping as it passed, erupting into chaff. It filled her compartment with an aroma not unlike bread, kindling memories of bakeries and cooking fires and sending shockwaves of hunger pain down into her stomach.

She had survived the past few days by eating snow, drinking melting ice, and by letting her tongue gather lichen from the ceiling. Regular food had been denied her. The night before, she awakened to the scent of roasting meat. She saw Bood and Deed squatting by a small pit and a makeshift rotisserie. They had killed something and were burning their fingertips in their eagerness to pluck the meat from the bones. Sounds of satisfaction tormented her, the sloppy smacking of lips and the grinding of teeth. She pleaded for a morsel, but they did not spare her a glance. She was invisible to them, just as she was to her father, just as she was to the people of Northendell. Aside from not being human, Emma's darkest fear was that, somehow, she did not exist, that her life was nothing but someone's dream. She spent the remainder of the night watching Bood and Deed fill their stomachs, watched them flick scraps from their fingers, hoping a bone might drop within reach.

Now she could see food, or a component of food, spreading to the edges of the world. She was not certain whether straw could be eaten raw, but if it could sustain a beast, she reasoned, it would do. She reached her arm through the window, feeling the stalks smacking and warping in her palms. It was more challenging than she thought. The stalks moved too quickly for her to get a good hold, and when she did catch one, it would slip through her fingers. Eventually, grains started sticking to her palms, which she did not bother to taste. The cramping in her stomach eased a bit with each hard swallow.

Emma had not thought about monsters since the last pines of Gloomwood faded on the horizon. She knew of the wilds of Aenya, knew of the unnamed creatures roaming the distances between civilizations. But she also knew that no place was more threatened than her home. It was the reason the city was confined by so many walls, for Northendell was founded in the deep north, on the edge of perpetual night, at the gates of Gloomwood. Yet, two days travel from that place and Emma began fearing her future life as a slave, or as wife to some cruel husband, more than any monster. That was until she saw something moving powerfully through the rows, thundering the ground, its scaly hide mottled and green. Never faithful to the gods, she muttered a less than sincere prayer to Strom, that the monster pass by, that it not come their way. But the gods did not notice her either.

The thump of mammoth hooves paused and the window of wheat came into focus. Reeds of gold changed directions like a phalanx in unison at the whim of the wind. She considered tugging one from the ground, but was too frightened of what might be waiting, of what might be considering her as its food. She rushed to the front of the cart, pressing her face hard against the partition. Splinters were poking her earlobes, but she could hear them, Bood and Deed speaking in hushed, measured tones.

The monster was much closer now, obscured by beams of iron and waves of amber. But she could make out its broad body, its ridged spine poking above the grain, its long curving horns. It snorted through powerful nostrils, and let out a high-pitched whicker loud as a trumpet. The pace of Emma's heart slowed. It did not sound the way she imagined a monster would. *Nothing but an animal,* she considered, *a beast of burden.*

It was a strange dialect that turned her ears now. Others were speaking to her captors. Was she to be sold to them, she wondered? No. She could hear the hesitation in Bood's voice. He did not sound pleased.

In *The Epic of Thangar and Sint*, Prince Thangar sought the aid of the hero, Sint, to rescue his princess from the three-headed dragon, Polykephalos. If Emma were a princess she would be valued enough to be fought for. With sudden inspiration, she pressed her cheeks against the bars and yelled out, "Help! I have been captured! I am the daughter of . . . King Frizzbeard!"

She could hear Bood demanding that she shut up. Then, a moment of calm, followed by shouting. The green creature was stomping away, breaking stalks as it went, and then came a sudden flurry. Emma could feel the ground beneath the cart quake and the beams rattle. Through the window, the view was rapidly changing. Amber parted like a curtain, disintegrating into clouds of chaff, and the green became alarmingly vivid. She could make out the rim of its fan-shaped skull, the wrinkles about its eye, its nostrils gaping, horns a blur. A clash of noises came all at once, competing for her attention—Bood and Deed yelling, the mammoth's deafening blare, the splintering of wood and groan of the wagon's axle as it tipped off its wheels. Emma found herself in weightless chaos and, when gravity returned, it pulled more forcefully. Her hip ached where she landed. Everything was rearranged. Broken reeds poked through the window in the floor—the other window was now in the ceiling. On tiptoes, she reached the bars and pulled herself up. The center bar, having taken the brunt of the impact, came loose in her hand, allowing her head into the open air.

Under a bright sun, Emma marveled at the mammoth's gigantic splendor. It tromped free of its harness, its knees rising above the tops of the grain. It was a short-lived sight, however, as a saurian crossed into view, its leathery muscles flexing. The mammoth twisted to meet the attack, its shaggy coat ruffling, threatening with its blaring trunk. As if reconsidering its action, the saurian hesitated, but the two were locked in a combative circle now, trumpeting at one another, pummeling the ground. The saurian, though smaller, with a frill no taller than the mammoth's foreleg, proved more agile, strafing the other's broadside. The mammoth's ivory teeth curved inward, and so were unable to penetrate the scales of the other, but the tusks were also long, the length of its shaggy body, which kept the attacker's horns at a distance.

Bone cracked on bone.

The mammoth turned and turned, meeting horns with tusks. It was a brutal standoff, an unnatural clash of behemoths. Emma was fixated on the duel, wondering how long the mammoth could fend off the saurian before tiring. But other blood was being spilt—human blood, she knew—and the sounds of it pulled her attention to the spaces between the reeds. She spotted Bood, looking dreadful, his eyes peering through the sockets of his skull helm.

"Face me, cowards!" he bellowed, nervously twisting the shaft of his ax, but the threat sounded forced, desperate.

Emma noticed that the saurian was harnessed and saddled with supplies. But she could see no trace of the drivers. She scanned her surroundings and was startled when her eyes fell upon Deed, the tail end of an arrow protruding from the center of his forehead as if placed there by someone's hand, his dull pupils staring up from the ground. She thought he looked more serene than he had in life, and that, in this way, no one could imagine the cruelty he had been known for. A trickle of blood coursed across his long nose and over his lips, staining the dirt next to his face. Despite how he made her suffer, she took no pleasure in seeing his corpse. Now she wondered whether she had been a fool to call for help. Perhaps there were worse things in the world than Bood and Deed.

She lowered herself back into the cart and peered over the edge of the window, shaking in her cloak.

The background was moving. Some animal was moving through the field, camouflaged in amber, in the shadows of wheat on wheat. Bood charged, his ax catching the sun's rays, and for a moment Emma thought him heroic. Not knowing what manner of creature lay in wait for him, she watched, bewildered, unsure whether to pray for his demise or for his triumph. She strained her eyes to penetrate the cover of reeds, but all she could make out was the surrounding space coming alive to meet him. Her ears made up for lack of sight. Challenges were exchanged, grunts and ringing steel.

Behind her, a clearing was forming. She glanced over her shoulder, forgetting herself as she lifted her head from the window. The behemoths continued their battle in a haze of pulverized straw. Burgundy shapes spread across the mammoth's hide from unseen wounds. Its trunk hung lifelessly, mangled, clumps of bloody hairs sprouting from where the saurian's beak had clamped on it. In a final, desperate attempt at self-preservation, the mammoth bent on its hind legs and came down with all the force and weight of its forelimbs, shattering the saurian's bony frill. A horrid bray sounded from the injured animal, and, as if deciding to sleep, it folded its legs and touched its head to the ground. Across from her, another sound came, like a knife chopping through meat and bone. Emma gripped the remaining bars of the carriage window, as repulsed as she was fascinated, watching Bood's head roll out of the field in a brilliant spray of red.

Monsters! Strom! They'll be coming for you next!

Not bothering to wait for Bood and Deed's killers to emerge, Emma crouched into the cart, tucking her garments around her, stuffing herself into a corner. Every sound was magnified—her heart thumped in her throat and splinters crackled against her robes. Despite her best efforts at not breathing, her lips sucked loudly at the air. Beyond the walls, footfalls crunched the ground.

Perhaps if you remain perfectly still, they'll forget about you and go away.

The beam slid away and the door tore from its hinges, forming a blinding white square. A human shape squatted in the light. She saw coppery skin and a scraggly beard and piercing, topaz eyes.

"Give me your hand." His tone was reassuring, but she trembled at the sound of his voice. "Give me your hand," he repeated.

She felt an urge to obey, felt her will dwindle against his. She fumbled for a moment to find her hands among her sleeves and reached out. His palms were like sandpaper.

"I am Xandr."

As her eyes began to focus, she was taken aback, her initial dread changing to an emotion she did not recognize, a feeling welling up from her gut. He was like a statue she once found in an alcove, crafted centuries before, as a gift to the then-king of Northendell, and had stood in the center of a fountain, but the water no longer flowed. The head and torso were long worn by neglect, caked with lichen, pitted by rain and sand. But what had fascinated Emma was the sculpted penis. She had never seen a naked man or woman before, and so she found it peculiar. Now the same rough features, corded muscle and intense brow confronted her. Just like the statue, the man looked weath-er-beaten. She imagined that, if thoroughly scrubbed, he might resemble a god.

A strap crossed his breast, in line with a winding scar, and a layer of dirt coated his every pore. Parts of him were colored, by splashes of blood—Bood's blood—but other-wise, he wore nothing at all, not even a loincloth.

Emma promptly guessed what he was. She had heard rumors of such people, *wild humans*, hardly more than halfmen, murdering and raping with abandon, drinking their own urine, fathering children with their own chil-dren. It was not a wonder her city needed such high walls. The outside world was a nightmarish place, full of night-marish creatures, and so she was much better off, she had decided, with Bood and Deed. Then again, wild humans were not known to speak above a groan.

"Don't be afraid," he said.

Strangely, Emma was possessed by a sudden urge to cover herself more completely. But before she could re-spond to him, a female emerged from the thicket, looking just as savage, just as free under the sky, balanced on the balls of her feet.

When preparing to bathe, Emma was certain to check and recheck that nobody was nearby, that the bathhouse door was firmly prodded shut by a plank of wood. After hurriedly dousing herself, she would don her robes quick-ly, which would always stick to her damp skin, and then sprint, nearly freezing, the short distance home. She had never even bothered to look at her naked body herself. And now, with a glance, she was becoming intimately fa-miliar with this strange woman's every adjoining crease and follicle. The wild female stood, invulnerable, in her bronze, armor-like flesh, and Emma found herself studying the woman like some new specimen of beetle, marveling at the definition of muscle beneath the skin, how it flexed with every movement. Emma could not help but wonder how she kept warm during high moon, how she walked barefoot without pain, whether she covered at all. Not being an insect, however, the wild woman did not care to be studied. She caught Emma's stare with a fierce expression and eyes that burned like emerald fire, and Emma was overcome by shame, as if she were the oddity.

To her male companion, the female spoke with hard consonants, in a language that sounded to the Delian like an exotic but deadly flower. She then moved forward with quick, deliberate steps, shoving Emma against the doorway. A quiver slipped from her shoulder and Emma realized, with dismay, that she had been the one to kill Deed.

"We're not going to harm you," the man interjected.

Emma blinked, became fraught in not knowing where to look, in not remembering where people looked when looking at other people. "I—I'm sorry, I've never seen . . . I mean, I've never met any wild humans before."

"We're Ilmarin," he corrected. "Are you all right, princess?"

The title startled her. Had she forgotten so soon? Did she even look anything like a princess? She tried to remember how Lady Sif appeared during her trial—her only glimpse of female royalty—tried to mimic that proud stance, that confident stride, a regal bearing that, Emma was puzzled to note, was more evident in the wild woman, despite her total lack of regal attire, or any attire for that matter. But Emma was unaccustomed to standing fully up-right, to throwing her shoulders back, to lifting her heels. Delians often remarked she was of short stature, when she was in fact of average height. Emma was used to being invisible, to hiding in black garments, between walls nobody ever bothered to look between. *But what do wild humans know of royalty?* Their ignorance was her only hope.

"Please," she murmured, inflecting her voice with a royal air, "my name is Emmalina."

"Emma-Lina?" he repeated clumsily.

"No," she stammered, "just Emmalina. Call me Emma." *You're such an idiot! They'll never believe you're a princess!*

The wild woman turned sharply, her chestnut braid following her well-defined shoulder. "Well I hope she's worth it. We lost Rurk because of her!"

"Who's Rurk?" asked Emma.

"Rurk was our trike," she replied. "Your stupid mammoth killed him."

"I'm sorry," Emma said. "But he wasn't my—"

"Just shut up!" the wild woman answered, moving to inspect the fallen beast.

"Forgive her," the man said. "She's had a long, hard journey. And forgive our appearance. We've been," and he paused to take a long breath, "far from civilization." His topaz eyes exposed her, despite her heavy cloak.

"It's all right," Emma replied. "I sometimes find strange things beautiful." *Did I really say that? He's going to think you're stupid.*

"That is good, because you might be more alarmed by our other companion. He scares people wherever we go, but he is gentle among friends." He called out a name

and a figure rose up, the tips of grain no taller than its
waist. She imagined some savage creature, some shocking
custom worse than nakedness, but what greeted her was
fully adorned, in blue velvet with pieces of gold-bronze,
a brass hammer gleaming in its four-fingered hands. She
stood within arm's length of it, craning her neck to its
toothy muzzle. She did not recognize the monster, but felt
strangely comforted by its presence.

"You're not afraid?"

"No. I know I should be, but I'm not. Perhaps it's simply all the day's craziness." She smiled uneasily. "I suppose
I'm prepared for anything."

He looked pleased by her answer. "This is our guardian. His name is Grimosse."

"A guardian?" she exclaimed, looking upon the monster with fresh eyes. "Does he speak?"

"Grimm speaks," said Grimm.

"But not often," Xandr added.

Emma brushed a lock of hair from her face. If she was
going to be a princess, she could no longer hide behind
her hair. She turned from him to the mammoth stomping through the wheat, and the wild female caressing the
saurian's broken frill. She did not expect such affection
from someone who could so readily kill. Emma was also
surprised by herself, by how quickly she was adapting to
the sight of her, and his, exposed bodies.

"I suppose I should thank you," she told Xandr, con-
cluding they were not going to hurt her. "For saving me.
Will you take me back to Northendell now?"

"To your father, the king?" he asked.

She sensed the accusation in his voice. "Yes. Of course."

"We were headed that way."

"You were?" she said. "I've never seen your kind in the city before. You won't be welcome. I mean, wild humans aren't normally—"

"We're on a hunt," he said, in tone so grave that it frightened her. "It's moving quickly."

"What is it you're after?" she asked timidly.

His quietness was unnerving, as if he was afraid to answer, and she could not imagine what in Aenya could frighten such a man. And then he told her.

"We're hunting a god."

7

THE SECRET OF BREAD

Ingrid was a squat, wide-hipped woman resembling a stack of dough balls—a head, a bosom, and buttocks. Thelana had never seen such proportions before, never imagined a human could be so fat—it was strangely beautiful. Despite the woman's hefty frame and age—she looked old enough to be her grandmother—she moved sprightly about her small kitchen. Even as she addressed her guests, Ingrid's hands moved independently from the rest of her. Watching her work was a thing to behold, a marvel of economy born of decades' repetition. But she was anything but tidy. Much of the room, as was her second chin, her apron, and the rolling pin in her hands, was caked in a fine amber powder.

The fresh aroma emanating from the house had been intoxicating, conjuring memories of home, of Old Man oak. The Ilmar were drawn to the house like bees to ilms, helpless but to stand at the door, until Ingrid waved them inside. The hunger and thirst she and Xandr had suffered along the road from the Dead Zones seemed ages away.

"Are you certain the big one wouldn't like to come in?" Ingrid asked them. "He is perfectly welcome, you know."

The old woman's sincerity was disarming, and Thelana found it impossible to dislike the bread maker. "No," she said, "our companion is not . . ." *human* . . . "Hungry."

"In that case, I'll have to pack some bread for you to take to him."

Peering through the beaded doorway, Thelana watched Rurk circling the wooden post tethering it to the ground. Grimosse stood nearby, dutifully guarding their water-filled gourds, their pelts and salted meats, a hood hiding his face from gawkers. Despite Ingrid's exuberant hospitality, Thelana did not believe she would react well to the sight the golem.

Xandr was gazing into his cup of crushed tea leaves and sprig of mint. Catching Ingrid's eye, he offered a nervous smile through the dirty blond hairs of his mouth. Cycles had passed since his grooming in Hedonia and he was looking more the barbarian with each passing day. It was clear he was out of his element—that he was more accustomed to fighting giant snails in swamps than sitting at teatime in an old lady's house.

"We cannot repay you," he said uneasily.

"Repay me?" she echoed, as if the idea was absurd. "Pish-Posh! Nothing doing!"

Thelana looked to Xandr for a clue to Ingrid's meaning, but he could only shrug. From the Dead Zones to Kiathos, the Ilmar had come across many different languages, dialects, and customs—in towns, in villages, and upon groups of nomads. Often, trades were made, for food or water, with nothing but gestures. But even in the shared Kratan tongue, some expressions were incomprehensible.

"You're getting some bread in your stomachs first," Ingrid insisted, "and then a bath, and then fresh clothes! And no *ifs* or *buts* 'cause I won't hear of it." She placed her rolling pin on a long table and motioned to Thelana. "Now dear, if you would please help an old woman. My back isn't what it used to be."

Thelana hopped to her feet and the woman was immediately upon her, probing the young Ilmarin's forearms with stubby fingers. Ingrid seemed genuinely disappointed. "So skinny, girl! That won't do, won't do at all. We have to get some meat on those bones if you ever expect to have children!"

"Well . . ." Thelana started, "I haven't really thought about—"

"Grab me that pot there, will you," she said. "The big one there."

Dozens of ceramics of varying sizes littered the wall beneath a fold-up shelf. By their simple patterns and rough edges, Thelana could tell they were locally made. An alley of spinners had greeted them when they passed into the village, women with wet clumps of clay between their fingers, their younger children carrying pales of water as the more learned offspring carefully painted designs on finished pieces. She tugged at the largest pot with all her might, surprised by her weakness, when a chuckling boy suddenly tumbled out of it and onto the floor.

"Eli!" Ingrid cried. "How dare you play such a mean trick on our guests? When I catch you—!"

Eli had dusty, dark hair and skin, and bright merry eyes. He brought to mind her meddlesome twin brothers,

Lodr and Heimdl. They often played such silly tricks in their mother's kitchen. "It's alright," she replied, smiling at the boy. "Let him be." But Eli did not wait for anyone's approval, disappearing through the curtain to the outside.

Thelana stood with a hand on her spine. "Is he yours?"

"Mine. Yes," the old woman replied with a hint of sadness. "He's my godson. But the way he acts, you'd think he belonged to everyone in the village, popping up all over the place. Boy can't keep to himself—always has to go running off, seeking adventure. World's not big enough for him I don't think. So tell me . . . where've you three come from?"

"From very far," Xandr replied dryly.

Not wishing to be rude, Thelana was quick to add, "From Baartook."

"Baartook!" the woman exclaimed. "Haven't received anyone from Baartook in many years. My, my, that's a long ways off. You must be famished. Not many towns between here and there."

"We did not find many," Xandr replied. "We lived by the spear and the bow." It was a common turn of phrase, despite the fact that neither he nor Thelana ever used a spear.

"Hunters, eh? That's a good way to get yourselves killed, if you ask me," she said. "What you need is some good bread." She picked out a corked jar, prying it loose with her fingertips. "Few people around here know the secret of bread. Nobody even knows where it came from. Some say the gods whispered it in the ears of our forefathers. But who can know these things, truly? The secret has been in my family for generations. My mother taught me, and her mother taught her, and well . . . you get the idea."

"Not really," he said flatly.

"Of course, I suppose a hunter wouldn't. But I can show you part of the secret . . ." She dipped her hands into the jar, producing a hazel, clay like substance. "The magic is in this. Can't make bread without it." She bent over the pot, her belly fat rolling over the side. Thelana watched her work the substance into a soft goop, watched a handful of salt turn the clay into mud. The room smelled of baking and spices and simmering tea. She'd helped mother make bread countless times, and now, seeing Ingrid go about it brought warm feelings to her heart, so that, for a time, the horrors of Hedonia and the Dead Zones lifted from her mind.

"So what brings you to Kiathos?" Ingrid asked, and without giving Thelana a glance, added, "Go outside and bring up a pail of water, will you, dear? Thank you."

Xandr breathed deeply. "We have come in search of . . . a place."

"Another village?" she said, taking a long spoon from a hook on the wall.

"No," he replied. "Not a village, a . . . location. We want to know where the star fell."

"Ah . . ." she intoned, and for a moment, lines formed across her forehead, and her mouth lost some of its cheer. "I see." Thelana handed her the pail. It sloshed from brim to brim. Water sprinkled from a crack in the bottom. The old woman measured the water as it poured, handed it back to Thelana and dove back into the pot. "Now a bit of ollyp oil." She pirouetted across the kitchen to a bottle on the shelf. "You know," she said, as the oil formed sinewy, circular patterns atop the mixture, "much goes into making dough. It spins round and round and then it changes, becomes whole—it becomes one thing. I sometimes have strange thoughts when I watch it . . . about stars and moons. I wonder whether they're not so different, like big balls of dough made of many things that got mixed together. I know it's silly, me a bread maker and all. What do I know of such things?" She told Thelana to bring a bag from the stack in the corner. A cloud of amber formed about the room as the grainy material was added to the pot.

"Now if you would, dear," she said, offering Thelana the spoon, "this part hurts my back." Thelana was more than willing, kneeling to the task. The mixing of flour, water, and yeast was easy at first, but grew more difficult and slow as it solidified.

With one eye on the dough and the other on Xandr, Ingrid began to speak, more somberly now. "*Tooth of the Taker*, fell from the constellation of the Dark God—that's what they say. When it happened, nobody expected it. Who could expect such a thing, I ask you? Long as anyone can remember, the stars have stayed in their place." She fanned her cheeks briskly, as if the subject was making her hot. "The whole ground shook, as if Lunestes himself was shaking the pillars of Aenya! Strom protect us!" Her fingers drew quick shapes over her bosom in a gesture of faith. "Smoke filled the sky for cycles! And don't get me started on the fires! So many trees . . . the valley used to be green. Now it's just a mountain of ash. We thought the whole world would burn to a cinder. And that's not the end of it! *No!* The animals that drank from the river started dying, one by one. People too, grew ill, and the Taker took them. So many gone . . .

"For us here in Kiathos, Strom protect us, the gods showed mercy. We managed to keep on with our grain stores. It happened far enough for us to hear of it, to see the smoke, to suffer the bad water. But our neighbors to the south fared worse. They came in droves, deaf or blind or both. Burned. Sick. We offered healers. Our bread. I'd rather not talk more of it."

By the time her story was done, Thelana was struggling to turn the dough. She could understand what Ingrid meant by its remarkable meshing. Before her eyes, the varied colors and consistencies disappeared into a fat, supple whole. She had never seen so much dough before. It was enough to feed a hundred people. As if the dough wished to keep the spoon, it tugged back as she attempted to free it.

"Still too sticky, dear," Ingrid replied. "Turn it more, would you?"

Thelana did not complain, but would rather have been turning a weapon in a monster's gut. Even in Ilmarinen, she preferred hunting with the boys than cooking with her sisters. She glanced over at Xandr, who sat brooding with his tea, looking confounded. Like her, he was also tired of traveling, of searching blindly. They were within sight of Spire Mountain, to the west, and a valley of hills skirting north and east, but there was no trace of the Absent Mountain, or a fallen star, anywhere. She watched him sip the minty liquid nervously.

Ingrid made an impression of her fist in the dough. "Better, dear. Better. Now fold it and knead it flat with your hands. Have to get your hands messy to make good dough."

Pulling at his satchel, Xandr produced the leather tome with its crinkled skull. He flipped quickly to the last pages, finding the silhouette of the twin peaks with the enigmatic space between them, with a streak of something falling from the heavens. "We are looking for this place," he said.

Ingrid looked carefully over the page, stretched a bony finger toward the smear of ink in the sky. "That's the star, isn't it? Tooth of the Taker."

For a bread maker, Thelana thought her unusually sharp of wit. "Yes," he admitted.

"I've never been to that place," she said darkly, "but I know it is not far, to the south. A man came to us after the happening. He was raving mad, but I could see he had a kind soul—only refugee not to die of the sickness. He may be able to tell you more."

"Is he still here?" Xandr asked impatiently. "In the village?"

"Eli can take you."

He stood at once, hurriedly stuffing his book away. "Come, Thelana."

She glared at him. "But the dough isn't finished."

"We must hurry."

"Never mind that, dear," Ingrid said, taking hold of the spoon. "I've made enough bread on my own. But tell me, why do you seek this place so badly?"

Xandr looked at her for a long time without speaking, perhaps because he did not have an answer, or at least not one he understood. How could such a simple woman fathom what she and Xandr were witness to?

Ingrid called out for her godson, who was not far from the house. As Thelana lifted the partition of beads, she saw Rurk and Grimosse surrounded by wide-eyed children, their anxious parents close behind. Trikes were not a common sight in Kiathos, but were not so unheard of as to stir a panic.

The boy turned sharply. His thick eyebrows touched whenever he smiled. "Is it yours?"

"Yes," Thelana said.

"Can I ride him?"

Ingrid stormed out of the house waving her hand like a weapon. "Eli! Don't you dare go near that thing!"

The boy shrank from her without a rebuttal, and Ingrid seemed to forget the boy's impertinence at once, her doughy cheeks relaxing again into an easy smile. She gave Xandr and Thelana a basket of breads and teas and made them promise to return before nightfall.

Kiathos was like any other village on Aenya, but Thelana could see that the gods gave greater blessings to its people than to those of Akkad. The people here were of simple minds and pleasures, their days spent spinning pottery, haggling for local wares, laboring over the land, making love and bringing new life into the world. They made offerings to petty gods for good harvests and prayed for protection from plagues and storms and bandits, from conquering madmen and zealous empires, and from the nameless creatures that roamed the wild spaces between human settlements.

Huts of pine and straw formed a haphazard circle about a clearing in the village. Faded tents indicated a bazaar, but the vendors were shut up for the day. Only children remained, clouding the air with pounding feet, racing kites across the face of the turquoise moon. Two boys accosted Eli as they passed, asking him to join their game, but he acted the part of *man on official business*, waving his hand importantly. The boys eyed Xandr and Thelana with equal parts curiosity and apprehension, and returned to their games.

"Look at them," Xandr said wistfully. "They know nothing of the outside world."

"Neither did we," she replied, her chest tightening.

He held her gaze a moment, but gave no reply.

As Eli led the Ilmar through the village, he proved incapable of silence. Every thought and question poured from brain to mouth without filter. He asked about the trike, what it ate and how it slept and whether it ever fought any larger, meat-eating saurians. He asked Thelana—and she couldn't help but notice that he was more comfortable speaking with her than with Xandr—about her battles and her weapons. Is your sword heavy? Have you killed many people with it? Can I touch it? On and on it went. Despite the horrors abounding in her tales, he did not seem the least bit affected. He understood the finality of death, but was innocent to it all the same.

At the edge of Kiathos, where the dwellings became smaller and less frequent and foliage crept in from the dense wild beyond, Eli began to tell them of Omeron. After the star fell, which the boy described as if something

marvelous, Omeron came to the village half-alive. Ingrid
nursed him with bread and soups, but Omeron went mad,
raving about a dark god who walked the earth. Other refugees, before succumbing to the sickness, confirmed that
Omeron was a farmer and that his wife and children had
been killed in the fire that consumed their village.

The boy paused mid-sentence, staring ahead, and
pointed. The only thing Thelana could see, amid a cluster
of boulders and basil stems, was a cylindrical vase as tall as
a man. Eli seemed hesitant to go further.

"Are we near his house?" Thelana asked, puzzled.

"Yes and no," Xandr answered the boy. He stepped up
to the vase and tapped on it softly.

"Come out, Omeron!" Eli announced. "You have
visitors."

Thelana felt the boy brushing against her. She remembered her youngest brother, Baldr, when he was afraid,
how he would seek solace by staying close.

"Leave me be!" a voice from the inside of the vase
replied.

"He lives in there?" Thelana inquired. "He really is
crazy."

A haggard face with gray bristling hairs poked up from
the ceramic orifice. "Think me crazy, do ya? Yer the crazy
ones, all o' ya, standin' out there in plain view! This here's
my magic turtle shell, is what it is!"

The greenish vase was mottled with age, its cracks
spackled over with mud. Thelana remembered how the
Kratan refugees resembled turtles, with their shells like
armor, and she smiled despite herself, knowing she was
becoming like them, was becoming oblivious to the

long garment she was wearing, the traditional desert djellabah they'd found among Nesper's wares. And she wondered how soon they might leave the village, her body suddenly aching for freedom, for the feel of the world on her skin.

"Come on in if you like," Omeron bellowed, spittle hanging between the gaps of his rotted teeth. "It'll protect ya from the sky. Did so once, can do it again!"

"I don't think two of us could fit in there," she remarked.

"Fine!" Omeron replied with unwarranted drama. "Stay out! I didn't wantcha anyhers!" And he ducked his head back down like a weasel in a hole.

Thelana thought him unusually animated for someone living in so little space. She turned to Xandr reproachfully then. "You wanted to learn something from a man who lives in a vase?"

"Turtle shell!" cried Omeron, his voice echoing from inside.

"He may be mad," Xandr said, scratching under his beard, "but perhaps mad in craft. Amid his ranting, there may be grains of truth."

"What is it?" Omeron cried, popping up. "What is it?" he repeated, wiggling his shoulders free as the whole of his ceramic home wobbled, nearly toppling. "I be knowin' whatever the question may be! Ask away, please! Noberdy asks Old Omeron anythin' anymore . . ."

"Alright," Xandr said gruffly, his gaze making Omeron shrink down into his vase. "Did you see the falling star?"

"Did I see it, he asks? Did I see it? What a silly question! Where've ya been?"

"Well, did you?"

"I saw god!" Omeron replied. His eyeballs rolled around in his skull, looking too big for their sockets. "I saw 'im, I did."

Thelana could see that Xandr held his rage in his clenched fists, and feared that he would not keep it there for long. But when at last he spoke, it was softly, and with resignation. "Forget it. He's madder than the cuckoo."

"It was huge," Omeron muttered. "A giant."

Thelana bent to study the haggard face. The man panted like a dog, eager for attention, begging to be listened to. "A giant, did you say?"

"Yes, yes," he replied. "I seen 'im wit' my very own eyes. Tall as the highest mountain! Earth tremblin' under his feet as if *she* were a-feared to hold 'im!"

"Can you tell us what he looked like?" she asked.

The man's eyes became fixed upon a memory, possessing him with urgency, the present fading from his face. "Black as darkness," he murmured. "Eyes burning fire. Flesh heaped on flesh . . . hands of steel."

Xandr unclenched his hands. "Flesh and steel?"

"Do not seek 'im!" Omeron cried, as if waking from a nightmare. "He brings doom! Everythin' dies in his path, for he is *Skullgrin*, the Dark God returned! Quick, hide in my turtle shell and you'll be safe!"

Thelana could feel Eli's trembling. The boy was back-pedaling, crouching behind her thigh. Her stories of mer-quid and snake people did not faze him, but to Omeron's ravings he showed uncontrollable fear.

"No," said Xandr firmly. "We need to see it for ourselves. You need to take us there."

"To the pit?" Omeron exclaimed. "I cannot take you. But you can take me."

As Rurk carried them over dark, hilly terrain, Xandr surveyed the mountain horizon, hoping for the familiar pattern to emerge, the twin peaks and the inverted V of empty sky known as Absent Mountain. Among their belongings, there was a vase containing a chattering madman, whom Xandr had long stopped listening to, or at least had tried to. Every shadow and unexpected noise needed explanation. On more than one occasion, he was convinced that the Dark God was following them, and if not for Thelana's constant reassurances, they would not have been able to continue. Xandr found himself grumbling the whole while, having agreed, albeit reluctantly, to keep Grimosse in the village, far from Omeron. But where the land was barren of vegetation, Omeron became less of a guide and more of a nuisance.

The path of devastation was easy to follow. South of Kiathos, a great pine forest once thrived, but little remained of it but malformed husks, towering overhead like blackened spears, as if armies had been burned at the stake and nothing but clumps of ash were left of the bodies. In random spots, the tall tapering forms were bent, each in the same direction, outwardly from a center point far in the distance. Aside from the remains of the trees, there was no sign that life was or had ever been. Not a bird's song or an insect's buzz could be heard, only the wind's dying breath through the hollow timbers. Even Omeron found cause for quiet contemplation. A burnt stench stuck to Xandr's clothes, his hair, pervaded everything. Smoke hung over the ground like a shroud over the body of the forest, stinging his eyes. Or was he weeping? In a flash, his mentor came to him, QuasiI expressing his love of flora, and Xandr was thankful that his mentor was no longer alive to witness the terrible loss, not only of the pines, but of every living thing—the insects that made their homes in the bark, the rodents that burrowed under the roots, the treer that grazed off the shaded grasses, every woodland creature known and unknown to the languages of men. There was a void, an aching emptiness, where the Goddess should have been. Even the familiar nymphs, Wind, Earth, and Water, were absent. Xandr was sickened by it, like the sickness that comes from longing for a loved one. The layers of his djellabah could not shield him from the pain, from the wound deep in his soul, in the soul of the Goddess, and turning to Thelana he knew, by her mournful expression, that she was also attuned to it.

They continued on in silence. Though Xandr felt in his bones that this was a land of death—knew that Thelana felt it, too—there was no indication of a settlement. No ruined homes, no charred human remains. "Omeron," he called out. "Were there people here? Villages?"

"People! Oh, yes! I was here, wasn't I?"

Studying their surroundings again, as though he had missed something, Xandr saw nothing to suggest a house. "How did you survive?"

"I told yers before, don'tcha listen? Was my magic turtle shell!"

Breaking like the yolk of an egg against the turquoise moon, the sun spread yellow and orange across the sky, tinting the mountain peaks red. Increasingly, the horizon took a familiar shape, and Xandr hurriedly pulled at the book, matching hills and arrangements of boulders with shapes of ink on the page.

"Eldin was here." His voice sounded loudly amid the stillness. "It's unmistakable." But the expressionist work differed from the reality. Absent Mountain was there as expected, as predicted, but was no bigger than his thumb. It was too far off, he determined. In the book, the twin pinnacles loomed larger. Eldin must have stood closer when he painted it. But had he actually watched the star fall, as the image suggested? Could anyone have stood so near the point of impact, at the moment of impact, and survived? No. The pinewood forest, a half a day behind them, was turned to ash. Eldin could not have fared better. Or did he escape through one of his angles, which even now Xandr had trouble comprehending?

They rode under an empty sky, where not even the memory of trees, not even a single twig, remained. Closer to the point of impact, the soil became like charred papyrus, black and coarse and lifeless. There was a deep depression in the terrain, a gradual slope leading into a deep basin, a crater too vast around to see. As the ground shifted beneath Rurk's hooves, pebbles tumbling down, Omeron screaming with fright, Xandr and Thelana holding tight to the reins, a lakebed of soot emerged, a scorched-black plain speckled in white. The trees that once stood were obliterated in an instant. Only flakes remained. Ashen white flakes. The center was pitch and shadow.

"This was my home," said Omeron, daring to peer over his vase as the saurian regained its footing. "Here were my crops that I grew, and here was my house that I built with my own two hands, and here was the family that I sired from my own loins."

"This is it?" Thelana remarked. "Where is the star?"

Xandr stirred at the question. "What do you mean?"

"I thought it would be brighter, that it would be glowing down there."

Not knowing how to reply, he snapped at the reins about the trike's horns, and Rurk continued along the broken path.

They dismounted a short distance from the center, descending to the base of the crater. Xandr found Absent Mountain in his sights again, matching it to the illustration in the *Ages of Aenya*. He lifted the page to the sky, letting the sunlight shine through it, until the outline of the mountain matched the outline of the mountain.

"We're here," he said.

Something white and crystalline circled the pit in a ring of debris. The further from the impact point, the larger the pieces. It was volcanic glass. The rock bed disintegrated on impact, Xandr determined, becoming hotter than the sun, leaving something sharp and transparent behind, a kind of white obsidian.

Careful not to cut her knees, Thelana knelt to examine the pieces, turning a dagger-sized blade over in her palm. "This could be useful," she said. But she hesitated before collecting them. As her hands hovered over the rocks, the hairs on her forearms pulled up and away, and her fingertips buzzed and pulsated as if plucking at her bowstring. "These rocks . . . they're still warm," she remarked. It was unnerving, unnatural, unlike any source of heat she had ever known. "How is that possible, after all this time?"

"Don't touch them," Xandr warned.

The pit itself was ordinary, waist-deep and no broader across than Ingrid's kitchen. They searched the ground as they moved forward, Omeron peeking over the rim of his vase, trembling as if some catastrophe might befall them at any moment.

"Nothing," Xandr remarked, quietly, angrily. Disregarding his own advice, he bloodied his knuckles against the crystalline rocks. "There's nothing here."

Thelana walked over to him, up to the lip of the pit. "What did you expect to find?"

"I don't know. Something . . . anything!" He screamed. "What are we here to do but witness this . . . catastrophe? I'm powerless, Thelana, just like in Hedonia, just like . . ." he added, barely above a whisper, "in Ilmarinen." He gathered long, heavy breaths, as if waiting for some god or goddess to answer him. But no divine voice, no omen—no phoenix—manifested.

"You must have faith," Thelana urged. "Look around. Be patient. Wait." Her eyes drifted southward. There was something significant to be found there, she knew, but she did not know what, leaving her mind to catch up with her senses. "What is in that direction there?"

"Nothing," he grumbled. "It is where we came from."

"No," she murmured. "We came from south*west*. Southeast . . . is the Gulf of Sarnath, is it not?"

He nodded.

"Don't you see, Xandr?" She leapt with excitement. "Hedonia! The star! It hit the ground so hard that it, it . . . Ingrid said it shook the world, and like a bed sheet the land rolled, like a wave," she explained, waving her arms for emphasis, "through the ground, under the water."

"Hedonia is gone," he snapped at her. "There's no point in what you're saying."

"Xandr!" she cried, annoyed. How could he be so dismissive when understanding was dawning upon them at last? She was like a sleeper awakening to truth. She no longer felt like a marionette, helpless to the cruel jests of the gods. There was reason behind catastrophic events—cause and effect. The mysteries of the universe could be unraveled—Aenya could be understood, and if things could be understood, they could be avoided, possibly even changed. Perhaps there was some grain of wisdom to Ingrid's words—perhaps the world was nothing but yeast, water and flour. But Xandr was too angry, too stubborn, to see as she did.

"The dark god!" Omeron bellowed. "There! Look there!" Omeron trembled, and his vase teetered.

Thelana dropped to one knee, changing her vantage point, and a pattern emerged amid the tumult of rock and sand. She strolled alongside it, falling easily into the role of a tracker hunting wild game, crouching to reach into each impression. Glancing up again, she met Xandr nose-to-nose. "They're huge," she murmured. And to prove the point, she sat inside it, a hole wide enough to accommodate her folded thighs.

Following the edge with his fingertips, he shook his head, confirming what she already knew. The footprints were part of the rock bed. Something massive had walked across the molten surface as it was cooling.

"What do you think it is?"

His eyes were shifting like a restless dreamer's. She could tell his mind was turning.

"Could it be a saurian? One we haven't seen before?"

"No," he said. "Nothing on Aenya could have survived this. It walked out of the crater—straight from the fire— straight from a burning star that turned solid rock to glass. For all we know, it *is* the star."

"I told yers!" Omeron shouted from the echoing depths of his tiny house. "I told yers was the dark god! But did you listen? Didjya? Nooo . . ."

Thelana felt her palms go clammy. She looked from the haggard man to Xandr. "Could he be right? Could it really be Skullgrin, walking the earth, as we walk upon it?"

Xandr did not answer her. Rather, he approached the trike, removing a slender bundle from the saurian's side. The orange gleam of the horizon caught on its mirror steal surface as he unraveled it. Without blood to spill, the great sword limped heavily in his grasp.

"If this thing—whatever it may be—is as we fear, death must surely follow it, and where there is death, Emmaxis will point the way." He closed his eyes and raised the sword parallel to the ground, and the ground pulled on it. Thelana, still nestled in the concave depression, could see that its direction was without doubt. Like a compass, the long tooth showed them the way north, following the footprints of the star.

8

AT STERNBROW HILL

Having memorialized the fallen saurian, with a mound of dirt and a prayer to their Ilmarin god, the wild woman christened their mount Onehalf, as the mammoth was left with only one complete tusk after its duel with the trike. Undeterred by the overturned wagon, they fastened their sparse belongings to Onehalf's sides and Xandr took to the reins, steering from behind the animal's great leafy ears, as Thelana crossed her legs behind him, confident as a bird in a tree. But for Emma it was a terrible ordeal. Not only was she sandwiched between a golem and a wild naked woman, she was forced to sit precariously atop the beast's hump, which was too broad for her to straddle with her thighs but narrow enough to lose balance and tumble to a broken neck. That was, at least, what she kept imagining. But the mammoth offended Emma's senses in more ways than one. Its body emitted a stench she could not hope to escape, reminding her of a goat pen. Nothing seemed to bother the Ilmar, however, neither the chill morning air nor the scorching midday sun, nor the biting gnats clouding the mammoth's head. Despite their nakedness, they were utterly without feeling, as stony as their golem, and Emma was forced to wonder how distantly related she could be to them, how one human could differ so much from another. Once, after waking to painful welts in her legs, Emma found mammoth fleas—each the size of her thumbs—crawling between the beast's ropey hairs. But the fleas outright ignored the Ilmar, nibbling on Emma as if she were made of sweeter stuff, despite tight layers of clothing.

They journeyed for days, searching the rolling landscape, occasionally changing course, but always to the north. When they did speak, it was only to each other in their hard sounding language. Sometimes the wild woman slipped to the ground, to caress the dirt, tasting it, and with three quick strides was up and mounted again, a remarkable feat to Emma's eyes, who fought clumsily, even with Grimosse's aid, to seat herself atop the mammoth's hump.

Too shy to play her piccolo and unable to talk to herself without drawing attention, Emma could find no respite but to draw quietly into her thoughts, watching the landscape change from wheat fields to brush plains, from hills to rising mountains. She sat, and waited, feeling the swell of Onehalf's muscles as the moons pirouetted across the horizon. With long passings of boredom, she studied Thelana's sinewy backside, her breath rearranging the hairs between the wild woman's shoulder blades. She found it curious that Thelana should bind her hair when Emma often hid behind hers. If Emma were born among her people, she certainly wouldn't keep her hair in a braid but, rather, use it to at least cover her bosom! After a time, she came to see Thelana's body like a map in a book. Each line told a story, and Emma could not keep from daydreaming, conjuring misadventures for how every scar came to be—a gash from the blade of a cutthroat pirate, a bruise from the rock of an erupting volcano, a bite from the dreaded voorgaven—*no, not a voorgaven*, she decided, even Thelana couldn't survive that. But it was clear some creature had made a broad impression of its fish-like teeth across her shoulder. Despite days together, Thelana never told her a single tale, never offered a word other than to admonish the Delian for her lack of dexterity—her inability to climb up or down the mammoth's side. Emma was used to feeling nonexistent, but never in so awkward a position, as close as she was to another human being.

As the sun stretched fire-orange fingers over the sky, Onehalf was brought to a creek to drink, and the Ilmar prepared their tent and gathered kindling. Emma was greatly relieved, her limbs aching from lack of use. Pretending to engage in pleating her skirt, she stole furtive glances toward Xandr and Thelana. Every morning she half-expected them to cover, as though they were only forgetting their clothes, but from eclipse to eclipse they remained as they were, oblivious to their exposed genitalia. It was not long before Emma found it easier to look at them, to focus on their faces, without her eyes wandering all over their bodies. With each passing cycle, they had become less strange, nearly childlike in their naivety, until their nakedness no longer offended her senses. If she was at all concerned, it was that others might come across them, a traveling merchant to embarrass the four of them.

The golem was a greater mystery. She was familiar with the rumors, of men who sought knowledge of creation, of things meant only for gods—madmen destroyed by their abominations. Such rumors were at the heart of her people's fears. Grimosse, she did not doubt, would never be accepted into the city. If caught in his company, the four of them would be exiled, just as she was exiled from Northendell. But how did a simple people like the Ilmar come to control a golem? It was beyond her comprehension. And yet the monster, however bizarre, did not plague her thoughts as one might expect. Rather, it was the wild human she doted on, a mere man.

The first time she saw him coming out of the water, the blood and dirt of battle washed away by the river, he was every bit the icon of a Hedonian god, his hair long and wet against his lower back like streams of gold in the sun. Even his scar, disfiguring upon first glance, was like an emblem in her eyes. She delighted in the beautiful way his thigh muscle curved into his backside, wondering whether every Ilmarin male could be so chiseled, so well endowed, so . . .

Blood rushed to her cheeks and, realizing Thelana might be watching, she tore her gaze from him, her dark locks tumbled over her eyes, as if, by doing so, she might shake the thoughts from her skull. *What is the matter with you, Emma? Don't you know where that kind of thinking can lead?*

To a dangerous place, a voice inside her answered. Besides, the notion—she dare not think it—was absurd. A city girl like her could never find common ground with a wild man, especially him, someone as unpracticed in the most basic of civilized customs. Besides, should her feelings be suspected, she did not doubt his female companion would gut her without an inkling of remorse. Yet how could she help from feeling warmer whenever he neared? Or keep her pulse from quickening as he spoke? She would have to control herself, if she wanted to keep on living.

On the fourth cycle day, a herd of ziff raced across the plain, pursued by a green tiger. With their long necks and horns, and black stripes running down their bodies, the ziff were not entirely unknown to Emma. They sometimes grazed outside the city walls during low moon, when the snow melted enough to allow for grasses to sprout. But an entire herd was a sight to behold, hundreds dashing and leaping with a single mind. Thelana sat spellbound, watching. The green and yellow cat, on the other hand, was like nothing Emma knew. With terrifying grace, it pounced upon a calf with a lame leg, and as the herd dispersed in a ruddy haze, the fallen ziff let out a long, agonizing whicker, pleading for its brethren to wait, but there was no hope for the young animal. She could already see the tiger, splaying the velvety black and white hide, its scimitar-like teeth reddening as it tore into its prey.

Without a thought for social graces, Emma put a quivering hand on Thelana's shoulder. "Do you think maybe . . . it could get to us?"

"No," Thelana said. "It'll have its full and we'll be gone before it hungers again."

Emma nodded but was not convinced. The size and power of the green tiger gave her gooseflesh, and the savage way it went about its meal made her long for the comfort of walls. The wide open spaces of the plain were beginning to feel too wide, too open.

"Don't worry," Thelana added. "We have my bow. If I hit it in the right spot, I could take it down with one arrow, maybe two. Certainly make it rethink having us for dessert."

Onehalf continued its northward trek and the tiger became more difficult to see. Emma relaxed, pulling her hand away from Thelana's shoulder. But she feared a return to silence, to mental isolation. The tiger and the ziff had given them an opportunity for discourse that she did not wish to abandon. "How did you learn to shoot so well?" she asked, hitting upon the Ilmarin's pride.

Thelana turned slightly, sunlight and shadow casting her profile in sharp relief. "Hunger is the best teacher."

"You killed Bood," Emma said quietly. She did not know why she said it.

"Who?"

"One of the men who held me captive. He had an arrow in him."

"Yes," Thelana admitted, "that was my arrow."

The moment was passing too soon. Emma could feel the discomfort growing between them. She had to think fast. "Was it easy killing him?"

"It was," the Ilmarin replied. "He had a big forehead."

"Oh." It was not what Emma meant, but did the Ilmarin know that? Was she being teased? Rattling her brain for something more to ask, she added, a bit awkwardly, "Do you like being a warrior?"

The wild woman did not move, as if such a question never occurred to her, and Emma was again made to stare

NICK ALIMONOS

at the lines on her back, thinking the moment was over, that she would continue the day as silent as her shadow.

"I was never given a choice," Thelana said at last.

"Oh. I didn't consider that. Do you think *I* could ever be one?" It was a ludicrous idea. Emma knew it even as she said it.

"A *what?*" Thelana pivoted to face her now, a move Emma would likely kill herself attempting. She could only sit, as rigidly as possible, hoping not to fall.

"A warrior." She blushed, feeling stupid.

"Let me see your hands."

Emma surrendered her porcelain palms into the warrior's own. No wonder the fleas did not bother the woman—her hands were like sandpaper, the joints scabbed over like a rock.

"You've never swung an ax before." Thelana did not ask—she knew. Emma had no blisters, no rough spots between the fingers. "A shovel? A hoe?"

Emma shook her head.

"What good are you then?"

"I'm sorry, I—" she stammered, stunned by the insult. But she agreed with Thelana more than the Ilmarin could know. "I've never been outside the city," she said apologetically, "and I don't know much about the world. Not many women warriors where I come from. Are all women in your village like you?"

"Warriors?" she answered coolly. "No—not in Ilmarinen. But some are hunters. Most are gatherers, farmers, bearers of children."

"What was it like, Ilmarinen? Why did you leave it?"

Thelana's face became impenetrable—a statue's face—her eyes hardened to crystals. "It was home," she said. "Where my brothers and sisters were, and my mother and my father. They're not there anymore."

Emma nodded sympathetically, knowing she should not speak of it again. But her curiosity could not be sated. It was what stirred her imagination. What intrigued her most about the wild woman, about the Ilmar, however, also made her timid. But as before, her curiosity overcame her inhibitions. "Is it true that your people never . . . I mean, are you always this way? Naked, I mean?"

Thelana drew a deep quivering breath of frustration. "When you look upon a tiger, do you say, 'There goes a naked tiger'? Or the mammoth roaming wild in the plains, would you call it a naked mammoth? Why, then, call us naked? We are simply human. We are our bodies. There is no shame being what we are."

"But how do you—I mean—never?" Her objections were tangling up in her mouth before she could articulate them, but a life without clothing was impossible for her to conceive. *Surely there are times when a woman of a certain age must . . .*

The hard features of Thelana's face softened ever so slightly. "Clothing is still strange to me."

Emma felt her pulse quicken as Xandr flickered in her mind's eye. How did the Ilmar, with bodies so firm, resist thoughts of each other? Or did they simply give in to their basest instincts? "But it isn't civilized!" she remarked, a sudden sense of boldness coming over her. "It isn't decent! Surely you must see that by now . . . how regular folk live, that is."

"You know nothing!" Thelana shot back. "Do you think your people will dress the same in a hundred years? In a thousand? Your customs change like the wind. Only the body is unchanging, is sacred. The gods are not found in your temples or books—*they are felt*, in the rain, in the grass, in whatever touches you. You don't *feel* anything! In those robes, you're as good as blind."

Emma was beginning to feel foolish, arguing with a savage.

"Look, *princess*," Thelana spat, "I abhor your presence as much as you do mine. The sooner we can send you back to your ivory tower the better."

By sunset they came to a lone rise of boulders Emma recognized as Sternbrow Hill, where they stopped to make camp, its elevation offering defense against the likes of green tigers. Using the flat of Thelana's sword, Xandr smacked the mammoth's trunk, directing it toward the hill, and with Onehalf securely tethered, the guardian helped bring Emma to the ground, which always made her feel like a child.

Emma was relieved. Another arduous day was at an end. But her rear was sore from sitting, and her legs numb and wobbly. To the north, a white line formed along the horizon—the lip of the tundra. Westward, the hills became mountains, rising like white-capped teeth to meet the moon. She would soon be home, and yet she did not feel hopeful. In Northendell, she faced execution for witchcraft, and if she were to remain with the Ilmar, they would continue to alienate her, just as the Delians did, as everyone did. And what would they do if they learned the truth? That they fought and killed, and risked their lives, for someone who did not matter in the least?

The Ilmar noticed the change in the landscape also, searching as they always did. Words and gestures passed between them as if they were sparring. Emma wished she could catch a single word of it. In Northendell, eavesdropping was her special skill, but among foreign speakers it was of no use.

As Grimosse hammered posts for the tent, Thelana and Xandr gathered sticks for a fire. A howling gust swept down from the north, forcing Emma to tug at her robes. Sternbrow Hill was known for its harsh winds. But the Ilmar did not flinch at the sudden chill. They seemed impervious to weather, not even bothering to cover as, each day from the wheat field, temperatures continued to drop. Did they truly intend to remain naked throughout the coldest cycle in Northendell, when even the stoutest of men-at-arms could not leave their barracks without fear of losing toes and fingers to the cold? She shivered at the thought of her bare body exposed in the high moon air, but there was no warmth to be had in their camp. They had gathered enough for kindling, but Xandr was struggling to shield the emerging embers from the angry winds sweeping about the boulders of Sternbrow Hill.

Emma picked along the base of the hill, finding a strange plant growing from between the rocks. Swaying wildly in the wind, the orange-red bulb was coated in thorns and reached up to her chin. It was a good place to hide and make water, behind the rock face where she hoped no one would see her, not even Thelana, whom, she imagined, went wherever and whenever, like a dog. Then again, on more than one occasion, Emma had to be watchful of Delians tossing buckets of waste from their windows, which was no more civilized. Hiking up her skirts, all three layers jumbled in her arms, Emma relieved herself as the icy air prickled her pale skin, and just as hurriedly smoothed her tunic, robe and cloak over her thighs. She was beginning to smell, she did not doubt, like her wild human companions. Even a leaf would have sufficed—*how do the Ilmar do without leaves?*—but there was only the dry hilly countryside with its odd thorny bulb, and half buried beneath it, a small object glinting dully. She studied the object between thumb and forefinger, an arrowhead rounded by time.

At Sternbrow Hill, she knew, thousands perished in a battle between two great city states. Their names were long lost to the ages, but the memory of the battle remained, in the ballads of the Delians. In Northendell, children held hands and danced in circles, singing the simple chorus,

> *At Sternbrow Hill, the armies came,*
> *with copper on their heads all gleaming*
> *and copper swords in belts a-shining*
> *and copper spears in hands a-bristling,*
> *met men with men to kill and maim.*

> *At Sternbrow Hill they came—*
> *they fought till from the hills they bled,*
> *met sword with spear till all lay dead.*
> *At Sternbrow Hill, they came to die—they came*
> *to kill.*

In the song's final stanzas, the great *Batal* took his stand atop the hill. Overwhelmed by enemies, he fought alone, ankle deep in the dead of his countrymen, slaying hundreds by his sword, until a single arrow cut his heart in twain. His dying cry was so pitiable that even his enemies wept. Inspired by his courage, the victorious carried him on the bier, burying him with all the honors bestowed upon the greatest of their kings and heroes, and the city state settled peaceably with the Batal's people.

Remembering the ballad's notes made Emma's fingers twitch for her piccolo. But she was afraid by what the Ilmar might think, too embarrassed to expose such a core part of her being, and so she continued her search for historic treasures. It was not long before arrowheads filled her pockets.

As the last touches of sun broke across the lip of the moon, like jewels in a crown, Emma felt the coming cold numbing her tendons. She started back for camp, unprepared for what she would find, fearing some nomads had come upon their camp, for, as she approached, she did not recognize Xandr or Thelana in the least. Seeing them in clothes for the first time was almost as startling as when she first met them without. Fully outfitted in furs and pelts, the Ilmar were like any weather-beaten travelers. If not for their eyes—eyes that shone like colored glass—they might just as well have been from Northendell.

In the darkening sky, a multitude of black shapes was forming into a funnel, spreading out and over the hill. They settled on twigs and made nests in the underbrush. Following Thelana's gaze, Emma saw them, and the arrow being fitted to her bow.

"No!" she screamed, sprinting clumsily over the uneven terrain.

Thelana lost aim, slowly lowering her arms. "The light is going. Even I can't hit them in the dark."

"You can't!" Emma insisted. "Those are ravens!"

"They're dinner," said Thelana.

With a sudden change of direction, hundreds of birds transformed, from a funnel into an amorphous wave, their bodies like dabs of paint against the bloody canvas of sky. How could they not appreciate the beauty of their formations? Emma wanted desperately to show them how ravens play like children, how they collect shiny trinkets, but there wasn't time. "They're my friends!" she blurted. "That one there . . . the fat one," she was pointing, "that one's Hugin, and his brother there, is Munin."

Thelana gave her a doubtful look. "I suppose you won't be eating, then? Good. Less to share."

Xandr's topaz eyes caught Emma's own and did not let go. She was not invisible to him—she existed in his universe. "Let them be," he said, "perhaps they are sacred to her people."

"Food is what's sacred to me," Thelana grumbled. But without further debate, she replaced her arrow in its quiver. He gestured to the fire. "Come, Thelana, Ingrid gave us more than enough for the journey, and if we are to expect a warm table in Northendell, it's best we respect her wishes."

Darkness swallowed the world, leaving only the glitter of stars and moons and the embers of their fire. They sat in a circle about it, but there was nothing to eat but bread and berries. Thelana chewed noisily, glaring coldly at Emma, as they briefly discussed the Endless Plains, the vast stretch of land awaiting them to the north. Emma explained that the plains were endless in name only, due in part to the tundra, which was flat and featureless and impossible to navigate by, and for the impenetrable fog sweeping across it, confusing many a traveler into perpetual wandering. The information she was able to offer made Emma feel important, a valued member of a team, and for a while she sat contentedly by the fire, warmed with pride.

After the food was packed away, Xandr took Thelana under his arm and into his tent. Emma could see them embrace through the canvas, and wondered what sweet words passed between them. She then had to make the difficult choice between security and comfort. Lying directly beside the fire offered greater warmth, but could not protect against roving tigers. Grimosse stood away from camp, a silent, unmoving silhouette against the turquoise moon. Though it gave her a measure of reassurance that he never slept, she doubted his loyalties, whether he would come to her aid should a tiger— or some worse thing—come to devour them in the depth of the night.

Exhaustion forced her decision despite her fears. She swept the ground to make a clearing, midway between the boulders and the fire, lying down to a sleep she could not fathom succumbing to, as the air continued to grow colder, making her shudder uncontrollably. Deep in the night, a hunger pained her, like a hand squeezing her heart. Cold and loneliness became inseparable in her mind. She yearned for the warm touch of another, for a soft voice in her ear, but she could only hold herself tight and let tears form icicles on her cheeks.

9

SIEGE AT NORTHENDELL

The Pewter Mountains impeded the northward passage, stretching east and west beyond sight. The shimmering white peaks cut crookedly across the turquoise horizon. Looking closer, Xandr could see the parapets lining the base of the mountain, dotted with windows, suggesting a silver city emerging from the natural rock face.

Northendell followed the course of the mountain, its battlements curving like a curtain, with a tower at each foothill. Where pewter had refused to yield to hammer, the manmade wall was abandoned and the natural rock protruded like a peninsula breaking the shoreline. City and mountain were indistinguishable, the whole of it rising like some colossal spire. A massive drawbridge, with links as big as horses, was set deep in the center of it, beset on both sides by narrowing tiers of ballistas and perches for archers.

"This is my home," Emma said, sounding, to Xandr, as though she did not believe it. "I've never seen it from afar."

Xandr stood near the precipice, exhaling columns of air, his eyes roving the unfamiliar landscape. Beneath him, the plateau sloped gradually to a ridged valley, mottled green with frozen moss and rimmed white with hoarfrost. Tributaries of the Potamis River wove across it like threads of silver.

Something was moving between the plateau, upon which they stood, and the mountain city, a dark host from the east. It waded through streams and trampled over hills and kicked up frost. Xandr's heart failed a beat as recognition assaulted him. He had not seen their like since leaving Ilmarinen. They were more than a passing's walk away, yet he could make out the dull gleam of their swords and daggers, if that was what their weapons could be called, wicked tools fitted to their bony hands, each blade curving and twisting uniquely, raw metals, he knew, spewed like obsidian from a volcano. He had only to close his eyes to see the creatures more clearly—bogrens—gray and short and spindly. Some crossed the valley saddled upon husks of fat and muscle, their diminutive fingers corded to their brute cousins' brains. These were the females of horg kind, the tamer of the species, for no method could be used to control the full-grown bulls. Males could be but corralled—as they were now—to be unleashed upon an enemy. With pykrete shields of frozen wood pulp, large as tavern doors, the bulls moved in a mob-like phalanx at the fore of the onslaught. Other terrors moved through the land also, titan saurians, with necks and tails like cedar trees, siege-engine howdahs tall as towers ferried atop their long narrow spines, as bogrens and horgs scampered beneath their earth-crushing hooves. Even at such distance, the monstrous army was frightful to behold. Its aim was without doubt. They marched toward Northendell, to the drawbridge, to make their awesome presence felt.

"They throw themselves at the walls, throw themselves upon our swords . . ." It was Emma, speaking softly, as if trying to remember the words of a poem. Her robes fluttered in the chill wind. She brushed a lock of hair from her eyes, never turning from the parade of terrors. "We repel them, but not without cost. I used to watch the bodies carted under my window. The dying and the wounded were carried in the same way—we learned later who could be saved and who was to be buried."

Despite filling half the valley with their numbers, the bogren and horg forces could not hope to breach the walls, but there were villages to ravage, farmland to despoil, harvests to consume. Xandr wiped a trembling hand across his brow. "We must go down there . . . we must join in the fighting."

By the ashen look on her face, it was clear Thelana shared his anguish, but she did not reach for the jade pommel at her hip. "Xandr, remember why we're here. We are to deliver the princess and—"

"No!" he cried. "I'll not watch and do nothing!"

"But the *giant* . . ."

Xandr shut out the sound of her voice. His heart pained him the more he stood doing nothing. "Emmaxis calls to me!" Retreating to the mammoth, he yanked at the ropes, letting bundles and gourds litter the ground. Emma took a few steps back as the shaft of milky silver emerged, its skull face smiling. Xandr could see the dismay on her face. She was truly scared of it, and of him.

Even Thelana distanced herself. *Why do they look at me so?* The sword burned ready in his palms, and their lack of understanding made his blood run hotter. He could not resist the lure of Emmaxis.

Suddenly Thelana was upon him, clinging to his forearm like a wanting child. He shrugged her off, and she stumbled, nearly losing her balance. "Let me be!" he pleaded. "Grimosse and I will deal with them!" He waved a hand to the golem, who stood with hammer, prepared for battle. Groaning in reply, the golem followed Xandr to the edge of the plateau. But the battle was already met.

Trumpets blew from the parapets and drums were beating below—songs of courage echoed from the valley. Copper helms were rallying, with swords upright and lustrous, the mounted standard bearers at the fore. The symbols of Northendell, the Hammer and Mountain, swam in the air. Soon there would be screams and there would be dying. Archers rained upon the attackers, and spears launched from machines to crack against pykrete shields.

"You're too late, Xandr! Look at the lines—" She choked on the words. Her eyes were emerald fires burning into him. "They'll kill you!"

"Not before I take them with me!" he cried, clenching his fist about his sword, turning away from her lest she sway him. But he could not deny, nor ignore, the scene unfolding below. The armies of the dark hemisphere were surrounding the city, swallowing the human defenders. Yet the monsters attacked blindly, without commands, without leadership. Many of the horg waited helplessly at the rear, with no enemy to face, and due to either boredom or bloodlust, or both, settled upon killing their own kind. If he were to join the battle, Xandr would be unable to join the forces of Northendell—he would fight alone and be swarmed.

"What good will it do to kill a few bogrens, even a hundred, even if you could?" Little by little, her pleading blunted his anger, the melody of her voice contesting the urging of Emmaxis. "I've lost many of my own friends to the same fiends," she said. "I know your heart. Let go. It is not worth your life, not now, not like this. Remember who you are—you were meant for greater things."

Rage cut his insides, shook him to his heels. Needing release, he ran to the edge of the plateau, lips foaming with obscenities, sword sparking against the rock. His psyche mirrored the battlefield. But as the clash of arms continued to ring below, the madness ebbed out of him, fragments of it settling like smoke, into helplessness and despair. Whenever he saw bogrens, anywhere on Aenya, he sought vengeance, despite his mentor's teachings that every life was part of the Goddess. As a younger man, revenge was his driving purpose, what kept him sane, what kept him fighting for life. But as he grew tall and powerful, his obsession lessened, until all that remained in him was the wisdom of his mentor and an aching in his heart. And yet he still hoped to find the bogren and their kin, if not to murder each of them, at least to capture their leaders, to ask *the why* burned across his torso.

The two women drifted closer to the edge to stand next to him.

"Thelana . . ." he murmured. "Look for me . . . you're eyes see further than mine."

"What do you—?"

"Tell me what you see!" he cried. "I must know."

Delian long swords churned like a storm. Blood sprayed the air and hung like mist. Cutting the monsters down by the score, the men-at-arms were holding the field, singing snatches of old ballads. Still many, too many, eager to meet the enemy, fell under the cascading blades. Elsewhere, a horg mob rushed to join in the killing. With their icy shields pressed together, they were invincible, their bone clubs thrashing men by the score, entombing the city's defenders in bronze.

Into the fray, a creature emerged, crawling on six legs, a flame-red salamander. Saddled upon it was a thing much like a man. He was plated in bloody hues from head to heels, with spikes thrusting from his body in every direction, long as a man's heart is deep. Whether man or monster, he carried a chained morning star, and as this weapon whirled about him, the holes in it whistled, and those who heard it, even those who met horg without hesitation, shrank with terror. Zaibos, Emma told them he was called. "I have dreamed of him countless times without ever having seen him. He paralyzes the defenders, drives us to retreat. None who stand against him live." Xandr watched men die under Zaibos' morning star even as she said this.

Zaibos managed to turn the battle, barking commands, leading his ragtag forces by the awful sound of his mace. With bogrens and horg in tow, he cut a wedge of destruction towards the drawbridge. Men-at-arms collapsed about his salamander's six legs, failing to slow his advance. His morning star whirled and whistled, tearing men from their armor, scattering shields and breastplates and helms like leaves.

"Is he human?" Xandr huffed.

"No one knows," she murmured. "Some say he is a demon born from the deepest caves of the dark hemisphere. Some say the spikes grow straight from his body."

"He is not a bogren, nor a horg," Thelana remarked, "and yet he leads them. I never saw such a creature, not in all my time with the Kratan army." She plucked the string of her bow, anxious for action, to aid the men-at-arms in some way. "If we could only get a bit closer."

"Do not fear for my people," Emma said. "We consider it a great honor to die this way. The city will not fall. The walls will hold. Look."

From Xandr's vantage, the enemy advance was so brutal and determined, there seemed little hope for the Delians but to retreat behind their impregnable battlements. Zaibos' wake was lined with twisting human shapes, and a titan saurian with a siege tower on its spine followed close behind him. Launching from within the city, fireballs showered the wooden structure. Bogrens scrambled to douse the flames and to shield the howdah with canvas. The simultaneous firing of the ballistas was like the crack of a rope when a man is hanged. Missiles hurled down, fixing into the titan's serpentine neck, and an agonizing sound, like the honk of a colossal goose, pained every ear. But the saurian refused to fall. Rearing on its hind legs, the titan fought the air, crushing man and bogren alike as its hooves came thundering down, as horgs and bogrens tugged at the harnesses to steady the teetering tower strapped to its back. The advance of the second tower, meanwhile, went unchecked.

Xandr could only watch, agitated, helpless. He felt no particular allegiance to the people of Northendell, but the men-at-arms were human, and the enemy threatening the city could not be more hated.

When the violet moon passed about the dour turquoise moon, completing a single passing since the onset of battle, a postern gate opened from a westerly tower, releasing a torrent of hooves. Flowing manes swept across the valley at ferocious speed, the riders' swords glittering like stars. Leading the vanguard was a single black destrier. Like a hammer striking an anvil, the western flank struck the monstrous host, which fell into disarray between the cavalry and the Potamis. Bogrens and horgs, neither of whom could swim, drowned in the icy flow. Turning his attention from the drawbridge, Zaibos battled his way to meet this new threat, foes and allies alike falling on either side of him.

At the sight of the giant salamander, the horses became wild with terror, racing off uncontrollably. Even the bannermen were fled, having lost control of their destriers, the Hammer of Strom fallen. Only one horse remained, the arrowhead of the vanguard, an immense charger with black shining muscles, its mane the color of pitch. It hopped from hoof to hoof, challenging the salamander, boasting of its strength. Pale gold spilled from the shoulders of the woman saddled upon it. She eyed Zaibos with unflinching determination. Her forces drew back as did his, making way for a contest of wills. A sword rang as it was drawn. It blazed all around her like a silver torch and as she raised it, high above her golden tiara, the sword began to sing.

"It is late in the day," she said, "and you've outstayed your welcome."

Zaibos let his mace go quiet. His salamander licked the gnats buzzing about the dead. Her charger kicked the air, its breath like bursts of steam. Moving like a single graceful creature, rider and mount gathered speed across the field of eager faces, her golden hair flowing, her sword singing over her crown. The salamander lifted itself, snaking to meet the oncoming charge, and Zaibos' chain grew taut and fast, splitting the air with a terrible hum. As she moved into his looming shadow, he twisted for a killing blow, and not a breath escaped the onlookers.

Horns of victory blasted from the battlements. Men hooted and wept. With a single swipe, Zaibos' mace was silenced—the chain severed, the bloodied sphere rolling lazily across the hoof-pocked earth. He was unseated, wallowing in dirt, wounded and furious. Up on high, Xandr watched, spellbound. "*Who is she?*" he asked, his curiosity piqued.

"They'll sing her praises long after she's dead," Emma replied. "Sif, *Daughter of Thunder*, and Clover, her stallion. She is the king's pride—though many say she is not his, that she is the daughter of Strom, a goddess. When she was born, the sky quaked with thunder and lightning, or so they say."

"She's a princess?" Xandr remarked. "Your sister?"

"Oh!" Emma's cheeks flared a rosy hue. "Um, of course, she *is*. I mean—"

Her hesitation was short, blinks of an eye, but it was enough for Thelana. "You're not the princess, are you?" A dirk of Hedonian design was already in her fist, the one once belonging to the assassin, Deed Whoreson. "You deceived us!"

Xandr moved between them, but Thelana was swifter, scratching Emma's robes with the edge of her blade. Grimosse also came near, frozen with indecision, not knowing who to guard. "I ought to kill you!" she screamed. "You let us on. You . . . you—"

"Thelana!" Xandr shouted. Emma was on the ground, trembling with fear, weeping with remorse. She was a grown woman, but when Xandr looked at the Delian, he saw only a child. "What are you doing, Thelana?"

"She lied to us. She's nothing but a vagabond . . . an outcast. Worthless." She spit in Emma's direction.

"So are we. Remember?" He turned to the cowering girl, trying to soften his features. "Why did you say you were a princess?"

"Because . . ." she could not control her weeping, "because . . ."

"Stop your crying! No one has hurt you. Now speak truthfully. Who are you?"

"I am just a commoner," she admitted, drying her eyes with her sleeve. "I was banished, to be sold into slavery. I knew that, like in the songs, like in *The Epic of Thangar and Sint*, that only princesses are rescued."

He considered her answer, uncertain how to respond, when the rumble of approaching hooves caught his ear. Up from the valley, a single rider came climbing, his horse little more than a pony. He pulled to a halt, looking from Xandr to Emma and from Thelana to Grimosse.

"Is there some trouble here?"

Xandr glared. "Who are you?"

"Who *am I*, you ask?" He lifted his face plate, which closely resembled a stove door, from the bushy gray hairs of his mustache. "I'm Starvod!" he proclaimed, as if the name could not be more renowned. "Have you not heard of Starvod the Brave, Starvod the Invincible, Starvod the Inscrutable?"

"If you are so invincible, what are you doing here, so far from the battle?"

"I am guarding from the rear!" he insisted, letting his face plate clank noisily down. "What else?"

Xandr could see that the man was feeble to the point of uselessness, his dull armor sitting heavily upon his old bones. "We have brought you one of your citizens." He tugged at Emma's sleeve, pushing her forward, but immediately she began to sob.

"Really?" Starvod exclaimed. "How interesting. Where ever did you find her?"

"Please!" Emma begged, her raven eyes glistening. "I don't want to go home. No more walls. I want to go with you—I want to be free."

"Free?" Xandr's voice turned harsh, impassive. "Who says we're free? Nobody is free. Go with the knight."

"Well now, wait a blinking moment," Starvod began, but his palfrey bucked, making to leave, and his face plate banged against his nose. "Steady boy!" Turning back, he added, "She can't come with me. We're in the middle of a siege—can't you see? I cannot be troubled to march a defenseless girl into, well, into that!"

"When do you think the siege will end?"

"Haven't the foggiest," Starvod replied. "Could be days, or cycles. One year it lasted the whole of high moon!"

Xandr searched over the lip of rock. Siege towers lay like shipwrecks across the valley, titans collapsed into hills of blubbery flesh. Bogrens, horg, and humans were crushed beneath them. Archers moved about their trunk-like necks and tails, taking defensive positions, casting arrows at the retreating horde. But Zaibos' forces were not heading back into the woods. They were regrouping. "What does this Zaibos want? Why do they attack you?"

Starvod looked puzzled. His mustache twitched beneath the grill of his helm. "They do so every year. Always have."

"Ask about the giant," Thelana intoned.

The ground was rocky, caked with icy slush, with a few hardened clovers that grew from between the cracks. But there were no footprints, no signs of passage for even the best of hunters to track. They had lost the trail days ago.

"A giant?" the man-at-arms echoed. "Like a horg?"

"No. Bigger, like a house. It makes tracks like a . . ." he turned to Onehalf, which was sniffing shrubs with its butchered trunk, "a mammoth."

"Only true giants I know of are in songs," Starvod answered. "However, I did see some strangely broken trees, over that way." He pointed to the east, where the wood grew tall and crooked, casting long shadows. "If Zaibos has a giant, he must be hiding him in the forest. But I don't know why it would seem that the giant came *from* the south."

"It's looking for a way around the mountain," Thelana inferred. "Whatever it wants, it is to the north, always north."

Xandr considered the possibility, rubbing his beard. "Then that is where we must go."

"Are you mad?" Starvod admonished. "Nobody goes *into* Gloomwood! It's full of denizens from the dark lands, or didn't you know?"

"We are Ilmarin," Thelana said to him, eyeing Emma derisively. "We do not fear. But this one is not. Take her with you. We'll leave her either way."

Before Emma could object, a white flake dropped onto Thelana's wrist. It was cold and star-shaped. She looked down at it, too surprised for words, then looked to the sky, to the countless other twirling flakes.

"Snow!" Starvod said with delight, his mustache whitening. "How very nice!"

Thelana shrank in her furs. Without her sinewy muscles showing, she looked smaller, less imposing, like any other peasant woman. Now her eyes darted frightfully, as the flakes continued to fall, covering her. "What is it?"

Starvod leaned forward. His mount whimpered, its knees buckling under the knight's weight. "You mean to tell me you've never seen snow?"

But it was Emma who answered. "This land is strange and deadly," she said, brushing the dark strands from her eyes. "You'll need a Delian who knows how to survive it."

"In Gloomwood!" Starvod cried. "No one survives in Gloomwood! Especially during high moon."

"I am *not* afraid," Emma said loudly. "What I fear is not death. Take me with you."

Thelana's dirk quivered in her palm. He could feel the hatred emanating from her body. But if the gods willed that Emma be rescued, he could not cast her by the wayside. The path ahead was harsh, he knew, and even the Delian was innocent to it, to the horrors beyond her city, but he saw in Emma a glimmer of strength, a power he had not expected and did not yet fully comprehend. But, as with Thelana, she would need to know the risks, to understand the sacrifice. If she were to follow, he would be tough with her, tougher than the wild unknown awaiting them, should she hope to survive.

"If you are injured—if you slow us down in any way— we will not stop for you, do you understand? We will leave you in the woods. We will leave you alone to die."

Emma did not flinch or speak, she simply nodded, her dark bird-like eyes blinking contemplatively, adoring him.

10

STORIES

The name alone gave Emma gooseflesh. Gloomwood was the place where wicked children were sent to disappear, where monsters lurked in shadows. Stories of the forest were numerous and none ended happily. Most were variations of the same tale, parents warning their children not to go running off. But always the curious pair, a brother and a sister, did not listen. An old crone tempted the children into the wood with the promise of a delicious stew, and the children eagerly followed. Only after helping in some menial preparation, like cutting carrots or dicing ollyps, did the siblings discover, to their horror, the main ingredient. In other versions, the children's eyes were plucked out by ravens the witch kept as familiars, or the boy and girl were transformed into bogrens, or worse, eaten by horg, who favor the taste of human young. No matter the tale, the parents are left grieving by the edge of the dark forest, holding some lost article of clothing, a girl's tiny shoe, a boy's hat.

It was this scene of grieving parents that Emma could not help imagining as she, Xandr, Thelana, and Grimosse crossed under the shadow of crooked elms into Gloomwood. Xandr had considered taking the mammoth into the woods, only to reconsider when he saw how densely the foliage flourished. Onehalf stayed behind, grazing on clovers that grew from between the cracks in the earth, indifferent to its newfound freedom.

Walking into the dark forest was like entering a mausoleum. The surrounding growth was colorless and cold and seemed dead many years. Disturbing a single leaf, Emma felt, would be like rousing a corpse. Where sunlight dispelled the shadows, a muted canvas of browns and greens could be made out, but only vaguely. Gangly trees obscured much of the sky, the pall of the turquoise moon looming vastly beyond the boughs like an archway to another world. Foliage twisted up to their knees, each specimen entangled with another into a thick, inseparable mass. On occasion, Thelana's sword was put to use cutting a path through it, and at other times, Grimosse uprooted whole trees impeding their passage. Branches bent from above like the pained fingers of a beggar. In few places, flowers sprouted in clusters from between overlapping roots, their petals hard and jagged like a fish's teeth. Amorphous fruits of sinister color hung temptingly within reach. The plethora of alien forms was such that Emma could not help but think of the primordial age, when gods first seeded the world. For in Gloomwood—the Delians believed—the outcasts of the plant kingdom were gathered, the rejects of creation, things abhorrent to nature itself, things that should not be.

With some difficulty, the four managed their way deeper into the wood. Spurs collected at the hem of Emma's robe and branches snatched at her clothing. She often called to the others to wait as she unhooked the finger-like brambles holding her. After some time, the dense foliage gave way to a quilt of wet leaves, a little more pleasant to look upon, but the dirt beneath it was soft and yielded to her every step, which made the trek equally draining.

Slowly, the trees closed behind them and the sun grew more remote, until becoming ghostly pale, like the eye of a dead man.

Emma studied Xandr and Thelana's faces, watching for signs of doubt—of turning westward, but their resolve was unshaken. She was determined to prove her courage, to show that she could be like Thelana, but the Ilmar were not privy to the Delian myths, to the terrors dwelling in these woods, and she could not help but feel her terror growing the further they moved from the light, her heart beating so furiously she worried the others could hear it.

Sensing her discomfort, Grimosse turned to her, saying, "Don't be afraid. Grimm is here. Grimm will guard you. Grimm is made to guard."

"That's sweet," she replied, surprised by how easily she could converse with him. The monster was as big and hideous as a horg, but possessed the intellect and innocence of a two year old child. She wondered whether a parent, or anyone—for that matter—had once cared for him.

For a while, they followed Thelana, who avoided even the smallest thorn. Anyone raised without knowledge of shoes, Emma figured, would have mastered the art of watching their step. But even in her boots, Thelana moved with unusual caution. The dangers were such that even the nature-loving Ilmar seemed out of their element. The forest was teeming with snaring vines, poisonous exploding bulbs, nests of killer wasps, and tar pits hidden under smooth patches of earth—things Emma surely would have stepped into if not for Thelana's keen senses. But something else was amiss, even in Gloomwood. It was plain enough for even a city born to notice.

Movement became increasingly easier as they came to a broad, clear passage. Thelana sheathed her sword, grabbing onto the knots of a werewood tree to gain higher footing, to better survey the devastation. The trees were not cut down by the ax, but torn from their roots, their boughs crisscrossing along the path like the ribbing of some colossal ship. Saplings and centuries' old giants lay side-by-side, some too wide for even Grimosse's arms to reach around. Thelana informed them that, by the dull amber of the bark, it was clear that their quarry had passed days ago. Emma tried to picture the thing, that could cause such destruction, but her mind refused to linger on it.

With the safety of higher ground, Thelana led them more swiftly, leaping gracefully from each fallen log, Xandr and Grimosse following more slowly, as Emma stumbled and fell and stumbled again, calling for them to wait. They moved relentlessly eastward, into the cold, where the greater moon loomed higher and higher, until its dull turquoise glow became the sky.

Night was sudden and with it came a different kind of cold. Devoid of wind, the air was still as death, the chill ever-present. Emma dug her hands into her sleeves, but rubbing her arms was a futile exercise. Her own body was like a stranger, without warmth. The cold was in her bones. She suffered without complaint, prepared to die before admitting weakness, but as Grimosse started to build a fire, she could not hide her elation, giving a great sigh of relief.

Frozen in perpetual decay, Gloomwood was littered with branches and fallen bark. The dark wood burned fiercely despite the lows in temperature. In little time, the flame erupted into an enormous fire, the sparks rising high as Emma's bedroom window, rising up to join the stars. Emma tucked herself beside it, feeling sensation return to her limbs, but the bark blackened quickly and would not last the night. Thelana elected to go with Grimosse to forage for more kindling. Emma considered volunteering in the task, to prove her value to the group, but knew she would be fooling no one. She was exhausted, her uncontrollable shivering tiring her all the more. Wanting nothing more than to sit and be warm, she went unnoticed, finding comfort beside the orange twists of flame. They embraced her like a pair of warm hands—like Xandr's hands, she imagined, and as she watched him from across the fire, the fear that so possessed her upon entering Gloomwood lost much of its power.

"Trees are not to be feared," he told her, "though these are very old, and ill, and may seem frightening to someone like you."

"Oh," she replied. "I don't know much about nature—I mean, I only know from books."

"Plants are sacred. Animals are sacred. We are all part of the Mother Goddess, sharing the same essence, the same *life*. At least, that was our belief, in Ilmarinen, before the dark times."

"How can you say things like that," she remarked, "when you kill a man with such ease? Bood and Deed—"

"It is never easy for me to take a life, Emma," Xandr admitted, "but death is also part of the Goddess. The Ilmar only take what she provides . . . to live, to love, and to birth new life. If we kill a tree or a man, it is to survive. Anything more is shameful."

"People and animals, I understand, but how can you care for the life of a tree?" she asked. "It's not as if they can feel or think."

"They don't have to," he answered. "The feelings are ours to give to them."

She nodded politely. "I don't think I understand."

"To cut whole forests for cities, as you do, to value *things* above that which takes breath, these are symptoms of a diseased mind. Too much time between walls, I suppose, will make anyone go mad."

She should have been insulted, she thought, but what love did she owe her people, who did nothing but cast her away? More and more, she was finding herself in agreement with the wild man. His raw notions rang truthfully in her ears.

"Ages ago, men and women lived free of greed and hate and envy. Everyone on Aenya lived as simply and peacefully as the Ilmar. Even the word for 'man' and 'mankind' in our tongue is 'ilman'. That time is forgotten now. None but the Ilmar remember what it truly means to be human." He cast a stick into the flame and Emma watched as it was greedily consumed. "As Kjus says, 'we come into this world with nothing and leave with nothing.'"

"Who's Kjus?"

"He was the first of the keepers, the guardian of wisdom and knowledge, a great thinker. Kjus taught us of the Mother Goddess, that she is not some remote and dispassionate deity beyond the stars, but that she exists in the ground we sit upon and in the air we feel on our skin. The Goddess is Aenya itself.

"Before his death, the myths say, Kjus became one with Alashiya, one with the plants and the animals. It is said he could change his physical body, and that his spirit lives on in the phoenix."

Emma sat upright with sudden interest, letting her robes unfurl and her hair flow across her neck. "Isn't that like a . . . a bird?"

"Yes."

"I didn't know they existed, aside from story books. I love birds."

"They are rare and beautiful, like the ilm that blooms only on our land, but I have seen them—at least one, that I know of."

Embers lit the sky like migrant stars as he continued to stoke the kindling. She could see Thelana's scowling face now, shifting in the patterns of orange and red from across the flame. A skewered chameleon roasted on a stick in her hand. Torn between pangs of hunger and disgust, Emma's stomach grumbled.

"This fire," Thelana said, "and the story you are telling, reminds me of Solstice Night." Abruptly she stood, slipping the rabbit skin jerkin from her shoulders, pulling her breeches of makeshift furs from around her waist. Her thighs prickled in the cold air, but she did not seem to notice. Her boots followed her other garments in the snowy grass. Emma, still shivering, was tempted to borrow the furs, which looked terribly warm and cozy, but was too embarrassed to ask.

Emma could not help staring with a mix of shame, curiosity and envy. She could never be like Thelana, never possess the Ilmarin's brazen nature, never draw Xandr's gaze the way she did, as if he'd never seen her undressed before. Emma detested her own body, hated her milky, undefined flesh. But she hated her utter lack of confidence even more, the shyness that churned in her stomach and made her hide from people.

Turning her attention from Thelana to Xandr, she asked, "What is the Solstice Night?"

"The longest night of the year," he said, his eyes never straying from the dance. "A night of revelry and lovemaking."

Backing into the cold, Thelana dashed forward, vaulting over the fire. Emma let out a yelp. She landed hard on her heels on the other side, unscathed.

Xandr grinned. "That is one of our traditions."

Emma could not imagine having to jump over a fire, especially naked. Ilmarin customs were bold and needlessly reckless and somehow, wonderful. "What else happens on this night?"

"Families come from all corners of the land," he explained, "there is a ring of hands, and dancing about a great fire, and then two pair—a boy and a girl of age, who have grown hair about the loins—and together they leap the flame hand-in-hand. Those that do so are forever joined."

"Joined?" she asked. "You mean they are wedded?"

"Yes. Except for the Ilmar, those joined in fire do not part in death. A boy and a girl who come together on Solstice Night have always been one, having joined in their first lives, from when the Goddess was born. They are merely finding each other once more."

Thelana pirouetted beside him, luring him with serpentine arms. "But you forget, my love, the most important traditional of all. During this holy night, we remember our myths in song. In dance, we venerate the old gods who danced before us."

Emma could see the story unfolding in her movements, from her face across her twisting palms. Xandr sat spellbound, and Emma started to wonder whether the performance was not meant for him alone, whether it was not a mating ritual to contest the city-born girl.

"In the beginning there were two," she gestured with each arm. "Anu, the male god, and Eru, the female. The Creators . . . the most ancient of deities. They came from nothingness, infinite and eternal," and she crouched flat, palms on her feet, vanishing in the shadows of the flame. "But they are no longer part of Aenya," she whispered, "having moved to birth other worlds. Alashiya is their gift to us, their offspring. Nature herself." Thelana cradled an invisible infant.

"Anu and Eru were inseparable in their lovemaking. As they went about an empty and dark universe, they sang to each other songs of love, and with their voices vanquished Skullgrin, who was the darkness, and brought light into being by sun and by moons," and she cupped her hands to make circular shapes. "They sang the mountains into being and the flora and fauna of the world, and from the fires of the sun shaped the first man and woman in their own likenesses."

"Ah!" Emma wanted to clap. "So that explains the fire jumping!"

"Yes," Thelana went on. "What was sung at the beginning of time is what we sing during the Solstice. Through song we sustain the life essence in the plants and in the animals, and in ourselves." Thelana hopped and twirled in the flame, embers rising as if from her body, as if she were a part of it. Her motions were hypnotic, impossible to ignore. Emma could not imagine that Xandr's heart did not race at the sight it. As her eyes went in search of Solstice Night, Thelana slipped into the Ilmarin tongue, voicing what lyrics she could recall—words and traditions, Emma recognized, lost to all but a few. Thelana sang forcefully, her eyes glistening with memories, and Emma could tell she was unaccustomed to lifting her voice in such a way. Without thinking, Emma fumbled for the piccolo in her sleeve. She could not hope to match Thelana's wild-eyed intensity, but could keep pace with her instrument. And they did not stare at her awkwardly, or ask her to stop, or appear in the least surprised. Xandr joined in the act, his voice deep and tortured and not one for singing, but sincere. And Emma realized then that Delians and Ilmar were not so dissimilar.

They made music through the night, until Emma's lungs were aflame and Thelana collapsed in a sweat, shivering and tugging at her clothes. During all the time she had traveled away from home, Emma longed for her secret alcove, to play her piccolo in secret . . . she had never imagined she could feel so comfortable, so unashamed, exposing her music to others.

"Solstice Night sounds wonderful," she couldn't help gushing.

"There is no longer such a night," Xandr replied somberly. His eyes were wounded, like an animal's. "The tradition died with our people."

"What happened?" Emma implored. "I want to know."

"Bogrens," he answered, feeding a stick into the flame. "We had no battlements in Ilmarinen, as you do. No keys nor locks, and rarely even doors. In our tongue, there is not a word for naked or secret, for deception or murder. There is no word for soldier, no way to describe war . . . What made us free also made us defenseless."

Thelana moved to embrace him. Drunk with passion, her hatred for Emma seemed to subside. "What of your people?" she asked. "What stories do you tell in Northendell?"

"Yes," Xandr joined in. "Let us hear one of your songs."

Emma hesitated, drawing a line of spittle from her lips to the piccolo's mouthpiece. She could play when Thelana's dancing drew his attention away, but not with their eyes and ears on her alone. The dark forest was less terrifying.

"Well . . ." She thought hard, in how she might excuse herself, but how could she? When Thelana had danced and sang so fearlessly? If she did not play, she'd look all the more cowardly . . . worthless. Here was a chance, perhaps the only chance, to show the one thing she could do well.

Only one song surfaced from her heart. In playing it, she would expose the deepest, most guarded part of her, what defined her, but her lips could find no other music, and instead of shyness, she felt an unexpected thrill.

Exposed but free. Free like a wild woman—No, free like the Ilmar.

No longer hiding behind her hair, or trying to bury herself in her robes, Emma stood and cleared her throat. "This is called the *Ballad of Titian and Midiana*. But it isn't a Delian song. My people sing only of gods and giants and warfare, which I have no affection for. This song is about love and loss. It is very old. It originates from the lost island Aea, or so I've heard. Sailors sing snatches of it in the taverns by the river port."

Ever so softly, Emma started into the chorus, half-singing, half-telling the tale, mouthing her piccolo in-between.

> *Titian and Midiana,*
> *Titian and Midiana,*
> *Do you know the tale*
> *Of the warrior cast ashore*
> *and the priestess whom he adored,*
> *and the love that grew between them*
> *and doomed them?*

"Titian was a Nibian soldier at Sea, returning home from war. Along the way, he and his fellow men ran across a violent storm which tore their ship apart. Titian awoke, alone on the island shore of Aea.

"Suffering from hunger, he explored the island to find a great city of marble columns and flowered gardens. At the center were three temples, each devoted to a goddess. In the temple of Irene, he found ecstasy—in the temple of Zoë, wisdom. But in Maki's temple, he found what his heart most prized—a beautiful, braided priestess named Midiana.

"But it was a love forbidden, for Midiana was a virgin warrior, bound by oath to never know a man. Titian wooed her, and in time won her heart, and in the temple they made love, blaspheming the goddess beneath her cold, idol eyes. It was in that moment, in that embrace of love, that the marble facade of Maki came alive to curse the priestess, transforming Midiana into a grotesque monster, so grotesque no man could stand to look upon her. Even Titian, who had so fondly adored her, was forced to avert his eyes and flee the city. Long days and nights he spent in torment along the shore, his tears adding to the Sea. But finding his lost sword along the beach, he returned to the temple and to his love, and mercifully took her life."

Feeling his blade lodge into her flesh,
her blood sprinkling his bosom,
her anguished screams would have made any shudder,
yet he blotted all but his aim
and struck again
and freed his love.

Thelana went slack against her elbows, sighing, as Emma's piccolo came to a mournful climax. "By the Mother Goddess," she exclaimed, "for once I am happy to be Ilmarin." Even Xandr looked affected by it. But despite the ballad's tragic theme, Emma was overjoyed. It was as if, by playing the ballad for others to hear, the weight of it was lifted from her heart.

"You are a bard!" Xandr declared after a while. "You should have told us sooner—a musician's company is better than any princess! Music is what the cosmos is made of," he added matter-of-factly, much to Thelana's consternation.

Emma could feel the blood rushing to her cheeks.

"Play us another song," he said, "something to lift us from the gloom of this place."

"If you wish." She pressed her lips to her instrument, and as the fire danced down, she evoked notes that, though far from merry—for she did not know to play merrily—conjured places far off, and childhood memories, and dirges long forgotten. Xandr was lulled by it, as was Thelana. Even the stone faced Grimosse, ever watchful, looked more alive.

Their eyes grew heavy, but Emma continued playing, the music as much a part of the wood as the hoot of an owl or the chirp of a cricket. Even the turquoise moon seemed to peer over the branches at the summons of her piccolo.

When Emma was certain that all were slumbering, she laid her head to the ground, piccolo in hand. There was no need for tents—the raging fire was enough. But her heart was restless. They were spending a night in Gloomwood, after all, with bogrens and horgs about, and a giant as well. Even the presence of the mighty guardian, who fell into a kind of half-sleep, could not allay her fears. Her only comfort was in thoughts of *him*, in his confidence, his strength. She watched him through clenched lashes, as if studying his features might help her win his favor. In the pitch of night he arose, bringing the bundle with his belongings into the firelight. She hoped that he not reach for that dreadful sword, which she found inexplicably disturbing, and was relieved when he produced, to her amazement, a tome—a book so laden with pages, so brittle with age, it would have seemed a rare treasure even upon Mathias' arcane shelves.

The book was at complete odds with everything she knew of the Ilmar. Only the most learned of aristocrats possessed knowledge of letters. What could a primitive people, who did not know to wear clothes, be doing with a book? What secrets did it hold and why did Xandr feel the need to hide it from her? As with the silver key, curiosity swelled in the pit of her belly, and a plan started to form. She would only need to bide her time, which would not be hard, for she doubted the most intrepid of men-at-arms could snooze a passing in Gloomwood.

The fire was mostly glowing logs and cinders. Her fingers were numb, stiff, and pained by the cold. She could not keep from violently shaking the letters, making the page difficult to read, and memories of Mathias' sanctuary made her bosom ache. If she were to be discovered, would Xandr be as cruel as her father had been? Either way, she could not suffer to let secrets go unexplored. The unknown gnawed at her brain, as it did from the lower stair and the city's alleyways, until she inevitably sought out the truth, no matter the danger. The book splayed across her knees was tantalizing, each symbol beautifully inked, its serifs more elaborately drawn than by the hand of any Delian scribe. But she did not recognize a single letter. The meaning was hidden, lying somewhere off the page, disguised behind the ink. *Is it Ilmarin? No. Primitives don't have writing—that's what makes them primitive, isn't it?* Trying to read the tome was a fool's errand, she decided, and yet there were wonderful sketches along the margins, pages of artwork to tease her curiosity, which made not knowing all the more frustrating. Myriad fashions paraded at her fingertips—high crowned princesses presiding over public galleries, cityscapes clambering over mountain slopes, spider-limbed palisades hanging precariously from vast plateaus, solitary minarets of alien design arising from the Sea. Each and every image inflamed her imagination.

"You must be deaf and stupid."

Startled by the voice, Emma closed the book carefully. There was a deadly gleam in the wild woman's eyes and a dirk in her fist.

"Th-Thelana," Emma stammered as she slipped the tome from her knees. "I-I didn't hear you."

"Of course you didn't. Do you think I could have survived this long, making as much noise as you do? I could hear your breathing from across the fire."

Emma eyed the point directed at her bosom, the blade glowing turquoise in the moonlight. "I'm sorry I disturbed you, but I was too afraid to sleep—"

"Liar!" she hushed. "I should have gutted you before, at Northendell. But now, well, Xandr isn't awake to pity you." Emma fumbled backward, her skirt catching the ground as Thelana advanced. "What were you doing with the book?"

"Oh!" she said, getting to her feet. "I was just curious—"

"You were going to steal it, weren't you?"

"What? No!"

"Lie to me again and I'll cut out your tongue!" she said, half whispering, half shouting. "It takes a thief to know a thief. Do you have any idea what we suffered to find that?"

Emma shook her head, not knowing whether to answer.

"You cannot imagine!" The dagger wavered. Thelana looked like she might weep.

"Forgive me," said Emma, desperately searching for words, anything to keep from harm, "but—but, wait—you mean to say you found this, that it isn't Ilmarin? Can you even read it?"

"That's not the point!" Thelana cried, raising her blade. "*This* is!"

Surrounded by the icy darkness of the wood, there was no place for Emma to flee. And she was exhausted, not only from the day's trek, but from running, and hiding, whether from her father or from bullies or crazed barbarian women. Without ever knowing love, Emma lost all fear for her life. Tears spread like frosted webs across her cheeks. Matching Thelana's menacing stare with her own, Emma stood taller than ever before, screaming, "Do it then! But be sure to cut out my heart, for I no longer want it."

Thelana did not move.

"What are you waiting for?" said Emma. "There is nothing in this world for me. Nobody will miss me."

The Ilmarin's eyes were deeply and intimately set on hers, and still she did not move. "Quiet," she mouthed.

"Quiet? Why should I be—!"

Thelana smacked her in the lips, keeping Emma from speaking. "You really are deaf, aren't you? Get out of your own head and *listen*." The sound was subtle at first, but became more intense and terrifying the longer she listened.

Trees groaned. Branches snapped. Leaves crackled. Something was moving in the woods. Massive. Close. Emma felt her forearm becoming tight. Thelana was yanking on it, leading her beyond the dim circle of their campfire into the darkness. "Run!"

Emma, so bold a moment before, so prepared to die at the hand of the wild woman's dagger, was again seized by fear. They were consumed by darkness, by cold, and by the unknown. Blindly and clumsily she ran, over roots she could not see, stems catching in her hair, thorns grazing her cheeks and wrists and ankles. But the Ilmarin was there, leading her by the wrist, her presence reassuring. Could it be a ruse? Was she being led to the slaughter? No, she refused to believe that. Something was in their midst, something terrible—even Emma, with her dull senses, could feel it.

They stopped. Emma searched the darkness for the female silhouette. "What?" she implored. "What is it?"

The Ilmarin's eyes caught the moonlight and glittered like emeralds. And it was there that Emma first saw it, reflected in her irises, a dark mass. "I said run!" She screamed it now, letting go of Emma's hand completely.

Like a hare rustling through the bush, Thelana was gone. Emma tried running but forgot how, her knees catching in her skirts, her heels sinking at every turn. She could not see where she was going or what she was escaping from, but if it was bad enough to frighten Thelana, she knew it wise to keep moving. *What could it be, unless . . .*

. . . the giant?

She hesitated. If she could only go back to their encampment, rouse Xandr and Grimosse, but every direction was the same subtle outline of forest, a maze of shadows and silhouettes leading into pitch blackness.

"Oh Strom. Oh Strom . . ." She repeated the mantra aloud for the gods to hear, but she was alone in a vast dark nothingness. The only other sounds were her irregular gasps for air, and the flailing of a weak heart, which she was certain would fail her.

Calm yourself, Emma. You can think through this.

She looked to the moon and stars to find her bearings, as she knew sailors to do, but the heavens were gone, utterly and inexplicably gone. The darkness was a solid mass she could reach out and touch, and then the sky was moving, and Emma was seized with such terror that reason abandoned her completely.

A hand pulled her into the bushes. Thelana was there again, invisible. She pointed through the prickly leaves with her blade. "Do you see it?"

"I don't see anything," Emma replied, as quietly as she could. She had spoken in haste, without willing herself to look. But it *was* there, waiting, pondering, and perhaps searching. Following Thelana's dagger, she could make out the broken line of trees in the vast gloom and the orbs like glowing embers. The air was crackling around it and Emma's hair was prickling, the long strands twisting and writhing in the current, and somehow she knew the orbs to be eyes, knew that those sentient embers were focused upon them. She could feel them seeing into her. This was neither giant nor horg, but a being of an entirely different order.

"It knows we're here," Emma murmured.

"No—" Thelana began, but she did not have time to argue. The bush whispered and Emma felt herself alone again, a fleeting voice calling back, imploring her, "Move!" When she looked again, the dark mass was expanding in her direction.

Wet leaves slipped under her soles, making it difficult to gain traction. She groped blindly for a limb or a trunk. The stomping of some immense, bipedal thing shook the small bones of her ankles and rattled her eardrums. Wood shattered—an explosive cracking sound—followed by the hiss and thump of felled trees. Whole elms toppled next to her, shuddering as they struck the ground, groaning as they collided with others. Branches smacked her face, bloodying her lips, but there was no pain, only the primal urge to continue moving.

Descending into a depression, deep in the twisting paths of Gloomwood, she reached the limit of exertion, where even terror could push no further. Emma caught fleeting snatches of moonlight and silver streaks of stars. She paused, her lungs full of fire, each breath coming short. All was quiet.

A severe sense of aloneness hit her. She felt like a small child having lost its mother, and realized she would have liked to look upon her father once more, that she longed for even Thelana's company. *I was alone in this world and shall die this way.* "It can't be far behind," she murmured, finding comfort in her own voice.

The thing had not given up pursuit. It was at arm's length, as it had always been, silent as a shadow, and with awful clarity Emma came to accept it. She turned, seeking its description, but was left with only vague impressions. Like something beyond the boundaries of natural law, the moonlight seemed unwilling to reveal it.

She considered running again, but was wracked with fatigue. Resigned to Fate's loom, she awaited whatever was to happen.

Many voices filled the silence. They spoke as one. It was so strange and unexpected a sound, she could not be certain whether it came from her own mind. A glove blotted out the moon and her feet lifted. She was weightless. He was holding her like a marionette, on invisible strings, its ember eyes glowing all around.

She could feel his presence like needles in her brain. Her every memory flashed across her mind's eye—every shameful thought, every guilty association, every desire— even those she was too ashamed to admit to herself. Her essence lay open, like a book, helpless as he poked and prodded within her.

Reality was torn away like a veil. Stars and moons and the surrounding woods became immaterial. She saw Titian and Midiana, Anu and Eru, and all the places in Eldin's book come into vivid focus, sights that defied possibility, that could only be dream. She felt herself lifting, far above the realms of her own thought into that of the *other*, into worlds beyond and *behind* the one she was born into. Her mind was open to his, a window to the frightful images that were flitting by it, things her psyche was ill-prepared to decipher—she was like a fish falling from the sky, an infant born a thousand times over, the scenery ever-changing. There were landscapes with glassy mountain towers and acid oceans and impossible canyons, and clusters of suns and cities in drifting bubbles and crustacean-like beings arguing the politics of their civilization. There were cephalopod-like monsters of unthinkable vastness, and life forms of such perplexing arrangement as to challenge the most basic assumptions of biology. The images continued to flow, violently, beyond her capacity to maintain her sense of self. Knowledge was drowning her, would kill her, she knew, and for the first time in her life she was desperate for ignorance. It was not long before she could not remember whether Northendell had been her home, or just another of the falling vistas. The colossal intellect behind those glowing eyes was the only constant, radiating such gravity that she felt her sanity disintegrating, yet among these many images, one caught hold of her, and like a raft she clung to it. It was Thelana, staring in horror at what Emma could only guess was her own floating body. Try as she might, Emma could not hold the image long. A vortex was opening somewhere, swallowing all realities into a dark void and she was being swept into it.

WE ARE HORDE, the voices said. *STATE THE PURPOSE.*

11

RETURN TO NORTHENDELL

Grimosse stood over her body, his hands tense about his hammer, his torso heaving heavily, his hideous muzzle lined with concern. Xandr's fingertips worked delicately to find life. Her hair was spread over the roots, patterns of morning sunlight splayed across her peaceful eyelids, robes draped heavily over her body like a funeral shroud.

Thelana peered over Xandr's shoulder. She was suited in furs, unable to bear the cold now that the hot rush of adrenaline had left her. "Is she dead?"

"I don't think so." Ever so carefully, he lifted Emma's head, and suddenly her lashes were fluttering like a moth's wings. Her pupils were impossibly large, swirling wells of black, and when Xandr looked into them he saw only his reflection.

"Emma. Can you speak?"

"Light," she answered, softly as a sigh. "Very painful."

"Are you wounded?"

"Only my head," she groaned. "Feels like Grimm hit me with his hammer. Hurts to think."

With that, Grimosse came alive, his leathery neck shrinking to reveal lines of thick veins, his jaw jutting with stubby teeth. "Who hurt Emma!" he cried, hoisting his hammer to attack. "Who hurt her? Grimm crush him!"

Everyone was startled. Even Thelana, instinctively, took a step away. Xandr had never seen the golem behave with such pathos—it presented another piece to the puzzle. She showed no fear when introduced to him just as he seemed overly concerned to protect her. What was their connection? And why had he not acted to protect Emma from Thelana? Did he sense no real threat? Or was he torn between allegiances?

"Calm yourself, Grimm," he said. "Emma was hurt by the thing we have been seeking. The giant. Remember?"

His hammer glinted gold in the morning sun. "Grimm crush giant!"

"You shall," Xandr assured him. "But we have first to find it, my friend."

Despite its inhuman face, the golem's expression was one of disappointment. He had failed his directive to protect. "But . . . Grimm guardian," he murmured.

"We know," Xandr replied. "And you will have your chance to guard all of us, but this is not the time for fighting. Do you understand?"

"Oh." The golem lowered his enormous arms with resignation, letting the hammer down gently against the ground. "Grimm understands."

Regaining strength, Emma lifted herself on her elbows, and feebly but urgently, began to relate her tale. "I was running, running from that awful thing, and then it—it," she stammered, fighting through the pain, "it forced open my mind. He was studying me, my thoughts, my . . . everything."

Thelana lost no time in adding her perspective. "She was just floating, her arms outstretched like how the Hedonians used to kill murderers—like on a crucifix—and the giant's hand was over her, I think holding her up."

Xandr's eyes widened. "You saw it! What did it look like?"

"I couldn't tell you. It was dark. I only know that it was huge, like a small fort, and its eyes . . . I'd rather never see them again." Thelana had not slept the night. He could see the redness ringing her emerald irises, the subdued panic. Exhaustion weighed her movements and even her heels, which almost never met the ground, were fallen from fatigue. Things were being hidden from him, he knew, for how could both women have run from the giant when neither he nor Grimosse chanced to wake and take notice of it? No doubt there had been some quarrel between them to distance them from camp. He was not blind to Thelana's growing hatred of Emma.

"You saw it, but it didn't attack you?"

"No." She sighed. "After it did what it did to Emma, it marched off, like I wasn't even there."

"Which way did it go?"

She lowered her face, letting the shadows divide it, and shook her head. A chill wind rattled the leaves in the trees, drawing chestnut threads across her sharp cheekbones. "It was dark . . ."

"Which way!" he demanded.

She shrank, motioning to protect herself. Grimosse did not budge. "West."

"To the city?"

With her palm shielding her eyes from the morning light, Emma managed to find the ground and stand. "I know to navigate its streets. I know where the walls are weak. It didn't study Thelana because she knows nothing of use."

The Delian girl stood taller than Thelana, not bothering to hide behind her tattered sleeves. Her complexion was even paler than before, utterly drained of color. The raven locks tumbling over her cheeks were streaked with white, as if she had aged many years overnight.

"So the giant is attacking the city?" he said to her.

"Perhaps not," Thelana interrupted. "I tracked it to here in Gloomwood, east of Northendell. It may be seeking a way around the mountains."

"That's not possible," Emma remarked. "The Pewter Mountains link to the Crown of Aenya, which circles the world. Why do you think no one in history has ever breached our walls?"

"But what could the giant be after?"

"Wait . . . it's coming to me now." Emma motioned as if to swoon and Xandr prepared to catch her, but she found strength, pulling back to her feet. "There was a voice—many voices—and it said, 'state the purpose.'"

Thelana continued to stare, her scowl replaced with a look of fascination. "What does that mean?"

"I wish I knew," she said.

Xandr furrowed his brow, felt his fists clench automatically at his sides. "So the giant comes to Gloomwood, studies and releases you, and then marches off to Northendell? None of it makes sense, and yet it must."

"Well, I agree!" Emma exclaimed, clasping her hands together. "But it would certainly be easier if we did not keep secrets from one another! If you want me to join your quest, I must know all that you know."

With each passing day, Xandr thought her more a woman and in measure more beautiful. "She's right," he said to Thelana. "Fate has made her as much a part of this as we are. And it is her home the giant is headed for."

"Tell her," she said, crossing her rabbit-lined sleeves. "It's all still a mystery to me. She'll do no better."

Xandr could feel the silence of the surrounding wood like a silk clot in his ears. In morning, the forest was far less foreboding, its ghosts vanquished like shadows. But a sense of doom still hung in the trees. Were they dead? Or just dreaming, waiting to awake? Perhaps, millennia ago, when the trees were only saplings, Gloomwood had been vibrant and green.

He ran his fingers through his dirty blond locks, turning, finally, to Emma. Her pupils were shrinking to normal, their opaque blackness becoming clearer, more human. "I'll tell you everything, but for the sake of your people, if you are able, it's best we make haste for Northendell."

Much to Thelana's disdain, Xandr helped Emma navigate the twisting roots and low-lying boughs until reaching their encampment. After Grimosse packed up and shouldered their belongings, they set out for the sun, casting final glances at the dark circle of ash where the fire burned brightly the night before.

Following the tunnel of broken trees, Xandr began to tell of how he met Thelana and Grimosse, of the city by the sea, and of the star that dropped from the heavens to raise the waters and doom that proud and wondrous capital. But it was the *Ages of Aenya* and the Prophet Eldin that brightened Emma's face. He explained how the book, written millennia before, prophesied what became of

Hedonia, and the greater destruction that would ultimately come to Aenya. Emma listened with only minor inquiries, and when, at last, the shadows cast by Gloomwood's skeletal limbs faded under the western light, Xandr told her of the crater near Kiathos and of the mysterious prints leading out from it.

She waited for a moment, before asking, "Why you?"

Such a simple question! And yet, for how long did it torment him, eluding any reasonable answer? Stunned by her insight, he was unable to speak, and losing hope that he might ever answer, she looked elsewhere.

"It's my fate," he answered at last.

The towers shone like veins of silver above the clouds. Over the valley, a gray haze ebbed like phantom waves, mercifully shrouding the horrors of previous days. Pale flickers of light streamed through the damp, heavy air, and at first the companions did not know what they were seeing. And then the wind came, opening transient pockets through the fog, and the lanterns came into view, swaying in the hands of wives and sisters and mothers. Husbands had not been counted among the returned. Fathers were not found among the dead. Families drifted like ghosts in roving candlelight vigils, calling names, seeking bodies to possess, to load onto biers or wheelbarrows. Helmets, swords, and spears poked up from the ground like weeds of iron and blood. Along the wall, armored forms lay scattered like fallen leaves, misshapen, contorted, frozen in acts of defiance.

"What is this?" Xandr asked Emma.

"I've never seen so many," she murmured. "Every year there are sacrifices, but never like this."

Mistaking Xandr for a Delian, a woman of middle years went to him, tugging frantically at his sleeve, her agonized voice upsetting the stillness. "Please, kind sir, have you seen my husband?"

Ashamed, because he had not taken part in the battle, Xandr turned away, but when she continued to plead with him, his anger turned outward. "Off of me, woman!"

Emma took the woman by the hand. "Forgive him," she said, "for he is not well. He lost many in his family."

The woman gave no reply. Xandr could easily see that all her mind was in finding her husband. "Will you help me?" she begged. "I know he's here someplace, calling to me . . . He was a brave fighter," she added, balling a weary fist into the sign of the hammer. "Almighty Strom always watched over him. He is wounded is all . . . I know it in my bones."

"I will help her," Emma said to Thelana. "Go with Xandr."

Thelana hesitated, made as if to protest, but continued on, allowing Emma to stay behind. Together, they made for the wall, which was further than it appeared, until coming upon a body that lay flat on its back, the copper grill pulled down below the chin. A ribbon of smoke and an unbearable stench was coming off of it, a mix of decay and burnt flesh, searing the insides of their nostrils. There was no face, only bone and bits of charred flesh, suggesting eyes and a nose and lips. Xandr doubted the man's own mother would recognize him.

Burying her mouth in the crook of her elbow, Thelana knelt by the corpse. "By Alashiya, this armor is still warm! And look!" She pointed to something in the grass, dully catching the morning light, within reach of the dead man's outstretched palm. The hilt was intact, but there was no blade attached to it, only a husk of metal like melted candle wax.

"How did this happen?" Xandr said to her.

Thelana shook her head, quick to distance herself from the reeking body.

A desperate noise drew their gaze towards the city. It was a knight emerging from the haze, waving and shouting like a madman. "Get away, you blasted buzzards!"

Bodies were gathered around him in a circle, each burned to a varying degree. Those with flesh to offer were crowded by ravens. Their beaks poked through gaps in the copper plating, through chinks in the chainmail, plucking human entrails like worms from the earth, and blackened eyeballs from between brittle helms. The lone man-at-arms continued his desperate battle to stop their scavenging with his erratic left arm, but it was a futile effort. As he managed to clear one felled soldier of ravens, the birds simply alighted upon another. Xandr could see that half the knight's face was missing, and that his right arm, clinging tightly to a sword, seemed a great burden to him, causing him to hobble about.

Xandr seized him by the shoulders. "You do the dead no favors!" he cried. "These men are gone to the Taker and the pickers of carrion will have their day!"

"Let me be!" the other man screamed. Only one eyeball remained in his head, and the lid was burned off so that it appeared to wheel freely in its socket. "I knew these men! I supped at their houses! Their women set tables for me!"

"You do not honor their sacrifice to suffer them this
way," Xandr protested.

The man's lone eye fixed on the Ilmar, and sense came
back to him. "Who are you?"

"I am Batal."

"The *what*?" The man-at-arm continued to stare, astonishment turning to laughter, and then to fits of coughing.
"I would never believe so bold a statement," he said, "but
after the previous night, I think I could be made to believe
anything."

"Tell me your story," Xandr implored.

"We were overrun by Zaibos' forces," he admitted, resting himself on a piece of rubble. "They entered the city.
Set fires to the houses."

"The bogrens are gone now?"

He nodded, his grill and copper breastplate chiming
as they made contact.

"Where did they retreat to?"

"To Gloomwood, of course. But their giant continued
on into the city."

"*Their* giant?" Xandr echoed.

"Aye, was the giant breached the walls. Last night we
saw him coming out of Gloomwood. We hit him with everything we had—arrows, spears, firebombs! Nothing! It
moved *through* our defenses. We were like fleas in a mammoth's hide! Those few who braved to cross his path were
mangled beneath his iron feet, snatched up like mice in a
hawk's talons, crushed, rent piece by piece as a leg is torn
from a hen!

"When he arrived at the foot of our walls, we met him
with strength, a hundred men-at-arms singing to the gods,

to Strom, not a craven in our company. But those hellish eyes—I'll take the memory to my tomb. One look from him and those brave souls burst as if all their blood was turned to fire!

"All perished, but one. And I was that one. Alone I stood against him, without an ounce of fear. When he went for me, I gave him my shield, and he crushed it like pottery in those gauntlet-hands of his. And then I thrust at his underbelly, watched his black blood spill down my blade. His bindings were all a throb, as if though he might rupture from the framework that kept him whole, and believing him fatally wounded, I let go of the hilt and stood back. For a moment he did pause, to glare at me through those burning, faceless eyes, but as I went to free my sword from his flesh, I could hear the groan of iron against iron, realizing, to my terror, that he was no mortal being, but something more—flesh and steel. Undeterred, I lifted my weapon again to strike, and that is when he set me ablaze with his stare, doing *this* to my face, and fusing my sword to my glove! I still cannot let go of it.

"I watched, as he simply pushed through the mortar, letting the stones—the very same set by my grandfather's grandfather—collapse and tumble over him. We channeled molten lead over him as he traversed the wall and still—nothing!

"Zaibos moved in afterward, to pillage and wreak havoc. Our inner forces rallied to rout them. Their numbers counted for little between our narrow streets. But the damage was done. The men-at-arms of Northendell have never failed in their duty to protect the innocent, until today. If only we had known they possessed such a monster!"

"Duncan." It was Emma, staring with astonishment and pity. "Did the giant say anything to you?"

"Aye," he replied. "He did indeed. If my memory serves me right, it was . . . it was very odd."

"Tell me."

"He did not speak the common tongue," Duncan replied. "And his voice was . . . like many speaking together. But he did say one thing that I recognized. It said that its name was Horde, and it asked me to 'state the purpose'."

Duncan was breathing with difficulty now. He was without sleep or nourishment, had likely spent the whole of the night fending off bogren and raven alike, and yet Xandr could not help but press him. "What else can you tell us, Duncan? Did the giant join with Zaibos' armies?"

"No," he replied, "he did not. From what I have been told, he went straightway to the mountain, ravaging only what came into its path."

"The mountain . . . what's up there? What could it be seeking?"

"Forgive me," he said, his chin propped by his sword, as if he might collapse without its support. "My weakness, it would seem, is catching up to me."

"You must tell us!" Xandr insisted.

"Up on the hill is the mead hall of old, seat of the king, but the giant did not go that way." He coughed, a harsh guttural noise, and banged his fist against his breastplate. "I know nothing else. Now leave me to my misery. I beg you."

Thelana laid a hand on Xandr's shoulder, her face sour. "Enough. Can't you see he needs a healer?"

Too weary for farewells, Duncan limped toward the city, his sword tapping the broken stones. They watched him as he shrank from view and, through the shifting fog, Xandr could make out the great fissure in the wall, yawning like the mouth of a cave. Frosted blocks of limestone lay strewn about, each the size of a wagon, what a hundred men could not lift.

Emma eyed Xandr, her dark lashes flashing. "Xandr," she murmured, "doesn't the book speak of this? Of the city being breached? If it is a book of prophecy, can't we follow its predictions? Prevent the next disaster from happening?"

"We have only the illustrations, which are few in number," he replied somberly. "It is the words that matter, but no one can decipher them. Alas, the language of the Zo is lost to the ages."

"That may not be true," she replied, her lips easing into a smile. "I think I may know someone who can help us."

12

REVELATION

Emma could hardly keep from crying out. Tension rocked her from heel to toe. What would she say to him, she wondered? How would he react to seeing her again? The wait, the not knowing, was unbearable. She felt as if her entire life's purpose settled on this moment.

State the purpose . . .

Xandr and Thelana followed her along the snowy rutted cobblestone, looking uncomfortable in what, for the Ilmar, was clearly an alien environment. Ropes heavy with laundry crossed from windows above. Post and lintel doors decked every avenue, pillared or arched, splintered or riveted in iron. Walls meandered like rivers up and down the city, vanishing into side streets, narrowing to passages where one could touch the homes on either side, which opened after some distance into niche neighborhoods. Crowds pressed them at each turn, aristocrats in embroidered silks, merchants shouldering fruit baskets, children busy at hopscotch. If they were to pause and listen, a thousand stories could be heard from just as many mouths. All what Duncan had related was gossip for the day.

Emma suppressed her laughter as Thelana's pupils—wide with apprehension—sprang at each new thing. The solitude of Gloomwood was nowhere to be found. To be caught undressed in such a crowd, even in knickers, was to invite a lifetime of gossip and jeering, enough to cause one's death by humiliation. Fortunately, no one heeded the newcomers, as the Ilmar—when clothed—looked no differently than the other bronze-skinned merchant travelers peddling their wares. Only Grimosse attracted undue attention, despite the hood drawn over his face, as he could not hope to hide his awesome size.

Rooftops were stacked like piles of paper overhead, haphazardly climbing the slope of the Pewter Mountains. They followed the course of what seemed an endless, zigzagging array of steps built into the natural rock face. Many of the stones were recently set, while the less traveled path was worn by time and by weeds growing between the cracks. For some length they ascended, up to the northeast section, into a less dense suburb, passing the boisterous tavern with the swaying sign that read, *The Moon-Talon Dragon*. The sun was still rising from behind the moon, but recent events drove many to drown sorrows in mead. Drunken song and the twang of lutes floated from the windows, summoning revelers. Even the Ilmar were drawn to it, but Emma shooed them away. It filled her with an awkward sense of empowerment to do so. No one had ever listened to her before.

Following the wall that led her home, they came to a bend with few houses. Frost glazed the streets and the spaces between the stones were packed with ice. Drop fruit, long out of season, spotted the quarter in purple. A forlorn tower, looking long-abandoned, reached feebly into the gray sky. There was but a single window in it, but even this was tightly shuddered. For how long had she sat by that window, memorizing the fissures in the masonry, watching year after year as roots of fig trees tore through the city walls? In seeing the tower again, the past cycle seemed even more remarkable and her home all the more oppressive.

"It's not the same," she said to no one in particular.

"What's not the same?"

Emma met Thelana's gaze. "Oh, it's just a feeling, that my home is not my home anymore."

Xandr came up beside them. "How much further?"

"It is here," she said, and suddenly the thought of having to confront her father again overwhelmed her, made her stomach ache to expel its contents. *Perhaps this was a mistake. Perhaps we ought to go back . . .*

But before she could choose a course of action, Grimosse lurched ahead. "Here!" the golem exclaimed, with all the enthusiasm of an overactive toddler. "It was here!"

No one was more surprised than Emma, who approached the monster with an equal measure of eagerness and dread. *He knows something about me . . . about my past. Could it be true? Could I be some sort of construct also?*

Xandr was quick to join Grimosse at the doorway. "You've been here before?"

"Grimm been here," he admitted. "Brought little girl."

"Who was she?" Thelana asked. "Was it the same girl you spoke of in the desert?"

"She first to guard," he answered. "What Grimm made for. Emma."

Unable to conjure any emotion, Emma listened to him relate the tale. She was in a stupor, detached from the words she was hearing, as if acknowledging them might choke her. But despite her resistance, some part of her brain was processing it, making her tremble all over and feverishly perspire.

I cannot let this destroy me. Not when I have come so close . . . I must go on, without thinking, yes. Thinking is the enemy!

She rested her slender white hand against the golem's massive forearm. "Grimosse," she said, "*I* was that girl."

"No," he argued. "You not same Emma! She little girl. So little, she fit in Grimm's hand."

"I grew up," she explained.

The golem stared hard at her, his barrel chest expanding and contracting heavily, the breath from his equine nostrils turning white. He was not made for thought, yet the others could see in his tortured mug the struggle for understanding. Finally, his all-black eyes softly shimmered and, carefully, he caressed a single thread away from her ear, saying, "You are my master. You are Emma."

Warm feelings washed over her as she gazed upon him. She could no longer see a monster. "Grimm," she said softly, "if I am your master, then I ask that you knock on this door. It's time we had some answers."

After rattling the hinges and shaking the snow from the lintel, a small man emerged from a dark antechamber, looking as if he'd just arisen from bed. He had ash-white whiskers and a pouf of hair all out of place and he was wrapped snuggly in a gray blanket. At first, he looked annoyed and aloof, but as his deep-set eyes touched upon the golem's snout, the man made as if to faint.

"He is the man who has hurt me!" Emma cried, and Grimosse grabbed the man by the shoulders, violently shaking him from his semi-conscious state. The golem then tossed him through the open doorway.

"Emma!" the old man cried feebly, his body crumpled against the opposite wall, "What are you doing—!"

She felt no pity. The power she now wielded roused something deep within her, something monstrous, tempting her to command the golem to kill.

"No!" Xandr protested. "The gods know you have your reasons, but we need him alive."

Watching Mathias be pummeled by the golem's fists began to feel less appealing to her, and before Grimm could do further harm, she calmed herself and regained her reasoning. "Leave him," she commanded, and turning to Xandr, added, "You're right. If I were to do it, I'd be no better than him."

The old man was slow to rise from the floor, and when he found the strength to do so, he cried out in agony. "You-You broke my back! Why have you done this to me, Emma?"

Xandr, Thelana and Emma followed the golem into the tower. The door swallowed the light with a resounding thump. In the dim glow of Mathias' lantern, their faces flashed savagely. "How dare you ask me such a question?" she snapped. "As if you do not know! You deserve worse."

"I . . . !" he exclaimed, his mouth agape. "After all I've done for you? Fed you when you were hungry, clothed you when you were cold . . . protected you from the evils of this world? This is how you honor your father, seeking vengeance upon me, bringing these people to murder me!"

"You locked me in a room for a year!" she spat. "You kept me a—a prisoner!"

"It was for your own safety. I never wished ill upon you! You simply have no idea the forces I contend with! Please believe me."

"Oh, so now you show me courtesy," she replied coolly. "Now you give explanations. You are a liar. You locked me up to punish me, no other reason . . . to punish me for going into that accursed den of yours!" She glowered over him, but there was no trace of the cruel father she remembered. Where was the man who terrified her with his presence? A feeble old man, trembling at her wrath, had taken his place.

"The knowledge I have collected, if you could have comprehended it . . ." he began. "Trust me when I say it would have destroyed you, brought destruction upon me and all I have worked so long to achieve."

"Well," she said, "the day has come for you to open your door. And you *will* tell me everything."

Mathias turned from her, to each face in turn. "C-can they be trusted?"

"They are my companions," Emma replied, "and have my confidence."

Mathias hurried down to his study. Emma followed closely, having ten years and an adventure with the Ilmar to build her courage to brave those few steps, which she was surprised to find, were little more than half her height, short enough to jump down from. Rummaging in his pocket, Mathias' ring of keys chimed in his hand. He poked nervously at the keyhole with the silver key, now dulled with age, until the sound of falling tumblers echoed through the tower.

The mass of books had grown considerably since Emma's ninth year. So much so, it did not seem as if the six of them could find room to stand.

"Please," Mathias murmured, "be careful. These books have been meticulously arranged."

The Ilmar nodded politely, marveling at the pages towering over them, lining every wall, piling in every corner. The taxidermy halfman that had once frightened her was entirely lost in the mess. It was as if the room was entirely composed of paper.

Thelana squeezed through more easily than the others, remarking, "I never knew there could be so much to write about."

His desk was as Emma remembered it—a clutter of candles, astrolabes, compasses, maps, quills, skulls, and other oddities. Holding fast to the edge of the tabletop, he hung up his lantern and descended gradually into his chair.

"So," he said, breathing heavily, "what do you intend to do now?" The flickering candles cast an eerie pall upon him, revealing a man of ghastly complexion. The balls of his eyes hung so loosely, they looked to fall from his skull, the rims so bloodshot, it was as if he never knew a night of sleep. "Without proper study," he began, "none of you shall comprehend a thing. I doubt your friends possess even the capacity to read. You are peons, utterly insignificant, going about the motions of your pitiful lives without any idea the enormity that is existence."

Emma went to speak, but Xandr stepped forward, silencing her. "I am Xandr, Ilmarin, and Batal of Legend."

"Ilmarin," he intoned, sitting up in his chair. "I did not think your people still existed."

"We are few," Thelana remarked.

"And you say you are the Batal," he asked. "The same Batal who fought on Sternbrow Hill?"

"I do not know of Sternbrow Hill," Xandr replied, "but I know men of destiny. My great ancestor helped free Aenya from the rule of the Septhera. I was raised in the Mountains of Ukko, by the Order of Alashiyan Monks, to confront the awful fate that now, even as we speak, climbs the mountain that surrounds us."

He leaned forward, his face split between skepticism and enthusiasm. "What you say is intriguing, but how do I know any of it is true?"

"I have this," Xandr replied. As the cloth fell away from the sword, the room took on a silvery brilliance, its milky surface mirroring the cluster of candles.

Mathias sprang at the sight of it with a power he did not look to possess, his mouth agape, his fascinated visage contorting about the nodes of the silver skull. "This is neither bronze nor iron," he remarked, his fingers moving anxiously across the metal. "It's simply flawless, like a diamond. The element is too heavy for our sun to produce— it is dead matter, stardust, an artifact that could only have been forged by the Zo!"

"There is more," Xandr said, reaching into his sack. "There is—"

"Not yet!" Emma searched the faces of the Ilmar. "I promised to help you, but I've waited too long for this."

Mathias leaned over his desk. "No, Emma, can't you see that this is more important—"

"The guardian obeys me!" she cried. "You will sit yourself down, and if you wish to know about the sword, you will first answer my questions."

"Oh, by all the gods above," he grumbled, the century-worn wood of his chair creaking as he settled into it. "I have dreaded this day."

"You've dreaded my knowing the truth? Learning who I am?"

"No, Emma—"

"Enough! First, tell me why . . . why do you persist in sitting here? Day and night? Night and day? What is it about this infernal room and these damnable books that so needs occupy your life, making you less than a stranger to me, a mere shadow?"

"All right." He pushed his fists tiredly into his eye sockets, studying each face anew. "If you believe the answers will ease your burden to know, I will give them to you. But be forewarned, you may not find comfort in what you hear. The truth of things, you will discover, is often disturbing."

"I don't care," she said adamantly. "I want the truth. I am prepared."

"Very well, then," he said. "But where to begin? I suppose, the very beginning is best."

"Long before you were born, Emma, I came to Northendell as a physician. My services were greatly in need, as the annual sieges were the cause of much suffering. At that time, the Delians did not even know what was required to keep a wound from festering, and more often than was necessary, men were deemed too far gone to be brought back from the brink of death. I saved many lives my first year that otherwise would have perished, and I taught my art to any who cared to learn. But I could not save everyone who was brought before me. Many died in my hands. Too many.

"After a time, my failures to return husbands to their wives and sons to their mothers weighed heavily upon me, rendering me sleepless. Despite my youth, the specter of Skullgrin followed me, and as I battled to keep men from slipping into the void, I could feel *him* watching, waiting to take the deceased as a fisherman reels in his catch. Unlike the Delians, I found no respite in mead, no solace in songs of valor. I did not believe in their gods, or in Strom, or in the Happy Hunting Grounds said to await the brave beyond this life. For me, death is final, ultimate and absolute, and there is no escaping it. This understanding oppressed me to such a degree, that living became nothing but a tiresome wait for the end. Even when I managed to pull a dying soldier from the grip of that accursed god, my effort felt wasted, knowing that I was only prolonging the inevitable. What did it matter that I save a man for the following siege, or, surviving conscription, another ten or twenty years? It was almost a mercy to let them slip away. For I knew that in the end, no matter my efforts, the Taker always wins out.

"My singular purpose, the task I am now devoted to, was discovered after meeting a historian named Dak. He came to me one day beseeching my aid. You see, King Frizzbeard abhors excessive knowledge, just as his father and his father's father, who outlawed the practice of, what the Delians call, witchcraft, but which the Ancients called science. All books brought to the city by learned men are burned if discovered, but owing to my services as a physician, my books were tolerated. So Dak suffered me to keep his histories, his philosophies, his science, from the fires of ignorance. I hid them here in this den. Other scholars quickly learned of our arrangement and followed his stead, and thus my collection grew.

"My nightly despairing, however, went unabated. Thinking continually of the death that would take me, I found myself incapable of sleep, with many more passings in the day than other men possess. To occupy my nights, I took interest in the histories secured in my home, and the more I studied them, the more I saw possibilities which, at first, I shuddered to imagine. It was a means of escape, escape from this trivial mortality, from the eternal darkness awaiting all living things, a passage once paved by the Zo.

"You see, the ones you call Ancients, who lived millennia before us, did not suffer death as we do. Indeed, they were immortal, possessing a secret that men of this age do not yet know of, and I became determined to discover it.

"To aid me in this pursuit, I sought other scholars, but the fools made me an object of ridicule, calling me mad. Only Dak shared my optimism, my vision, and for a time— following closely to the designs of the Zo—we labored over the creation of a construct. Knowing we faced immolation should we be discovered, we shunned the company of other citizens, acting in secret. I even changed my name, from Mattathias to Mathias, though Dak thought such precautions excessive.

"Everything was going splendidly, until that damnable creature came into his life! Dak abandoned me and all our years of work over love of a woman—a *woman*!" Mathias cried. "Instead of building a body that we might become immortal, he fashioned that abomination which affronts my sight." He waved an aggrieved hand at Grimosse.

"So I labored on alone, deserting my profession as physician to learn all I could of the Zo, to conquer Skullgrin or *die in the pursuit.*" Here he paused to catch his breath, trembling with passion.

Emma marveled at the story, almost forgetting her years of hurt and neglect. She had to remind herself of the day she was locked in her room. Her rage was her confidence, her strength, and she could not lose it. "And what does all that have to do with me?" she asked.

"Don't you see? I was much too busy to know a woman's touch. Knowledge was my mistress! My lover! I could not have bothered to father a child."

Before she knew why, her eyes became moist, and the sight of him began to blur. "Then that means . . ."

"The construct that Dak built, the guardian—he finished it to protect his unborn daughter, to protect *you*. Dak was your father."

Her tears fell freely and shamelessly. She did not think to wipe her cheeks. She could not even blink.

"Now you have your truth," Mathias continued. "Your father was discovered by a young, idealistic knight— Duncan, I believe his name was, and by king's command, Dak and his wife were murdered, burned alive in their home along with their books."

"His wife?" she murmured, longing to hear the name she knew in her heart was her mother's.

"Ilsa," he said. "She left something for you, a gift for when you would be old enough to appreciate it, but you were clever enough to find it on your own."

She slipped her hand into her robes, feeling for the piccolo she kept close to her heart.

"The guardian rescued you from the king's men," he added, "bringing you to me when you were but an infant. I suppose there was no one else Dak could trust."

"Why . . ." *didn't you tell me?*

"I never told you because I cared for you," he said coolly. "You must believe that. When you were first brought to me, I saw you as nothing more than a burden, something to steal time away from my research, but as you learned to walk and to speak, I became fond of your presence. Remember, I was not the one who bore you, so I was under no obligation to keep you . . ."

"You should not have kept me!" she wailed. "You—you should have thrown me in a ditch!"

"I owed your father much," he replied. "Without his books, I would not be as close to immortality as I am now."

Standing at the foot of his desk, her face in her hands, Emma could do nothing but sob. Xandr took her by the shoulders, whispered something softly, and pulled her away. The *Ages of Aenya* dropped with a thud on the desk.

"What is this?" the old man asked.

"A history," Xandr answered, "written by Eldin."

Emma looked up, steadying herself on an adjacent stack of tomes. Mathias examined the book with slight interest, feeling its heft, the wrinkles along its spine. "Is this why you've come here? For this?" He produced a choking sound in an attempt to laugh. "I have dozens of these. Which translation do you prefer, Vermond of Hysperia? Khaledan of Shemselinihar?"

"It's not a translation," Xandr said to him. "It is written by the hand of Eldin himself, and it is complete, with books one through seven, which, I believe, even in Hedonia they did not possess."

Mathias' chair smacked against the floor as he took up the book, his hands trembling like a father lifting his newborn for the first time. "Were you careful with it? Is it missing pages? Where did you find it?"

"In the desert," Xandr replied. "Near the Septheran ruins."

"Of course!" he exclaimed. "The ruins of Shess, most ancient of ancient cities—the dry air would preserve it." The spine cracked open to the first page, and he gasped. "It is the protolanguage, the language of the Zo!"

"Can you read it?" Xandr asked him.

"Of course I can. But it'd take years, decades, to translate the whole thing."

"No!" Xandr cried. "We don't have even a passing! Something has come to our world, has come down from the stars. It's laid ruin to the people near Kiathos, has broken through the walls of your city, and is now making way for the mountains. We must know what this thing is," he exclaimed, turning the book over, to the illustration of the Absent Mountain and the falling star. "This is an omen of doom."

Mathias righted his chair and collapsed in it, defeated. "You wish for me to tell you what this book means, simply and precisely, when you have no knowledge of history, no understanding of anything that is in heaven or on Aenya? Bah! Easier teaching alchemy to a baboon!"

"You claim to be so wise," Xandr answered him. "Yet you are foolish enough to imprison yourself, wasting the precious years Fate gives us, when by your own admission you dread the god of death! I do not see a man nearing immortality. I see a deluded fool."

Without thinking, Emma found herself hovering over the book. Looking at the words again was a lot like the game of clouds, when after gazing long at the various amorphous shapes in the sky, rabbits suddenly appear, or flowers, or fish. In Gloomwood, the words were nothing but random juxtapositions of ink. Now, like finding images in the clouds, she found meaning on the page. She could not understand how she knew—she simply knew. And the process was accelerating. Soon, interpretation came effortlessly, her mind like a sieve draining knowledge from the page.

"It's all so simple," she murmured. "I couldn't read it before, but now I can."

Xandr turned to her, his face masked in shadow, his eyes flickering orange in the candlelight. "When Horde looked into your mind, it must have changed you."

"I suppose so," she said. "It's like remembering something I'd only forgotten." She saw Mathias staring in wonderment and it angered her that he should take an interest in her now. Part of her wanted nothing but to storm from the room, to burn the book and let the world be damned.

"I can help you," she said at last. "We'll study it together. We have only to find the prophecy, the part about the world ending, to learn what this . . . this Horde monster intends to do."

"No," Mathias said somberly. "I know the ending. I always have. We will start at the beginning." He lifted heavy eyes upon Xandr and Thelana, saying, "Give us until tomorrow. We'll work through the night. You may lodge upstairs, in my daughter's—" he coughed into his fist, "in Emma's room."

13

TRUTH AND FIRE

H er breathing came in short, sharp bursts, and after much groping and thrusting, he pulled away spent, lying beside her.

She could still feel his warmth in her body, his sweat tickling her skin, her thighs sodden with his seed. But a vacant spot remained whenever they separated, a lingering, aching emptiness. She stared at the trellised ceiling, following the arrangement of supporting beams. Moonlight shone faintly through a lone window, illuminating an empty hearth and a chamber pot and a chest. Except for the dozen or so books lining the walls, the room showed little evidence of life, and Thelana quivered at the thought of being trapped in it for a year.

She had slumbered in worse places, on city streets peopled by beggars and harlots, in jungles where carnivorous creatures growled and stomped, under cold rain with only leafy fronds for cover, but her mind was too full for sleep to penetrate. She was not blind to Emma's lustful stares, nor did she fail to notice the way Xandr's eyes lasted on hers. Restlessly, Thelana sprang to her toes, studying herself like a finished statue, her hands moving across her breasts, waist and thighs, hating every bit of it. When Xandr made love to her, she could not keep from thinking what teeth and steel had done to her body, scars his fingers were certain to discover. Thelana's ribs showed like a pubescent boy's, and she was too muscular in the calves and forearms. Her palms were scabrous from hoeing the field and plucking at bows, and the soles of her feet, having walked countless sun-scorched hills, were hard as aurochs' leather. Emma, on the other hand, was shapely in all the right places, like Anja, who never wanted for suitors, and being city born, was no doubt soft as an ilm. Worst of all, Thelana, *who should have listened when Mother warned not to stay too long under the sun,* was burnt a ruddy bronze, whereas Emma was pale as milk. Even when the Delian girl spoke, it was with wit and charm, but her unrefined self never managed anything clever to say.

If only Thelana could have met him on Solstice Night, to have jumped the fire with him and joined with him. It was too late now, and without tradition, they were like two people groping in the darkness. Her body coddled him night after night, yet she did not know what she was to him, or, if he fancied Emma, whether she would be expected to share him as Hedonian wives did their husbands.

As greatly as these thoughts plagued her mind, they made her feel silly. It was not becoming of a warrior, of the Batal's consort, to compare herself to another, and yet she could at least manage such concerns. After all, she was not wise to the importance of the book they'd found, or what role Xandr, as Batal, was meant to play in it. History was too big for her. The world was too big. She was raised to cultivate crops by a family with simple concerns. The Ilmar specialized in survival and nothing else. It was what drove her into the jungle to hunt, and to the field to wage war, and to the city to pilfer. The giant, or dark god— whatever it was—was too otherworldly, an intrusive reality pushed to the far corners of her mind. And yet, with the charred faces of dead Delians fresh in her mind, she could no longer pretend that it did not exist.

Surrendering pretense of sleep, she laid back down, the floor hard against her side. Emma's bed had been too soft for them. "Xandr, are you awake?"

He only nodded.

"My heart is heavy tonight."

"What would you have me do?" he grumbled.

"Nothing," she replied. "But I have been thinking . . . if we do find this monster, what will you do? How will you stop it?"

"I don't know."

"You saw what it did here to these people. What makes you believe you can succeed when they couldn't?"

"I do not know," he droned, not bothering to open his eyes.

"Men!" she cried with exasperation. "Do you only know to rush into things? Do you never think . . . ?" *About me?*

"Please, Thelana. I've long to rest. Fate only knows when the chance will come again."

"But what if Emma's right?"

He lifted onto his elbows with resignation. "I suppose the gods are too unkind to grant me even a single night's peace. Now what is this about Emma?"

"She asked why it had to be you," Thelana said.

"Emma meant nothing by it," he replied. "It was a simple question and you heard my answer."

"What answer was that?" she asked, her voice bitter. "That it's your fate? All you talk about is fate!" She did not want to become angry, could not endure the rift an argument might make between them. She started again, more softly, "Could the Spinster not have chosen another path for us? Why not leave this place, find somewhere to build a home, and someday, perhaps—?"

"Please, Thelana, do not fill my head with fantasies."

"But why not?" she pleaded, leaning into him, sliding a finger across his torso, along the ridges of his great scar. "We are survivors, the very last of our kind. Why throw our lives away for these people? For anyone? They only hate and fear us. And should we pursue this monster any further, I dread I'll find your body a smoking carcass.

"I've lost everyone," she murmured. "You are all I have left. I could not bear to lose you also." She waited for a reply, but there was only a deep silence that seemed to confirm the worst of her fears. "Would you have me be the only one?" she cried. "Alone in this world of misers and deceivers? My heart grieves to think of it."

"Quiet," he said, shushing her, "or they'll hear."

"I don't care what anyone hears!"

"Thelana." His voice came hard, dispassionately. "Apart from the sayings, what do you truly know of Kjus?"

She shook her head without listening, choking down her emotions.

"In the monastery, I was taught many strange and wonderful things. Our Order possessed all the knowledge, and wisdom, in the universe. Despite everything I've seen in my travels, I've no doubt of that.

"Our people were the first humans, Thelana, and in the river valleys between the Mountains of Ukko, we prospered since the beginning of Time, hidden from the Septhera, and later, from the Ancients. But it was Kjus who, millennia ago, gave the land of ilms and the people who lived there a name, and built the monastery where I was raised. We—the keepers and I—are his descendants. His philosophies codified what we as a people had always known, that 'knowledge not tempered by wisdom sows destruction'."

She stared at him blankly, still seething, but curious. "Why are you telling me this?"

"Today, I could not help but think of Kjus."

"I still don't follow."

"Thelana," he began, "if Kjus founded Ilmarinen, he must have come from elsewhere. What if he was of the Zo? What if everything known to the keepers, and taught to me, was passed across the ages directly from the Ancients? It's the only way the keepers could have known of history and astronomy, the only way to explain my sword, made of alloys beyond even the capabilities of Hedonian metalsmiths. Our people could scarcely produce simple cloth."

"Are you saying we're descended from the Ancients?"

"No," he said, "only that we share their blood. Kjus fathered many children in Ilmarinen. But his philosophy shows that he rejected the Zo. He abandoned them, their power and their promise of immortality—he chose to die to become one of us.

"After meeting Mathias, I understood what Kjus meant by knowledge without wisdom. Emma's stepfather studied the Zo and it has driven him to madness. What if the Zo were of like mind? In their mad pursuit of immortality, to what depths might they have reached? What abominations might they have unleashed?"

When Thelana was a child, the fact that buried seeds could produce food was miracle enough to boggle the mind. Now she was made to contemplate powers beyond nature: a star falling to the ground, ancient civilizations overcoming death, the doom of the entire world. Without fully embracing the implications, she played the part of listener, saying to him, "You believe that Horde came from the Zo? From thousands of years ago?"

"That is what I'm saying, and I am beginning to think that Kjus knew of it. The secrets of the Ancients were not written by our people, but were encoded in myth, in song.

I knew a monk named Zoab. We gazed at stars together and he told such fantastic tales, spoke of a Wandering God, a being who journeyed beyond the realms of Alashiya, roving the universe from star to star, forever seeking."

"Seeking what?"

"I wish I knew," he replied stiffly. "Zoab told me that the Wandering God would return someday. What if that day is upon us now? What if the keepers were preparing me, to *be* the Batal, to save the world as the Batal is prophesied to?

"So you see, Thelana, this is my fate and mine alone. Of all Aenya's people, only the Ilmar remember the Wandering God, and only I remain of the Order of Alashiya, keeper of their wisdom. If I should fail . . . what hope have we, or anyone, for a home, or for children, or anything? If Alashiya dies, the world dies with her."

Weighed against such matters, how trivial did Thelana's dreams for love and children seem? How ridiculous her envy of Emma? Even if Xandr were taken from her, like Borz and Dantes, like her sisters and brothers and parents, what would it matter if the world were doomed—every home and family. Perhaps, if Xandr were to defeat the monster, a future could exist for them. But she could not ignore the hopelessness clutching her heart. After all, she spied the thing in the woods, saw how it uprooted whole elms and paralyzed Emma with merely its presence. It was as if her hopes hung on Xandr having strength enough to lift the greater moon.

"Think no more on these things," he said with finality. "You'll need your rest."

Careful not to bend the floorboards lest she wake him, Thelana paced the short passages of Emma's home, feeling a prisoner.

Long ago, when Baba stopped eating and Nicola was growing pale and sickly, she might walk the whole of Ilmarinen, its lush beauty never failing to ease her worries. As long as she continued moving, troubling thoughts failed to follow. But in the tower, she could go nowhere, nor did she dare wander the avenues of a place that was, for her, strange and foreboding. Thelana used to think that people in cities, wealthy enough for proper homes, lived without cares. With bazaars full of meats and vegetables, running water from aqueducts, and walls to keep out predators and cutthroats, what could trouble them? Now she was finding Emma's life less enviable. In Ilmarinen, she'd known freedoms no Delian could dream of. On her twelfth year, she and Britannia went scouting, a cycle's journey from home. They found footpaths over the hills of Ukko, crossed valleys into unnamed lands, swam the tributaries of the Potamis to wherever the water flowed. That was freedom, that was—

BOCK! BOCK! BOCK!

Thelana froze on one foot, forgetting that she was in a house and that no creature could see her. The noise came again, echoing more loudly, rattling the decrepit beams of the ceiling. She waited for it to go away, but the knocking persisted, sounding angrier by the moment. Against her better judgment, she hurried down the stairs, keeping some space between herself and the door.

"Um . . . Who goes there?" she mustered, unaccustomed to answering doors, or to greeting strangers in a city.

"Open up!" a man demanded.

Thelana could not imagine who it could be, but the voice did not sound friendly. She felt her breathing quicken and her muscles grow tense, and her palms perspiring for want of a weapon. Pressing an ear to the door, she heard the muffled sounds of boots in snow from at least a dozen men.

"State your business," she called out.

"Open the door in the name of the king, or we'll force our way in!"

"Alright," she said, "give me a moment."

Thelana considered her choices. She could remove the beam barricading the door and let the angry men in, or go downstairs to warn Emma and Mathias. Or she could go upstairs, retrieve her bow, and wake Xandr. A warm glow emanated from the lower level, so she was certain her Delian hosts were continuing their study, and if they were coming upon some bit of wisdom to increase Xandr's chances of survival, she was not about to interrupt them. As the door continued to shudder, she bolted up to the bower, remembering she did not need to wake Xandr. All she needed was Grimosse.

"Don't let them through," she told the guardian as she seated herself midway up the stairwell, stringing her bow.

"Grimm not," he said oafishly, hoisting his massive hammer over his shoulder.

The knocking was followed by numerous demands, all of which related to the opening of the door. Thelana gave no refusal, only half-hearted assertions that she would, given time, yield to their wishes.

"You've been warned," she heard a voice say, and then another remarking, "Bring the ax."

The door quaked from a more powerful blow, the tip of the ax having yet to break through, but the wood swelling from where it was struck on the other side. Thelana remained calm, fixing her aim where the door would splinter.

After a successive series of blows, a piece of planking fell to the floor, and a man's helmeted face poked through the opening. It was all Thelana needed to send him reeling. On the other side of the tower, panic was setting in, as the victim of her aim started to scream, "Take it out! Take it out!"

"No, Thelana!" It was Xandr, sounding fatherly and disappointed. "You may have killed him!"

"I thought that was the idea . . ."

"Not here," he admonished. "We can't fight the whole city—!"

But there was no time for discussion. The panic beyond the door turned into a frenzy. More axes were coming through. Just then, Emma emerged from below, giving a short yelp and starting back at the sight of the splintered door.

"Go back down!" Xandr commanded her.

She stared at him, her eyes wild and bright. "What have you—?"

"No arguing!" he cried. "Let us handle this!"

Large gaps were beginning to appear now. The axmen retreated to make way for a multitude of hands. They were searching for the beam blocking the doorway. Emma stood petrified, fascinated by the intrusion into her home, but Xandr was quick to escort her away. Thelana, all the while, reached the entryway in two quick strides, snapping a soldier's mailed wrist with her bare foot, removing another's finger with her teeth.

"Some kind of . . . monster!" she heard someone say.

But the barricade would not hold. Openings were being made large enough for a man to crawl through. If they were so intent to enter, she figured, she would oblige them. As one man-at-arms came crashing in, chips of wood flying every which way, she pulled him to his knees, where Grimosse's hammer rang against the back of his armor. A second intruder came at her belly with a short sword, but she joined her knee with his groin, forcing him back into the wall, twisting the helmet from his head to pummel him with it. A host of men-at-arms gathered up behind her, spying her with their blades, but Grimosse sent them flying, smashing the armor from their bodies, hurling one against the stair, another three back through the doorway.

Having beaten her assailant into unconsciousness, Thelana turned her attention to the jagged pieces of what had been the tower's entrance. Outside, a dozen or more men-at-arms were gathering in the bailey. Snatching up a felled sword, she buried her ankles in snow to meet the invaders head-on, but before she could strike, Xandr's palm fell hard on her shoulder, forcing her away.

"Get Emma!"

Thelana's heart was a monster in her ribcage. Her veins were like molten steel, her breath like fire in the frozen air. She was more alive now than when bonding to his flesh, and she wanted to disobey him, to meet the Dark God with all her fervor. But his scowl overpowered even her resolve, and she shrank behind the doorway, choking down her bloodlust.

Reaching the base of the lower stairwell, she could hear Mathias' frantic voice, "They've found me! Found me at last!"

"Emma!" Thelana called out. "Xandr says it's time to go!"

But the Delian was unable to turn from her adoptive-father. He looked more ghoulish than ever, his face loose against his skull like a mask of skin, his bloodshot eyes jolting frightfully.

"Come with us," she pleaded. "It'll be alright."

He put a hand through her robes, touched her belly as if she were with child. "Is it safe?" His voice wavered with uncertainty. "Do you think they'll find it?"

"They won't," she assured him. "They know me. I always wear my robes this way."

Something in the way Mathias fussed over the book was unnerving, as if he were giving his daughter a parting gift. It turned Thelana's thoughts to her own secret, hidden in the hilt of her bow-sword—the ilm her father had given her before leaving Ilmarinen.

"Remember not to stand too straight," he said, "or they'll question the bulge, and you know what they do with books and to people with too much knowledge . . ."

Thelana did not know what Xandr was doing. Now that her blood was cooling, she was able to focus, to consider possible actions. Was he planning an escape? Or was he going to surrender? Either way, time was their enemy. "Hurry!" she cried.

Mathias sent her a frustrated glance, and returned Emma's gaze. "If you value my words, despite all I've said and done, I beg you this small kindness that you listen to me."

She nodded, looking doubtful, afraid.

"I've been a fool, Emma—an utter fool! I sought an escape from death, but before the Taker came for me, I buried myself in this . . . this damnable tomb! I brought myself to the grave by not living."

"This is not the time for sentiments," Emma said to him. "The men-at-arms, outside—!"

"Permit me to finish, I beg you," he said. "The day your father was killed, he tried to share a gift with me, what we had both sought for so long, *immortality*—you, perpetuate his being." His voice collapsed to muttering. "Dak's life continues through *you*. And I was too much the fool to realize it.

"I've never been a father to you, Emma . . . and I know that I am undeserving of it, but—"

"It doesn't matter," she murmured, blinking the tears from her lashes. "You're not so old. We still have days ahead of us."

For an instant, beneath his tired façade, Thelana saw in him a look of yearning. But like a smothered candle flame, the expression went out, and Mathias gestured for Emma to depart. She started for the doorway, but hesitated, turning to the spot behind his desk from which he made no motion. Her dark, raven-shaped eyes glittered in the chamber's many lights, questioning him.

"Give me a moment," he said uneasily, lifting the kerosene lamp from the wall, "to collect my belongings."

She offered a puzzled expression, but he rushed her out by the arm, where she joined Thelana at the bottom of the stair. And then the door slammed shut with an echo of finality.

"Mathias!" Emma checked the doorknob, yet it was as she feared, locked from within. "What are you doing?"

"They cannot find these books," he sounded from the room. "And they can't find me . . ." With that, Thelana could hear the ting of splintered glass and a rush of air, followed by a flash of gold about the seams of the door.

"By the gods!" she screamed. "*Father*, open this door at once!"

Thelana watched Emma's porcelain hands grow pink about the brass knob. Her raven colored hair tumbled about her face and neck as she struggled with the barrier, forcing her weight upon it. The handle twisted and groaned in her delicate fingers, but the door refused to yield. Her screaming mixed with sobs. For Thelana, the scene of a daughter and a father separated by a door was all too familiar, and when she looked at Emma again, weeping miserably, childishly, the Ilmarin was unable to harden her heart to it. A deep sorrow, whether for Emma or for herself, drained away her rage, her strength.

"There's still time," Emma repeated, in a kind of frantic mantra, pounding the door with her fists, pounding until collapsing against it. "Father, there's still time." She continued until her voice gave out and smoke, black as the ink from Mathias' inkwell, swirled about the doorframe. The scholar had immolated himself without uttering a sound.

Emma stood mechanically, her face a mess of hair and grief. She brushed at a tear and tried the handle again, burning her fingers. "Bring Grimosse," she said.

Thelana knew there was nothing to be done. "He's gone."

"No," said Emma. "Bring Grimosse."

"We'll go together," she answered, tugging at her robes.

As the two women made for the upper level, they could see the dull copper of men-at-arms. The intruders scurried across every available surface, bustling up and down stairs, a number of them, for reasons unapparent, clutching Emma's story books, tracking dirt and snow over loose pages of *The Epic of Thangar and Sint*.

Thelana's fist tightened against the jade hilt of her sword. They were to blame for Mathias' death, for the loss of Emma's only family. She felt a surge of hot blood once more, a need to kill everyone in the room, but, as if sensing her desire, Emma reached out. Her eyes turned dreamily between her dark lashes as she took Thelana by the hand into the cold night.

Xandr and Grimosse stood beyond the threshold with their wrists in knots. A pair of men-at-arms were heaving and swearing over the guardian's hammer. Emmaxis lay half-buried, fading against the pale snow, no one daring to touch it. Across the street, lights started to burn, heads poking from neighboring windows curious as to the goings-on. Knights were arriving from every avenue. Thelana's heart skipped. Unconsciously, her sword slid from her fingertips, ringing against the ice rimmed cobblestone.

She did not bother to see what strange hands were groping her backside. The ropes were coarse, cutting into her skin as they tightened, pinning her arms against her buttocks. Emboldened by her submissive state, a second soldier—a knight, she figured, by the finely embroidered look of his armor—approached from the front. His eyeballs rolled over her body. The other men-at-arms were no less observant, staring and snickering, sharing in the unexpected pleasure. In the heat of battle, Thelana had completely forgotten the taboos of civilization, and now she found herself wishing against all her nature for something—anything—to hide her shame. Noticing her sword, half-split into a bow, the knight's expression turned suddenly to outrage, remembering the men that were wounded, possibly killed, by her hand.

"You bitch!"

She clenched to receive his mailed fist, stomaching the blow without complaint, staggering while keeping to her feet. As he looked on in disbelief, she pounced, crushing his nose between her teeth. After some thrashing and howling, he tore away, clutching his face to staunch the flow of blood. Now the eyes were on him. He was humiliated, her shame overshadowed by his. Enraged, he threw a hand over the pommel at his hip.

"Do that and I'll reconsider!" Xandr warned. The Ilmarin looked vulnerable with his hands roped behind his back, his bare breast taking on a bluish hue in the cold night air, the cobblestones glazed with ice and snow looking hard beneath his bare feet. But his voice and the certainty in his eyes gave the knight pause.

"Consider what?"

"My stance on killing you," he replied. "See, I did not surrender to spare our lives, but to spare yours. Lay a hand on her again, and you die—the whole lot of you."

"You against all of us?" the knight replied. "I'd like to see you try."

"Grimosse," Xandr intoned, "show him."

The guardian growled, snapping the ropes with a twitch of his muscled arms. A number of soldiers cowered back. Others pressed forward, training their lances against the monster's throbbing torso.

"Hold off, Grimm." A delicate white hand eased the golem into submission. It was Emma. Thelana and Xandr had made such a show that the young girl was able to pass among them unnoticed. She proceeded to search the faces of the Delians for any she might recognize. Two of the younger men shuffled away fearfully.

"Who did this!" she cried. "Who's responsible here?"

A white destrier cut through the gathering, clopping softly before her. The rider's greaves and the pattern on his breastplate were familiar. But she did not seem to recognize the closed helm with the single spike—long as her forearm—extending from the forehead.

"I'm in charge," he said, his voice echoing weirdly from his faceplate. "And it would appear, considering my wounded men, that we should have listened to the king and had you executed."

"This is my home," she cried. "We've done nothing to warrant this intrusion. You know me, Duncan! We're not witches!"

He brandished the long sword fused to his copper glove, to the plates of his arm and shoulder. "My wife cannot bear to look upon me. My children flee from my face. The man they once knew as Duncan Greyoak is no more. Henceforth, you may call me, *Swordarm*."

As the men-at-arms led them away, Thelana turned back to the tower, watching the smoke rising through Emma's bower window as blackened bits of philosophy rained on the city.

14

TWO GENESES

*B*efore humans separated from the halfman by walking upright, before the avian learned to fly, before the merquid awakened to coral cities beneath the oceans, on a pinpoint of light in the sky, the Xexaz civilization was, ancient beyond measure. None can say from whence they came, what they looked like, or whether they evolved in this universe or the next, but that they looked to the same sun as we on Aenya. Scant mention of their kind exists in the annals of history, but what is known is hereto recorded:

The Xexaz were masters of the universe. No secret of the physical or the spiritual lay beyond their sphere of knowledge. It was during this final epoch of omniscience and immortality that their civilization fell into ruin. Having achieved all that a species can achieve, the Xexaz lost the will for life, which permitted a far lesser yet more ambitious race, the Septhera, to grow in power. The history of the Septhera is written in blood. Their society was one of carnage, where the strong devoured the weak, and the feeble-bodied and listless Xexaz were conquered before they could remember how wars were fought. Towering repositories of wisdom, built upon the *aeons, were laid to waste. Devices of science, greatly beyond the usurpers comprehension, were made awesome weapons of devastation. Devoid of wisdom or empathy, the Septhera left no trace of the elder species. What had been the Xexaz homeworld became a den for serpents, and that once-great race would hence become known as the Forgotten. This is the oldest record known to history and nothing further can be written of it.*

Though men of reason say otherwise, god-fearing acolytes will claim that the powers beyond sought to purge this evil from the universe. Whatever the cause, our shared star began to swell, and great plumes of fire reached across the void to smite the Septheran world. The sky turned red and orange and the air to flame, and all the waters of every sea and ocean and river boiled into the ether, and the mountains melted like candle wax. Countless species perished, but in an ark borrowed from their predecessors, the Septheran royals would continue to thrive, as would the lower castes attending them and the great saurian beasts of burden native to their homeland.

Sailing the void in a Forgotten vessel, as one might cross the Sea, the Septheran royals set their pitiless eyes upon civilization's cradle, now an ember in the darkness, a cinder consumed by swelling white fire—

Thump! Thump! Thump!

The door rattled, echoing dully about the cramped space. Emma jolted, thrown from the window where she watched a planet be consumed by fire into the dull reality of a water closet, the book nearly slipping from between her thighs into the straw-lined dung pit. Looking over her shoulder, she could make out a man's eye, poking between the weathered beams.

"Are you done in there?" a man griped from beyond the door.

"Ah—!" She stuffed the brittle pages under her dress. "Almost finished!"

Slouching to hide the book amid the folds of her robes, she went out into the hall. Having to relieve herself was no ruse, but she had been unable to resist the history once her business was done, was made powerless by the lure of knowledge, by the archaic lettering both alien and familiar to her, what she only recently discovered she could read.

Hoarfrost was as vast and hollow as she remembered it. But the quivering, whimpering girl marched before the king's presence no longer existed. *That* Emma lived a lifetime ago. Xandr, Thelana and Grimosse now stood where she had been tried, occasional silhouettes in the intermittent torchlight. A smooth mahogany table glittered with brass goblets and copper platters. There was whole roasted boar glazed with honey, with apple in mouth, and piles of steaming turkey legs in beds of chopped carrots, potatoes and ollyps. The aromas arrested Emma's senses, wetted her mouth and made her stomach protest. She was not like her traveling companions, could not go days without food, without real food, anyway. Her fears of subsisting on prison rations were quickly allayed, however, as they were brought before the king. They entered with hands bound, but were soon released and invited to sup at the table. Frizzbeard went so far as to summon his courtiers to clothe the Ilmar. Not knowing their custom, he believed to have caught them in an act of passion, and was all the more apologetic for it. Xandr's lordly samite vest and leggings looked uncomfortably snug, and Thelana, standing awkwardly beside him, was no better off, lost in the frills of a scullery maid, complete with apron and bonnet. Dressed as she was, the Ilmarin could pass for any peasant in the street. Emma never saw her so miserable, and was grateful for her own long robes, which Frizzbeard and the assembled host failed to recognize. Going unnoticed was, she surmised, her special talent.

King Frizzbeard was as fat as ever, his head like a bush in desperate need of pruning, overgrown with flame-colored hairs. What little was visible of his face was red like a raw steak. This was the man who'd robbed her of the life she so longed for—for the loving parents she could have had but never knew. *He* was responsible, she told herself, for Dak and Ilsa's deaths, and for Mathias also, whom she pitied now more than hated. She watched the king wet his beard with mead and imagined dashing across the table, to the large two-pronged fork in the roasted boar. If she were quick, she could skewer the king's jugular with it, if a neck could be found beneath that beard. But was he truly to blame for all of her sorrows, or the Delian people as a whole, who feared and hated anything they did not understand? Whatever the truth of it, she could not reconcile what she knew of the king with the jovial fool now seated on the throne.

"Enough with the formalities and the legalities!" he bellowed, much more loudly than was necessary, which left Emma wondering whether the king was deaf or close to it. "Let us talk of swords! Of bravery! Sir Greyoak, if you would—"

"Swordarm," Duncan corrected, his voice shivering from the grill of his helm.

"*Sword arm*, quite right," Frizzbeard said, too distracted by his chief man-at-arm's appearance to be angered by the interruption. "Terrible what's happened to you. But you must admit it'll make a good song. Now . . . where was I?" Sif, the warrior princess, leaned into his ear, but he waved her off. "Yes, of course—we must treat these three—er, four—as our guests, not our enemies!"

"Allow me to intercede, your Grace," Duncan said. "These two are in league with this witch, the selfsame you banished. And they brought this monster to our city also, no doubt a thing born of forbidden crafts." He gestured to the hooded, silent figure of Grimosse.

"Ah!" the king retorted, as if a clever thought suddenly came to him, "but look at *that hammer*, Duncan—a finer standard of the Thunderer I have yet to see! Do not forget the Trolls of Thralla, who aided the god when giants robbed him of his hammer."

Emma's focus shifted from the immense, bell-shaped weapon in the guardian's palm to the tapestry beside him. The standard was in gold stitching, the Sigil of Northendell seen on banners and shields and in miniature throughout the city, the hammer which was sold as toy, or trinket, and as a holy relic used by clerics. The resemblance was uncanny.

"This is no troll!" Swordarm insisted, forgetting protocol. "Surely, your Grace, the hammer is mere coincidence. We cannot go about distinguishing allies from enemies solely by the choice of their arms. Not to mention they killed two of my men!"

"Poppycock!" Emma recognized the aging knight from the hill overlooking the battlefield. He was still having trouble with his faceplate, holding it from slamming shut as he addressed the king. "Both are due for full recovery. Sir Melak suffered a mere flesh wound, and Sir Taz took an arrow to the eye, which is fortuitous as he hasn't got much brain to injure. He'll have trouble with his aim, perhaps, but shall live to defend the city again."

"Spoken like a true knight of Northendell, Sir Starvod," Frizzbeard said, waving Duncan away. "Besides, I know witches' consorts when I see them, and these are not! More like the girl was taken as a spoil of battle, as this other lass," the king added, eyeing Thelana lustily. "I know a man of my own heart when I see him!" He took a swig of mead and slammed it down, and with laborious effort, squeezed his buttocks from his throne, tottering to the other end of the long table to address Xandr. "Just look at that noble stature, that heroic build . . . and the *sword*, a weapon of the gods if ever there was one! Truly, this must be the Batal reborn."

A wave of groans and murmurs swept across the mead hall, evidence that not all, if any, of the men-at-arms shared the king's appraisal.

"Him!" an effeminate voice called from a dim corner. "You jest!" An ash-encrusted orb of embers—a single dying torch—knitted ribbons of smoke over a pale face.

King Frizzbeard rounded on him, his beard erupting like fire. "And what know you of battle, or of heroes, Aldric? Where were you when Zaibos called for blood at our gates? Where were you when the giant toppled our walls? Cowering in your bedchamber, no doubt, like a *woman*!" He spat the word, as if there could be no greater insult.

"I was . . . plotting," Aldric answered icily, his ornate-ly-patterned breastplate heavy atop his bony shoulders. "Would you have the future king endanger his life for the sake of . . . honor and glory? Can honor be spent? Can glory procure the forces needed to defend our fair city? Or conjure strategies to rid ourselves of this demonic Zaibos once and for all? Better that my brain remain secure behind our battlements, where my talents may be better spent, than to risk some errant missile from some fool's bow."

"And what talents are those, my son, to talk and talk, and bewitch men with talking? If I was not the wiser, I might think *you* in league with witches!" Frizzbeard moved his arm in an exaggerated arc to slap his forehead, like an actor overdoing his performance. "Would not that I, who fought so valiantly in my younger days, have lived to see the shame of it—a daughter who fights more bravely than a son!"

"Well," Aldric replied with a sneer, "you *do* know what they say. That she isn't yours—daughter of thunder . . . offspring of Strom." Despite the insult, Sif did not stir, nor betray any emotion in the slightest.

"'Tis better to be a cuckold, than father to a craven!" the king bellowed, stretching his arm about Xandr's shoulders. "Now then . . . come, come! Sit! Let us drink and be merry and sing songs of valor!"

With hesitation, Xandr lowered himself into a chair, saying nothing. The king moved close enough for their beards to intertwine, taking a swig of mead and pushing a goblet into Xandr's unwilling fist. "I've many children, you know—bastards the lot of them. Alas, of my rightful heirs,

Strom favors me only with maidens, as if I did not please him in battle, as if I did not slay a thousand bogrens with this hand . . . which reminds me, did I ever tell you about the time that I—?"

"Ahem!" Sif cleared her throat. "Perhaps now is not the best time, Father."

Frizzbeard was like a child reproached by his mother. "Oh, alright, but I never get to tell my stories!" He cleared his throat again, of a seemingly never-ending supply of phlegm. "And now to the business at hand. Tell me, son— why you have come here? And leave out no detail. I wish to hear everything."

With some reluctance, Xandr related his tale, and the king sat rapt, as if nothing could have delighted him more than hearing of the slaughter of merquid, of Hedonia's crumbling walls, of their daring, aerial escape from the giant caw. He was careful to leave out many particulars, saying nothing of the Serpent's Eye, or of their encounter with Emma. The more the king listened, the greater he showed his love for the Ilmarin, leaning in more closely, laughing more heartily, inquiring after the most outland-ish of details. He wanted to know how great was the caw's wingspan, and precisely how numerous the merquid had been, even going so far as to ask Xandr to mimic the nois-es they made when killed, a request Xandr pretended not to hear. And the king never bothered to challenge the truth of any part of it, though many listeners shook their heads in disbelief. As for Thelana's equally heroic feats, Frizzbeard showed no interest, and of the Ilmar's origins, he asked nothing.

When there was nothing more worth saying, the king raised his goblet with a guttural "Huzzah!" and the aging knights dutifully followed, downing their mead. Considerable chatter then passed between the assembled host, in praise of the Ilmarin's courage, and they drank to his honor. Only Duncan and Aldric remained impassive, their goblets untouched.

As the ruckus began to settle, Duncan moved to address the king. "Your Grace, what we have heard is well and good, but do you truly believe a single man can defeat this *thing*, when it hardly took notice of our defenses? I beseech you all, my king . . . my countrymen," he added, waving the long sword fused to his arm about the room. "Heed my words now if ever you have, for I alone have faced the monster and lived to speak of it, and I assure you it is no mere giant.

"It tore into my mind, made revelations to me of things I dare not speak of!" Swordarm quaked beneath his suit as he said this. "If anything, we should not be sitting idly, sharing stories and drinking. We should be rousing our soldiers, marching battalions into the mountains! Strom only knows its evil designs!"

There was another round of murmurs, much in agreement. Duncan Greyoak commanded the ears of the Delians, Xandr could see, and the recent encounter that had left him mutilated appeared to have elevated his status, equal, by the looks of many in the room, to that of Batal.

"Bold words," King Frizzbeard replied, his belch erupting like flames from a dragon's mouth. "I drink to you as well, Sir Knight, but do we dare forget the songs?"

"Sire," Duncan replied, "I fear I do not see the relevance—"

"*The Song of Strom!*" the king exclaimed, throwing his furrowed brow about the room. "All this—everything we've seen and heard this day—does it not only confirm what we have long, already known?" With a proud strut, Frizzbeard marched along the table, eyeing each and every man in turn. "If you do not know our lore, you do not deserve to drink at my table! Now, raise your goblets all, and listen to my song!"

Hoarfrost fell silent as the king's voice, emboldened by mead, rang out, powerful and deep. Xandr listened, as engaged as the king had been with their story.

> *I am wanting to arise and go forth singing*
> *hymns ancestral of our kindred lore.*
> *Lay ear to me and listen—*
> *hear my song and be inspired.*
> *Ages past my forefathers sang them,*
> *and my father as he carved his ax*
> *and I nipped my mother's teat.*
>
> *When the world was in its youth,*
> *there were but gods and giants*
> *and their wars were bloody, endless,*
> *until the day that Magmus, King of Giants,*
> *sent Peace, a Nymph, to the gods,*
> *who spoke of truce between gods and giants.*
>
> *One god and one giant were to meet atop Mount Krome,*
> *highest of mountains.*

Being bravest and strongest,
Strom the Thunderer, Red-Bearded,
Red-Knuckled,
set forth to meet Magmus, King of Giants.
They talked peaceably, dividing the world in
twain—
one half each for their kind.
But there was but a small patch,
upon which Hoarfrost stands,
which both giant and god claimed for their own.

As they could not agree on this small parcel,
Magmus, King of Giants, challenged Strom.
Each would drink his full, and whoever drank
more fully
would lay claim to this land.
So Magmus filled his cup—massive as a
mountain—
and drank until done.
But Strom the Thunderer, Mightiest of Gods,
Red-Bearded, Red-Knuckled,
said unto him,
Fool giant, who thinks I can be bested, drink you
so little?
So Magmus offered up his cup—massive as a
mountain—
which his sister Wizzeria hath made
from the stars for Strom to drink.
Strom drank from it, and drank and drank and
drank.
But when his belly was to bursting,
he saw that he had not drunk so much.

*Look you, sayeth Magmus, your cup is not yet empty,
you dranketh less than I, and so the disputed hill
is mine!*
*And Strom hung his head in shame, leaving from
the mountain.*

*Distraught as was the Thunderer,
he went down to the Open Sea,
to his brother Sargonus, White-Eyed, Foam-Haired,
and saw that Sargonus was deeply troubled.
My Sea! Sargonus declared,
The waters have fallen! Look you, Brother!
And when Strom looked, he flew into an awful rage,
knowing he had been deceived, and his cup
bewitched,
refilling from the Sea again and again as he
drank from it.
Outraged, Strom the Thunderer, Red Bearded,
Red Knuckled, took up his hammer
and flew in a storm of rage atop Mount Krome.
But the giants lay in wait for him, to ambush him.
THREE there were!
Lunestes, the Four-Armed, Whose Head Scrapes
the Stars, Brother to Magmus,
and Wizzeria, Hag, Bewitcher, Mother of Bogrens
and Horg, Sister to Magmus.
But Strom's fury could not be matched,
the battle lasting not days, not cycles, but seven
times seven years.
The heavens blazed and thundered from the din
of battle
and the earth trembled fearfully.*

Never was there such battle known,
and henceforth the world was torn asunder,
into the Light and into the Dark.
Magmus and Wizzeria were fallen,
their skulls crushed by the Thunderer's mallet,
and from Magmus' bones did the god fashion
Mountains,
and made he the Hills from Magmus' teeth,
and made he the River from the giant's blood,
and made he Men, and all the races of men kind,
from the god's own sweat,
and from Wizzeria's eye did he cast up the evil
moon, which we call Eon.
But Lunestes, Four-Armed, Whose Head Scrapes
the Stars, he let live,
binding the giant between earth and sky,
so that he may lift the greater moon to the heavens
and in eternal penance keep it,
so that oath-breakers and deceivers may look
upon the moon and be dismayed.

When the battle was won,
the giants of the world lay down in the earth,
fearing the Thunderer's wrath,
craven before Strom's wrath,
and there they remain to this day,
asleep in stone.

But weary from battle,
Strom the Thunderer, Mightiest of Gods, Red-
Bearded, Red-Knuckled,
lay down his hammer—

which neither god nor giant could lift—
atop the sacred plateau known as Strom's
Hammer.
And Strom went into the mountain and lay him-
self down,
to awake when giants come again to lay claim to
the world.

Emma had heard snippets of the song many times before, resonating from many a tavern, but never in its entirety. It embodied much of Delian society, she knew, but she found the tale to be long-winded and preposterous, the melody nearly non-existent.

When the king finished singing, he settled into his throne to empty another goblet of mead. It poured over his lips and dripped from the frayed wisps of his beard. The hall was thick with silence, until Aldric said, with a mocking tone, "And how exactly, Father, is that supposed to help us?"

"Silence," the king bellowed, froth flying from his lips, "lest I forbid you from speaking again!" He turned from his son, his brow dark with disappointment. "Don't you see? Certainly, you all can plainly see?" He eyed Xandr, clearly awaiting some sort of affirmation. "The giants have returned!" he exclaimed, brandishing a turkey leg, the same he used to demonstrate the hammer in the song. "They seek revenge upon the gods, and us as well, the offspring of Strom himself! The giant that attacked us moved up into the mountain, did he not? Doubtless, he is going to that place which is sacred to our people—*Strom's Hammer.*"

Emma's mind reeled. The contrast between Eldin's history—with regards to the beginnings of the world—and

the king's song, was considerable. And yet there were similar-
ities. Both spoke of cataclysm and rebirth and a world divided. Could there be a measure of truth to the ballad, waiting
to be discovered atop the peaks of the Pewter Mountains?

As if hearing her thoughts, Xandr addressed the
throne. "King Frizzbeard, are you trying to say that the
hammer is still there? The same used by Strom?"

The king stripped his meat to the bone before answering, in a slurred voice, "Of course! When I was a lad, my father took me to see it—the pilgrimage is the duty of every
king, to lay eyes upon the hammer."

Emma could not believe it. Of all she had learned from
Mathias and Eldin's history, there was nothing to suggest
that the gods were anything but nature given human attributes. Strom was no more than a phenomenon, thunder and lightning, a way to give men courage in battle.
How could the rumble and flashing in the sky be from a
weapon, sitting idly in the snow above them?

"We'll need to know where to find it," Xandr said.

Frizzbeard jumped to his feet, spilling a flagon across
the table. "Excellent!" he belched, laughing drunkenly
and slipping to the floor, to his daughter's embarrassment.

"Father," the princess entreated, helping him to his
throne, "will you permit me to escort a scouting party?"

"No, my child. Who'll sit by me, by my right hand,
if you go? Better you remain to defend our walls should
Zaibos return. Strom knows we cannot count on Aldric!
Besides, if this man here is what he claims . . . and, well, I
believe that he is . . . he'll not fail us. We'll send him with
a hundred men, a hundred of our best rangers, to kill or
capture the giant!"

"Your Grace, if I may intercede." Duncan cleared his throat. It was a tortured, painful sound, as if some mechanism in his throat was burned beyond usefulness. "The mountains are treacherous as is, and at high moon a man's blood can freeze in a passing. Here on the battlements, where we are best fortified, more than a hundred perished defending the city against that thing—good men, all of them. Any who braves those mountains, in search of the giant, will find only death."

"And this is why you are no hero," the king retorted. "A true hero would—"

"I'll go alone," Xandr interrupted. "Myself and my companions."

"We'll still need a guide," Emma said, to him and to the king, "your Grace," timidly curtsying.

"Low moon, high moon, bogrens, horg, giants, or woman's treachery . . . what does it matter to me?" It was Starvod, his mustache twitching under his rusty helm. "A true knight does what he must for the realm. I led the king when he was a boy and his father before him. I will show the Batal the way to Strom's Hammer. I'll need but a squire— these old bones don't carry loads like they used to."

King Frizzbeard cast a wandering eye about the room. "Take Duncan's squire, then."

A helmet fell noisily to the floor and a boy came chasing after it. Emma could not keep from smiling. Ovulus was as she remembered him. His eyes white with panic, he looked anything but heroic.

15

REVELATIONS

If you stare long enough into fire,
you may see past and future.

—Kjus

From the precipice, he watched Aenya unfold. Hills meandered down and down, spotted with fir trees, green on white. Rooftops bunched like mushrooms, wisps of gray rising from their chimneys, audacious settlements fitting the palm of his hand. In the silvered arms beyond, mountain faces turned into smooth, geometric shapes, into walls. Northendell spread along the base, a rocky shore against a tide of ice and snow, a sprawling labyrinth crowned by Hoarfrost, built on high of wood and straw, the upended longboat of Strom. Further south, a golden thread cut across the blue-white tundra, the mighty Potamis, lifeblood of the world, which ran from the Pewter Mountains to the Sea. And somewhere in-between, Xandr could make out the hazy outline dividing land from sky, the Mountains Ukko, where, a decade ago, a boy of fourteen fled from home.

If we die here, so far from home, will our bones grow into roots? You never taught me, Queffi.

"It's ready," she said, her voice clouding the air.

Beneath her many layers of pelts and a woolen overcoat, Thelana could have been a stout woman. Only her face was recognizable to him. But even that small part of her was changing, her windswept strand of auburn hair turning stiff with frost, her lips altercating between shades of purple, her cheeks and nose going from a ruddy bronze to cherry red. On a less somber occasion, he might have laughed. But nothing could sully the beauty of her pale emerald eyes, the seat of the soul, eyes that searched and doted on him, and waited for him. On the night of their capture, she had been shameless with her fears, and he'd longed to comfort her ever since. But what could be said? She was much too clever for hollow words, for false hopes. There was no confidence to be had in the long cold trek, only an oppressive sense of doom.

"Come on," she said, "the fire." He felt the weight of her gloved hand on his arm and followed. It was their first night on the mountain. With Starvod's guidance and the aid of the king's horses, they had made good progress, but as the pass narrowed and grew steeper, and the terrain threatened to break their mounts' fetlocks, they were forced to continue afoot, making camp when the sun began to dip below the moon.

The wind did not allow for tents. Their camp was little more than a fire pit, a tripod and a kettle, with rolls of mixed furs to sleep in. It was set in a rocky niche beneath an oblique, glassy overhang, which helped to shield against the frigid gale.

As if sensing the depths of his dour mood, Thelana offered him a smile. He clasped her gloved hands in his and drew her close, sharing his warmth. A fierce flame was twisting and changing shape between them, casting golden ellipses across the faces of Emma, Starvod and Ovulus.

"Heresy!" Starvod's face was pink and shrunken, like a rotting, mustachioed peach.

"It's not heresy—it's the truth!" she insisted. "The world is born of the sun and will die of the sun. It is written!" Emma was looking more animated than usual. She was up on her knees, glowering at the aging knight, her overlong sleeves flapping in the wind.

"Blasted sun-worshipper," he grumbled, tearing a piece of salted pork with what remained of his teeth. "I would have liked a Delian witch instead."

"Do you believe the song, then?" Emma asked. "That this mountain's made from a giant's bones?"

"Magmus' bones," he offered. "You have faith in the old songs, don't you, lad?"

Ovulus was huddled beside her, shivering in his armor, his expression vacant. "D-d-don't look at me," he managed. "All I know is it's cold!"

"Stupid boy!" Starvod rapped his mailed knuckles against the youth's helmet. "No wonder they call you *Sir Obvious!*"

"Hey, I'm n-n-not *that* obvious!" he protested. "And don't call me stupid. My father was Sir Edmund, Edmund of Lakshmir!"

"If you'd be a man-at-arms, best start acting like one."
He shook his head with disapproval, his mustachio swaying
this way and that. "Now help me get this stew going if you
don't want to die in your sleep—a full belly keeps the blood
from icing," he said, scooping balls of snow into the kettle.

Looking at Ovulus, Xandr was reminded of another
soldier in the dawn of his manhood, a Hedonian. Finias
was just as bald about the chin, just as uncertain and eager to prove his worth to his countrymen, before dying
alongside them. Xandr prayed to never see another young
man stare into him when the Taker comes, to never have
to witness the hope and ambition of youth wash from a
boy's eyes.

"Grimm brings sticks," Grimm reported. The ground
crunched under enormous gilded boots as the golem
walked over to them, dumping the bundle from his hands,
the flame crackling and flashing and spitting embers.
Starvod stirred fitfully, never bothering to acknowledge
the monster. His squire was no less squeamish, but could
not resist stating the obvious. "It speaks!"

"Well, of course he does," Emma said. "Doesn't
everyone?"

"But it's a . . . a troll!" Starvod objected.

"*He* is no troll! Grimm is our guardian. I'm teaching
him to be more . . . personable." Ovulus was lost for a reply, as was Starvod.

In the sky, bands of reds and pinks were darkening
to indigo, and the silver-veined outcropping under which
they sat turned opaque. Embers popped and spiraled upwards, mingling amid the emerging stars and moons that
were coming into focus.

"Emma." Xandr watched her between absences in the fire. "You've had time, I hope, to understand it, to find some clue as to what we're after?"

She shifted onto her knees, like a woman heavy with child, her eyes drifting tenderly to her belly.

· "It's alright," he said. "You're safe here."

Her face growing wild with excitement, Emma reached between her breeches, producing, to Starvod's and Ovulus' consternation, the *Ages of Aenya*.

"A book!" the squire exclaimed.

"A forbidden book, you dolt!" the mustachioed man-at-arms declared. "I know it when I see it! Nothing honest needs so many words!"

"There's so much here," she admitted, ignoring the knight and his squire as she thumbed through the pages, "but what is most remarkable, is the beginning. The giant isn't mentioned directly," she added, her raven locks wreathed in embers as she leaned across the flame, "but I have a guess as to what he is."

Like the boy he had been, a pupil full of questions, Xandr could scarcely conceal his eagerness. Would she finish the lesson his mentor started? Would his life find new purpose from what she was to reveal? It seemed strange, impossible even, that one so innocent could show him the way, and part of him resented her for it. He had traveled too many roads and spilled too much blood.

"It all began with the Forgotten . . ."

She spoke for a passing, describing the expanding, exploding sun, the white hot fires turning the world of the Septhera to ashes—her eyes aflame as she related the tale—and of the ark sailing the void of stars. Starvod and

Ovulus listened incredulously. From the looks on their faces, the story seemed no more plausible than the *Song of Strom.*

"The Septhera came to our world millennia ago, when Aenya was covered in water, when merquid cities flourished across both hemispheres. Of the land, Eldin says, there dwelled two races, the halfmen and their progeny, proto-humans."

"Wait." Xandr held a hand to her lips. "Who were these . . . proto-humans?"

Emma glared at him, as though the answer could not be more obvious. "Well," she stammered, "we are, of course."

Thelana's face twisted with revulsion. "Do you mean to tell me that we have . . . some relation to halfmen?"

Catching on, Starvod and Ovulus both cried out in protest. "We are born from the sweat of Strom!" Starvod said matter-of-factly. "And Delians from his armpits!"

Emma stood abruptly, looking to smack him with her book, but she directed her gaze, instead, toward the Ilmar. "You may take heart in knowing that before the Septhera, men and women everywhere lived as your people do. Afterwards, humans became slaves, bred to be devoured or to fight. It was the first Dark Age, and into this age, the Batal was born.

"The Batal," she continued, "changed everything. He proved that men could be strong, could fight their oppressors. After centuries of revolution and warfare, the last of the Septhera were destroyed and an age of peace ensued. A golden age. But no victory comes without cost. The price paid for freedom was man's innocence. In his desperation, man had become much like his old master, having learned to kill, to subjugate, and make war. There were some who preached a return to the old ways, to a life of simplicity, but those voices were drowned by the masses, by those who hated and feared other races. The peace did not endure. A mere decade after the last Septheran stronghold was taken, men turned against men."

A terrible hollow sensation welled up from the depths of Xandr's being. He could not help but feel some affinity for the people of the tale, having looked through the Serpent's Eye himself. It was impossible to believe his struggle against the snake men had not occurred cycles ago, but thousands of years in the past, and it grieved him terribly to learn how briefly prosperity had lasted after his sacrifice.

"To achieve victory in these civil wars, those who hungered for power sought relics of power, tools the Septhera themselves wrested from the Forgotten. They called themselves the Zo, after the Goddess of Life, and when they had conquered all of Aenya, a second golden age began."

The further they delved into the history, the more agitated Thelana seemed, until she looked ready to pounce through the fire. Sitting and listening had never been her strong point, Xandr considered. She was a woman of action, a huntress, a fighter. "What does all this have to do with the giant?"

"Still your mind and listen, Thelana!" Emma snapped. "Remember the expanding sun? What destroyed the Septheran's world?"

"W-wait," Ovulus interjected, raising his hand. "How did the sun destroy the whole w-w-world again? I mean . . . it's just a ball of f-fire? I didn't understand that part."

"I'll explain later, if I must, but for now let me speak." Emma sighed and continued, pressing her palms against the heat of the flame. "Now the star, our sun, still hungered to devour worlds. Just as before, it grew, and Aenya was to come into its circumference, just as the Septheran world had been. The Zo, who achieved far greater understanding than the reptilian brains ever could, did not sit idle and wait for doom—no, they took action.

"They built, deep in the core," she hesitated for emphasis, as if she were to reveal a thing more unbelievable than mountains made of giant's bones, "a *machine.*"

"What kind of machine?" Starvod asked, tugging at the gray white hairs of his face.

"A machine to move the planet away from the sun," she managed. In a trance, she flipped through the pages, until coming to a sketch. It was a kind of map surrounded by stars, Xandr realized, but its only feature was a range of mountains and a line drawn from it, reaching down to the center of the circle.

"Something went amiss," she said, "and here the historian, or maybe it's just my understanding of it, becomes unclear. It would seem that Aenya drifted through the void, coming into confluence with Infinity."

The gloom pressed in, confining them to darkness, to the black, star-filled void above and below, more stars than any man could count if he lived a thousand years, the world they knew becoming as remote as the Septheran horizon. The fire was their only constant, eternally erupting to form ever more suns, and she was like a goddess at the center of it, weaving worlds between her lips and fingers.

"Long ago, our world *turned*," she explained, "like meat on a rotisserie, you see." She took up the tongs, moving the salted pork over the fire. "Once, the sun warmed each hemisphere in turn. Before, the desert known as Ocean was entirely water, like the Sea. And the Dark Hemisphere," she said, "was not dark. Sunlight allowed for plants and animals to flourish. And then this rotation stopped." She pulled the tongs away. One side of the meat was crisp and black.

"It burned!" said Ovulus.

"Yes. Aenya became fixed in place, by the greater moon that held it. With a new moon broaching our sky, our world was now separated, into perpetual night and endless day. Where the sun touches the West, the land is scorching hot. In the East—frigid. This was the end of the second golden age," she whispered, her face vanishing, veiled by her sleeves, "the end of the Zo, nearly the end of it all."

"The Great Cataclysm," Thelana murmured.

"Precisely," Emma replied. "Millions perished, beast and man. The waters boiled away, leaving the merquid little more than bleached carcasses in the sand. Only the gill settled in what we call the Sea remained.

"In the lands of dawn and dusk, life continued to thrive, but this narrow divide, this hospitable middle, could not sustain the masses. There was . . . warfare, beyond anything Aenya has known, then or since. As Eldin put it, *there can be no worse bloodshed than when men vie with men for want of food.*

"Wars of attrition have no victors, it is said. Starvation was ever-present. Only a few held onto the middle ground—our great ancestors—and in time they became prosperous, founding great cities—Hedonia, Northendell, Shemselinihar . . . Those ousted from the light sought new means of survival, digging into the depths of the dark hemisphere, becoming a new species, horgs and bogrens.

"I believe," Emma added, her attention on Starvod and Ovulus, "that for a very few, the wars never ceased, but persisted through the ages . . . until the reason was lost to history. Year after year, we fight our ancient cousins for the sake of battle alone. It makes sense that after so many generations, we should come to not only tolerate the killing, but rely on it, as tradition."

When she was finished speaking, Emma folded into her robes like a shadow, exhausted. No one spoke until the sun was eclipsed, the turquoise moon hanging bright in the sky.

"I don't know about you people," said Starvod, "but I prefer the Song of Strom!"

"It's not a story. It's the truth!" Emma asserted. "How does your silly song explain anything? It does nothing but inflate your already overblown pride!"

Xandr sat quietly as their arguing became an indecipherable cacophony. There was a gulf between Emma's mind and the rest of theirs. In Ilmarinen, she would have been a keeper of the highest order, and yet she was little more than a child. Even with Quasil's teachings, he was at a loss for words. It was no wonder Mathias had shut himself away, for how could the Delians, so proud in their ignorance, not have thought him mad?

"Enough!" Xandr cried. "What you've said is well and good, but you've not yet given us the answers we need.

You've not explained to us what this giant is . . . or why it's come to our world."

Fingering her bottom lip, Emma pointed to Grimosse. The guardian remained impassive but for its continual, toothy grin.

"*He* was built by my father to achieve immortality," she said. "Mathias believed that by transferring his consciousness into an invincible body, he might cheat death. But the knowledge to fashion such a body did not come from imagination alone, but was borrowed, just as the Zo borrowed from the Septhera, and the Septhera from the Xexaz. The giant, I believe, is a golem made by the Ancients."

So it was as Xandr suspected.

Starvod snatched the burned meat from her tongs, declaring, "So the only ones who've ever originated anything, were these Forgotten, am I right?"

"I—I suppose so."

"And so it's safe to assume," he went on, coiling his mustache about his forefinger, "that nobody really knows anything about these so-called Forgotten, because, as you say, they're forgotten? Correct?"

She nodded, her brow wrinkling.

"But—" he argued, "and *here's* the rub—how can we be certain they lived at all, if we've already forgotten them? Ah? Ah?" He crossed his arms with a smug face.

Emma was too baffled to reply, allowing Starvod time to gloat, but it was Thelana who cut-in. "So the giant is like Grimosse?"

"Only more," Emma replied. "He is what Mathias hoped to become. In Gloomwood, when Horde possessed me, I heard the voices in its mind, speaking to me . . .

showing me things, so many unimaginable, unthinkable things . . . I can't say what it all means."

"So then why is he climbing the mountain?" Starvod asked.

"To g-get to the Hammer of Strom, of course," Ovulus answered. Everyone looked at him, puzzled, but he merely stared back, equally puzzled. "Isn't it w-where we're going?"

"Grimm has hammer," the golem muttered, startling the men-at-arms. "Need hammer? Grimm has."

Placing a hand on the monster's shoulder, Emma gave him a look of sympathy, like a sister might her dim-witted sibling, and then turned sharply to her detractors. "Strom, is, a, *myth!*"

Without ceremony, the old knight stood, brushing icicles from his mustache. "Bah! You're all loony, the whole lot of you, and I still say the Song of Strom's a better story."

Xandr stared through the fire, knowing that it was he and he alone, who was meant to unravel this knot of myth and history. He remembered his mentor's teachings, how truth was found in all stories. Out of darker passages of memory, he recalled Brother Zoab, from when, together, they stared at constellations and spoke of a Wandering God.

Horde is the Wandering God come to destroy the world. The Ilmar guarded the secret for thousands of years and now Xandr—as Batal—would have to act upon it. But how was he to stop such an otherworldly thing, when he did not even know its purpose? Could QuasiI have told him, or Zoab, if they'd lived? The *Ages of Aenya* offered no more answers than they, and its failure to do so infuriated him, made him want to tear the book from Emma's grasp to let it smolder.

Or was no answer given simply because there were none to give? Was it that raising him to become the Batal was but a vain attempt at hope? Both the Xexaz and the Zo, despite their godlike wisdom, were powerless to prevent their own extinctions. *And we are next in line.* It was no wonder Eldin's history ended as it did, its last page black with ink stains, revealing but a lone, solemn shape . . .

16

THE HERMIT

Silver-veined walls rose to their left as the world unraveled to their right, firs clinging to the hillsides, tiny as basil leaves, houses like pebbles across the base of the mountain. The ground was a perilous mix of slick ice and ankle-deep sludge. Every step seemed higher and steeper than the one before. They ascended to perches of twisting rock and precarious footholds, crevices hidden beneath the blue-white surface catching their boots like pincers. One hasty step could mean a broken foot, or worse, a fatal fall. The path narrowed as they climbed, sometimes receding entirely, so that only the wall remained, angling to push them toward empty sky.

Emma thanked the gods that it was not her place to lead them. It was the Batal who chose whether to go forward or turn back, to risk a dangerous crossing or seek a safer route. Rarely were these decisions made without argument. But despite his eagerness to ascend, Xandr more often than not accepted Starvod's advice, avoiding places where the ice looked too thin or the passage too narrow.

By mid-moon, level ground became a rarity, until nothing remained but sheer rock. They circled back, descending what they so tiredly had climbed earlier that day. Xandr profaned the mountain as they did so, despite Starvod's assurances that the giant was simply too massive to take the path they were on, that they were certain to reach Strom's Hammer before him.

There was no rest to be had in the days that followed. The mountain seemed to go higher and higher, endlessly, as if to the starry heavens, and the air grew thinner and colder. Whatever they could see of Aenya was lost to a gray haze of clouds. By the fourth day, their voices were stolen by the howl of the wind, so speech was abandoned in favor of gestures, at least when they were climbing.

When no safer purchase could be found, when it was understood that trailing back might cost them a day's trek, they continued vertically, with plodding, delicate movements, anxiety swelling in Emma's throat. They crouched on all fours. They formed chains of helping arms. They hugged the rock like one might an infant its mother, prayers billowing from their lips that the mountain embrace and keep them. Emma mostly dreaded the broken precipices, rifts wide as the avenue she grew up on. Nothing but pale sky yawned below her feet, and she was expected to simply walk over it—to jump even. One misstep, one failing ledge, and she'd be gone. The very thought screwed up her insides, shook her so violently and made her so dizzy, she feared to lose balance. *Why? Why in Strom's surly beard did I agree to this? I am not meant for adventures!* After all, she was not like her ravens, could not take to the air effortlessly as they did, though she often dreamed of it. Despite

her envy, she could not change who she was, could not
become like Thelana, who hopped from one precarious
outcropping to another as surefooted as a mountain goat,
shoving Emma's buttocks when the Delian impeded her,
catching Emma's boot whenever it started to slip.

Higher they went, beyond the point of reason, where
no sane man would think to tread, where the air was difficult to breathe and the wind combative. Once, shimmying
across a ledge the length of her sole, her cloak billowed
up like a sail and before she could think to scream, she
was groping at empty space. The next thing she knew,
Grimosse's palm was closed firmly about her arm, each
of his four fingers the thickness of her wrist and, for a
terrifying instant she was suspended in his grasp, flailing helplessly. One look into his beady, all-black eyes was
enough to still her heart. He would never allow her to be
harmed—she could be certain of it.

The cold was another matter entirely—a slow, methodi-
cal killer even the golem could not defend her against. The
wind was like a scythe, relentlessly cutting through their
trappings, freezing the marrow in their bones. Sinking her
leg into the sludge was always a danger. Moisture could
build up in her boots and turn her feet to ice, to dead flesh.
To Emma and her countrymen, the effects of high moon
in the Pewter Mountains were terrible, but familiar. For the
Ilmar, it was insufferable. Whenever they found a stretch of
rock to rest upon, Thelana balled up in her furs, and when
Emma's eyes met hers, there was no animosity between
them, only the kinship born of the need to share warmth.

When the moon waxed fully across the sun, which happened often in that part of the world, they huddled closely

to one another, the wind battling their efforts to sustain a flame. And in the narrow ellipses of light, Emma labored further into the *Ages of Aenya*. She read of extinct tribes, of kings and heroes and obscure words that became a jumble in her mind, preoccupying her dreams. But there was no mention of Horde. She could hardly turn the pages in her gloves, but without them, she could not keep her fingers from trembling, from tearing the delicate papyrus.

After days of grueling, treacherous climbing, and with nights growing longer and colder and offering little sleep, hopelessness began to set in. She could see it on all of their faces. Felt the truth of it herself. Despite her fascination with the Ancients, translating the runes became exhausting work, and she even doubted its worth. *How much can it help, anyway? We're off to face a giant, not a schoolteacher.* Of all the companions, Ovulus made the most sense, and it frightened her. The boy put questions to her no one else had bothered to ask, like whether the giant could be killed by any of their weapons, or whether he could ever understand their speech.

"Have you been eating?"

Lifting her face from Orath's Remarkable Aqueduct System, she met Xandr's sullen eyes. He looked so little like the wild man she had seen through the cell wagon door. His beard was white with frost and his flowing mane was tucked under layers of animal hide, yet he exuded the same power, still made her wet between the thighs. Thinking hard for something clever to say, Emma heard herself mumble stupidly, and then the words came to her.

"That stiff-as-a-shoe pita?" She found the 'p' in 'pita' painful to form with her cracked lips. "Think I'd rather go hungry."

He looked far from amused. "Force it down if you have to. You'll need to be strong."

"I'm all out of strength, to be honest." She motioned her wind-burned cheeks into a smile. Over his shoulder, she could see Thelana, swaddled like a newborn, her eyes half-open. Sleep was becoming elusive despite their exhaustion. Or was she spying on them?

"There's plenty to drink, at least," he said.

Her fingers wrapped around an icicle, but she didn't feel like sucking on it—had no desire to feel the water burn her lungs. Besides, she hungered for something other than food and drink, or knowledge of the Ancients. "Xandr," she whispered, "if we fail to do what we've set out to . . . I mean, if we can't stop it—"

He hushed her, his finger on her lips. That one simple touch was enough, electrifying her. She pined for him, for his warmth against her every particle. Would that she had the courage to express that sentiment, but even in the face of world-ending catastrophe, she was craven, and despised herself for it.

A pallid sun emerged warily across an expanse of icy blue, looking as though it, too, would rather be sleeping. The mountain was a barren wasteland, without a twig to be found, nor a single bit of green, and yet there were vistas of dreadful beauty—vivid rock formations adrift in the ether, vapors flowing all around like running water that, in the dawn and at dusk, changed from white and gray to fiery oranges and yellows. It was what looked like morning in the Pewter Mountains, and Emma managed to pack up her sparse supplies, a rope and a tinderbox and a package of salted meats, and wordlessly set out.

A dull ache permeated her thighs, and her feet felt no longer a part of her, but like lifeless stumps attached to her ankles. On more than one occasion, Grimosse had offered to carry her, but she refused him. The thought of being cradled like an infant made her feel weak and pathetic. Since no one else, Thelana especially, was given favored treatment, she resolved to walk until unable to, accepting that, afterward, she might never walk again. At least, in Northendell, no one questioned missing toes or fingers, extremities turned black and hard and lifeless.

They ascended a slippery hill to a wide plateau, the translucent surface refracting the sun with icy, bluish, luminous hues. If Emma had gods to thank, she would have thanked them now. Starvod, who had made the journey with the king decades before, suddenly remembered the place and was overcome with excitement, taking the lead from Xandr. They crossed over the glazed elevation and Emma could see the divide cutting across it like a frozen, deep-set riverbed. Icicles had formed along the ridge like crystal teeth, weeping droplets of water where the sun glared off of them.

"This is where the Potamis begins," Starvod explained. "During low moon, the ice melts and flows down this way. The great river forms where the streams join below. Any higher and we'll be over the clouds, in the hall of the gods."

"And that is where the hammer is?" Thelana asked, her voice weak, almost lost to the whistle of the wind through the rocks.

"Aye," Starvod said. "Shouldn't be more than a day now, maybe by tonight. This is the Gate of Kings—no other way to Strom's Hammer but through here."

Xandr did not seem to share the knight's confidence. "Are you sure? I see no sign of the giant."

"We must have beaten him here," Starvod answered him. "He's much too big to have come our way. Come the morrow, we'll be sitting at the top, waiting for him!"

Xandr gave no reply, turning away in search of something, Emma could only guess at what. That was when she noticed it, plain as a fly in milk, a dark blot in the sky. All along the base of the hill, there were lines, circles, and interlocking ellipses. It could not have been a natural phenomenon, but was more than art. The angles were too perfect, too meticulously etched into the rock. Even in Northendell, stonemasons needed some knowledge of mathematics, and she knew enough to recognize the lines as a kind of geometry. Had she seen them before, in her stepfather's study?

She called out, her mouth dry, laboring to be heard. "Um . . . does anyone else see that?"

"It looks like a m-man!" Ovulus blurted.

Seated casually atop a crop of boulders, they could see him, aged beyond belief, his beard in his lap, white as the snow around him, his head bald as the mountain above the tree line.

"By Strom!" Starvod exclaimed, lifting his faceplate to gape, "a hermit. I hear tell they live in the mountains, but this is unsung—a man living this far!"

The hermit did not appear to notice them, but continued to sit, his eyes half-closed as if he were only pretending to sleep, or in a trance, or dead and frozen stiff.

"Eldin!"

Starvod turned to Xandr, his mustache twitching on his bewildered face. "You *know* this man?"

"Wake up, Eldin!"

The man's eyes fluttered like a moth's wings. His expression, if one could be discerned upon that ancient, weathered face, was of annoyance. "Go away, if you please."

"But it's me!" Xandr exclaimed. "Don't you recognize— No, of course you wouldn't. You don't look quite the same either. But I'd know those damnable circles anywhere."

"You . . . you know about my circles?" the hermit replied. He was like a man carved into the rock, a fixture upon the mountain's face suddenly coming alive.

"Of course, you old bastard—now come down here. We need your help."

"Who, exactly, is we?" the man asked, his voice ringing surprisingly from his emaciated body, his accent so foreign, so different from the common tongue, Emma first thought he spoke a different language, the sharp inflections reminding her of the Zo.

"I am Xandr . . . I am *the Batal*."

The hermit stood uncertainly, his knees wobbling like a newborn fawn's, looking to collapse at any moment. "D-do we know each other?"

"Know each other?" Xandr repeated. "We spent a fortnight in a Septheran pit!"

"A Septheran pit, did you say?"

"Tell me, truthfully, are you Eldin or not?"

The man nodded. "That is my . . . *true* name, the name given to me by my father. But if you know who *I am* . . .," he said tiredly, brushing the icicles from his beard with spidery fingers, "we must have met in my future, which would of course be your past, which would mean that you, too, travel through space-time."

Eldin? The prophet? Here of all places? Without knowing how it could be, Emma accepted the situation and stepped forward, the *Ages of Aenya* tight against her bosom. "Excuse me, sir, but I believe I am reading your book."

"M-my . . ." he stammered, looking away. "Don't show me that! Put it away, my dear, put it away quickly!"

"But why?"

"I've not finished it yet!"

Sir Ovulus lowered the grill from his face. "This is all very c-c-confusing."

The hermit's annoyance seemed to grow. "Look, you people . . . there's a *reason* I'm hiding up here!" He paused, breathing hard and long, gathering strength to continue, "I'm trying not to interfere with history! I am only an observer!" He paused again. Emma waited anxiously, gooseflesh prickling her from head to toe, forgetting the cold, the exhaustion, everything. "Would you have me jeopardize the future? For all we know, the whole of the universe could be destroyed!"

"But we need your help," Xandr insisted. "We're chasing this giant, this thing that calls itself Horde, and it seems to be going somewhere called Strom's Hammer."

"Really?" Eldin said. "How very interesting."

Xandr reddened with rage. "Will you help us or no?"

"I . . . I can't," the hermit answered. "I am only supposed to observe. I moved into this body, at this time, to witness something remarkable. In fact, there's very little life left in me—I'll soon be escaping through the angles, so whatever it is you're looking for must be," he glanced around curiously, "over there."

There was nothing but the flat surface of the cracked, icy plateau, and a lone, snow covered hill not more than thirty paces ahead. *Just a hill*, Emma thought, and yet it wasn't. Betraying its size and weight, the entire mass turned to face them, clumps of snow tumbling from it, and she let out a low scream as the book slipped to her ankles. Ovulus tried to free his sword, realized that it was frozen in its scabbard, and tripped, falling on his face. The hill was walking fast now, closing the gap between them. Its eyes were deep-set furnaces, ablaze with churning fire. Before anyone could even move, it spoke, the voice cutting through the whistling wind as if there could be no other sound in the world. Many voices speaking as one.

STATE THE PURPOSE.

17

THE THING THAT SHOULD NOT BE

*To know immortality is to know infinite
death. That is not beauty or joy which
does not perish. To live is to struggle and
to make choices against that struggle.*

—Kjus

Emma's mind failed to process what it was seeing.
The giant was as tall as three men and of equal
girth. Its flesh—if flesh it could be called—was
slick and tar-like, and so black that it absorbed the light.
It was a mass of pulsing, hulking muscle, yet otherworldly, ethereal. When it moved, it was like something far
heavier than even something of its size implied—when
its elephantine feet met the ground, the mountain
trembled.

Hundreds of voices, of varying pitch and volume,
sounded again from that place where a face or a head
should have been. STATE THE PURPOSE.

Thelana moved by nature—knowing but to fight to survive—reaching for bow and arrow. Across from her, shifting its hammer from hand to hand, Grimosse stood, his beady eyes betraying no emotion other than a readiness for action. Only Xandr did not hesitate, crossing into the giant's shadow without an inkling of fear—incredibly, Emma thought—unraveling his great sword from its shroud. The men-at-arms of Northendell, meanwhile, seemed to vanish.

The Ilmar and their golem were preparing for battle, but Emma knew their efforts to be wasted, that they could no more influence the being that stood before them than an ant could wrestle with a mammoth. She had known it since Gloomwood, but had been afraid to admit it, to the Ilmar or to herself. If anything could be done, it was a task for her alone. If Emma could touch the mind of a god and survive, she could do so again.

Come on, Emma, this is the reason you've been studying. You must not fear.

She clenched her eyelids, her lashes tight on her cheeks, as if not seeing that awful throbbing mass might bolster her courage.

I do not fear.

Her boots crunched the hard snow as she moved ahead of Xandr, the book outstretched in her arms like a talisman, the wind perusing the open pages, undecided between MCXVII and MCXVIII. Each word was a rune of protection, the leather binding itself a shield. Or so she hoped. All her focus was on the history, her sanity walled up by knowledge, and in that moment, whether the air was cold or scorching, she could not have guessed.

I do not fear.

Giving a tremulous curtsy, she addressed the thing in words she did not know she knew. "We humbly request an audience with you," she found herself saying.

Without a hint of intent or emotion, the measured voices came again. STATE THE PURPOSE.

"What's it saying?" Thelana had grown tense, her fingertips flushing, the string of her bow warped like a broken lute. Emma could see how badly she wanted to shoot—would have shot at it—if not for the fear they all shared.

"It asks what we're doing here . . . I think . . . what we want. No, it can't be that simple . . . it's seeking to know, the purpose of, of everything."

"What in the Goddess' name is that supposed to mean?" Thelana barked.

"Please! Lay down your weapon for a moment. Give me a chance to communicate." Emma lifted her head again, her eyes soaking up the dark mass. It was less a physical being and more an absence in the sky, she realized, and in thinking that her stomach pitched with doubt and uncertainty.

Again a voice that seemed not to belong to her came forth from her lungs. "Stranger from beyond the void, we are but lowly mortals, and do not comprehend. Tell us, so that we might answer: what do you mean by, 'state the purpose'?"

The giant's shadow bled over the pale snow, giving her an unnerving sense of smallness, of insignificance. For a time, she feared he did not hear her, that no answer would return, but its brain was buzzing like a hornet's nest—she could feel it. WHAT DOES IT MEAN TO EXIST? it dead-panned, its indifference somehow terrifying.

"You mean you don't know? How can you not? It's easy, even a child knows."

THERE ARE TOO MANY VOICES. CONFLICTING THEORIES.

"To exist is to *feel* . . ." she answered matter-of-factly, ". . . to love."

DEFINE LOVE.

Love? On long, lonely nights atop her stepfather's tower, pining for what she could never have, she pondered the question, and now knew the answer. "Love is connection. To another. Two together."

WE ARE HORDE. WE ARE CONNECTED.

"That isn't the same. Horde is one. Love is connection and separation."

THIS IS INSUFFICIENT. THIS IS A PARADOX.

"No, it isn't." She did not know from where this font of courage was coming, but faced with that awesome other-worldly intellect, death no longer seemed to matter. Thoughts of Xandr and Thelana, and even Grimosse, anchored her mind against the tide of insanity.

HORDE EXISTS FOR THE PURPOSE.

"What is that purpose?" She gazed long and fretfully into the fiery recesses of its eyes, but when no sound came from it, she approached from another angle. "If you travel across the void between worlds, how is it that we find you here, on this mountain, afoot?"

FOUR HUNDRED AND FOURTEEN YEARS IN ORBIT. SOLAR FLARE UPON REENTRY, ANTI-BOSON

FIELD COMPROMISED, RECALCULATED COLLISION COURSE.

If you can be damaged, you can be killed . . . But she regretted the thought, and tried to bury it, certain the construct could see into her mind. "I don't . . . I don't understand . . . what do you seek to find here that you cannot elsewhere?"

PURPOSE CAN ONLY BE FOUND AT THE ORIGIN. AT CREATION. THE PAST IS TO BE REALIGNED.

Whatever the meaning of its answer, Emma was certain it boded ill.

Xandr was shaking her now, his voice a distant, hazy sound, a shout through a long tunnel. For some time she did not, could not answer him, separated from her immediate reality, her mind one with Horde's, until the words reached her, each syllable dropping in turn in her ears.

"What . . . does . . . it . . . want?"

Xandr . . . She mouthed the name without speaking, having nearly forgotten him, his existence altogether. "I am not sure," she murmured.

"What do you mean?" he cried. "You're not sure or you don't know?"

"I'm not sure!" she snapped. "But it isn't . . . it isn't good."

As if they were no longer present, the colossal shape turned from the gathering, forming trenches in the ice. "Wait!" Emma cried. "Please tell us why you're here!" But it continued on without changing pace.

With Emmaxis tall and gleaming in his arms, the dull light of the moons reflecting from its surface, Xandr chased after it. "I'll make him listen!" Thelana and Grimosse charged behind him, as the knight and his squire, Starvod and Ovulus, hesitantly followed. Emma shouted at their backs, tried desperately to explain how foolhardy any attack would be, but her voice was less than the howl of the wind.

If only they saw what I saw, in Gloomwood, when it had me . . .

THOOM!

Emma steadied herself against a boulder as the mountain shrugged. A wave of snow and ice cascaded from the intricate arrangement of steel pipes and iron rivets that was Horde's fist. Xandr and Thelana were unharmed by the impact, having moved at the last moment, but the giant was now fully engaged with them.

Thelana rolled into a crouch, her bow drawn to her cheekbone, an arrow loosed between its eyes, but the bronze tip rang off, its tar-like face deflecting it like a shield. Horde's tree trunk arm swept in a violent arc, but she caught onto its finger like a mouse, stealing its strength to fling herself into the sky. Opposite, Xandr's battle cry clouded the cold air. Watching from a ring of boulders, Emma watched him drive his milky steel, five feet of it, deep into the giant's muscled thigh, and for an instant she hoped against reason that the construct was not beyond their power to destroy. But hope was short lived. The golem made a quick and calculated response, snatching Xandr in its metallic fingers. Emma heard, or thought she heard, the snap of ribcage and pelvis—could feel it in her own bones. The scream erupting from her beloved was horrifying to the ear, echoing from each column of ice, a final desperate cry for life. And before she knew what she was doing, Emma's numbness gave way to fevered passion, and she was running toward him, and the monster clutching him. But

Grimosse arrived first, pounding his hammer against the giant's spine, again and again, each blow powerful enough to pulverize marble. For Horde, the assault was sufficient to take notice of, to swat at the other golem, to send Grimosse reeling against the cliff face.

Released from its crushing grasp, Xandr dropped against the weather-beaten ice. Emma could only pray that he survived, to gods she kept no faith with, and then the Batal arose, reaching for the hilt of his sword, which still protruded from the giant's thigh. Emmaxis cut a long swath across the dense muscle. A substance like pitch oozed from the wound, spattering black glossy droplets across the frozen landscape.

It bleeds . . . By all the gods, it bleeds!

Horde's eye sockets constricted in a manner revealing, not pain, but concern, regarding Xandr and his sword, and its raised arm came down again. Emma shut out the image, unable to watch her beloved die, knowing a blow from such a mass would turn any man to pulp. But when she found the courage to look again, Thelana was engaged in the battle once more. Her sword was a jade and gold blur, hacking furiously. She directed the edge of her blade to where a knee or elbow should have been. With uncanny deftness, she dove between its thighs, to force the point of her steel into its groin. But for all her efforts, she could have attacked the glacier. She was no more than a nuisance, a distraction for Xandr to free the ancient weapon. Running nimbly across an arm and over its shoulders, Thelana's fists found the lit recesses of the golem's eyes, as Emmaxis, black to the hilt with blood, was again in Xandr's gasp, its tip directed at the golem's heart. And for an instant Emma's hope turned to pity, that they should destroy an immortal being, a life of such vast intellect, and then the mouse was caught. Between gauntlet-like fingers, Thelana was stretched from wrist to ankle.

Strom on high . . . she'll been torn apart!

Her jaw locked with agony, so she could not scream, and suddenly Grimosse emerged—a guardian to the last—crashing a boulder larger than himself over the dome of Horde's body. Its eyes blazing, the giant dropped Thelana in one piece, swinging back to meet the golem. Fire flashed from its palm. Emma shielded her eyes as heat washed over her at twenty paces, searing the exposed hairs of her body. Now blinded, the sounds of struggle intensified, becoming terrifying. She imagined being pummeled into a soup of flesh, her bones flayed with fire. Blinking once, twice, a blackened husk came slowly into focus, Grimosse lying dead in the snow. Xandr and Thelana were also fallen, likely dead, but where were Starvod and Ovulus? Where were the men of Northendell?

Horde's eye sockets turned in her direction. She could feel them like branding irons, burning through her forehead. He was not about to let her be. Mindlessly, she lifted the *Ages of Aenya* like a shield, but the giant was only growing closer. She turned to flee and stumbled. Sir Starvod's mangled body lay at her feet, a mess of bone and copper and smoking blood, a ghastly scream frozen on his face. Emma had no time to mourn him, or to fret over the lives of her friends. Like a wild animal in her chest, her heart was leaping, and the thunder of footfalls was amplifying in her ears, vibrating through the heels of her boots.

"Emma!"

Ovulus pulled her into a shaded recess and together, they waited, and waited, watching their terrified breathing escape into the air.

When the sounds of pursuit grew distant, Emma crawled up from the icy riverbed. Horde was a dark blot in a white haze, indistinct amid the Pewter Mountains. She glanced toward the hill, where they had seen the old hermit, but he was no longer there.

The squire tugged, shame faced, at his frozen sword. "I d-didn't even get to s-swing at it. What k-kind of knight am I going to be? Running away . . . cravenly."

"Obi," she murmured, "you saved my life."

"I know," he said, "b-but—"

"You saved my life!"

"Yeah," he admitted, "n-now who's being obvious? Besides, I j-just couldn't live with what I'd done, before . . ."

She looked at him, puzzled.

"Giving you up t-to those two, to Bood and Deed . . . I m-mean, it just wasn't right, the way we t-treated you all those years. Sure not befitting a true knight, even if you are a w-witch."

Emma looked into his eyes, wanting to offer some word of gratitude, but nothing came to mind. She ran off, careful to avoid Starvod's mangled body.

By the time she reached the Ilmar, her chest was so tight she could hardly breathe. Xandr was alive, with one hand clutching Emmaxis buried in snow, the other brushing a lock from Thelana's pallid face.

We've been chasing Death all along.

"Is she—?" Emma started, afraid of the answer even as she asked it.

"She's breathing," he said, his voice dead, soulless.

Emma intoned his name, as sympathetically as she could manage. "I'm so—"

"Don't be sorry!" he shouted at her. "I know what I need to do, and what you need to do. It's our destiny . . . our . . ." He pulled his hair over his face, and he pummeled the ground, flecking the ice red with his blood. He was weeping, she could see. "Not *her*," he sobbed, "take the world away, take it all away!" he cried to the heavens, to the gods, "but not her!" He was looking every bit the madman, tugging to remove his clothes. "Stay here," he commanded, "and keep her warm."

She wrapped Xandr's overcoat around Thelana's body, and when Emma looked again, he was utterly naked, his veins rushing to turn his body a pale turquoise, the violet bruising across his sides and crimson pustules marking where the blood was broken beneath the skin.

"Xandr! You can't go on like that!"

"Look!"

Ahead of them, the ground had been cracked open by Horde's fire. A river of water ice flowed across it, dividing the plateau, blocking passage to the mountain's peak.

"I'll have to swim across."

"Xandr," she murmured, "you'll die."

"I've always known that, but without her . . ." He could not speak.

"You'll die before you reach the top!" she cried. "Listen to me, please, I know these mountains! You're throwing your life away—making her sacrifice amount to nothing."

"I am Ilmarin," he said. "The Goddess will protect me."

"How will you find the way? Without Starvod?"

"Emmaxis has tasted its blood—it shall lead me—and I will kill it."

Before Emma could think how to dissuade him, he was gone, a wild thing of flesh against a backdrop of blue white and silvery rock.

For a long while she knelt beside the body, fearing to abandon her, waiting and watching. Snowflakes billowed sideways from adjacent clouds, whitening her robes, turning her raven-like locks the color of ashes. Thelana's complexion, once bronze and fiery with life, was turning to chill, dead hues.

You showed such bravery and cunning and for what? To die here? To fade in this sea of white? And here you are, Emma, alive for all your cowardice, alive along with him. No, I won't accept such favors of Fate! She belongs with Xandr, Ilmar with Ilmar, not I . . . not—

"Go to him."

Thelana's eyes were hard as glass, the tears frozen before they could roll from her cheeks.

"He told me to stay. With you."

"No." Thelana shook her head. It seemed to take all her strength. "I'm off to join my family, to be one with ilms. Do not mourn. It is a happy fate."

"You can't die," Emma asserted. "Xandr told me . . . you're not allowed to."

Thelana smiled wanly, pulling Emma's hand into hers. "My body is broken," she said, so softly that Emma had to lean in to hear. "Feel for yourself." Tremulously, Thelana directed Emma's hand. Beneath layers of furs, she could feel the vertebra in all the wrong places, knobby bones tossed like dice along the spine.

"I'll not you let you," Emma was saying. "It doesn't matter how broken you are. I'll find a way. I'll—" Her eyes stung as Thelana's face became a watery blur. *My god, this sense of hopelessness, this despair . . . is this what Mathias was fighting all these years?*

"The Goddess is not with me." Her breathing came in short, sharp gasps, and she was wincing with every intake. Some tremendous weight was on her, Emma could see, a weight she had not the strength to continue holding.

"I know you care for him," Thelana whispered, her emerald eyes glistening. "Be good to him."

What am I to do? Obey Xandr, leaving him to die, when there might be a way to save him? Or betray his trust by abandoning the woman he loves?

The sound of sloshing snow roused her from her thoughts. "Go after the Batal," Ovulus said. "I'll stay. I'll watch her."

"But what can I do?" said Emma. "I can't fight. I can't even . . ."

Something was fluttering, trying to escape from Ovulus' hand. It was page two thousand and twelve. Without saying a word, she reached for it, just as he said, "It f-fell out of your book when you were running. The old hermit g-gave it to me, just before his h-heart gave out. Poor b-bastard. It seems he died."

Emma searched each line. Of the thousands of words on the page, one stood out like a firebrand,

KJUS.

The first of the keepers, the guardian of wisdom and knowledge, a great thinker.

"Obi, quick, bring me the book!"

The *Ages of Aenya* landed on her lap, and never minding the cold, she removed her gloves to search through it, finding where the missing page belonged, and started to read,

Before the foundations of our world collapsed, circa 5 BGM, there came to pass a meeting of great minds. Kjus and Kzell sat across from one another in the Compass Tower at Tyrnaiil. They were to duel not with swords, but with words. At the end of a long chamber, raised over Kzell's shoulder like a dead giant on the bier, lay the Golem.

Never one to hide his emotions, Kjus slammed his fist on the quartz table dividing them. "That thing is an affront to nature . . . an abomination!"

Kzell answered him, ever patient and soft-spoken, "Do you not think you are being a bit narrow-minded?"

"No, I do not!" Kjus insisted. "You will never get me to agree! You know how I feel about transference."

"I know you are stubbornly conventional, and that you have always had a quaint, romantic sensibility for tradition—but if we do not learn to reconsider the fundamentals of existence, humanity and all of its achievements may cease to exist altogether. You cannot deny the findings. Solos is unstable, has been for millennia, shedding heavier elements by the nano. At best, it will expand into a new stage, at worst, go nova. Either way, our species faces certain extinction. Our only hope is transference. Regrettably, there was not the time to create a body for each of us, so we must join as a collective."

"And what of the millions of others, in our cities, in the villages? What of the avian and the merquid races? Do you plan to transfer them all?"

"We cannot. Even as is, we risk certain madness."

"What of the Mass Hammer? It is not beyond hope!"

"That was a dream born of desperation, when we had no other alternatives—you knew that when we began. Move the planet, indeed. Whoever could dream such a thing?"

"It can still be done—" Kjus argued. "They're not yet finished in the mines. We have the power. You simply lack the will to see it through, now that you've found a way out for yourselves!"

"It is impractical if not impossible," Kzell retorted.

"Impractical! We're talking millions, no—billions of lives! Countless species not yet to be discovered! And as far as I am aware, the plan defies no laws. Dead sun matter, pushed through the portal into the core, should shift the planet's mass sufficiently to elongate its orbit. Further out from the sun, Aenya may last another billion years!"

"Yes, yes, we've debated this endlessly. I am not a child that you need repeat it. But there is too much conjecture and a zero margin of error. Even if it does work, and we manage to move the entire world into a safer orbit, there are massive stresses to contend with. Simply turning the Hammer on will wreak global havoc on weather systems, shift tectonic plates, cause earthquakes, floods, eruptions—it is doubtful any ecosystem could survive it."

"And your suggestion is to simply allow the planet to die?" Kjus cried. "Abandon it to roast in the corona of the sun?"

"The Zo Ascendency will live on," Kzell answered. "In this indestructible form, our civilization will thrive forever. Allow me to elucidate. The golem does not age—its cells replicate without flaw and without sustenance of any kind. It is impervious to heat, cold and physical harm. It can survive the rigors of space and will travel the stars, perhaps to find new worlds upon which we might repopulate the human race. The zero-boson field renders its mass insignificant, and since time is meaningless to one that is immortal, the vast distances of space will come to mean nothing."

Kjus stood angrily. "I'll hear no more of this!"

"Please, Kjus, sit down and think! Think what you will be missing! Eternal life! Limitless knowledge! Is this not the apex of evolution? Might this not be the noble goal of our species? To become—"

"What? To become what, Kzell? Gods?"

Kzell rubbed his knuckles against his forehead. "Not this again. Look, I understand you maintain some academic fascination for primitive societies, but your tongue strays too closely, I fear, to theism."

"Fine, then! Cast your body aside like an old suit. Become one with that thing, but when you are no longer human—when you are so far and beyond that our species will look to you like a germ, what then, Kzell? On a distant shore across a sea of stars, will you give up immortality to become a lowly human? And what of the life forms on that other world? Will you show them compassion? Or, with your vastly superior knowledge, will you treat them as the Septhera treated us?"

"We are nothing like the Septhera!" Kzell cried.

"And yet you follow the exact same path! You crave knowledge—to become masters of the universe—but without an ounce of wisdom!"

"Wisdom? What is wisdom? Philosophical musings, with no pragmatic value whatsoever."

"You possess the knowledge to live forever—that is true—but without wisdom you will never know what living is for." Kjus turned to leave.

"Wait, Kjus, do not go! Perhaps I spoke in haste. Your perspective—call it wisdom if you will—the golem is incomplete *without it. I am saddened to think of a mind such as yours going to waste. And consider how it will seem, when the council learns that someone of your stature and lineage, a direct descendent of the Batal, has rejected the plan? You may doom others to following your idealistic example."*

"If I go into that thing, I lose my vulnerabilities, my weaknesses, my pain and my grief and my fears, everything that makes me human, and in losing that I lose myself. Besides, the planet needs me . . . Aenya and all its myriad life forms have a spirit. When the world ends, I must perpetuate that spirit should anything remain alive."

"You realize there's a good chance of total extinction, of Aenya becoming as inhospitable as the other planets in the system."

"It's a chance worth taking."

"Where will you go?" Kzell called after him, as Kjus turned to leave.

"To the mountains of Ukko," he answered, "where lives a race untouched by your hubris, quite possibly unchanged since the genesis of our species. For decades I have studied them. I go there to continue my research."

"You're going to become one of them, aren't you? You won't accept my offer of immortality, and instead you choose to retreat into the dark ages, to become an animal no less! Indeed, you are either the epitome of stubbornness or truly mad, and for that I pity you."

"Did you ever stop to think . . . that perhaps this has all happened before? You speak of mankind's ultimate future as if history has an end. But time is cyclical. Stars burn out and are reborn from the atoms. Civilizations perish to make room for the new. Ilms bloom where the old have wilted. Man was meant to die so that his offspring might inherit the world. History repeats. It is the nature of the universe."

"I admire your eloquence, but you are being foolish in this. Make no mistake, if you go into those mountains, you go there to die, if not by the changing orbit or the death of Solos, then inevitably, by the slow decay of your mortal body."

Kjus laughed. "Die. Yes, die indeed, but I will die as a man! I'm four hundred years old, and have seen enough."

The *Ages of Aenya* slid down to her knees, the sense of déjà vu debilitating. She had been in that room all those ages ago. Buried beneath a million fleeting memories, she could piece together Kjus' expression of outrage, could describe the phoenix-shaped fibula pinned to his chiton, and even smell the terraced valleys beyond the arches. Kzell was buried in Horde's subconscious, was a part of Horde, and after Gloomwood, was also a part of her. Now, with sudden, awful understanding, she read the passage again.

"Simply turning the Hammer on will wreak global havoc on weather systems, shift tectonic plates, cause earthquakes, floods, eruptions—it is doubtful any ecosystem could survive it."

"What does it s-s-say?" said Ovulus, trembling beside her.

"He is going to do it again!" she explained, almost screaming. She glanced at Ovulus, then at Thelana. "I am sorry. I have to go."

Thelana's bosom swelled and contracted. "My sword. Baba gave it to me, when I left home . . . Put it in my hand."

"I'll find it!" Ovulus cried, already surveying the white landscape. "You go on!"

With the words of Kzell fresh in her memory, Emma trekked away, her feet suddenly heavy, her body cold and hollow, the wind moving through her like a breath through her mother's piccolo. Snowflakes smacked hard against her cheeks, slowing her movements, impairing her vision. She glanced once behind her, to where Ovulus knelt, where Thelana clutched her sword to her bosom like a man-at-arms readied for the pyre, until everything Emma knew washed away in a flurry of white.

Despite that she could not hope to swim across the icy river, could not climb, could not suffer the cold, was too ungainly to manage her way over the least perilous of passages, she soldiered on. The snow kept beating against her, blinding her. Steep, jagged slopes met her in every direction.

I do not fear.

She could no longer feel her body. Or mind. Her thoughts became a nightmarish mishmash of imagery: Thelana dying, Starvod's mangled body becoming Thelana's mangled body, becoming Xandr . . .

I do not fear. She mouthed the words, spoke them aloud to make them true, but her voice was weak, less than a whisper. She *did* fear.

Emma collapsed. For how long she lay unmoving, she did not know, but in the stillness of death was not alone. The ravens were there, perched along the rocky shelves above her, everywhere.

Hugin! Munin! My friends. My only friends . . .

It had to be a hallucination. After all, she was freezing to death, and it was known that fond memories become realities before joining the Taker. No raven could survive such harsh conditions, and yet, they were here, Hugin and Munin, her friends since childhood, never failing to appear in times of loneliness. And was there anything ever so lonely as death?

Come fly with us. It was what they always told her, whenever they flew by her windowsill, to rescue her from her bedroom. *Come with us, raven girl. You know you want to fly. You want to be free.*

Either she was suffering from some dementia, or Emma was coming to new understandings after what Horde had shown her. It frightened her to follow this line of reasoning, in that she might go mad, or lose her humanity, as Kjus feared. But didn't Kjus become one with the Goddess? Did he not take the shape of a phoenix?

Magic is only a word, for the ignorant, for those of limited intellect. She shared the infinite mind of the Zo, and of the Xexaz of aeons past. She had looked through Horde's eyes to witness the transparency of matter, and knew, knew to rearrange herself, particle by particle, to reach the Batal.

Wild, exotic energies engulfed her. She could feel the surge in her fingertips, warping the fabric of substances, felt the change in the pit of her stomach, the vertigo, wanting to vomit. The moment passed. Her bones were breaking down, whittling away, and her hands were stiffening, growing hooked. Her hair became coarser, stem-like. At last, the pain subsided and she weighed close to nothing. Emma spread wings and was loose from the tether of gravity. Was free.

18

THE SECRET OF THE SWORD

*I have been asked, 'Why have you enshrined
the god of death upon your sword?' In truth,
I do not love the darkness. But Skullgrin is
a part of Alashiya. They are two faces of the
same coin. Without death, there is no life.*

—*Kjus*

His feet damp with blood, fourteen-year old Xandr sprinted toward the monastery across corpses of men and monster. Ash rained across his path, dusting his blond locks and bare skin. Blinking to clear his vision, he could make out a vague shape, of what had been his place of sleep and contemplation, dissolving in an inferno of oranges and reds, opaque vapors stretching from the colonnade of arches to the swirling darkness above. He groped at the bronze rings, singeing his fingers, and the door came apart.

Muttering to the Mother Goddess that the temple not collapse upon him, he moved through the aperture, his every breath burning like an ember in his lungs. He stumbled blindly through rolling clouds of soot, his forearm shielding his eyes, uncertain as to how much of the structure remained intact.

Xandr knew the way to the *Chamber of Forbidden Knowledge*. Often he had gone to stare at the great arched double-doors, to wonder at its secrets. Once, when Quasil went with Brother Zoab to meditate atop the mountain, he had even dared a peek within. He had been twelve, and memories surfaced now from that time, of muted colors and unnatural shapes, followed by the approaching footfalls that had frightened him off.

Turning the corner, he came to a place thick with smoke, though he could still picture the intricate patterns etched into the door. A grinding echo met his ears as he wrenched the door ajar and slipped inside. As the soles of his feet met cold marble and his lungs began to swell with fresh air, tides of energy broke against his bosom.

It was like entering an entirely different world. There was no smoke, no heat, none of the sounds of the fiery chaos outside the door. Shafts of lurid color cascaded through mosaic windows from a domed atrium, making the dust glitter, reflecting from the tessellated walls. Alcoves met him on either side, but in his haste he caught only glimpses of wondrous, indescribable things, metallic seashells oozing liquid fire, moths with mosaic wings of crystal, geometric shapes that were not quite cubes, not quite spheres, yet somehow both. Nothing seemed like a weapon, much less a sword, and so he pressed on, resisting the urging of his curiosity. Further inward, his shadow lengthened across a concave mural. It was a circle of monks in glass, kneeling before a sleeping child, where a great phoenix of orange, blue, and white spread its wings. A hollow beneath the mural led to a spiral of steps. He went down and down, his heart racing with equal parts anticipation, for what he might find, and with dread for his mentor, who may be dying as he lingered.

At the base of the stair, Xandr found himself in a cavern of cream-colored stone, its dimensions lost to the gloom. Life was as abundant here as it was above ground, he could feel the rich, wet earth underfoot, and the boy considered that he did not know Aenya as well as he thought. The roots of Ilmarinen spread like a nebulous brain, green with vegetation and moss. Phosphorescent mushrooms gave the whole of the cavern an otherworldly pastel glow. He moved on, searching for what might resemble a sword, until a peculiar sensation on his skin gave him psuse.

Cold.

It emanated from the place where the roots were ashen and brittle, making the small hairs of his body prickle, making him want to shake and rub his arms against his body. Subterranean plant life lay choked in beds of barbed weeds that appeared to be creeping in from the east. That was a place of darkness, he knew, though he could not understand how the darkness had come so near to Ilmarinen. Turning away, he followed the light of thriving fungi, to a gradual sloping of the cavern floor.

Concentric tiers sloped down into a depression, ringed by luminous vegetation. The deepest part, the center, was bright as a bonfire. It was the light of the *Star Tree*, the *Tree of Knowledge*, what the elder monks spoke of only in whispers. Its fruits were bright and round and swirled with color like bands of clouds. But the tree was decaying, he could see, its bark black and hard and flaking.

Buried beneath a tangle of roots and dirt, in a niche in the trunk of the Star Tree, he could make out a human outline raised in stone, a sarcophagus, and a shrine to the founder. Kjus wore only a sash across the breast, fastened by a golden phoenix. A narrow band running the vertical length of the shrine caught the light, glittering between the greens and browns of the tree's roots—a hard, smooth, unnatural substance topped by a handle.

Xandr broke away stems and brushed at centuries of dirt, until the weapon was unearthed. It was extraordinarily long, the length of Kjus' body, and would surely reach over his head. How could he ever hope to wield such an ungainly thing? No matter, he thought, tugging at the weeds with determination, until his fingers bled and the blade mirrored his charred and bloodied face with surreal clarity. An eerie feeling washed over him as he stood, his forefinger over the pommel, prepared to free the sword from its resting place, from where it had rested untouched for untold ages. It made his palms clammy to think on it, and with his touch the alloy quivered like some living thing, but with a minimal effort the sword came free of Kjus' grasp. The sound of steel against stone was deep and resonant. Lifting the hilt upright and into the light, he eyed the yawning skull on the hilt. It was like some ghastly apparition fighting to escape its casting. Gazing into the metal cavities that were its eyes, the world began to spin and fade, and a universe of potentialities loosed upon his mind: waves swallowing empires, serpents taking the guise of men, stars falling from the heavens, and bloodshed, always bloodshed. It was a hunger in himself, a longing for slaughter not all his own. Tearing himself away from these visions, at once alluring and repugnant, he heard the sword calling him, whispering its dreadful name.

I am Emmaxis.

Remembering his mentor, the boy awakened from his trance, carrying the sword under his arm toward the stair.

Sunlight pained his eyes as he emerged from the ruins of the monastery. Gasping for air, he descended the steps, coming to a field of bodies. Numb and trembling, he stumbled through the haze, over friends and mentors.

"From nowhere." It was a voice, a breath like a gust through the branches, passing in step with the boy.

"Zoab! What's happened? Who still lives?" Xandr leaned his ear against his mentor's black and hardened lips.

"They came from nowhere, the gray devils. We were . . . unarmed, unprepared." His voice trailed, but he continued in an attempt to speak, until the rhythm of his breathing relaxed and gave way to quiet release.

Xandr recoiled, taken aback by the sudden trespass of the Taker, at its utter lack of ado, at the mundane way in which the cords of Life came unknotted. No longer would Zoab's folktales enflame the boy's imagination.

"Rest," Xandr told him, cupping shut unseeing eyes.

He continued through the carnage, until brushing against the wrist of Pawn, the sword of his old sparring partner dull and sullied with use. The youth looked peaceful in his repose, his body cushioned by wild grasses, and if Xandr had not seen his bosom wet with streaks of crimson, he might have thought his friend asleep. But where was QuasiI, he dared ask himself? He called out the name, unwillingly searched the endless supply of dead faces, dissected between hope and fear.

Amid a scattering of gray corpses, a lone scalp shone whitely in the sun, and Xandr cursed himself for all the times he'd mocked him for his baldness. The dull sheen of many hilts could be seen, rising and falling with his mentor's bosom, a pool of blood changing shape beneath his mentor's form, and the boy collapsed to his knees, his legs unable to carry him.

"I am here, Queffi! . . . I am—!"

QuasiI's parched lips cracked to address him. "The trees . . . we must save the trees!"

"The fire has subsided, teacher, but the temple is gone."

Whether saddened or relieved by the news, Xandr could not tell, as the dying keeper's face became a mask too weary for expression. "I staved off the Taker, for your return."

Xandr tugged the handle of the sword into QuasiI's cold, crumpled palm. "Here, I've brought it, as you commanded me."

"The sword has but one use," he struggled to say, every syllable bringing pain. "It's your burden now. Watch the sky. Watch for the omens!"

The boy turned, letting his braid hide his eyes, wet, in part, from smoke. His hands trembled over the sunken daggers as if his will could undo the act. "We could have fought them . . ." he protested. "We could have fought them together. You taught me to move without thought, but I hesitated. I doubted."

"Weep not, son, for life is more than a body, or a mind. I am in the trees, in the ilms . . . in you."

"But I don't want to be alone," the boy pleaded.

"Remember," his mentor said, coughing. "Remember . . ." Blood came bubbling up to froth across the old man's lips, and then his eyes drifted, as if seeing into a world Xandr could not. At once, the boy knew the sword would remain an enigma, and that what he was meant to become—what the *Batal of Legend* meant—he would never learn from his mentor.

A howl erupted across Ilmarinen, through the timbers of the oaks, over the orange and violet valleys of the ilms. Against the sunken breast of his mentor, he wept, cradling the inert skull in his arms, laying gentle kisses upon the bald scalp.

Upon surrendering the body to the earth, the blood streaming from it turned into a clear liquid, into water. The knobby fingers of his mentor became brittle, and the limbs expanded into branches. Before Xandr realized what was happening, the body of QuasiI was no more. Where it had been was now a tree, a tree he could not name.

Nothing was left to the boy but the hideous sword, and his hatred swelled as he gazed upon it, the skull face mocking his loss, reminding him of the unbearable finality of death. He wanted to be rid of it, to cast it back into the ruin. Why had QuasiI told him to retrieve it? The weight of the question collapsed him like a marionette, and for a time he lay hidden in the tall grasses with his brothers.

After a long peace, an answer came to him, like a whisper in the wind, or from the will of the sword, directing his eyes through sinuous belts of gray to a pair of orbs returning his gaze. Was it a lone bogren admiring its handiwork? Spying upon him in his misery? Before he could move closer to inspect the copse, the face was gone, but it was enough to turn his misery to rage. He would have vengeance on the demented minions who had done the deed. It would become his driving purpose.

The tracks led every which way, but he followed, under the trees, through a weave of light and shadow. All that mattered was that he run, even should his life become a matter of pursuit. And the thorny seedling in his sole dug deeper, becoming part of him. He vaulted over moss-covered boulders and through trickling ravines, the sword clutched awkwardly under his arm or in his hands, the five-foot blade snapping branches and sparking against the rocks. But Emmaxis was his now. He would make a belt for the sword and wear it always, no matter how cumbersome.

At last he came to a hill overlooking the whole of Ilmarinen, where the wind frolicked freely in hair and the bare sun washed over his exposed body. The valley spread at his feet in a thousand myriad colors, but already it was becoming despoiled. He could feel the change in his skin, the deathly chill from the east. The land was breaking, crumbling apart like stale bread, and bogrens were spilling from the rifts. Forests were turning bright orange with flames. Fleshy behemoths, things like bogrens but bigger and more hideous, were uprooting trees and tearing through straw rooftops. Not knowing to fight or defend themselves, naked bodies spread across the valley, seeking sanctuary in the hills or in the woods—men, women and children, moving in panic and confusion and then falling, falling as monsters descended upon them, the ground reddening beneath their soft, lithe bodies.

I am Emmaxis, the sword said to him. *I am what you see.*

19

SONG OF THE BATAL

Vertical cliffs met his fingertips, without hardly a niche to set a foot upon or a slope to scale. There was no way to know whether he could reach *Strom's Hammer* or whether he would ever cross paths with Horde again. Lost in a haze of white, he desperately sought crags to hang from. His muscles ached, pushed beyond exhaustion, and the thin air cut like a knife in his lungs, every two gasps counting as one. And yet he fought the unrelenting wind, which bludgeoned his body against the hard edges of the mountain. He was driven to be free of destiny, to be rid of the questions burdening him since birth. There was also vengeance. Thelana was an ever-present spirit, though he kept her twisted body at the fringes of his brain. Despair would only cripple him. When he could bring himself to hope, to believe that he might look upon her emerald irises again, he found the strength to climb.

When his rage was spent and his blood cooled, his body was like a lifeless thing, a suit to be discarded. He was aware of the deathly temperatures and of the wet mist that enveloped him, but was detached from these sensations, knowing more than he could feel. Vaguely he remembered QuasiI's lesson, that a man freezing to death feels warmth within his core, the body abandoning the extremities to preserve the organs necessary for life. But he could not imagine his body giving out yet, not so close to the end—the end of the world at the mountain's peak—where answers awaited him if he could keep himself moving, if he could will his tortured frame a step further.

Alashiya . . . do not abandon me. Give me strength.

Words of prayer came stuttering forth, mashed and broken, from bluish quaking lips.

For the thousandth-thousandth time, he groped blindly for a perch to hook his fingers into, only to find a vacancy of empty air. With childlike eagerness he searched for a rim, finding a rough surface of ice-rock as hard and sharp as iron. Hope is a powerful thing, he thought, as he hoisted himself onto a step cut into the mountainside, and climbed, the mist thinning into silvery translucent bands to reveal the peak above the clouds, and a meandering stairwell. What ancient culture had built the steps and for what purpose, Xandr had not the will to ponder. He took satisfaction in that it was there and that, despite its weathered edges, it continued unbroken.

A sea of white and violet, limned with golden light, roiled and drifted beneath him. He was far above the clouds. There was no snow, only rock and iron ice, formed from the time of the mountain's formation. Mist flowed like a ghostly stream over the surface of the plateau, shrouding his feet and the bases of jagged pyramids that floated like ships through the ether. This was a home for gods.

In the vacant sky, the sun shone like a golden chalice, and Xandr shut his eyes to bask in its life-giving warmth. *Thelana would have loved this*, he thought, and then her mangled body flashed in his mind and the moment of serenity passed.

Warily, he started across the plateau, wincing and clutching at his ribs. The pain reminded him of Horde, how it had nearly crushed the life from him. He was grateful to Grimosse for attacking when he did, but could spend only fleeting thoughts on the golem and its well-being. Those half-formed thoughts were quickly interrupted when a human shape stepped from between the ever-shifting curtain of vapor and rock. It was Eldin, come again through a wormhole, or so Xandr believed at first. But the face that greeted him, with its silver-streaked beard and shimmering scalp, harrowed him to the core. Scrambling backward, tripping over his own feet, Xandr's heart swelled with equal measures amazement, horror, and hope.

"Queffi?"

"You've done well, my son," his mentor said to him. "Well, indeed."

Xandr kicked further away, unwilling to accept the proof of his senses. "But . . . you can't be! How can you be . . . here?"

QuasiI offered a broad, knowing smile, making Xandr feel childish, inept. "You've still much to learn. So much to learn! But come, you've proven yourself worthy of your ancestor, worthy to carry the name, Batal. I asked you to bring me the sword, and so you have."

Xandr's mind was at war, torn between reason and his heart's desire. He longed for his mentor's embrace, for the assurances he could only find in the old man's wizened arms. The world was such chaos and with no one to guide him through it. But now QuasiI was returned, someone to show him the way, to lift the burden of Aenya's troubles from his all too weary shoulders.

"B-but you *died*," his reason argued, the last word a whisper.

"Death is but an interlude," QuasiI replied. "I have taught you nothing if not this. The body passes on, becomes one with the trees, with the Goddess, but the spirit lives. Now, come to me, my son, and give me the sword. It's burdened you for far too long."

Feeling like a boy, Xandr hobbled toward his teacher. "Queffi . . ." he said, as he slowly lifted the sword, "I've missed you so much." In the cold of the mountain, his tears burned upon his cheeks. "Forgive me." Emmaxis came down in a flash over QuasiI's balding head, and if his mentor had been flesh, he would have burst into clumps of blood and brain, but the image merely dissolved into the mist.

Xandr stood alone on the mountain, staring at the empty space where his mentor had been, pining for the thing he knew could never be, and then his surroundings washed away like a ripple in water. Rock and ice and mist were gone and he no longer felt the cold. He now stood on an elaborately trellised rooftop. Waves were pounding the foundations, splashing his knees, washing across his ankles. Splendid architecture was crumbling around him, collapsing marble columns, tossing people into the Sea. The merquid were rising from the briny depths, murderous intent in their bulbous eyes, jagged coral weapons in their webbed hands. It was all happening again and Xandr was powerless to help them.

He tried to shut his mind to it, to fight the images, but it was all too real. Even with his eyes closed, he could feel the wind on his face, could hear the screams of the drowning. Clammy limbs were tugging at his wrists and thighs, wrestling him down into the violent Sea. He gasped for air, only to suck in water. The angry current gushed through his lips and nostrils, filled the pockets of his agonized lungs. He was being drowned.

As he struggled to lift his face from where the merquid held him, he saw, or thought he saw, Emma's face amid the throng of highborn women, peering from a balcony between the columns. It was a thing so remote from his mind, he could not help but focus on it, and the merquid seemed to grow weak then, and the water evaporated from his lungs.

Emma was shouting, pleading with him, but he could not make out the words. Another illusion, he thought, like his mentor had been. *But why her? Why now?* When the only one that mattered to him was . . . His mind was spinning. It was a dark night and he could smell the salt and the blood in the air. Thelana's body lay crumpled on the shore, dressed in Finias' armor. Merquid surrounded them, threatening to tear them to pieces, and out of nowhere, Emma's voice came again. She wore a white silk chiton and her hair was bundled up in gold lace.

"Listen!" she cried, as merquid rushed past her, ignoring her. "Doubt whatever you see! None of this is real. Horde can enter your mind, he can—"

Hearing the giant's name sent him into a rage. Tossing the frail amphibian bodies into the sand, he took Emma's hand in his, as though he might lose her in the illusion, and, lifting Emmaxis, swung at the sky. The world shattered around them like broken glass. A reddish horizon, an alien landscape, lay beyond it. They were in the arena, with tens of thousands of eyes upon them, cheering, hissing.

Emma was sprawled on the hard-packed earth, entirely naked, in a body not her own, bronzed by the desert sun, emaciated by hunger, scarred by torture. "Is this your nightmare?" she asked, fingering the gashes in her bared bosom.

He was too distracted to answer, his eyes trained on the Septheran in their midst. Sunlight glinted off dark purple scales, and the twin-moon blades were dripping with Emma's blood, and as it circled them, the reptilian mouth pulled back to reveal black, syrupy fangs. "Can these illusions kill us?" he asked her.

"I—I don't know, but it hurts real enough . . ."

Xandr could see the terror in her eyes as the snake man descended upon her. Knowing the illusion did not seem to matter. The instinct to survive, to know fear, could not be abated. He thrust himself between them, reaching for a weapon that was not there, and felt its claws rip through his guts, the muscles in its neck flexing in his hands as he wrestled the fangs away from his throat.

And again, Emma's voice came to his aid. "The pain isn't real, Xandr! None of it is! Just as Horde used my yearning for knowledge against me," she explained, "he is using your fears and doubts."

He could not see Emmaxis, but believing it was there, imagining it in his hands, he lifted his arms and split the hooded skull in two, and as Purple Death Adder came apart, Xandr was stricken by the sudden cold. He was on the mountain again, as was Emma, but he could not help questioning whether she, too, was an illusion. After all, how could she have reached him, and why was she without her robe? It was too unlike her to be real.

"Emma? What are you doing here? I told you to stay with Thelana."

She was still naked, but in her own pale Delian body, shivering against an embankment, her arms tight about her bare breasts, her prickling skin turning a sickly shade of blue. "Xandr . . . Thelana is . . . sent me to you."

"But how did you get here? And where in the Goddess' name are your clothes?"

"No time for explanations!" she said, her voice wavering, her hair falling like black velvet across her bony shoulders. "If you don't stop him—if you don't stop him now—

we're all going to . . . to die." She paused, shaking. "Life on Aenya will be no more!"

"Wait," he murmured. "How do you—?"

Taking him by the wrist, she led him to where the mist dropped away like a waterfall. A gorge cut across the plateau, and a lone bridge arched across it, wide enough for a single person to cross. There was no railing nor any struts, nor any apparent means of support. It looked to be made of ice, but was too perfect a parabola to be formed by nature. Beyond the bridge, on an island in the sky, there was an iron gray structure, its face buried crookedly in the mountain. Pinpoints of colored light flickered like stars from inside of it, radiated in a haze of green and blue and red, and a complex latticework of lines and shapes were etched across its length and protruded from its surface. The handle was taller than the obelisks in Hedonia, the pommel eclipsing the smaller moon—Frizzbeard could not have made room for the head alone in his mead hall. If this was Strom's hammer, the thunder god would eclipse any giant in the songs, could have his bones turned into tiny hills.

"Do you see him?" Emma said. It seemed as if she were harnessing every ounce of will to keep from crouching into a ball.

A miniscule form stood beside the structure, the giant working fervently and methodically, its crimson fingers probing invisible cords like a bard playing a harp.

"It's the machine," she said in a voice drained of strength, "from the history. It reaches down to the core of the planet. Horde's going to use it. He's trying to move Aenya again."

Xandr gave her a puzzled look, unable to reply, or think.

"He means to right a wrong, but the planet cannot be moved without . . . well, imagine Hedonia, but on global scale . . . coastal cities drowned, volcanoes blackening the sky for decades, earthquakes the likes no one has ever seen. Every living thing wiped clean, like, like lichen from a stone." Xandr could see her growing whiter by the moment. She had not long to live, he knew, and instinctively he pushed his body into hers. The warmth passing between their conjoined bodies was enough to buy them another passing, but she wanted more than to survive. The pent up longing in her bird-shaped eyes was clear. He could feel the frantic rhythm of her heart, her icy nipples softening against his bosom, and his manhood came alive, pulsing with fresh blood. She wanted his kiss, needed his lips on hers like a fish needs water, but before he could act on it, the ground pitched like a galley caught in a squall, pulling Emma out of his arms and onto her back, her hair dashing like black chalk against the white frosted plateau. A distant rumble echoed, a thunder from the bowels of the world, and his knees dipped again as the ground began to swell and lurch. Countless shapes were rising, forming dark curtains over the pale sky. Ravens beyond number were abandoning the surface as if sensing the destruction to come.

The mountain was breaking apart, and if the bridge were to go with it, he could never hope to reach Horde. He ran to the edge of the gorge. On either end, the sheer walls were buckling, twisting, tearing.

"The machine!" Emma's voice was barely audible, lost in the tumult of crumbling ice and rock. "Go! Do what you were meant to do, Batal!"

When he looked for her, she was gone, as was the ground where she once stood. Ravens were soaring up above the fissure. He blinked, unable to decide whether she was dead or become the birds, and tearing himself away, he did as she bid him and made for the bridge. The ice was shattering as he crossed it, but with no time to consider the gap, he shut his eyes and kicked into the air, and came crashing down on the other side.

The sky was like a pale glass dome, and the stars shone with a greater luminosity than he had ever witnessed, each point of the horned constellation of Skullgrin winking like jewels in sunlight, each of Alashiya's feathers burning like the wings of a phoenix. It was as if he were standing beyond the atmosphere, above the world.

Despite his proximity to the machine, there was an eerie calm about it. Horde paid him no heed, engrossed in its task. Moving with trepidation, the sword close to his side, Xandr studied the hammer's remarkable intricacies, never doubting its Ancient origins. From each of the giant's fingertips, threads of blue-white fire interlaced and broke apart and rearranged, where a cube was rotating in the air, defying the planet's pull. Xandr could see the recess in the machine from where it was removed. The cube reacted to the giant's every gesticulation. It was a kind of controlling mechanism. If Xandr was to save Aenya, he would have to distract the giant away from the cube, to destroy it, if possible. Sensing his intent, the giant paused from his work, and the cube, losing momentum, waited in mid-air.

STATE THE PURPOSE.

For so long, Xandr's purpose had been to reach this point. He never considered what he would do after. Remembering how Thelana and Grimosse surrendered their lives to free him, Xandr could not imagine how he was to destroy, or even subdue, the giant. Here was a thing that had walked through Northendell's walls with every spear and arrow aimed at it. Here was a god dropped from the stars to shake the world. What hope was there for him? For mankind?

"Stop!" The word sounded weakly from his lungs. "You're going to kill all of it," he added, choking for air. "Everything on the planet."

SMALLER SPECIES WILL SURVIVE. MICROORGANISMS WILL ADAPT. EVOLVE.

"But *we* will die!"

ORGANICS ARE SUBJECT TO MOLECULAR DEGENERATION. LIFE IS BUT A MEASURE OF TIME. ORBITAL SHIFTING WILL INCREASE SUSTAINABILITY BY NINETY-PERCENT.

A hole was expanding in Xandr's consciousness, from which he could sense every living thing, every ilm and treer, pleading to him for life, and yet he was beginning to understand how futile existence truly was. "All our people . . ." he muttered, as thoughts became agony, " . . . how can it, mean nothing to you?"

HUMANS ARE IRRELEVANT. EXTINCTION IS A VIABLE OPTION FOR GREATER SPECIATION. There was a finality to the collective voices that made him shudder. Horde's physical power was trivial when compared to its mental faculties. Xandr was little more than a termite justifying the value of its existence.

"If I am so irrelevant . . . why even speak to me?"

Horde turned from him. The cube threatening to destroy the world and remake it anew tilted in the air.

"Part of you, is listening, isn't it? One of those voices inside you remembers what it means to be human. To be truly alive." There was no reply. But Xandr was finding a new source of strength. The machine was generating enormous heat. "The people you once were . . . those people are dead," he continued, sensing the wisdom, the life of QuasiI, within him. "Kjus was right. I am more than this mortal coil. My life is others, those that I love—it is in the trees, in the ilms. The Zo sought immortality by moving into that . . . that *body*. But if nothing can harm you, nothing can touch you. If you *feel* nothing," and here he clenched his fist, pounding the heart in his chest, "you *are* nothing, nothing but a pale imitation of life!"

The construct turned, faster than Xandr thought possible, the wind breaking hard against its hulking shape. A single voice echoed from beneath its featureless face. In tone and timber, it was like Mathias, but distant, dreamlike. Xandr had the impression that the voice was of a drowning man surfacing for breath. "You're a madman, Kjus! A madman! You'd rather go off, deny progress and live like a primitive, as we embark upon the final stage of evolution!"

"Whoever you are," Xandr started, "stop what you're doing . . . stop or the children of Kjus will—"

IRRELEVANT. The collective swallowed the memory, along with Xandr's hopes. Horde turned with inhuman precision toward the controls, the cube and all of Aenya rotating between its fingers.

"Enough!" Xandr cried, as Emmaxis surged into his palm. "If you can bleed, you can die!"

For ten years in the swamps, he had believed that the sword was meant to make him a hero, the Batal of Legend. But that was never its purpose. The keepers were guarding it, along with every other Zo artifact—powers which humans had not the wisdom to control— powers that the primitive warring civilizations would only use to destroy. But Xandr could also see the wisdom in keeping Emmaxis. For centuries, the Ilmar watched the stars, waiting. They knew that only a weapon forged by the Zo could destroy a construct of the Zo. Here was the reason QuasiI had sent him to retrieve the weapon, his final words being to watch the sky, so that Xandr might someday destroy the Wandering God.

Horde did not waste its energies on illusion. Detecting the threat posed by Emmaxis, a white fire erupted from its palm, crossing instantly between them. The brilliance overwhelmed Xandr's eyes, yet he held to Emmaxis blindly, trusting that the Zo forged weapon could resist the blaze. The beam continued to rent the air with a deafening pitch, the deflection rattling his fists and arms and the whole frame of his body, forcing him to his knees, but he did not surrender his hold, even as the handle turned red hot, even when his fingers began to cook and his beard began to fray and the fibers in the bones of his hands started to unstitch.

The beam was hotter than fire, was the stuff of lightning, Xandr realized, and did not subside. His hands were aflame and he was leaving them to smolder. The agony was beyond measure, and yet, to permit himself relief was to doom the planet, to fail the people of Aenya as he had failed those in Hedonia, as he had failed to save his people from the bogren.

No!

He pushed against the stream, but without the strength to lift from his knees, he could not hope to move the blade any closer to the golem's heart.

Pain was crowding his mind, forcing out all other thoughts. The world was disintegrating, along with the universe, along with himself. There was nothing left but pain. And the will to suffer it.

He reopened his eyes, and could see the machine far beneath the mantle of Aenya, the crust of aeons breaking away, unearthing ageless gears the size of cities, pistons driving white hot magma from the center, the whole of Northendell sinking into a recess as the ground rotated under it like an enormous coin. He did not know how, but beyond the searing glare he could see the entire world, all that the Goddess was, every innocent who was going to die, Ouranos and Ingrid and the children in Kratos, Grimosse and Emma and . . .

Thelana.

Xandr screamed.

Xandr wept.

With a tremendous surge of love feeding back into its mind, the stream extinguished, leaving the ground scorched and the air crackling. Xandr's hands were eaten away, the threads of muscle raw and red and sticking to the handle, but the milk-silver blade was still gleaming, as untarnished as ever.

The Wandering God was staring at him now, the glow of its eyes dimmed, and he knew that it was trying to remember. Xandr could feel the tenuous connection between their minds, understood that Horde was rummaging through memories, from hundreds of worlds, only to find . . .

Loneliness. And emptiness.

Long ago, the people who became Horde knew wives and husbands and children, but each voice drowned out the other, resulting in madness. With its collective consciousness open to him, Xandr could sense its thoughts unfolding and, rising up from a well of identities—a gaping, terrifying vacuum. But the connection would not last long. Horde was pushing his mind away and time was of the essence.

With his last breath, the Batal thrust himself into the golem's arms, and collapsed, his charred palms slipping away from the sword at last, the grinning skull of Emmaxis planted in a sternum of steel, through a heart of flesh.

Standing in triumph over the Giant, the Batal took in his hands the lever of the world, and with it, held back the waters of the Tsunamis, and stilled the pillars of the earth, and pushed back the fires from swallowing the cities of men. For the races of Aenya, Cataclysm would not come again, nor would history come to an end, but continue anew into the dawn.

—From the *Ages of Aenya*, Volume VIII, by Emmalina Ravenborn

20

LAMENT OF THE ILMARIN BRIDE

. . . the words . . . I know them . . . the singing
by the crackling fire, the leaping lovers . . .

The chorus faded as the weight of the world began to press on her. Pain radiated from the tips of her hair and toes, an awful reminder of life. Soreness, weakness and delirium followed, and a dryness of the tongue. There was a touch of silk, and a pillow, and for once she was thankful for something other than dirt and leaves to rest upon.

A face was coming into focus, a scraggly beard and a sharp nose, and those soft topaz eyes which always caught her unguarded. Ornately-furnished walls, and chairs and cabinets and rich velvety fabrics, swam about that face, drifting into position like ships coming to port. Her name was in his voice. He was calling her from a distance, summoning her from the dead. She blinked to make certain he was real, and stirred, testing whether her body still functioned.

"I was . . . dreaming," she heard herself say.

"What of?" His voice was like the bed, warm and tender.

"I . . . I'm not sure . . . but it felt . . . weightless, like air, like . . . being free."

"You sing sometimes," he offered. "Snatches of old dirges from Solstice Night."

A tear clung to the pit of her eye, glittering like an emerald. She brushed at it with aching fingers, but was unable to place the source of her melancholy. "How long?"

"It's been almost four cycles. Forty days. The healers were certain you were dead, but I said to them . . . I said they didn't know you like I do." His lips were hidden under his beard, and whether he was smiling or scowling, it was not easy to tell.

"You need a blade." She lifted a hand to his cheek. His face was rough to the touch, like weeds.

"That was never our custom."

"It's how I remember you," she murmured, "in the temple, when you caught me." She shifted onto her side, but her body erupted in spasms of protest. All of her organs seemed to roll and bunch against her ribcage and she was forced onto her spine again.

"Be still. You're still weak."

"I am not weak!" she protested. To prove it, she pushed herself into a sitting position. Ascending the headboard was like climbing the Mountains of Ukko. "Now tell me, what is this place?"

"A house of healing," he said, "by the river port. Best in Northendell, or so Lady Sif assures me. The apothecaries are acolytes of Zoë, refugees from Hedonia."

"You've never left," she said. "I could always feel you."

"I just thought . . . well," he was like a boy, flushing, "to lend you my strength, so you might stave off the Taker. But in truth, it was your medicine that kept you with us. That sword of yours," he added, "you never let on about the hilt or what was in it."

"A thief must have some secrets," she answered with a wan smile. "My father gave it to me when I left home. It was all I had of him, of them . . . At times I wanted to eat it, but even in the woods, when I was alone tending to a bite from some creature . . . I did not dare take the dream journey. I was afraid to lose myself."

"It stilled your heart and your breathing, and insulated you from the cold. Alas, there are no longer such flowers in the world."

"What of Emma? I sent her to you . . . Is she . . . alright?"

"She calls herself Emma Ravenborn now, and she's writing, always writing. She's continuing Eldin's work. Whenever she fills in the last page, a new, empty page appears. It's our history now. Only . . . she won't let me read any of it."

"You're fond of her, aren't you?"

"How could I not be? The ilm kept you alive, but she fixed you. Only a matter of knowing how, she said. She has her stepfather's spirit.

"Grimm was also dead, in a sense, but his body regenerated. Emma learned how Mathias did it. Not all of his books perished in the fire. She even had help, sneaking around the city at night, meeting with those who once aided him. There is an underground cult of knowledge in Northendell, she tells me."

Thelana jerked upright, suddenly frightened. The bones of her spinal column were tender and strange to the touch. "You mean I am . . . part golem?"

"No," he said, "nothing so extreme. But you have in you a capacity to regenerate, like Grimm does, like an infant in the womb, or a tree cut from the stump, or a saurian its lost tail. The Zo learned from the Goddess, borrowed from her, just as the Ilmar did. They were only blinded by their hubris, unable to see how much a part of nature they were."

For a time, he was quiet, and Thelana was comforted by it, in holding to nothing but the rough features of his face. The window by her bedside was ablaze, and she was like the ilm after a long period of darkness, returning to life in the golden warmth of the sun. Swinging her legs away from her body's groove, she forced herself upright, despite the punishment.

"I want to know everything."

"It's a long tale," he murmured, "which you will hear, I am sure, again and again." The bed frame strained with his added weight, and she could feel his warmth, his hair tickling her shoulders. "For now, at least, know that Grimosse did as he was made to do. He carried you and Emma, and Ovulus, of course. There were even times when I needed his arm."

"You!" she said with a wry grin, "Batal of Legend, carried like a helpless babe? Is that how the songs will go?"

"I suppose," he admitted, and she shared his laugh through tortured ribs.

"What of the old man?"

"Starvod?" Xandr shook his head. "It was his last adventure. He went as he would have wanted, I believe.

"We managed our way down to the valley and were taken in by a man and his wife. Their house collapsed in the quake, killing two of their sons, but they'd not given up on kindness. 'Always good to be kind to strangers,' the wife said, 'you never know when one might be a god.' They never lost faith, see . . ." his voice trailed off, choked. "After losing everything, they helped us make the rest of the journey here."

"You look . . . different somehow," she murmured. "Where is Emmaxis?"

"It is safe."

"You do not carry it around like you used to."

"I . . ." he began. "It does not speak to me as it once did." There were still many things left unsaid between them. Even now, she could see the past lingering in his topaz eyes, like a tempest.

Leaving the bed was like stepping off a cliff. The room was a kaleidoscope of shapes and colors. And the weight of her body was crushing. "Help me to the window. I want to look out."

"Thelana," he protested, "you're not strong enough—"

"Not strong enough!" she cried, pushing herself forward. "I'm strong enough for you, aren't I? To accompany the Batal on his journeys."

Without further argument, he took her hand, and she was shocked and dismayed by its coarseness. It was like a bird's talon. She resisted the impulse to pull away—she was his, after all, and her love for him could not be diminished no matter his deformities. And yet it saddened her to think he might never again know life's myriad textures, never caress her body as he once did, at least not with his fingers. For the Ilmar, touch was as vital as sight, and now a part of him was blinded.

They walked toward the golden square where the city opened before her eyes. It looked more splendid than she remembered. To the north, shingled rooftops, with chimneys billowing smoke, were stacked up along the mountain, climbing the parapet walls. Elsewhere, precariously-placed balconies grew beards of tangled fig trees heavy with drop fruit. To the south, leading out from the city beyond a broad arch, an expanse of water glinted in the sun, where longboats and galleons were tethered in rows, their multi-colored sails rippling defiantly in the wind. Thelana watched the ravens swirl over the masts as sailors cursed and waved them off, remembering Emma and Grimosse. She looked out for a long while, without a word. Despite all she'd seen and done, she was not much changed. She was still the young girl leaving home too soon, and the world was just as strange and uncertain without her parents or sisters to reassure her.

"If it's all over . . . why do I still feel lost?"

"Perhaps," he answered, pondering the question, "there was never any place to go, to not feel lost."

"I'll never see my family again . . . will I?"

"I wish I knew."

She fought to maintain her hardened exterior, but could no longer maintain the emotions dammed behind her eyes. Tears streaked over her cheekbones and down from her chin. It felt a long time in coming. "I thought if I could just climb every hill, search every forest, I might find them, or at least forget them. But it just sits there, a dull aching in my bosom, and that won't ever leave me, will it? Sometimes, I miss them so much, the pain rises in my throat and I can't breathe. I wish I'd never left home,

Xandr. I wish that whatever happened to them happened to me." She paused, unable to look at him. "I cannot help but wonder, was this meant to be . . . everything we've endured? Was it the plan of the gods?"

"The gods are cruel," he answered. "If they can hear us, they do not listen, and if they can see us, they do not care. All that matters is us. Our actions."

"Forgive me, but I'm just a stupid farm girl, I don't—"

He cupped her hands in his. "You told me you returned to find your home abandoned, and Ilmarinen ravaged, and I know you have been searching, as I have, not just for your family but for a place to belong. But if we keep each other close, all is not lost, Thelana. Ilmarinen is not out there, on some parcel of land. It is a place within us."

"But what of our people . . . our way of life? There has to be more than you and I . . ."

"When I looked through Horde's eyes, I could see the world in a way I never could before. Every life is connected and dependent on the other. Quasil tried to teach me as much, but I was too stubborn to listen. He told me that the Batal is like the camphor tree, a sanctuary for many species, and now I must become that sanctuary. I will remake it, Thelana . . . remake Ilmarinen, but not just for our people, but for all of Aenya to know peace."

"You want to change the entire world? No one can do that. Not even you. Not even the Batal—"

"If I can move a planet, I can change the people in it."

Xandr's words rang truthfully, but even now she doubted him, and what she was to him.

"Will you not, at least, wipe away my tears?"

"No," he replied. "You are more beautiful in weeping." He held her questing gaze in his own, caught her heart just as it was falling. "If the Solstice was tonight, Thelana, I would choose you, and no one else, to jump the fire."

She pounded her fist angrily, lovingly, tearfully against his scar. "If you knew this, would you have suffered so to have told me?"

"I was afraid," he said, "that in knowing you, I could not be Batal, that losing you would destroy me. But when I was up there on Strom's Hammer, the only thing that kept me alive was you, was the thought of seeing you again. And what defeated Horde, in the end, was what he could no longer feel or understand. From the moment I saw you dangling like a fool from that rope, I've loved you."

Thelana looked across the sprawl of towers and hanging neighborhoods, to the Pewter Mountains looming ominously beyond, finding it incredible how close, and yet how far, the device that nearly doomed their world had been. Along the outer wall, under which the Potamis flowed, angled ships bobbed against their moorings, their hulls creaking, their tethers snapping and going slack. Xandr had kept her prisoner for two days before allowing her to visit the port, and her newfound freedom to roam, albeit slowly and with some pain, was a joy beyond her capacity to express.

For the first time since leaving home, there were people she longed to see, and they were not Ilmarin. Eagerly, she searched for faces across colored sails and crisscrossing ropes, among the bustle of sailor merchants rolling barrels and fishmongers dragging nets, and if not for the distinct black on black pattern, Thelana might never have spotted her. Emma, with her raven hair combed behind her ears, shimmered darkly in splendid new robes tailored to her voluptuous figure. Grimosse was not far off, his hideous face bared, his garments—Hedonian blue and gold—newly mended.

"Back from the dead, are we?" Emma chided. "For some time we feared you were lost to us. Quick now, I have something to show you." Before Thelana could respond, Emma turned excitedly to the golem, saying, "Alright, Grimm, do as we rehearsed."

The golem towered over Thelana. To anyone that did not know him, he would have appeared quite menacing with his leathery muzzle and soulless, black-olive eyes. "Nice to see you today, Thelana," he said, his voice as gravelly as ever. "How are you feeling?"

Thelana was robbed of speech, but it was to Emma she turned, for there were words she needed to say. "I learned what you did for us, for Xandr and . . . me, and I wanted to say, well, it's only right that I . . ." *I'm such a fool! An unread fool!*

"Don't say anything. A friend shouldn't have to."

"But you are not my *friend*," Thelana remarked. Emma was shaken to hear it. "No! I mean, in my culture, when someone gives their life for another, they become, well, family."

A plethora of contesting emotions roiled in Emma's raven eyes—she looked like she wanted to pull her hair over her face again. "I've always wanted to belong to a family."

Without hesitation, Thelana pulled Emma close and held her tight against her bosom. She had found one sister after all.

Sif Redhair stood at the bow of a great ship, one hand over the sword at her hip, her hair the color of lava over her bare shoulders. Not two steps away, Ovulus moved to and fro like an impatient toddler, sweltering in his polished armor. But at the foot of the pier, Thelana saw something to make her stop and gape in wonderment. Never again did she think to lay eyes upon so elegant a creature, not in Northendell of all places. The avian princess was as majestic as ever, with her azure plumage and willowy limbs, her accouterments of gold and lapis lazuli and ivory radiating in the sun.

"Avia," Xandr addressed her, equally startled. "What brings you here? Where've you been? What of Ouranos?"

The bird woman lowered her massive, almond eyes, shaking her head slowly from side-to-side. "The caw took him. And when you and your mate fell from the ib, I feared you were lost to it as well. I searched the Great White Flat for two days, but the sands leave no trace. Forgive me."

"There is nothing to forgive," he said. "We owe only our thanks."

"In answer to your other questions," she chirped, "you should know that there is not an ear on Aenya that has not heard of your valiant deeds. Delian sailors recite the *Song of Batal* at every port from here to Shemselinihar. That is how I suspected that you might have survived. To see you well, and your mate also . . . Ouranos would have been soaring. But first, you must pardon me. I have duties to attend to."

To Sif, she gave a bow, stretching her wing to catch the light. "Your Highness, I bear dire news from the South." The princess motioned for her to rise, and Avia straightened, her bright blue plumage darkening to violet. "Civil war," she said, "terrible losses. They say *the trident is broken*. As you know, the trident was the empire. As the coastal states no longer sail under Hedonia's standard, they have taken to fighting amongst themselves."

"Which of the city-states are at war?"

"Most rally under Thetis or Thalassar," Avia answered, "though there are villages and small landholders who resist conscription, who desire only independence."

The redheaded Delian looked troubled, though Thelana could not understand how the news affected Northendell. Could the war reach so far to the north?

"I carry another message," Avia informed them, and from the baldric at her waist, she produced a finely embroidered roll of parchment. "It is sealed," she said, "with the Royal Compass, the crest of Tyrnael."

"Tyrnael?" Sif echoed the name as if it were something preposterous, news from a fairy tale.

Thelana gave a questioning stare, but it was Emma who explained, "Tales of the Kingdom of Tyrnael, or Mythradanaiil, as it is better known, are utterly fantastical. It is said to have been once the capitol of the entire world, the seat of the Zo Ascendency, the last remaining Ancient city, hidden in the Crown of Aenya."

"There's nothing in those mountains," Sif asserted. "The top of the world is nothing but rock and ice. If there was any way through it, the Delians would have found it by now."

"The myths speak truly," Avia attested. "The Zo used ships of the air to fly between cities, as we do. Without wings, you could never have discovered it, your Highness, which is why only the Council of Azrael keeps diplomatic ties with its people. But alas, their prosperity has given way to considerable strife, following a coup, after Tyrnael's young ruler was deposed."

"Give me the scroll," Sif said.

"I—I cannot," said Avia, looking abashed. "It is addressed directly to . . . the *Skyclad Warriors*."

"Demacharon!"

Everyone turned to Xandr. Even Thelana was staring at him with confusion. "Don't you see?" he said, excitement rising in his voice. "The old bastard's alive!"

"Who's Demacharon?" Ovulus dared to ask. "Is it a man?"

"Before jumping, he spoke something into my ear. He called me—us—" he added, acknowledging Thelana, "the *Skyclad Warriors*." Xandr turned his attention to the bird woman. "How did you know to bring this to us?"

"It was handed to me with some urgency," she answered. "I was told only that I might find the recipient by searching for the Batal, but as there are many claiming to that title, the letter was addressed thusly. Knowing what Ouranos told me of your peoples' customs, I had no doubt for whom the letter was intended." Her arm stretched out, fan-shaped with feathers, and Xandr accepted the scroll.

"I beg to take my leave of you now, your Highness," Avia said finally. "The world has been thrown into chaos and winged couriers are needed by many."

Biting her lower lip, the princess nodded approval. But the bird woman hesitated, turning again to the Ilmar. "To you, Batal, and Thelana, I bid good journey."

"It shall not be long, I hope," Xandr said, "before we cross paths again?"

"As the avian flies, the Tower of Heaven is never far." Her wings ruffled in the gale, changing hues, and with that she swept upward and away.

For a while they watched the bird woman shrink to a single black dot against the turquoise moon, and when she was entirely gone, Sif called to her oarsmen to lower the gangplank. Xandr, Thelana, Emma and Grimosse walked to the edge of the pier, across a broad hull of maple with its fifty oar ports and its towering masts. Lettered in gold across the starboard side were the words, *HORIZON CHASER*.

"You may *not* call me lady, or highness, or princess," Sif Redhair declared as she boarded the vessel. "If you are to sail upon my ship, you will address me as captain."

Thelana considered the places they might visit. What of the Sea she knew only from afar? Or Thetis and Thalassar with its warring factions? Or fabled Mythradanaiil? What did its ruler want with Xandr now that he was known to the world as the Batal? Any who chanced to hear of Xandr's victory against Horde would be sure to seek him out. After all, this was still the Dark Age of Aenya. And the more Thelana thought on these things, the more heavily they weighed upon her heart. *Without a home, there can be no real future for us, no place for family.*

"Where are you headed?" Thelana called up.

The captain licked her fingers and lifted them to the air, gazing long across the wide berth of river. "Away from here."

Thelana stepped onto the plank. It was damp and grainy and cool against her bare soles. But before she could move, a talon-like hand closed about her wrist. Xandr's topaz eyes looked hard upon her.

"Are you well enough for travel?"

She yanked her arm free, snapping, "Would you prefer I remain here? Do you wish to soften me? I am no princess to be pampered!"

"Thelana—?"

"Or would you make of me a simple housewife?"

"Well, perhaps someday, we might—"

"Never," she said to him. "You think me to wake, day after day, like some fattened heifer, to the same walls, to the same chores? *Better to chase through fields unblemished, over a thousand lofty hills, through summits high and low and plains forever long, to die someday without aching bones and timeworn flesh, but as a young maid, with my beauty about my corpse.*" The song escaped her lips, the *Lament of the Ilmarin Bride*, recited by maids chosen on Solstice Night. "That is the way I will die, Batal, and do not forget it."

Half her heart was broken by the lie. The other half believed.

His fingers found her cheek, his touch coarse, the flesh having burned away. It reminded her of all that they had lost. "We will die as we have lived, Thelana. Human."

Oars dipped into the waters and pushed the ship from port. The sailors tugged at the ropes, raising the standard of Strom's Hammer across each lateen sail, and every eye turned with delight toward the blue and orange phoenix, to the Goddess' herald gliding alongside the ship. It was a good omen.

With the *Ages of Aenya* fluttering in her lap and a piccolo on her lips, Emma sat against the mast, under the ravens that looped about the crow's nest. Grimosse was never far from her, ever vigilant.

Leaving Xandr's hand, Thelana leaned freely into the spray of wind and water. She could feel the wooden frame of the galley in the soles of her feet, the flow of the current below and the life teaming within. Aenya was a part of her body, the rhythms of its hills, the whisper in its trees, the song of countless beating hearts and mating calls. And when the wind changed, the *Horizon Chaser* tacked south toward the Mountains of Ukko, toward the valleys of Ilmarinen.

Made in the USA
Las Vegas, NV
05 April 2024

88296950R00371